# Splinter in the Blood

Ashley Dyer

corsair

CORSAIR

First published in the UK in 2018 by Corsair
This paperback edition published in 2019

1 3 5 7 9 10 8 6 4 2

Copyright © Margaret Murphy, 2018

The moral right of the author has been asserted.

A CIP catalogue record for this book
is available from the British Library.

ISBN: 978-1-4721-5102-5

Typeset in Granjon LT by Hewer Text UK Ltd, Edinburgh
Printed and bound in Great Britain by Clays Ltd, Elcograf S.p.A.

Papers used by Corsair are from well-managed forests
and other responsible sources.

MIX
Paper from
responsible sources
FSC® C104740

Corsair
An imprint of
Little, Brown Book Group
Carmelite House
50 Victoria Embankment
London EC4Y 0DZ

An Hachette UK Company
www.hachette.co.uk

www.littlebrown.co.uk

For Murf

A woman stands in the middle of Detective Chief Inspector Greg Carver's sitting room. She is holding a 1911 Colt pistol in her hand. To all appearances, she is calm; there are things she needs to do. She pivots on the ball of her foot, turning full circle, taking in every detail of the scene. Nothing has been disturbed. An empty whisky bottle lies on its side on the floor. Greg Carver is slumped in an easy chair, one leg bent at the knee, the other straight out. Looking down at him she feels anger and contempt, but also regret. His eyes are open, blood oozes from a bullet wound in his chest. She shifts the weight of the gun in her gloved hand, flips the catch to safety. The place reeks of alcohol, gunsmoke and blood, and her stomach hitches, but she snuffs hard, purging her nostrils of the stench.

She carries the gun through to the kitchen; his laptop is propped open, his files spread out across the table. The floor, ankle-deep in balled-up paper, looks like the aftermath of a massive hailstorm. On a chair beside the table is a cardboard filing box. She drops two of the files into it, gingerly wraps the gun in clean paper and carefully lowers it on top of them.

Under the litter of papers on the kitchen table, she finds a framed photograph, laid face down. DCI Carver's wife, Emma, on their honeymoon, seated on a stony outcrop near a waterfall. Emma is blonde and slender. She is wearing skinny jeans with wedge sandals, a blue peasant top. Her hair, silky and long, is combed in a centre parting. She is smiling. The woman carries the picture through to Carver's sitting room, wipes it for prints, and places it on the top of the cupboard, where it always sits.

In the bedroom, A3-size wall charts Blu-tacked to the walls. On one, smiling photos of five female victims alongside hand-written notes:

1. Tali Tredwin – DOD: 3rd January. Age 27, 5ft 4", brown hair, brown eyes. Divorced, 2 children. Back & shoulders tattooed – blue ink. Severe ink bleed, speckling. Maori symbols & eyes – all closed. *Berberis* thorn.

2. Evie Dodd – DOD: 10th March. Age 25, 5ft 5", black hair, hazel eyes. Married, 3 children. Torso, neck, arms, legs, feet/soles, hands, palms, all tattooed – blue ink. Stylised plants, magical sigils & eyes – closed/ half-open/open. Ink bleed. *Berberis* thorn.

3. Hayley Evans – DOD: 6th June. Age 28, 5ft 3", brown hair, brown eyes. In civil partnership, 1 child. Torso, neck, arms, legs, feet/soles, hands, palms, all tattooed. Stylised plants, thorns, magical sigils & eyes – closed/half-open/open. Blue ink. Less ink bleed. *Pyracantha* thorn.

4. Jo Raincliffe – DOD: 2nd September. Age 35, 5ft 6", brown hair, brown eyes. Married, 2 children. Torso, neck, arms, legs, feet/soles, hands, palms, all tattooed – blue ink. Stylised plants, thorns, sigils, etc. No ink bleed. *Pyracantha* thorn.

5. Kara Grogan – DOD: 22nd December. Age 20, 5ft 10", blonde hair, blue eyes. Torso, neck, arms, legs, feet/soles, hands, palms, all tattooed – black ink. No bleed. Stylised plants, thorns, magical sigils & eyes – a lot of eyes. *Pyracantha* thorn.

She peels the charts away from the wall, folds them, carrying them back to the kitchen, where she scoops up the rest of the papers – balled up notes and all – and stuffs them inside the file box, jamming the lid onto it.

She wipes down the door handles, light switches, his chair. Hefting the box, she makes her way out of the house, treading carefully on the fire escape steps at the rear of the building and down the driveway. It has recently been cleared of snow, but her shoe marks are visible in the fresh fall. It's very dark, and the curtains are drawn up and down the street; she doesn't think she's been seen.

Minutes later, she returns ungloved, without the box, and climbs the steps to the front of the house, wipes the bell push, then presses it. She doesn't wait – but takes a key fob from her back pocket and uses one of the two keys on it to open the front door. Inside Carver's flat, she retraces her steps, touching surfaces she has just wiped down. Finishing her journey at Carver's chair, she sees the drained bottle again and something niggles at the edges of her consciousness, like an itch she can't quite reach. But she doesn't have time for this – what's done is done.

She crouches in front of him, gripping the armrests and staring into his face.

She gasps, springing to her feet.

Panting, her heart hammering, she watches him for a few seconds. *You imagined it.*

She lowers herself, holding her breath, her eyes fixed on his. Greg Carver's eyes are light hazel, flecked with gold. Sometimes those gold flecks seem to shimmer, but not now. Now they are dull, dead. She leans in closer, watching, barely breathing – and sees again a flicker of movement in one eyelid. Her shoulders slump and she swears softly.

3

*Day 1*

The woman held Greg Carver's front door open for the para-medics. They took the steps slowly on snow now trodden to slush and ice. Her own footwear impressions leading from the fire escape at the side of the house and down the drive had been quickly covered by the steady fall of snow. A police helicopter clattering overhead shut off its NightSun beam and moved off in an abrupt manoeuvre, most likely recalled as the snow whirled and thickened. Lights flashed on emergency vehicles, arc lamps lit up the driveway of Carver's house and crime-scene tape was strung fifteen metres either side as an outer cordon to keep gawkers at bay. She followed the medics to the waiting ambulance and spoke a few words, watching until Carver was lifted inside.

A Scientific Support van was parked inside the cordon. Two CSIs and the Crime Scene Manager stood at the rear, suited up, ready to move in when they were given the okay.

The woman took a breath before heading over to them. 'It's all yours,' she said.

'Is it true?' The CSM said.

'It's Carver,' she said.

'Jesus, Ruth.' He touched her elbow.

Detective Sergeant Ruth Lake edged away. 'Eyes everywhere,' she murmured. She'd seen two local journalists outside the tape already.

'Where are they taking him?' he asked.

'The Royal.' Her throat closed and she couldn't say any more.

'Anything I can do?'

'Just be thorough.'

'Goes without saying.'

Lake tilted her head, a gesture of apology.

'I touched the doors – handles and locks – ' She frowned as if trying to recall. 'Light switches and the chair – in the sitting room at the front of the flat. He was – that's where I . . .'

He nodded. 'Understood. We'll need your footwear.'

She scratched her eyebrow. 'I'll get it to you.'

'How'd *you* get in?'

'It was wide open,' she said, avoiding a direct lie. But her hand closed involuntarily around the key fob in her coat pocket, and she looked away.

He ducked his head, forcing eye contact. 'If there's evidence in there, we'll find it, Ruth.'

She blinked, twice. 'I know.'

'Trained by the best,' he said.

She couldn't manage a smile.

A car turned into the street and a beefy man got out, fastening his overcoat and striding through the crowd of onlookers as if they were invisible. Detective Superintendent Jim Wilshire wasn't media-friendly police.

Taken by surprise, the two journalists at the tape turned a little too late to get a decent shot, and he ducked under and was fifteen feet away by the time they regained their equilibrium.

'Superintendent,' one of them called out. 'Sir – is it the Thorn Killer?'

Ruth Lake exchanged a look with the CSM. 'I'll catch up with you later,' she said.

The CSIs headed inside, and she straightened her back, waiting for the superintendent.

'Detective Sergeant Lake,' Wilshire said.

'Sir.'

'Join me.' He walked to the far side of the outer cordon where there were fewer people. There, he unfolded a huge black umbrella, more to shield them from the crowd, she suspected, than as protection from the weather.

She stepped under its canopy.

'Greg Carver?' His voice was lighter than you would expect in a big man.

She nodded.

'Who's the First Officer Attending?'

She looked guilelessly into his face. 'I am.'

'You got here fast.'

'Actually, I found him.'

He frowned. 'This was, what – thirty minutes ago?'

'Thereabouts.'

He checked his watch. She knew it was ten past midnight.

'Odd time of night to be making a social call, Sergeant.' His tone was speculative, inviting explanation rather than demanding it.

'He wanted to talk about the case.'

'Odd *time and place* for a meeting,' he said, sharper, now.

She nodded, felt her eyebrow twitch, but didn't comment.

He watched her for a few more seconds, and she forced herself to breathe slowly and stay calm.

Behind her, the road lit up and she heard the sound of an approaching vehicle, followed by the creak of tyres on fresh snow. She glanced over her shoulder as a large vehicle braked to a halt. *Mersey View* – a local cable TV company. Wilshire hated those people more than all the others.

6

'Sir?' she said.

He looked past her at the broadcast crew scrambling out of the van.

'All right, I'll let it pass – for now,' he said. 'But you heard the press when I got here. They're already asking if this is the work of the Thorn Killer. So you need to brief me.'

She took a breath, exhaled, put herself in the right mindset to give her boss the details he needed to hear.

'He was sitting in an armchair in his front room,' she said. 'He's been shot in the chest at close range.' She cleared her throat. 'It looks like a small calibre bullet.'

'You know this because . . .?'

'I was a CSI,' she said. 'I've seen a few shootings. And . . . there wasn't much blood.'

But she'd smelled it well enough. The coppery stink rose in her nostrils again.

Wilshire said, 'Are you all right?'

'Fine,' she said. 'Just—'

He nodded, then shifted position slightly, and she realised he was blocking the cable TV crew's view. 'It's understandable. But you need to hold it together. It's your scene till the OIC gets here.'

'I said I'm fine.'

He drew his brows down, and she knew she'd sounded snappish. To hell with him. 'Who *is* the Officer In Charge?' Wilshire's nostrils flared, and she added, 'If you don't mind me asking, sir.'

'DCI Jansen,' he said, his tone stiff. 'He'll be here in twenty. He'll want to know if you compromised the scene in any way.'

Her heart stopped for a moment, then began again, a slow, thick thud in her chest. 'I'm a trained CSI,' she said.

7

'Even so, in the heat of the moment . . .'

'I was careful,' she said, truthfully.

'Did he say anything?

'Carver?' she said stupidly.

'Yes, Carver. Did he *say* anything?'

'I thought he was dead.' She felt a horrifying bubble of laughter surge up in her chest, and gripped the keys in her pocket so hard she felt the cut edge break the skin of her palm.

'That doesn't answer my question.'

She bit her lip.

'Sergeant Lake?'

Ruth swallowed the humiliating urge to laugh and shook her head, focusing on a patch of pure white snow that reflected the light of the emergency vehicles stuttering red and blue, seeing Carver's eyes staring back at her, the flicker of the lights recalling the slight tremble of his eyelid, the moment she realised he was still breathing.

She started to shake.

'*Sergeant*,' Wilshire hissed, moving in so close that she had to take a step back.

She looked into his face and the shaking stopped.

'Look, the ambulance is about to leave. Go with him if you want – these media clowns will be on at you until they get a comment.' More press had begun to pile in – national outside broadcast crews, already in town reporting on Kara Grogan, swelled the numbers of local journalists. They set up their own arc lamps and called from the edge of the cordon, agitating for an update on the situation.

'I need to work,' she said.

'You can't work the scene, and you can't work the case – you know that.'

8

'More use on the j-job,' she said, then clamped her jaw shut to stop her teeth chattering.

'Where's your car?'

Lake jerked her chin towards her Renault Clio, parked opposite Carver's house inside the police cordon, with Carver's files and the gun still in the boot. She should have moved it after she'd called emergency services; right now, it was officially part of the scene.

'Come on.' Wilshire took her by the elbow. 'We'll talk in there.'

'What?' *The files. The gun.* 'No!' She pulled free of him.

'Lower your *voice*, Sergeant,' Wilshire hissed.

'Sorry, sir. I – I mean I should stay.'

'You're showing signs of shock,' her boss said. 'We need to get you out of this storm.'

He meant the snowstorm, but she thought he had never said a truer word.

'Get in your car, I'll wave you out after the ambulance – unless you want me to get someone to drive you home?'

Relief washed through her. 'No – I can drive. Thanks.' She fumbled her car keys from her coat pocket and got behind the wheel, staring straight ahead as uniformed police moved the media vans out of the way to let the ambulance through. The ambulance's emergency lights and the press cameras strobed on her eyeballs, half-blinding her, but she gripped the wheel till it creaked with the tension and gritted her teeth and kept the wheels turning until she was out of the street.

Sounds buzz and zip through Carver's ears like radio interference; alien sounds like telemetry from a distant planet.

He is lying on his back. Which doesn't make sense: he should be sitting up in his chair, drinking – that's what he was doing, isn't it? Yes, he remembers with a burst of triumph, as if remembering will make sense of this crazy confusion of light and noise. He was drinking. Whisky – a lot of it.

Then the world tilts and swoops, and he loses all sense of up or down. He feels the rush of air beneath him, hears a roar of jet engines and feels a panicky flutter in his chest. *I shouldn't be here, I've got a case to investigate*. Lights whizz by overhead, like runway lights on an airstrip – another nonsense – runway lights aren't *overhead*. Above, or below, either way, he shouldn't be seeing this; he would have to be outside the plane to see what he's seeing.

*Jeez, Carver, you're drunk*. But he feels the dull throb of a headache beginning, so maybe he passed out and this is the morning after.

A shadow moves in front of the lights: human, but strangely formless.

*This is freaky*, he thinks, and suddenly he's standing in St James's cemetery. The sheer sandstone walls of the sunken cemetery loom sixteen yards high either side of him, across a wide, flat space – remnants of the old quarry that provided sandstone to build much of Liverpool in the seventeenth and eighteenth centuries. On the westerly side, the escarpment rears up to Liverpool Cathedral. A biting wind screams from the Mersey River, a mile away, gaining momentum as it crests the hill and plunges down into the old quarry bed.

DS Lake is looking at the body of a young woman laid out on a table tomb, hard against the cemetery's sheer sandstone walls.

'This is freaky,' she says, echoing his own words. But she's looking at the first of the Thorn Killer's victims, and that was a year ago, so really, *he* is echoing *her*. And wasn't he somewhere else a minute ago – with jet engines roaring and lights racing overhead?

The victim is fully clothed, but with enough bare flesh showing to see what had been done to her. The patterns have been etched into her skin: eyes, half-closed, hiding something. *Hiding?* Now where did *that* come from? Tali – Tali Tredwin, her name was. They didn't know it then, but it seems important to remember it, now.

Someone is calling: 'Greg. Greg Carver?'

At first, he thinks it's Ruth.

'Fuck's sake, keep it down,' he wants to tell her. 'Can't you see I've got a headache?'

But he's plunged into darkness, and Ruth is gone. A blinding flash, and pain sears behind his eyeballs like a knife.

Someone says, 'Pupils equal and reactive to light.'

Carver doesn't recognise the voice. He tries to speak.

'Positive RAPD, left eye,' the voice says. 'Can we get a portable CT in here?'

Carver thinks he should answer, but still he can't speak.

The shadows pass like ghosts above him. At least the jet engine has shut up. This is wrong. He was in his flat, drinking.

Someone else was there. A woman. He remembers having sex. *In the flat?* No, somewhere else, but it feels familiar. He's yelling at the woman. A gun. *Was I holding a gun?* That blinding flash again, then more shadows. Someone is moving around his flat. *Now – or then?* Time is messed up. *And anyway, you weren't in your flat – not with the woman.*

Then where? Suddenly, he understands: being there / not being there; ghosts; jet engines; and airstrip lights that float above – this is the logic of dreams. He just needs to wake up.

Instantaneously, he's back in his flat, and the presence in the room feels tangible, a shadow, a dark *something* just out of his line of vision. He wants to turn his head, but he's paralysed; the fear is crushing, like a physical weight on his chest. *Night terror*, he thinks. He's had them before – usually after his drinking binges. If he can just move – a finger, an eyebrow – he'll wake, and the nightmare will end.

The shadow swoops in, stares into his face. *Ruth*. Relief floods through him.

He wants to say, 'Ruth, I'm *off my face* drunk, and this is a bastard horrible dream. Wake me the hell up.'

But he blinks, and she's gone.

Sounds, movement. His eyes won't focus; he still can't move, but the frightening presence is gone, and the crushing pressure on his chest is lifted – he can breathe again. Blue lights strobe beyond the curtains of his sitting room, and he thinks of a rave he once went to with Emma. He hears the clatter of a helicopter's rotor blades.

Then darkness again.

# 4

Across the Mersey River, a twenty-minute drive from Greg Carver's apartment, in a 1930s house on a quiet lane, the Thorn Killer watches BBC News 24 on TV. Paramedics carry their patient on a trolley down the steep front steps of his home; the drone of a police helicopter drowns out the voice of the reporter as it hovers, its beam focused on the scene, and for a few seconds DCI Carver is drenched in light. He looks dead.

The killer stands impulsively and paces the room. Months of planning followed by three weeks of backbreaking toil, fingers calloused and sore, hands cramped and aching, eyes burning under the glare of the lamps. Three weeks' work on Kara's skin art, preparing her, making her ready – for *this*?

Carver, as good as dead. And even if he survives, what possible use could he be?

An irritated glance at the TV reveals Ruth Lake following the paramedics down the steps of Carver's house. The camera zooms in on her, huddled in an overcoat. She breaks away to talk to a CSI, although her gaze is fixed on Carver as they slide the trolley into the ambulance. Her face is empty of emotion. The killer stops mid-step and turns to face the screen, wondering, not for the first time, what she's thinking. Snow gathers like confetti in the cascade of Sergeant Lake's hair; it looks dark under the arc lamps, but the killer knows those curls are a light brown; in the right light, the highlights appear auburn.

The imposing person of Superintendent Wilshire appears suddenly, already on the other side of the police tape, his back to the camera, and a couple of journos scramble for a comment.

*Oops – missed that one boys.*

'Superintendent,' one of the newsmen yells. 'Sir – is it the Thorn Killer?'

Detective Sergeant Lake says a few words to the CSI and turns to meet her boss. She draws herself to her full height, shoulders back, chin up.

*Now, there's a woman steeling herself for something.* The killer's suppressed rage retreats a little, tempered by curiosity about this sphinx of a woman.

The detective is lost from view for a moment, hidden under Wilshire's protective umbrella. *How symbolic.*

A cable TV van slides to a stop on the far side of the cordon, and a fraction of a second later, the news team cuts to a more revealing perspective. The recording has been nicely spliced with the original footage, but the lighting is different. The execs at the hand-to-mouth cable TV station that got *that* angle must be rubbing their hands at the money coming in from news teams, eager to get the stricken face of DCI Carver's right-hand woman on their screens. Except it's impossible to read any emotion at all on that pale, pretty face.

From this angle, the crowd is visible and the killer switches attention away from Ruth and her superintendent, focusing instead on the rubberneckers, seeing curiosity, excitement in their faces. Everyone loves a good murder.

The superintendent says something and DS Lake replies, confusion written in the furrow of her brow. He speaks again and her shoulders go rigid for a second. *So tense.* Then she lifts her head and the whites of her eyes catch flashes from the

14

emergency vehicles' light bars. Could Ruth Lake actually *care* about Carver?

Is she *shaking*? She *is* – she's losing it. The killer moves in closer: this just got interesting.

A sharp word from Superintendent Wilshire brings the sergeant to herself again, but her control seems tenuous. She nods towards her car (it *is* her car – the viewer knows this, and a lot more besides about Ruth Lake). Wilshire takes her arm, and she jerks free. She can't be heard, but it doesn't take a lip-reader to see that DS Lake is saying, 'No.' She leans back, body angled away from the direction the superintendent wants her to take – classic signs of refusal, literally digging her heels into the snow. She *really* doesn't want to leave. And then suddenly she does, and she's moving fast, dragging her car key out of her pocket so fast that it practically turns inside out.

*Well, now that's . . . odd.*

A rewind, pause, replay reveals a little more. The viewer reads alarm, and then relief in Sergeant Lake's face. This isn't just odd, it's *fascinating*.

Playing the sequence one more time, the viewer leans forward, looking for the instant that alarm turns to relief.

The camera zooms in on Ruth's face as she follows the ambulance past the tape. Her jaw is clenched tight enough to break a molar.

'Sergeant Lake, what *have* you been up to?'

# 5

Forty minutes later, having safely stashed the files and the gun, DS Lake headed over to the hospital. A marked police car was parked in one of the emergency bays; the driver stood under the awning, out of the steadily falling snow, taking crafty puffs on a vape. He tucked the e-cig out of sight when he saw her.

'You brought Emma Carver here?' she said.

'Half an hour ago, Sarge.'

'And you're hanging around because . . .?'

'It's quiet, and I thought . . .'

'You know what you should do when it's quiet?' An answer didn't leap readily to the constable's lips and she said, 'Bimble about; be seen, *deter* crime with your highly visible presence. Help someone out of a snowdrift. The glow of righteousness will keep you warm – and it's better for your health.' She cocked her head to let him know that she'd seen him sucking on his e-cig.

She walked through the staff entrance and the doors slid shut behind her. She stamped her feet on the rubber matting and shook herself to shed some of the snow that had gathered on her shoulders and hair. A nurse hurried out of one of the cubicles opposite the nursing station; she glanced at Ruth, beckoned to someone out of her view, but carried on.

'Greg Carver?' Ruth called.

The nurse slowed, and at the same moment, a security guard appeared. 'Are you family?' the nurse asked.

16

'Police.' She showed her warrant card.

'He's in no state to answer questions,' the nurse said, walking on. 'And I haven't got time—'

'Emma arrived half an hour ago – Greg's wife. I was wondering how she's—'

The nurse frowned.

'You see,' Ruth went on, 'Greg is a friend, and—' That word, 'friend', almost undid her. A spasm twisted her mouth, and she took a breath, letting it go slowly.

The nurse stopped, considering her for a moment. 'Let me see that warrant card again.'

Ruth handed it over. The nurse checked it and, with a nod to the security guy, gave it back.

'We've had reporters trying to get in,' she explained. 'Mrs Carver's in the waiting area – through the doors on the right.'

'Before I talk to her,' Ruth said, detaining the nurse for just a few moments longer. 'Is there anything I should know?'

'He had a few problems in the ambulance coming over,' the nurse said, keeping her voice low. 'But he's stable, for now.'

'For now? What does that mean?'

'It means his BP dropped dangerously low for a short time, but we got it under control, and now he's being assessed.'

Not much of an answer, but Ruth understood that medics had their protocols, just as police did, and she didn't push for more.

Emma was seated alone. When her eyes finally focused on Ruth, she leapt to her feet and seized her by the hands. They were desperately cold. Her skin usually had a peaches-and-cream complexion Ruth envied, but tonight it was paper-white, and seemed stretched too tight over the bones of her face.

'They said he was shot?' It came out as a question, as if it was too implausible to be real.

Ruth nodded.

'And what they're saying on the news – is that true?' she asked. 'Is it the Thorn Killer, Ruth?'

'I don't know,' Ruth said, keeping her answers short to avoid building lies she couldn't keep track of.

'Had Greg made a breakthrough? He'd tell you, wouldn't he? They said you found him – did he say anything?'

'He wasn't . . .' She looked into Emma's blue eyes and saw Carver's staring back at her, unblinking. 'He couldn't . . .' *Shit*. 'He wasn't conscious,' she said finally, as the closest to the truth that she could manage.

Her mobile phone buzzed in her pocket, and she checked the screen. John Hughes, the Crime Scene Manager. She excused herself, walking through to the emergency treatment area to take the call in private.

'You need to take that outside, Sergeant.' The nurse had returned with box of nitrile gloves.

Ruth apologised and stepped into the freezing night before moving the slider to answer. The sky had cleared, leaving eight inches of new snow on top of the ice-crusted remnants of the last fall. It softened the contours of the taxis and emergency vehicles parked on the forecourt, and reflected the ghost-white glow of the streetlight LEDs.

'How is he?' Hughes said, without preamble. 'Have you heard?'

'I'm at the hospital now. He's still being assessed,' she said. 'How about you – did you find anything?' Hughes getting in touch so soon meant one of two things – they had found something, or they didn't think there was anything to find. She held her breath.

'A small amount of blood spatter on the chair. No signs of struggle, a whisky spill on the floor – could be he passed out, didn't hear the shooter come in.'

'Footwear marks, fingermarks?'

'The paramedics trampled all over the scene,' he said. 'But we did get a small size footwear impression on the rug in the bedroom – could be a woman's shoe.'

*Crap.* Leaving her shoeprints in his living room was one thing, but in his bedroom . . . Wilshire was right – she must be in shock, missing something as simple as that. But she would hand over a different pair of shoes for comparison, so it wasn't a major problem.

'It looks like surfaces, light switches and door handles have been wiped down,' he said. 'The only fingermarks we've found are yours.'

She sighed, hoping it didn't sound too theatrical.

'And a void on the carpet of the bedroom – looks like a heavy square object has been sitting there for a while – a box most likely. It looks like Blu-tack has recently been removed from the walls in there, so maybe he used the bedroom as his unofficial war room?'

'Maybe.'

'Come on, Ruth, don't be so tight-lipped. If *anyone* would know, it'd be you.'

'He didn't invite me into his bedroom, but I'd say it was a fair bet he worked on the case at home.'

'Jansen's the OIC, isn't he?'

'Yeah.'

'Well, you'd better let him know.'

'I don't see why.'

'Jesus, Ruth – you're not thinking straight! Let's say, for the sake of argument, that Carver *did* keep a private dossier: whatever you've got on the murders –'

'– could now be in the Thorn Killer's hands,' she finished for him. 'And if that's the case, the whole investigation is screwed.' Hughes was right, she wasn't thinking straight. Couldn't get that image out of her head: Greg Carver in his chair, blood oozing from the bullet wound in his chest, his eyes fixed on her while she cleared up the evidence.

'So, are you going to tell Jansen, or shall I?' Hughes said. 'Only, it might be better coming from you.'

'I'll do it,' she said. 'Just give me an hour to find out what's happening with Greg.'

'All right,' he said. 'And Ruth?'

'Yeah?'

'When you've done that, go home and get some sleep.'

As Ruth returned to the waiting room, a doctor in scrubs came through a side door and called for Mrs Carver. Emma gazed round in panic, seeking out Ruth. The two women reached the doctor at the same time, and for a moment the medic looked confused, and a little embarrassed.

'DS Lake – I'm a friend and colleague of Greg's,' Ruth explained.

'Best we talk in private,' the doctor said, holding the door.

Emma seized Ruth's hand.

'Sergeant Lake can come, if you want her to,' the doctor said.

He showed them through to a private room with armchairs around a low table, a box of tissues within easy reach. The nurse Ruth had spoken to earlier hovered next to the door.

'Is he all right?' Emma said. 'Can I see him?'

'We've performed a CT scan,' the doctor said. 'The bullet is lodged about here –' he pointed to the centre of his own chest '– between the aorta, which is *the* major artery, and the spinal cord. We need to give Greg antibiotics to lower his chances of infection. Does he have any allergies?'

'No,' Emma said.

The doctor turned to the nurse. 'Tell them they can make a start.'

'A *start?*' Emma said. 'Haven't you operated on him, yet?'

'It's a complicated picture,' he said, his tone calm and firm. 'He's had a blood transfusion, and his vital signs are stable, so we don't have to rush in. But your husband also has some swelling of the brain.'

'I don't understand,' Emma said, her voice shrill with anxiety. 'You said he was shot in the chest.'

'He was,' the doctor said. 'The head injury isn't obvious, but it's something we routinely check for in cases like this. It may or may not be related to the shooting.' He looked at Ruth. 'He was found sitting up in a chair?'

'Yes,' she said. 'I found him.'

'Is it possible he fell and hit his head after he was shot, managed to crawl to the chair?'

Ruth thought about it. There was no blood spatter, no blood anywhere in the room, except for on the armchair. She shook her head. 'Unlikely.'

'Well, brain swelling can happen quite a while *after* the trauma. Has he been involved in a fight, or a car accident recently?'

Emma turned helplessly to Ruth.

'Greg and Emma are separated, just now,' she explained. 'He and I work closely, and I'm sure he would have mentioned something like that. But when he rang to ask me to call round this evening, he sounded, uh –' she glanced at Emma '– intoxicated. So I suppose he might have fallen *before* the shooting.'

'Okay, so the injury is probably very recent – which is good, because it means we're treating the injury fast.'

'You seem more concerned about the brain swelling than the bullet lodged near his spine,' Ruth said.

'Greg has significant build-up of fluid, and that's causing pressure on his brain,' the doctor said, tapping the top of his own head lightly. 'Reducing the intracranial pressure is our first priority. So, a neurosurgeon will insert tubes into his brain cavities to drain the extra fluid off. That should do the trick.'

'And if it doesn't?' Emma said.

'There are other, more radical, options. A team of specialists at the Aintree Neurosciences Centre is ready to operate.'

'But that's miles away,' Emma wailed. 'Why can't you do it here?'

'It's his best chance, Mrs Carver,' the doctor said gently. 'They have the best resources in the north west for injuries like this.'

She gave a juddering sigh.

'We'll airlift him, which is quicker, and safer, because there's less risk of any jarring on the journey. But before I give the word, I need to ask you something, and it's important you're honest with me.'

Emma blinked. 'Of course.'

He looked into her face, as if watching carefully for her reaction. 'Greg's blood alcohol is dangerously high. Now, we can still operate, but the team will need to know if this is a one-off, or if Greg has a long-standing problem with drink.'

'He's been drinking heavily for some time, but I can't believe it got so bad.' Emma looked to Ruth for confirmation.

'He drinks. Maybe a bit more than most,' Ruth said, being honest in this, at least. 'But . . .' She recalled the empty whisky bottle lying next to Carver's chair. 'This is . . . unusual.'

The doctor nodded. 'That's helpful.'

Emma took his words as a good sign, and smiled gratefully at him.

He glanced at Ruth. She had been a cop for long enough to know that the prognosis for habitually heavy drinkers was never good in trauma cases. She explained this to Emma.

The doctor went on: 'Greg's drinking pattern means there's an additional risk attached to anaesthesia, even before we operate,' he said. 'But the risk of permanent and catastrophic brain damage is even greater if we don't.'

Emma nodded, dumbly, and the doctor turned to Ruth with a slight lift of his shoulders. He looked young to be doing this kind of work. Not dealing with death as such – Ruth herself was just twenty-four when she worked on her first murder scene – but what came after. She had always been grateful, back then, that the task of breaking the bad news to a victim's family was on others' shoulders. How much harder it must be to talk families through life-and-death situations, helping them to make decisions that, should things go badly, could make life worse than death.

'Emma, he's asking for your permission to operate,' she said.

'*Mine*? But we're – I haven't even *seen* Greg in over a month. We . . . oh, God.' Her shoulders slumped. 'I asked for a divorce.'

'You're still listed as his next of kin,' the doctor said, his tone apologetic. 'If there was *anyone* else . . . But as I understand it, he has no other family.'

Greg's wife pressed her fingers to her lips.

'Emma?' Ruth prompted.

Emma slid her hands to her cheeks, as though physically holding herself together. 'Tell me what to *do*,' she begged.

Given what she had already done, it really wasn't her place to say, but Ruth said what was expected of her, anyway: 'I don't see that you have a choice.'

Emma brought her hands down from her face and clasped them in her lap. 'Then you have my permission,' she said.

# 6

In the critical care unit, Carver dreams.

Sefton Park, seven days ago, a light dusting of snow, and bitterly cold.

She is seated on a flat stone under a tree lit by fairy lights, a frozen waterfall as the backdrop to the staged scene. He sees her first from a distance of thirty feet, and his heart stops. Blonde and slender, she is wearing skinny jeans with wedge sandals, a blue peasant top. Her hair, silky and long, is combed in a centre parting.

The backdrop, her blonde hair, the centre parting, her clothing— it's a tableau of the honeymoon photograph he keeps on the dresser in his sitting room.

*Emma*, he thinks. Before he knows it, he is running.

Twenty feet in, he slows, every nerve crackling with tension, his heart stuttering.

It isn't Emma. He murmurs, 'Thank God', though he is not proud of it.

'Greg!' Ruth calls to him from the pathway. 'Stop.'

He turns, sees his shoe marks tracking back through the frosted grass. There are no other tracks. Already, he is thinking timelines – the exact time of the snow flurry and the frost that came after it will tell them when the body was placed here.

'Do *not* touch the body,' Ruth commands.

He swivels to look again. Tattoos covering every inch of her flesh make it seem that she is wearing a long-sleeved top. A wash of light from LEDs festooned in the tree gives her face a bluish cast, and frost glitters like tiny jewels in her eyelashes.

'Walk back to me,' Ruth says. 'You know the drill: take the same path; match the footwear marks, if you can.'

Next he is in the post mortem room, although he doesn't remember getting there. The body is laid out on the table. By now, he knows that the victim is Kara Grogan.

As he watches, the mortuary technicians undress the body, taking pictures as they go, and the tattoos inflicted on Kara Grogan's body are revealed. The camera flashes illuminate the ink patterns: heads on grotesquely elongated necks, their faces upturned, featureless. There are gaps between the clusters, and from these spaces eyes stare out – thousands of them.

But the eyes scored on Tali's body were closed, or half-closed. The ink on Kara's body is black, when all of the other victims were tattooed using blue ink. And the eyes tattooed on Kara are all wide open. Some have an avid look, others appear almost threatening. He is feverish to write this down in case he forgets, because in dream-logic, he knows beyond all doubt that the tattoos hold the answer to the puzzle – and to the identity of the killer.

The mortuary technician lifts a hank of Kara's hair, ready to comb it for trace evidence, revealing a pair of Ola Gorie silver millennium earrings. Carver knows exactly what they are, because he'd bought a pair for Emma as an engagement gift. She had worn them on their honeymoon; was wearing them in the honeymoon photo.

'What the f—?'

Ruth says, 'Greg?'

He is breathing hard, seeing sparkles of light in front of his eyes.

26

'Greg, you're hyperventilating,' Ruth says.

'If he's going to pass out, mind it's not over my body,' the pathologist says.

Ruth edges him to a corner of the post mortem room.

'Those earrings,' he says, 'They're Emma's.'

'*Like* Emma's, you mean?'

'No, they're hers. They were a limited edition – hers went missing when I moved out. We had a row about it – she thought I'd stolen them.'

'We'll check them for Emma's DNA,' Ruth says.

Suddenly, he's back at the post mortem table, and Kara's body is naked. He hears a high-pitched *snick* – the sound of a sharp knife through flesh. He glances in question at the pathologist, but the doctor spreads his hands to show he isn't holding a scalpel, and Carver knows he has not even touched the body, yet. They look down at her in unison. As they watch, a line opens up along the length of one of the tattooed necks. *Snick, snick, snick, snick, snick* – and the line becomes a gash.

Kara's skin splits along the lines of the markings, and begins to peel back in bloody strips. Kara screams, writhing in pain as her skin sloughs off, exposing muscle and tendons. Beneath the bloody strips of skin, something is moving.

Horrified, Carver backs away, but he cannot tear his eyes from her, and suddenly the skin of the girl's face pares back and falls away and Carver sees Emma's face, gory with Kara's blood, her eyes huge with horror. His heart hammering, Carver turns to the people around him, begging them for help, but they are looking at him, and not at the body on the table. A sudden sharp beeping, and someone says, 'You've set off the fire alarm.'

\*     \*     \*

27

Nurses rushed to Greg Carver's bedside. A deep-throated buzz almost drowned out the rapid beep of the cardiac monitor.

'He's tachycardic,' the first said.

The second touched Carver's hand. He twitched, throwing her off.

'Reactive to touch,' she said with a quick glance at her colleague.

Then she spoke directly to Carver, raising her voice over the noise of the machinery. 'Mr Carver? Greg – you're in hospital. Everything's fine. Greg – you're safe. You need to calm yourself. Try to keep still. The doctor is coming.'

Carver's right leg flicked, once, then, as the doctor arrived at his bedside, a series of shuddering contractions ran through his body.

'Hold him,' the doctor said. Swiftly and with steady hands, she increased the flow of propofol into the IV infusion.

Inside two minutes, the crisis was over, and Carver was stabilised. The doctor checked the time and made a note on Carver's chart. The three exchanged a look that said, 'That was close.' One nurse remained to check the monitors one last time, and saw that tears were squeezing from under Carver's eyelids and the thin strips of tape holding his eyes closed had lifted a little. She gently wiped his eyes and dried his cheeks, using a sterile swab, then applied new strips of tape.

Distraught, Carver reaches in to the mass of skin and blood that had been Kara, trying to recover his wife from the girl's tortured remains. At last the pathologist seems to have noticed what's happening on his post mortem table, but instead of helping, he places a blindfold over Carver's eyes.

'So you don't contaminate the scene,' he says.

## 7

Ordered to go home, Ruth Lake tried to get some rest, but every time she closed her eyes she saw Greg Carver staring at her from his armchair. She finally drifted off at around five a.m., jolted awake fifteen minutes later by her phone. It was Emma, calling to say that Greg had experienced some kind of seizure.

'Is he okay?'

'They're doing another scan to check that the bullet hasn't moved.'

'They haven't removed it yet?'

'No – they need to insert a drainage tube into his brain first. The doctor said they had to sort out the brain swelling before anything else – remember?'

*Did he?* 'Yes. Yes, of course he did.' *For God's sake, Ruth – you've got to get your shit together.* 'Sorry,' Ruth added. 'But I thought they were sedating him?'

'They gave him a lower dosage of the anaesthetic than usual because of his blood alcohol levels. He came out of the coma very briefly.'

Ruth sat up straight. 'He woke up?'

She almost blurted out, 'It's too soon!' Said instead, 'Did he say anything?'

'He wasn't fully awake,' Emma said. 'But he was getting there. They said it's a good sign.'

'That's – that's great, Emma,' Ruth said, thinking she needed to get to Carver before he spoke to anyone about what happened. 'I'm guessing they'll keep him under until they get the pressure in his brain down to normal?'

'Yes.'

She suppressed a gasp of relief. 'Would you do me a favour, Emma? Would you ring me when they decide it's time to wake him up?'

'Of *course*,' Emma said. 'You do know you saved his life?'

Ruth tasted bile at the back of her throat and swallowed hard. 'This is important, Emma – you need to tell me before you talk to anyone else. Okay?'

'Okay.' She heard uncertainty in Emma's voice. 'Ruth, is there something you're not telling me?'

*Oh, so much* . . . 'I just need to know what's happening,' Ruth said.

'Ruth, I'm sorry – this must be awful for you, too.'

'I have to go,' Ruth said. 'Work.' This, at least, was true: DCI Simon Jansen, the Senior Investigating Officer investigating Greg's shooting, had called a briefing at eight a.m.

Ruth arrived a few minutes after the hour. Jansen welcomed her with a nod and, with standing room only, she took up position at the back of the room, dropping her shoulder bag between her feet. Simon Jansen was a tall, sombre man with dark hair, turning grey. He had thirty-five years on the job, but as a European Police Champion in Judo, and one of three coaches to the national team, he wasn't expected to retire anytime soon, and he was known to keep close control of his investigations. Ruth knew him as efficient, rigorous and dispassionate to the point of ruthlessness. He had a team of ten detectives already in place, and another thirty uniform police were helping with house-to-house door knocking. The inquiry would be run entirely separate from the Thorn Killer investigation – standard procedure.

The owner of the flat downstairs had already been interviewed: he was out at a party, didn't get back until the early hours. He said he'd neither heard nor seen anything unusual over the last few days. The house stood in its own grounds, and none of the street's residents noticed anything suspicious – most of them had been roused from their beds by the police and ambulance services lights, or the chatter of the police helicopter as it searched the area.

CSIs were still going over Greg Carver's house, but John Hughes, the Crime Scene Manager, was at the meeting, and he reported that key areas had been wiped down, and only Ruth Lake's and DCI Carver's fingerprints were present in the flat.

'So, if we're going to have any chance of finding the shooter, the timeline for the hours leading up to the shooting is going to be crucial,' Jansen said. 'What've we got?'

'He had no recent run-ins with local criminals, as far as I can make out,' a Detective Constable she didn't recognise said. 'And no meetings last night. At least none he'd logged on his schedule.'

'DS Lake?' Jansen said.

She leaned off the wall. 'I can't help much,' she said. 'But I guess my after-hours meeting to talk about the serial killings wasn't on Carver's schedule either.' It sounded like over-explanation, and Ruth was known as someone who didn't say more than was strictly necessary. But she didn't like to be caught on the back foot, either, and judged it best to get the fact of her rendezvous with Carver in before Jansen asked her directly. A few of the men shifted in their seats to take a sly peek at Carver's late-night visitor.

'Did he say *why* it wouldn't wait until today to have that conversation?'

She was ready for that. 'He said he didn't want to talk over the phone – but it was urgent.' Her answer contained a simple truth, and a complicated lie. Of course, she had already lied about her time of arrival, pushing it back by ten minutes; a few eyebrows raised over an unscheduled meeting was the least of her problems.

Jansen grunted. 'So, we've got Carver's Decision Logs and Policy Files for the investigation to date,' Jansen said. 'If he kept personal notes, I'd like to see them.'

John Hughes swivelled to look at Ruth and widened his eyes at her, as if to say, 'What the hell?'

She had promised the CSM that she would tell Jansen about Carver's missing files. *You screwed up again, Ruth.* Under normal circumstances she would never have expected John Hughes to cover for her, but these were not normal circumstances. Either he would, or he wouldn't, so she took a breath, and said, 'He didn't share those with me, but I imagine he kept them in his flat somewhere?'

After a pause that seemed to last a minute, but was only a second or two, Hughes said: 'If he did, they're not there now, or in his car. We did find an imprint on his bedroom carpet that suggests a large, heavy box had been resting there for some time. Also, A3-sized sheets of paper had been tacked to his bedroom wall until very recently.'

DCI Jansen rubbed a hand over his chin. Nobody spoke. At last, Jansen said, 'What about his laptop?'

'The computer techs are looking at it,' Hughes said. 'But, it's fully encrypted, per protocol.'

Jansen sucked his teeth. 'Of course. It's just *paper* files he leaves lying around.'

'There *is* a chance the password is written or encoded some-where in his official paperwork, or on his mobile phone,' Hughes suggested.

'But we can't rely on that.' Jansen gave a tight smile. 'Well, we'll just have to hope Carver didn't give away any trade secrets, won't we?' He took a deep breath and exhaled slowly. 'All right. His mobile phone has already been taken into evidence – we need to know who he was talking to – and when.'

'The good news is he doesn't password protect his mobile,' Hughes said. 'So his phone logs, texts and so on will be immediately available. His police email account wouldn't be accessible via his phone, but if he has a private account—'

'Okay, tell your guys to prioritise his phone.' Jansen located the DS who was managing task allocations. 'We're going to need multiple copies of his Decision Logs and Policy files.' He pointed to two detectives seated near the front of the room. 'You and you will sift through his paperwork for passwords, logins, codes – whatever.' His attention switched back to the task manager. 'And I want someone to go through his credit cards, bank statements, cashpoint withdrawals – we need to know Carver's exact movements for the last week. If he met with anyone, if his spending patterns changed, if he's had a run-in with anyone – I want to know.'

Finally, he turned to Ruth Lake. 'Meanwhile, if anything pops into your head, Sergeant . . .'

'I'll let you know, sir.'

John Hughes was waiting for her as the team filed past in the corridor.

'Got a minute?' he said.

She nodded towards the fire exit, and they walked up to the next landing.

'I thought you were going to tell Jansen about Greg's unofficial file *before* the briefing.' Hughes had the weathered skin of a man who had enjoyed hiking and sailing since his schooldays. The lines on his face usually bore traces of laughter, but not right now.

'Yeah,' she said. 'I meant to.'

'Why didn't you?'

If she was honest with herself she hadn't really forgotten: telling Jansen that the files were gone when she knew exactly where they were was one lie too far, and she'd just put it off until it was too late to say anything.

'I'm sorry, John,' she said. 'I dropped the ball on that one.'

He peered into her eyes. 'Did you get any sleep?'

'Some.' Ruth reached into her shoulder bag and handed him a pair of shoes, already bagged.

He held them up to the light, peering in though the cellophane window of the paper bag.

'These are the ones you wore to meet with Greg?'

He seemed perplexed and she felt a spurt of anxiety. 'That's what you asked for.'

'Just – they look in good nick for having been through a snowstorm.'

'I was on the *street*, John, not walking up Ben Nevis. And I took them off as soon as I got home.'

He said, 'Hunh,' eyeing the contents of the bag dubiously.

'What?'

'I've already taken a squint at Carver's phone logs – and right off the bat, I found an anomaly.'

Ruth felt a momentary stab of fear. *He doesn't know what you've been up to*, she told herself, widening her eyes and clearing her mind of guilty thoughts.

'Great,' she said. 'Anything I can work with?'

'Something you can explain.'

She stared earnestly into his face, repeating to herself, *He doesn't know*.

'In your report, you said Greg called you at eleven twenty-five. But he actually called you twelve minutes before that.'

'Did he?'

'Ruth, what's going on?' John said.

'I don't know where my head is at, just now, John.' The lines and wrinkles in his face realigned to an expression of sympathy, and Ruth shrugged, even smiled a little. 'It was snowing – driving conditions were slow.'

He raised a finger, another question forming on his lips.

She checked her watch. 'Sorry, John, I've got to go – the boss wants to introduce me to my new DCI.'

The distraction worked.

'Already?' John said. 'He's not letting the grass grow.'

'He thinks we've got the Thorn Killer backed into a corner.'

'Does he know TK's got Carver's case files?'

Ruth bit her lip. 'I haven't told him the files are missing, yet.'

'You need to start communicating with the SIOs, Ruth.'

'I know,' she said, thinking she would have to be very careful precisely how much she communicated. 'So, there was no sign that anyone else was at Greg's flat?'

He lifted up the evidence bag with her shoes inside.

'Only the shoeprint.' A shadow crossed Hughes's face. 'This guy is a ghost,' he said. 'We searched every inch of the place

35

– there's no sign that *any* man other than Greg was ever in his apartment.'

That was dangerously near the truth, so she gave him a sympathetic grimace and wished him luck, then headed off to talk to Superintendent Wilshire.

# 8

*Day 3*

New Year's Eve; BBC News is running a feature on the 'Thorn Killings'. Most news coverage over the two previous days has been focused on Carver: looped video of the scene outside his apartment; reports on his status – 'critical, but stable'; press conferences with appeals to the public for information. But with no information forthcoming, and Carver's condition unchanged, press interest has returned to the killings.

The subject of the programme sips coffee and watches, conscious of being a part of history in the making.

'It is nine days since Kara Grogan's body was found,' the reporter intones, his solemnity a fair approximation of sincerity. 'Apparently the fifth victim of the so-called "Thorn Killer".'

Images of the five women appear one after another on-screen.

'In a pattern that has become chillingly familiar, Kara, a student at the Liverpool Institute of the Performing Arts, disappeared just over three weeks before she was found,' the commentator goes on. 'Police believe she was alive until shortly before her body was discovered in Liverpool's Sefton Park, at a place known locally as "The Fairy Glen".'

The reporter speaks over footage of the rock feature and the tree where Kara had been found, the foot of which is now littered with cellophane-wrapped flowers, some half-buried in snow. The camera pulls back to show a waterfall, complete with picturesque drifts of snow on its rocky outcrops and a few twinkling icicles hanging from the topmost rock formations.

Kara was the most beautifully staged of all of them. The backdrop was dramatic; the dressing, lighting, makeup brilliantly conceived and executed. That night's frost had heightened the scene, taking what was already gorgeous and rendering it truly exquisite.

'Like the other four victims, Miss Grogan's body had been extensively inked with tattoos which the police believe were made using a sharp thorn.'

Her skin – so pale! The ink seemed to float above it, so that the eyes etched in her flesh appeared alive, active.

The snowy scene at the glen melts to an image of a smiling Kara Grogan side by side with a recent photograph of Emma Carver, helpfully captioned with her name and her relationship to DCI Greg Carver, described as 'the detective in charge of investigating the murders'. Emma's picture has been airbrushed and retouched to make her look younger, but even without the photoshopping, the two women are strikingly similar.

The reporter rehashes how Kara's body had been posed, as all the others were, in a place where they would quickly be discovered. 'But on this occasion, a text message was sent from Kara Grogan's mobile phone to Detective Chief Inspector Carver, with a photograph of the scene, and instructions as to where he would find her.'

He maintains a poker face, but can't quite contain the excitement in his voice as he adds, 'A confidential source revealed to us today that when she was found, Kara was wearing a pair of earrings which have since been identified by DNA analysis as belonging to Mrs Carver.'

They switch to a photograph of earrings labelled, in the interests of clarity, as 'the same design' as the pair Kara was wearing when she was found.

'Oh . . .' That's new. Someone has been tattling to the media. The killer feels a return of the dull fury experienced after first discovering that Carver had been shot. The earrings were a message for Carver to reflect on; they were not intended as a topic for vulgar gossip and public speculation.

'In an extraordinary turn of events, two days ago, Chief Inspector Carver was shot in his own home. Police say they are keeping an open mind as to the possibility that the shooting is linked to the so-called Thorn Killer inquiry.'

Obligingly, they show a press conference at which DCI Jansen regurgitates the usual platitudes about police objectivity, and the unhelpfulness of speculation, ending with a request for help from the public.

His appeals don't seem to have got through to the media. The most popular theory to date is that DCI Carver got too close to finding the Thorn Killer, and had narrowly escaped becoming his sixth victim. By shooting. How could they compare Kara's grotto with the ugly mess in Carver's apartment, and call that the Thorn Killer's work? It was insulting, offensive.

'Detective Chief Inspector Carver remains in a critical condition under twenty-four-hour guard at the Aintree Neurosciences Centre, on the outskirts of Liverpool,' the reporter says.

It's a matter of public knowledge that Carver was airlifted to the neurosciences centre, but it is still somewhat puzzling, since the killer is one of the few who knows for a fact that Carver was shot in the chest.

'Merseyside Police have also placed Chief Inspector Carver's wife under armed protection.'

'*Really?*'

The newsreader turns to his left and introduces a retired Detective Superintendent from the Met and an elderly forensic psychologist. The ex-cop explains that the physical similarities between Kara and Emma Carver, and – more chillingly – the DNA match to Mrs Carver on the earrings, means that Merseyside Police had to consider the possibility that there is a credible threat to Mrs Carver's safety.

'Oh, for heaven's sake . . .'

In fact, Merseyside Police have declined to comment on this speculation, but the reporter asks the ancient forensic psych for his take on the new evidence. The old man grumbles and wheezes through a psych 101 explanation of transference, makes a feeble attempt to jazz it up with a confused bit of psychobabble about 'misidentification of the object' – a misidentification of his own, ironically, since he seems unintentionally to identify the entire female sex as 'objects'.

The fact of the matter is there *was no* misidentification. Kara was chosen as a facsimile of Emma Carver as she had been in the early days of her marriage. Kara wasn't intended as a *threat* to Emma. She carried a message to Carver.

The psychologist rumbles on: 'The murderer could be substituting Emma for a hated figure in his early life.'

'Oh, spare me . . .'

'Equally, by selecting a victim who so closely resembled Chief Inspector Carver's wife, he could be threatening that which Greg Carver holds dearest because he – the killer – felt particularly threatened at that time.'

'Brilliant reasoning: "If it's not X, then it may be Y, and if not Y, then it could be Z.'" The BBC must really be desperate, seeking the opinion of this decrepit blowhard.

'And BTW psycho-hack: "Threatening *that which* Carver holds dearest"? Your female objectification is showing.'

Kara was never a threat – she was a *reminder* to Carver that he still cared for his wife. And judging by Carver's reaction on the night he found Kara's body, the message had got through loud and clear – at least to the one person it was intended for.

When the old man starts in on 'unfinished business' and the significance of the thorn as an object of penetration, it's time to reach for the remote control. But the programme switches to new footage of Detective Sergeant Lake leaving the hospital, and the killer stops, finger hovering over the 'off' button. Journos yell the usual expressions of concern and questions about the state of Carver's health. One voice, louder than the others, roars, 'Did the Thorn Killer shoot Chief Inspector Carver, Sergeant?'

On previous occasions over the last two days, DS Lake has ignored press questions, but now, she stops.

'I am not qualified to comment on Chief Inspector Carver's health,' she says. 'And I am not directly involved in the investigation into his shooting.'

*You've been briefed by the press office, haven't you, my darling?*

'The team assigned will be investigating all possibilities,' she goes on. 'It's too early to comment, and it's unhelpful to speculate, but I have full confidence that the person who did this will be punished.'

Lake ends the discussion with a curt nod, and steers through the crowd of reporters without a sideways glance.

'You're *saying* all the right things, but you don't believe a *word* of it. Now is that because you don't have faith in Chief

Inspector Jansen, or is it because you know something you're not telling?'

A rewind and replay is not enough to unravel that tangled web, but one thing is certain: Ruth Lake says one thing, but her posture and gestures tell quite a different story.

How marvellous! Sergeant Lake becomes more and more intriguing with every encounter.

# 9

Ruth Lake's terraced house in Wavertree was only a short step from the more desirable location of Carver's apartment, but it might as well be a world away. The house had belonged to her parents, bought from the council under Right to Buy in the 1980s. It backed onto another row of Edwardian red-brick houses, and a dozen more streets just like it.

A back entry running the length of the street was just wide enough to accommodate the wheelie bins on collection days. For a while in the late nineties they'd had a problem with addicts queuing in the alley to get their next fix from dealers who lived in the street. Ruth, just a kid at the time, was warned never to use the alley as a short cut. She'd promised, but of course she broke that promise, and had witnessed a fight between two junkies which ended with one of them being stabbed to death. A criminal prosecution, a couple of evictions and gates placed at strategic points along the alleys to restrict access had finally purged the street of drug touts, and now the area was again considered a safe place to bring up a family.

A two-storey extension was tacked on the back; housing the kitchen and bathroom, it took up most of the tiny rear yard, but Ruth had planted up the remaining strip of garden. In spring, the borders were filled with crocuses and narcissi, while in summer, honeysuckle rambled over the walls and filled the air with heady perfume.

Right now, though, her back yard was eight inches deep in snow.

She shivered on her back doorstep and took a drag on an e-cig. She hadn't had a craving for months, but stress, and the fear of being caught in all her lies, had triggered a jittery need for nicotine. Seeing that uniformed cop at the hospital puffing away like a steam train was more than she could take – she'd almost asked him if he had a spare she could bum. She had resisted – just – the urge to stop off at a newsagent and buy a pack of the real thing, but succumbed to the siren call of the vape later that same day. Another promise broken.

She blew vapour skywards and murmured, 'Sorry, Mum.' It was six a.m. and still dark, except for oblongs of light filtering through the bedroom curtains of the houses across the alley.

Since Detective Superintendent Wilshire had introduced him, she had managed to duck DCI Parsons, who had been drafted in to take over the Thorn Killer case. He had spent the best part of the last two days reading Greg Carver's key decision logs and policy files, trying to get up to speed.

These logs and files were described in the how-to manuals as 'crucial elements in the Senior Investigating Officer's decision-making process'. But in the year she had worked with Carver – and increasingly over the past four months – Ruth had seen him routinely make decisions on the spur of the moment and justify them after the fact. In reality, his policy notes were a joke, imposing a spurious logic over the intuitive and sometimes random actions he'd taken. So, while her new boss pored over Carver's near-fictional account of the investigation, Ruth was getting acquainted with his unofficial files.

She saw the light go on in next door's kitchen. She didn't feel up to a chat with old Peggy, so she turned off the vape and returned to her kitchen to pour a fresh coffee from the machine she'd splashed out on in the pre-Christmas sales. Warming her hands on the mug, she sat at the table, stifling a yawn.

Carver had done a lot of research on Kara, finding YouTube videos, SoundCloud podcasts and recordings of readings linked from a WordPress website the student had put together herself.

Ruth opened her laptop and followed one of the links to a YouTube recording entitled, 'Kara Grogan as Lady Macbeth – sleepwalking scene (dress rehearsal)', clicked on the image and sat down to watch.

An end-of-year student production, shot in semi-darkness, the audio quality on the recording wasn't great, but the strength of this young woman's talent was mesmerising.

Her eyes glistening with tears, dull horror in her expression as if she peered into the murky depths of hell, she held her spotless hand up before a candle flame and whispered, 'All the perfumes of Arabia will not sweeten this . . . little . . . hand.'

Her peers, arranged in a circle of chairs around her, shifted nervously in their seats as she began a soft exhalation. It rose in tone and volume to a wail of anguish. A male student shrunk back in his chair as she spoke to him, admonishing him for looking so pale, urging him to come to bed. 'Come,' she said. 'Come, come, *come*!'

Unnerved, the student glanced at those either side of him. For a moment, it seemed that he might even take her proffered hand. But she turned abruptly, snatched up the candle and swept it in a semi-circle so that it guttered and flared in the faces of the front row. A gasp, followed by a murmur of

45

disquiet from the audience and then the candle was extinguished and she disappeared into the darkness muttering, 'To bed, to bed!'

The picture faded to black, then a still photograph of Kara smiled out of the frame, her name and the dates of her birth and death in plain white lettering below the picture.

Ruth shivered, and not from the cold.

With Kara fresh in her mind, she turned again to the post mortem files. Kara Grogan, Jo Raincliffe, Hayley Evans, Evie Dodd, Tali Tredwin.

Tali Tredwin was the first, her body discovered almost twelve months ago, in early January. Tali's back and shoulders had been marked with circles and spirals, like a Maori ceremonial tattoo. At the centre of some circles an image of an eye – closed, or half-closed. The inking was unfinished, abandoned as the killer had just started etching a new spiral, extending from the corner of one of the half-closed eyes, as if he had lost interest, or been distracted in the middle of his task and never returned to it.

The other women were a different story. Although their faces were entirely unmarked, it was impossible to find a square centimetre of the rest of their skins that had not been inked. Their bodies, arms, legs and hands – even the soles of their feet – were covered in the crudely drawn tattoos: flowers, trees, circles, Celtic knots, snakes. Crowding the gaps between them, heads on elongated necks, or eyes at the end of long stalks. Some of the eyes were closed, some open. The ink had been applied too deeply, bleeding into the subdermal tissues and creating a cloudy effect around the pattern – blowout, tattooists called it, an amateur mistake.

The victims' skin had been manually punctured, not machine drilled; thousands of tiny, painful wounds, pricked and inked

46

over days and weeks to create the pattern-work. Two victims had shown signs of an allergic reaction, and some of the markings had become infected. It must have been an agonising ordeal. Minute traces of woody fibres found in the puncture wounds proved that the killer had used some kind of thorn. Within a week, the first 'Thorn Killer' headline appeared.

The pathologists had painstakingly extracted tiny splinters of thorn from the first three victims' skins, and sent them to the University of Liverpool's Institute of Integrative Biology for identification. Progress had been slow because of the small amount of material they had to work with, compounded by the fact that woody tissue doesn't contain much DNA, but they knew by April that the killer had used berberis thorns to ink the first two victims.

There was no apparent link between the dump sites, but trace evidence indicated that the women had been held – and killed – at one location. Somewhere cold and damp, probably underground: the pathologists had found the same combination of soil fungal spores in the victims' airways. Cause of death was asphyxia, but the precise manner and means was still unknown. All of them, apart from Tali, had been kept alive for weeks.

Chemical analysis had told them already that the 'ink' was, in fact, natural indigo dye most professional tattooists wouldn't touch because of allergic reactions, and the possibility of scarring. The killer had completed the tattoos on the second victim, Evie Dodd, but the result reminded Ruth of some of the bad prison tatts she'd seen over the years: messy, primitive, with a lot of ink bleed.

It didn't take an expert to notice that the inking of Hayley Evans showed greater skill, with less bleed into the surrounding skin tissues, and sharper definition, as well as denser patterning.

'Practice,' someone said.

'Ten thousand hours of it,' one wag had suggested.

But it was a botanist who had given them a more likely explanation: the Thorn Killer had swapped an imperfect tool for something more sophisticated.

Only a few members of the investigatory team were in the know that the Thorn Killer used thorns from a shrub that grew in millions of gardens across the country, and so far they had managed to withhold that information from the general public.

Hayley Evans's body had been found in June, and two months after that, Ruth Lake and Greg Carver were heading back up Brownlow Hill towards the biological institute. Dr Grace Furlong, the botanist who had made the original identification, had been working on samples extracted from Hayley Evans. It was the end of August, hot and humid. Heat bounced off the car park tarmac, doubling the effect of the late summer sunshine, and Ruth shrugged off her jacket as soon as she was out of the comfort of the car's air-conditioning.

'She didn't say what this was about?' Carver said.

'Just that it was "significant",' Ruth said.

The place was quiet, and they had to walk around to the front of the building and then buzz to gain access to reception. Dr Furlong arrived in under a minute. She was small and spare, with curly black hair turning to grey, and an energy that seemed to spark off her. She showed them through to the lift, thanking them for coming in person.

'It sounded important,' Carver said.

'I believe it is,' she said, nodding emphatically. 'Please – come through.' She led them to a small laboratory. Amongst other paraphernalia, an e-tablet attached to the housing of a digital microscope displayed a slide showing stacked tubular structures, stained pinkish-red.

'This is the thorn?' she said.

'This,' said Dr Furlong, 'is a longitudinal section – that is to say, cut lengthwise – through a *minute* fragment of the *Berberis stenophylla* thorn we identified from Ms Tredwin's skin tissues. The pink-stained structures are woody fibres.'

'Okay . . .' Carver said.

Dr Furlong deftly removed the first slide and replaced it with another, quickly focusing the image. 'Now, *this* is a fragment of thorn that we were sent from the most recent victim.'

Ruth Lake and Greg Carver stood shoulder to shoulder, examining the image projected from the microscope onto the eight-inch tablet screen.

'This is the same magnification?' Ruth said.

'It *is* – ' She seemed delighted by the question. 'Magnification two-twenty.'

'These fibres look darker, more densely packed.'

'Mm-hm?' The academic peered into Ruth's face, her eyes bright, inquisitive.

Ruth sensed that Carver was becoming irritated by the drip-drip of information, but for her own part she was loving it. Being back in the lab reminded her of all the things she had relished about her former work as a CSI. 'So . . . this is from a different plant?' she ventured.

The academic smiled, nodding encouragement. 'Indeed it is.' She scooted along the bench to a stereo microscope and invited them to take a look. Unlike the digital microscope, the stereo mic was designed to look at whole specimens under comparatively low magnification. This one was set to x15. There was no projector for this microscope, so Ruth went first.

'I've mounted examples of the two thorns side by side,' Dr Furlong said.

Ruth adjusted the focus: the thorn on the left was relatively short and slightly hooked, orange-tinted at the tip. She recognised it as *Berberis stenophylla* – the thorn their killer had used on the first two victims. The other was darker, more woody, four times the length of the berberis thorn and dagger straight, with a wicked point.

'*That* looks vicious,' Ruth said, stepping back to let Carver peer down the lens.

Dr Furlong raised an eyebrow. 'Doesn't it?'

She moved to a table nearby and handed a long plastic container to Ruth. Inside was a thin, russet-red branch, about the length of her forearm, but only the thickness of her finger.

'This is *Pyracantha angustifolia* – the firethorn,' Dr Furlong said.

Ruth lifted it out of the box. Vivid clusters of fire-red berries clung to the stem, amongst glossy green leaves, and thorn-laden side shoots broke from the main stem. The thorns, three centimetres long, appeared at intervals along the twig, and at such varied angles that it was almost impossible to handle the thing without being stuck painfully.

'So this is what he used on Hayley Evans?' Carver said.

'DNA analysis confirms it,' Dr Furlong said.

'Why switch?' Carver frowned at the branch. 'Convenience?'

Dr Furlong tilted her head, but didn't offer an opinion.

'Is this thing rare?' Carver asked.

'*Angustifolia is* less commonly grown in the UK than berberis and isn't as popular as other pyracantha species.'

'I can hear there's a "but" coming.'

Dr Furlong's dipped her head in apology. 'It *is* widely grown, and readily available.'

So it wouldn't help them to narrow the search to a particular location.

Still examining the branch, Ruth spiked herself on a thorn and winced. 'Maybe he just wants to inflict more pain?' she said, sucking blood from her finger.

'I couldn't say,' Dr Furlong said. 'But I did do a couple of quick practical tests – a pyracantha thorn is far less likely to bend or break than berberis when pushed into a substance of similar resistance to human skin.'

'So we have a *pragmatic* serial killer, honing his skills, improving the tools of his trade,' Ruth murmured, turning the branch cautiously in her fingers, focusing on a long side shoot. 'Speaking of which . . .'

The side shoot ended in a five centimetre terminal thorn.

'Nasty-looking thing, isn't it?' Dr Furlong said.

Ruth tested it with the tip of her index finger; it was *sharp*.

'What are you thinking?' Carver said.

Ruth cast a glance around the lab and spied a pair of secateurs. 'May I?'

Dr Furlong handed them to her and Ruth clipped the side shoot off the main stem. It was about fifteen centimetres long, with four lateral thorns plus the one at the tip.

'If I take these off . . .' She rotated the shoot, trimming off all the lateral thorns, leaving just the evil-looking spike at the end of the stem. Then she turned it point-down and gripped it between her thumb and forefinger, like a pen.

'You've made yourself a stylus,' Carver said.

Dr Furlong laughed. 'Ingenious.'

Carver didn't seem to approve of the academic's enthusiasm for the killer's choice of murder weapon, but that was because he was a cop, and not a scientist.

'It's a comfortable grip,' Ruth said, handing it to Carver to try. 'He'd have much better control of the depth of puncturing – which could explain why Hayley's tattoos have less ink bleed.'

'You might also want to speak to a toxicologist,' the botanist said.

'Because?' Carver asked.

'You mentioned in your lab request that the victims had died of asphyxia.' Carver lifted his chin, acknowledging the fact.

'The genus *Pyracantha* produces hydrogen cyanide – in small quantities, and mainly in the berries,' Dr Furlong said. 'Nevertheless, it's worth noting – because cyanide can cause respiratory failure – even death.'

Carver looked at Ruth. This felt like an important moment, even a turning point. Standard tox screens after a suspicious death tested for a fairly narrow band of commonly used poisons. They could take weeks, or even months, to search for more obscure toxins, and every time the lab performed a test it used up some of the victims' sample bodily fluids, so they had to be selective. This new information gave the analysts a specific toxin to look for, an area of focus.

As it turned out, there was bad news even before the toxicologist began the screening process. Hydrogen cyanide was only detectable in a body for two to three days post mortem, he told them. There *was* a possible ray of hope from a recent study that had identified raised levels of a chemical called ACTA in the liver tissue of HCN poisoning victims. This chemical, he said, remained in the liver tissue for weeks or even months, so it could be used as a stable bio-marker.

But once again, their hopes were dashed: although the victims' livers *did* show signs of inflammation, ACTA levels were normal.

When the fourth victim, Jo Raincliffe, turned up in September, Carver had asked the pathologist to look immediately for physical signs of hydrogen cyanide poisoning, and to include it in the initial tox screen; he even got permission to fast-track the results. But the tests came up negative.

Knowing that the Thorn Killer had crafted a new and more accurate tool from the pyracantha stems should have told them something about his methods and his psychology, but all it had proved in the end was that he was adaptable.

## 10

By seven a.m., Ruth had made a list of lab tests they were still waiting for and fired off emails requesting updates. The holiday period slowed everything down, even for a high-profile case like theirs. She'd held off pestering the lab during Christmas week, but this was January 2nd; the holiday was officially over, and she felt no need to hold back. First on her wish-list were the remaining toxicology screens. Even though the pathologist had ruled out cyanide as the means of asphyxiation, the fact that there were no signs of struggle or physical trauma on any of the bodies had convinced him that some form of neurotoxin had been used. He had yet to determine what that was, and how it was administered.

Only days before he was shot, Ruth had gone to DCI Carver with a question: since the killer was so hung up on the tattoos, what were the chances he had injected poison mixed with the ink he used to tattoo the victims?

She had spoken to Darshan Singh, a toxicologist with whom she had worked in her CSI days, and he had liked the idea. Poison applied to the outer layers of skin via relatively shallow puncture wounds would work more slowly than an injection into a vein. But to have any chance of isolating toxins he would need skin tissue from the most recent tattoos on Kara. Carver had okayed the samples and the cost of tests. Tox analysis could be grindingly slow, but she dropped Dr Singh an email anyway, asking for an update, then turned to Carver's notes on police interviews of Kara's drama school friends.

Pinpointing when and where a person was last seen gave you a target group to talk to. Interviewing witnesses, Ruth always hoped to hear the words, 'It's probably nothing, but . . .' That phrase always sent a shiver of anticipation down her spine. A throwaway comment, an apparently unimportant occurrence, could be the crucial spark to reignite a case that was going cold – could even point the way to the primary scene, yielding all the evidence that had eluded you up to that moment.

Carver had summarised every witness interview from the team of detectives assigned to the case, highlighting commonly used phrases in a neon rainbow of colours, as though working to some kind of language pattern analysis of his own design.

'Bloody hell, Greg,' she murmured. It was a wonder he'd ever found time to sleep.

He'd highlighted one phrase in Day-Glo pink: 'Kara was reserved and private.'

Carver had written in the margin, 'Why "reserved" – why not "quiet" or "shy"?' Later in the document, as the phrase came up again, he'd jotted a note – 'Rehearsed?' A half page down, he had written, 'The party line?!!'

The interview transcripts went on to describe Kara as 'private', that she had 'kept to herself'.

His comments degenerating into scrawl, Carver wrote: 'Kara delib. isolated?', then, 'Who's pulling the strings, here?' And later still, 'Talk to these little shits again!'

Ruth guessed that Carver was drunk as a skunk when he wrote this – the limits of his patience always had been inversely proportional to his alcohol intake. But she took his point – it did feel like people were struggling for something kind to say about Kara and coming up with platitudes. She needed to talk to Kara's classmates herself.

She turned to the photographs of Kara, seated under the tree in the grotto, snow on the ground, icicles glittering from the rocks under the waterfall, frost on her eyelashes. Some of that 'frost' had turned out to be craft glitter. Snow was forecast for that night, but maybe the killer wanted to be sure of the effect, didn't want to leave anything to chance.

Unlike most murder victims, too often denied any dignity in death, the Thorn Killer's victims had been carefully dressed, each left in a restful pose, artfully displayed.

*'Artfully'? Really?* Ruth examined the pictures of Kara again; it could be a theatre set: the ice maiden in her grotto.

*Yes*, she thought, it *was* artful.

Back when Ruth was just starting out in her forensic training, one of her lecturers encouraged all of them to dip into *The Adventures of Sherlock Holmes*. Being a dutiful student, Ruth had read the lot. That was more than ten years ago, and many of the stories had blurred into one, but the odd phrase did stick – one such being, 'Singularity is almost invariably a clue.' The fact that their killer took such great care preparing his victims *was* 'singular' in the old-fashioned sense of being unusual. Their killer was no 'women-as-play-things' archetype; the way he worked on his victims, and the manner in which he left them afterwards, showed a level of care. His behaviour contradicted the norms of serial killer behaviour. Means, method and disposal were all 'singular'. And the most singular of all these things was that he had selected Kara.

For the first time since she'd met him, Ruth Lake went looking for her new SIO.

It was seven forty-five when she arrived at Canning Place, and DCI Parsons was already in his office, still reading Greg Carver's files and compiling notes. Parsons was forty, pleasant-looking, as sober-suited as an insurance salesman and serious as an undertaker. His desk was laid out with five neat stacks of files, one for each of the victims. Carver's A4 bound notebook was set in front of him, and a yellow, ruled notepad lay to his right. The page on view was already filled with his close, neat script.

Parsons glanced up at Ruth, a little distracted, or possibly stupefied by the mountain of paperwork he had already tackled. He launched straight in: 'I've noted some . . . anomalies in my audit.'

*Dear God, we've got a cop at death's door and a new murder victim barely cold in the mortuary, and he's doing an audit.*

Ruth had met this type before: always up to the minute on the legislation, keen on protocols and procedures, meticulous with paperwork. Parsons's type memorised the manuals as if they expected to be spot-tested at any minute. Parsons had a reasonable clear-up rate because mostly the protocols worked. But he was not a risk-taker or a betting man, and sometimes in senior policing you needed to be both.

'Some of this stuff just doesn't tally, Sergeant,' he said, his tone accusing.

Ruth parked her expression in neutral. 'Oh,' she said, not inviting further confidences.

He tapped his notepad petulantly.

'Well, what can you tell me?'

'I'm sure DCI Carver will clarify, when he can,' she said, staring past his left ear at an empty picture hook on the wall.

'Didn't you two *talk* to each other?'

'Every day, sir.' She remembered what had been on that empty picture hook: a photograph Greg had taken of Striding Edge from the top of Helvellyn in the Lake District. A cardboard box of DCI Parsons's own photographs had been set on the floor by the desk. It looked like her new DCI was planning to settle in for the long haul.

'I'm waiting for an answer, Sergeant.'

'To . . . what, sir?'

'What the hell was Carver *playing* at?'

She frowned, still focused on the hook on the wall. 'I'm afraid you'll have to be more specific.'

He gave a snort of disgust. 'If you were as obtuse with him, I can see why he would keep you out of the loop.'

She let that one pass, and he sighed heavily. She waited, and finally, he looked up, as if surprised to find her still in his office.

'Was there something you wanted, Sergeant?'

'I've asked for updates and status reports from the labs,' she said, knowing that this would appeal to Parsons's need for order.

He gave a begrudging nod of approval.

'And I was thinking about Kara Grogan.'

'Victim five,' he said, glancing at the relevant pile of papers on his desk.

'The student,' she said. 'Kara is not the killer's physical type. Which is an anomaly,' she added.

He glanced at her sharply, his eyes dancing over her face, checking for signs of piss-taking.

She pushed on, giving him nothing. 'Kara was like a photonegative of the killer's type: she was fair-skinned and blonde, when all the others—'

'Yes, I've read the files,' he interrupted. 'I know they were darker, older and so on. But surely Kara was selected because she looked like Carver's *wife*? She was dressed to look like her – the earrings even *belonged* to Emma Carver.'

'If Kara's murder was meant as a threat to Carver, you'd think the killer would go for maximum impact – snatch, kill and dump her fast,' Ruth said. 'But he didn't. The pathologist thinks Kara may have been held for up to five weeks. And he took more care tattooing Kara, using a different dye, dressing her, "staging" her, than he did for all the others.'

'It was personal,' Parsons rationalised. 'Carver got too close. He wanted to put Carver – and the investigation – off balance.'

'The first Carver knew about Kara was when he got the call telling him where to find her body.'

'Shock tactic,' Parsons said. 'Proves my point.'

'But if the killer wanted to chuck a spanner in the works of the investigation, wouldn't he let Carver *know* that a girl was being tortured and murdered? A girl who was nothing like the other victims – a girl who looked like his wife?'

Parsons gave a nod of tacit agreement. 'What's your theory?

'You know how it works with your average woman-hating sociopath – they see what they want, they take it, and then they throw it away. "It" being whoever has a) the right attributes to feed their fantasy and b) the bad luck to cross their path,' Ruth said. 'But Kara wasn't selected as a physical type, so it must have been something else about her that got his attention. This guy takes his time, gets to know his victims. Which is why it didn't matter that Kara was blonde and slight when the others were dark and curvy. I think he's is selecting *people*, not "objects".'

Parsons leaned back in his chair, thinking about it. 'I'll run it past the forensic psych, see what he thinks – but I'm not sure how it will help us to find the killer.'

'If I get to know the victims as people,' Ruth said, 'Maybe I can work out what it is that attracts him.'

'Character traits?' he said, finally in complete agreement with her. 'Victimology?'

It seemed it was all about textbooks and box-ticking for Parsons.

Ruth said, 'Kara is fresh in people's minds. I need to get to know *Kara*, sir.'

'All right. You have the witness statements: go over those, see if anything stands out.'

'I've already done that, sir – I need to talk to actual people.' She immediately regretted the slip in her mask of politeness.

Parsons bristled. 'Your colleagues talked to "actual" people when they took the witness statements.'

'Even so, I need to talk to the witnesses again.'

He shook his head. 'That could take months.'

'It doesn't need to,' she said. 'I've selected a few that I think are worth a second look.'

'Because?'

'They're lying,' she said.

'Why on earth would you think that?'

If she was honest, it was Carver's angry scrawl in the margins of the transcripts that had persuaded her. She couldn't tell Parsons that, but she could quote her former boss.

'Their answers seem rehearsed,' she said. 'Too many of them use exactly the same phrasing. Everyone is being too *nice* . . .'

Parsons stared at her, flicking the corner of the log he'd been reading, his thumb making a repetitive zipzip*ziiii-ip* sound that quickly became irritating.

'So,' he said, eyeing her as though he suspected her of trying to trick him into something, and he wasn't about to fall for it, 'you want to re-interview anyone that you believe has been holding back or hiding something?'

'I do,' Ruth said.

He seemed doubtful. 'You must see how it looks, going back over old ground.'

'It looks like thorough investigation, sir.'

He tilted his head, showing that he was listening, but not yet convinced.

'It looks like maybe we've found a new line of inquiry.' It hurt Ruth to use that inclusive 'we', but she needed an okay from Parsons to do this – the detectives who had done the original interviews would not be happy having their work reviewed.

'It won't sit well with the superintendent, you dragging people away from their family fires at Christmas time.'

Who would have thought – Parsons, a sentimentalist?

'The Christmas vacation is almost over, sir. The academics may well be on campus already. Spring term starts in just over a week, and most of Kara's friends are final year students, so they'll be around, too.'

He considered a moment longer. 'All right,' he said, slowly. 'But this must be approached with tact.'

'Of course.'

'I'll want to see your list of questions,' he added, as if you could stick to a script when you knew witnesses were lying to you.

'No problem,' Ruth said, as glib as any sociopath, but at least aware of the irony.

'But before you start on that, I want to know who leaked the information about those earrings to the media.'

'The earrings went to a private lab for analysis,' Ruth said. 'There were CSIs, mortuary techs and a pathologist at the PM

61

– they all witnessed Carver's reaction when he saw the earrings on Kara. You could try, but I wouldn't waste my time.'

He held her gaze: she had more or less told him, 'Do it yourself, and good luck, 'cause you'll need it.' For a silent moment, she sensed he was teetering on the edge of bawling her out, but finally he nodded and sent her on her way.

The Major Incident Room was open plan, which was how Ruth liked it. Twenty-plus desks set out in a fairly haphazard fashion. As the killings had gone on over the past year, the number of officers allocated had increased, and they jammed a desk wherever there was space, adding sockets for power and computer jacks.

As soon as she got back to her own desk, Ruth contacted everyone she wanted to re-interview and made some appointments. A few were not around; these, she emailed, asking them to call her without delay.

At eight forty-five, she was compiling a list of questions that she thought would keep Parsons happy. She sensed a movement to her left and glanced up.

'Sarge?' The speaker was a young detective with fine, ginger hair already thinning at the front. He was pale and freckled, with the eager look of a starved whippet. Ruth recognised him from a house-to-house she'd led a couple of years before. He was in uniform back then.

She stopped typing and waited for him to go on.

He coughed. 'Um, DCI Jansen asked if you could spare a minute,' he said.

'Well, he must have developed some manners since I last worked with him.'

The young detective flushed a delicate rose.

'What did he really say?'

The young man looked at his feet.

'What's your name, Constable?'

'DC Ivey, Sarge.'

'Got a first name, DC Ivey?'

'Tom.'

'Okay, Tom, I'll take a wild guess.' She drew her brows down, dropped her voice a bit and added a slathering of north Liverpool: '"Tell Lake to get her arse in here." Am I close?'

Ivey gave her a rueful smile. 'He did call you *Sergeant* Lake . . .'

She leaned back in her chair and gave an answering grin of recognition. 'You're all right, DC Ivey.'

He flushed to the roots of his hair, and she let him go, taking her time to put on her jacket and log out of her account before sauntering through to the Carver Major Incident Room down the hall.

Jansen had a full briefing in session. He didn't acknowledge her at first, so Ruth leaned against the door jamb and folded her arms as if she'd popped in for a friendly catch-up. A crime scene photo of Carver's sitting room was up on the data projector screen behind him. The check on Carver's financials hadn't uncovered anything unusual, she learned. No credit card transactions, cheques or transfers that would help them with the timeline leading up to Carver's shooting. House-to-house was ongoing, but no suspicious activity had been noted.

When Jansen finally deigned to notice her, some minutes later, he announced her presence and thanked her for sparing the time. 'Although Ruth can't be active in this investigation, she will be consulted as someone who knows DCI Carver well, and has been working on the serial murders right from the off,' he explained.

Ruth felt eyes on her, but focused on Jansen, keeping her expression pleasant. It hadn't escaped her notice, or anyone else's, that he'd not seen fit to acknowledge her rank.

'How can I help, Simon?'

He stiffened, turning a little too sharply to the young detective he'd sent in search of her. 'Tom, would you bring Sergeant Lake up to date on the phone situation?'

DC Ivey was seated dead centre of the room, just two rows from the front. He turned to speak to her. 'The techs are still working on DCI Carver's mobile phone,' he said. 'The only thing they've turned up so far is a mobile number he's been calling on a regular basis over the past month. It's untraceable – a pay-as-you-go.'

'What's the number?' she said.

Jansen clicked the projector remote control and a screenshot of Carver's phone log came up.

'Does that mean anything to you?' DC Ivey asked.

'Nothing.' Looking past the younger officer, Ruth saw DCI Jansen watching her closely. Had he set Ivey up to ask the questions while he watched for her reaction?

'Could it be an informant?' Jansen said. 'Someone helping with the case?'

'It could be.'

'But you don't know.'

'No.' She left it at that, and after a moment, he went on.

'DCI Carver rang that number the night he was shot. We've looked at CCTV, traffic cams and so on, tracked his car from police HQ to home. At twenty-fifteen he made a stop, got out of his car and walked.' Jansen paused, still watching her.

'Okay,' she said, but she was finding it hard to quell the jittery feeling in her chest.

'We tracked him all the way to a hotel.' He clicked the remote again, and ran a section of footage. Ruth thought she recognised the hotel: a high-end boutique-style place near the business quarter of the city. People came and went along the street: the well dressed and the shabby, although only the well dressed turned and walked through the doors into the hotel lobby. Well-fleshed men in tailored suits; sleek women in cashmere overcoats, stepping out of taxis in high heels. Then Carver, seen only from the back, but his figure, his gait, were so familiar that she didn't need to see his face.

'He stayed for two hours, walked back to his car and drove directly home,' Jansen said.

Ruth nodded, as if accepting it as useful intel.

'Do you know who Carver would go to meet at the Old Bank hotel?'

'Do you know that he *did* meet anyone?' she countered.

'A member of the hotel's staff said they recognised Carver from recent coverage of the shooting,' Tom Ivey said. 'Saw him heading for the lifts up to the bedrooms.'

'Was he with someone?'

'He was alone, and there's no record of his having booked a room,' Ivey said.

'You've checked the CCTV in the lifts?' she said. 'If you have a picture, I might recognise who he was with.'

'They don't have security cams inside the building,' Jansen said, taking back control of the discussion.

'Then I don't see how I can help,' she said.

## 11

Kara Grogan had shared a house with five other students in Canning Street, only a few minutes' walk from the Institute for Performing Arts. This was the lately gentrified Georgian Quarter of the city, at the summit of a hill with views across Liverpool, from the Anglican Cathedral all the way down to the Liver Buildings on the riverside. At this time of year, a constant, cutting wind whipped up from the Mersey, and Ruth Lake buttoned up her coat and tightened the scarf around her neck as she locked her car. Kara's digs were in an impressive building, three storeys high, though the windows looked in need of repair. Ruth didn't envy the residents their single-glazed grandeur in this weather.

It was five days since Carver had been shot, and the snow clouds had blown northwards, leaving the city under ice-blue skies. The snowfall had turned to slush, then to packed ice, so Ruth trod carefully up the sandstone steps to the front door.

She had phoned the previous day to arrange a meeting, so they were expecting her. Hurried footsteps clattered down the hall as soon as she buzzed: a large girl in jeggings, a pink tunic top and a red tartan blanket scarf threw the door wide and waved her inside. 'Come on *in*, for fuck's sake,' she said. 'I'm freezing my *titties* off!'

'Shut the bloody door, Angela!' someone yelled from further down the hall.

Angela laughed, a throaty rich chuckle that sounded rehearsed. 'Swear to *God*,' she said. 'If the city planners allowed double glazing in these old ice-boxes, they'd save the fucking *planet*.' Although Angela swore like a trouper, her cut-glass accent betrayed her privilege and wealth.

Resisting the girl's efforts to snatch her up on a wave of laughter and obscenities, Ruth remained on the doorstep. 'Don't you want to see my ID?' she asked.

'Oh, *you're* no stranger, Sergeant,' Angela said, indulging in another throaty chuckle. 'You're practically a *celebrity*!' She flung her arms wide to emphasise the point, then turned on the ball of one foot and walked away, her stiletto heels clacking on the expanse of black and white tiles.

Ruth stepped inside and closed the front door just as Angela sang out, 'Hide the crack pipes, guys – it's the rozzers!' Laughing, she disappeared into a room off to the left.

Ruth waited for a second or two before making her way to the door Angela had gone through. It was a high, square room, incongruously furnished with ugly black leather sofas and club chairs. A slab of black granite on a steel base served as a coffee table, and a wood burner the size of an industrial furnace was throwing out enough heat to melt the ice caps single-handed. She loosened her scarf, taking in the four avid faces turned to hers; three girls and one boy. She used 'girls and boys' loosely – none of them would be under twenty-one.

Ruth recognised the boy from a video of Kara online; the one who had flinched, half afraid, as Lady Macbeth bade him come to bed. This, she knew, was Jake. He sat hunched on a club chair next to the wood-burner, warming his hands. The others were arrayed on the two sofas, Angela leaning over the back of one, her hands spread, fair hair curling over her shoulders.

'Well, here we are, foregathered in the drawing room,' Angela said, 'awaiting the *denouement*, Sergeant Lake.'

Ruth stared at the student, widening her eyes and allowing a small smile to play on her lips. From where she stood, Ruth could see the whole group. One girl, Lia, bit her lip nervously; the other, Helen, shot Angela a look of bitter hatred.

Angela became a little self-conscious under Ruth's gaze, but she was not the type to be easily intimidated. She raised her shoulders and spread her hands, pantomiming surprise and disappointment. 'What, no devastating insights?'

'I was hoping to gain insights from *you*,' Ruth said. 'Kara being your friend, and all . . .'

'Oh, that's so *sweet*.' Angela chortled, then rubbed her snub nose vigorously. 'We shared a *house*, Sergeant . . .'

Lia smiled, shamefaced, but Helen looked like she could happily strangle her housemate.

'Am I missing something?' Ruth said.

As she'd expected, Angela was the first to speak. 'Kara was what you might call . . . charismatic.'

'Reserved,' Lia said, nodding agreement.

'Yes, that word came up a lot in your witness statements,' Ruth said. 'Charismatic is a new one on me, though.' She put enough of a question into her tone to invite explanation.

Angela shot an amused look at Lia that said, *Poor plod needs a dictionary definition*. Obligingly, Ruth played to the stereotype, holding her pencil poised over her notebook, a carefully contrived look of fatuous interest on her face.

'Oh, I only meant that she was something of a mystery, but compelling . . . in her way,' Angela said, with a deprecating shrug.

Keeping her voice light, Ruth said, 'And *I* thought you meant opaque, but with a bit too much personality to be called boring.'

Angela flushed, and Jake scowled at the fire and began chewing on his thumbnail. Lia hunched her shoulders, clasping her hands between her knees. That wasn't good – she'd meant to shut down the ringleader, not put a damper on the entire group.

'Now look,' Angela began, 'We've gone to some trouble to be here today. *Some* of us have dissertations to work on, finals start next week. We didn't *have* to—'

'You're right,' Ruth interrupted, laying on the Liverpool accent a little heavier than usual. 'Down the station, they won't let me open my gob till I've had my caffeine fix in the morning.' She smiled brightly at Angela. 'How's about a nice brew, and we'll start again?'

It had the desired effect. Angela's eyes widened, and Ruth read a mixture of fascination and cold contempt in them. 'Well, jump to it – someone fetch the sergeant a "brew",' Angela said, in a fair imitation.

Helen said, 'I'll get it,' her voice tight.

Helen was interesting. Angela and Lia were dressed in elaborate layers, with flounces of fabric and a bright palette of colours. Helen, on the other hand, wore cords with a thick shirt and sweater, dark trainers on her feet. Helen seemed kitted out for efficiency.

'Helen,' Ruth said. 'Why don't you stay? I'm sure Angela and Lia will do the honours.'

The girls blinked. Lia looked as chastened as if her mother had just walked into the room and demanded to know why she was treating her guest so abominably. She tucked her hair behind her ears.

'Of course,' she cooed. 'We really should've asked.' She shot Helen a worried look. 'I suppose we do *have* tea?' Helen rolled her eyes, and Lia apologised again. She turned away and made towards the door, but Angela remained stubbornly behind the sofa.

'Sexist, much?' she said. 'What about Jake?' She jerked her chin petulantly at the boy, who was now scowling into the flames of the wood burner. 'He *does know* which end of a kettle is for pouring.'

'No doubt,' Ruth said. 'But I want to talk to Jake.'

Jake shifted uneasily in his chair, but still didn't make eye contact.

Suddenly protective, Angela said, 'You cool with that, Jake?'

Ruth saw the slow blink and the slight flare of his nostrils that said Jake would be *way* cooler without Angela in the room.

'He'll be fine,' Ruth said.

Angela sucked her teeth, regarding Ruth with obvious dislike. Ruth fixed her with that calm, mildly curious gaze and finally the girl shrugged and flounced out of the room. Lia, the nervous girl, made a move to follow her, but Ruth said sharply, 'I've changed my mind. Lia, *you* can stay.'

Lia's pearly skin reddened, and she looked like she might burst into tears.

## 12

When Angela left the room, it was as if the three housemates remaining heaved a collective sigh. Helen threw herself onto the sofa muttering an obscene insult; Lia smiled in answer, then bit her lip, apparently appalled at herself. The biggest change, though, was in Jake. He uncurled from his stricken posture and sat up straight.

'Look, I just want to catch whoever did this to your friend,' Ruth said, taking a seat on one of the club chairs. 'So if you have *any* insights . . .' When no one was forthcoming, she said, 'Okay, here's your starter for ten: Kara clearly wasn't well liked.'

'No – *no*! That's not true!' It came out as a wail of distress, and Lia seemed shocked by her own response. After a few moments' pause to get a grip of herself, she said, 'Kara – she was just . . . reserved, that's all.'

'That word again,' Ruth said. '"Reserved". Like a theatre ticket, or a table for dinner.'

The girl didn't understand the sarcasm, or maybe it was guilt that made her say, 'No – I didn't mean . . . I meant reserved as a *person*. She was quiet, you know?'

'No, Lia, I *don't* know. That's why I'm here,' Ruth said. 'I know she was talented – I've spoken to her tutors and I've seen the clips of her performances on YouTube —'

She saw a flicker of pain cross Jake's face.

'You're on the *Macbeth* clip aren't you, Jake?'

He nodded mutely. He was dark-haired and slender, and Ruth suspected that his sullen good looks made him something of a favourite with the girls.

'I was surprised by your reaction.'

'What d'you mean?' He sounded defensive, even alarmed.

'You must have known Kara well, but it was as if you were almost afraid of her.'

He didn't reply.

Lia came and sat near him. 'She could be intense,' she said.

'And that made her unpopular? I can see how it might.'

'No – it wasn't that,' Lia said.

'Your tutors said that rivalry between the students could become heated.' In fact, the academic in question had used the word 'bloody'.

'*Some* people were jealous, of course.' Unconsciously – tellingly – Lia glanced swiftly towards the door that Angela had just exited. 'But acting with Kara was, I don't know – special. She . . .' Lia looked to Jake for help, but he frowned, seemingly sunk again in his own misery.

Helen was eyeing the other girl coolly, and Ruth noticed that Lia didn't even look her way. She revised her estimate of Helen's age – she seemed more mature than the rest, older by a few years, Ruth judged.

'She was . . . demanding,' Lia said. 'But only because she wanted to get the performance right,' she added hastily. She frowned, clearly struggling. 'No, not just *right*. For Kara, it had to be *perfect*. She rehearsed for *hours*. And if you played opposite her, she expected you to do the same. I mean, she would make you go over and over a scene until you felt your brain would *bleed*. Even so, everyone – well, almost everyone – wanted to partner up with her.'

That tallied with something the tutors had said: 'They might resent Kara, but only because they wanted to *be* her.'

On their part, the academics were less apt to resent Kara's circumspection: more than one seemed to be convinced that being an introvert was a prerequisite to becoming a fine actor.

'If she pushed you so hard, why didn't you just walk away?' Ruth said.

Lia shrugged. 'In this business, if you want to *be* the best you can, you *act* with the best.'

'And Kara was the best?'

'She was a genius,' Jake said.

This was his first uninvited contribution to the discussion. Ruth turned to him, tilting her head to show she was listening, but he dropped his gaze and began to retreat into himself again.

'Genius.' She sniffed. 'Well, that's a devalued word these days.'

The provocation worked. Jake's eyes, a startling blue, flashed as he met her gaze.

'Kara had a gift that could make you better than you could ever hope to be,' he said, his voice rough with emotion. 'She could have been—'

A clatter of noise from the hall warned them that Angela was on her way back. Jake gave a little groan of distress, and shifted to face the fire again. Lia moved nervously to sit on the other sofa, nearer to Helen.

'I wouldn't drink the tea, if I were you,' Helen said quietly.

Ruth smiled her thanks. She hadn't intended to, but it was good to know she had made at least one ally.

Angela came through the door, grinning.

'Hot chocolate for the kids,' Angela said, handing one to each of her housemates in turn. 'Tea for the grownup.'

Ruth took hers, staring into Angela's eyes with the bland, open look that had served her so well over the years. She read gleeful malice in the student's eyes.

'So, now you're all here,' she said, placing the mug on the mantelpiece, 'did any of you notice anyone hanging around the house, or even the street, in the weeks leading up to the Christmas vacation?'

They exchanged blank looks.

'Did Kara mention anything out of the ordinary – anything that had happened?'

'What sort of thing?' Angela said.

'You tell me.'

Angela raised one shoulder. 'As I said, we shared a house, not a bed.'

'For God's *sake*, Angela,' Helen growled.

'All right,' Ruth said. 'Did she seem more anxious that usual?'

Nobody answered that, and Ruth got the feeling that they were avoiding each other's gaze. She let the moment ride until it became uncomfortable. Lia was the first to weaken, stealing a quick look at Jake.

'Lia?'

She jumped like a startled cat, 'What?'

'Did Kara seem particularly anxious?'

Angela answered for her: 'We had public performances to arrange for January, *and* research outlines to submit before end of semester. We were *all* anxious.'

Ruth kept her eyes on Lia. 'Anything you'd like to add, Lia?'

The girl clasped her hands on her knees, but Ruth could still see they were shaking.

'She *did* disappear off a few times, in the evening,' Lia said. 'That was unusual.'

'And nobody knows why?'

A ragged chorus of, 'No.'

Ruth sighed. Whatever they were hiding, she wouldn't find it out while they were all watching each other.

'Okay,' she said, half to herself. 'I'd like to see Kara's room. Can someone show me the way?'

'Is that it?' Angela said, trying to sound put out, but there was barely covered relief in the student's sudden buoyancy. 'Aren't you going to sweat us? Badger us till we break?'

'You're mixing your metaphors, Angela,' Helen said drily.

Angela flicked a hank of hair over her shoulder. 'And who made *you* the grammar police?'

Helen scoffed, and knowing that she'd lost points in the exchange, Angela turned crossly to Ruth.

'Well, aren't you at least going to drink your tea?'

'It was good of you to go to the trouble,' Ruth said. 'But honestly? That was just a ploy to get you out of the room.'

Angela looked from Lia to Jake. She seemed almost panicked for a second, but Lia leaned forward on the sofa, eyes wide, and Ruth thought she caught the tiniest shake of her head.

Angela slouched. 'Fine,' she said sulkily. 'Good luck getting in there. There's no spare key.'

Ruth smiled, patting her coat pocket. 'I came prepared.'

'Oh.' Angela looked around at the others, trying hard to control the hunger in her face. 'In that case, I'll show you up', adding with a tiny lift of one shoulder, 'That's . . . if you'd like.'

'*Christ*, Angela, you're such a disgusting ghoul,' Helen said.

Angela drew herself to her full height. 'It's perfectly natural to show an interest, under the circumstances,' she said, primly self-righteous.

Helen didn't respond, and Angela added, 'Like *you* aren't gagging for a peek at the scene of the crime.'

Helen shot her a contemptuous look. 'It's *not* a bloody crime scene.'

'You're right, Helen,' Ruth said. 'It's not a crime scene, it's just Kara's room. And I'd like to see it.' Perhaps Helen would be more communicative one-to-one? It was worth a try: 'So, if you wouldn't mind . . .'

As Helen made her way out ahead of her, Ruth fished some business cards out of her pocket. 'If there's anything else you think of – anything *at all* you want to tell me . . .' Jake's jaw tightened, and he drew his eyebrows down as if engaged in some inner dispute; Lia looked alarmed; Angela fiddled with her hair and turned her head slightly, refusing the card in a gesture of defiance. Ruth left one for each of them on the coffee table. 'In case you change your minds,' she said.

Helen was waiting at the end of the hallway, at the foot of the stairs. She stalked ahead.

'You *do* know those three will been be using you as a character study before you've even left the house?' she said. 'Improvising dialogue, honing their "authentic" local brogue.'

'That's all right, I'm thick skinned.' Deciding that a direct question might get a more helpful response, she said, 'So, was Kara picked on?'

Helen slowed on the turn of the stairs. 'You don't think they had anything to do with . . . with what happened?'

'No,' Ruth said. 'I'm just trying to get a handle on Kara.'

'Okay . . .' Helen waited for her, and they walked the rest of the way side by side. 'Kara was never really accepted by the others, but I wouldn't say she was picked on exactly. Angela and Lia can gang up a bit – but only because Lia is terrified of Angela. Jake is . . . well, Jake is just a moody bloke with some good looks who'd like to think he was Colin Farrell.'

'Ouch.'

Helen tilted her head as if to say, *You did ask*.

'And Angela?'

'Angela is the only one I have a real issue with.'

'So, she's more than just irritating?'

'She can be cruel. And even when she's only being irritating, she's the worst kind of influence on Lia.'

'What kind of influence did she have on Kara?'

Helen smiled, starting up a second flight. 'Zero. Kara's influences were the greats of film and theatre; she didn't really care about the wannabes in this place.' She stopped on a narrow landing at the top of the house. 'Well, this is it.'

Crime-scene tape had been put in place after the CSIs had finished, and the landlord had been instructed to leave it untouched in case they needed to return.

'It's a long way up,' Ruth observed. *Isolated* was what she was really thinking.

'Kara liked the view.' Helen hesitated. 'You know, the crime scene people were all over her flat for three days. They took her laptop and tablet.'

'I know,' Ruth said. 'But I'd like to get a feel for her personal space.'

'Okay – I'll leave you to it.'

'No – stay,' Ruth said. 'I feel I got more from two minutes talking to you than I did in the last twenty with the others.'

Helen nodded. 'They're definitely hiding something. '

'Any idea what that might be?'

'I wish I did,' Helen said, adding with a self-deprecating shrug, 'Kara wasn't the only outsider in the house.'

Helen really didn't seem a good fit with the place. Listening to her as they'd chatted on the way upstairs, Ruth had detected a hint of Liverpool in her speech, while the others spoke in the clipped accents of the privileged and privately educated.

'Lia seems to look up to you,' Ruth said.

Helen's mouth twitched. 'Like a big sister – useful for tips on STDs or the morning-after pill.'

'Why would she ask you?'

'Well, it's not exactly the sort of thing you'd talk to your classmates about – unless you really wanted it splashed all over campus by the end of the day.'

'So, you're not studying at LIPA?' The interview report had listed Helen as a student – someone was in for a bollocking when she got back to the office. But she covered her annoyance, saying, 'I thought this was a student house.'

'Eighty per cent,' Helen said, with mathematical accuracy.

'So, what *do* you do?'

'I'm a nurse.'

That explained the practicality of her short, bobbed hair, the sensible cords and sweater. Ruth raised an eyebrow. 'Nice digs.'

'Yeah, well it comes at a price.' Helen's mouth twisted in a bitter quirk, and Ruth got the impression she wasn't talking about financial cost.

Ruth took the key from her pocket and sliced through the scene tape before opening the door, but Helen balked.

'I don't know if I can—'

'It's okay,' Ruth said. 'It's just a room.'

Helen stood with her back to the stair rail, and for a second it looked like she might bolt.

'You knew her,' Ruth said. 'And I think you cared for her.'

Helen's eyes shone with tears.

'There may be something in here that I'd miss, but would mean something to you.' She went in, hoping that Helen would follow.

The room was right in the eaves of the house. Laid out as an open-plan living space, it was rammed with books, and every available patch of wall was taken up with posters of actors in the great roles from Shakespeare to Beckett; Miller to Pinter.

Three sash windows, smaller than those on the ground floor but still generous in size, let light flood in. An en suite wet room was tucked behind a curved wall on the left, and a small kitchenette off to the right.

'It's quite self-contained for a shared house,' Ruth said.

Still hovering at the door, Helen said: 'That's Kara for you. She was willing to pay extra for her privacy.'

Ruth looked into her face, but saw only affection for the lost girl.

Helen came into the room and sat on a chair by the desk, her gaze shifting from the blank notepad to a jam pot filled with pens.

'Jake wasn't exaggerating, you know – Kara really was a genius.'

'You saw her perform?' This didn't sound like the outsider she claimed to be.

'I went to a few of her end of term productions – even did line rehearsals with her a few times.' Helen shook her head, lost for words.

'She was really that good?'

'Kara could draw the light to her. Sometimes, it felt like she had you physically in her two hands, so you could hardly breathe . . .' She trailed off, staring out of the window for a few moments. 'But she couldn't compromise. And that can be difficult to live with – especially for a mediocre talent.'

'Like Angela?'

'Not just her. I've seen a succession of these guys, been to their stage shows, even seen a few make it big. But most of them plod into doing the odd TV commercial, or corporate training videos, filling their "resting" periods temping, before they finally come to the realisation their big moment is *never* going to happen.'

'Sounds like you know something about it.'

She gave a short laugh. 'You're thinking I was one of the many who ended up getting a proper job?'

Ruth raised her eyebrows as if to say, 'What am I supposed to think?'

'I lived here when these houses were still owned by slum landlords and the streets around Canning and Huskisson were teaming with prostitutes and kerb crawlers.'

Ruth nodded. It wasn't that long ago.

'Then things got crazy in the build-up to Liverpool's Capital Of Culture year in 2008.'

'I remember the buying frenzy,' Ruth said. 'London property developers scooping up grotty housing stock around Kensington, Liverpool like it was Kensington, London.'

'A lot of people got burned,' Helen said. 'But Angela's daddy hit the jackpot. Bought this house for a couple of hundred thousand sight-unseen at a property auction in 2005. It's now bringing in twenty thousand a year in rental – and that's with Angela living rent-free.'

Ruth whistled. 'I hope you were on a protected tenancy?'

Helen smiled. 'Low rent, too – I mean a *quarter* of what the others are paying. Even better, I can stay as long as I like. Or at least until I act on the *powerful* itch to slap Angela's self-satisfied face.'

'I get the feeling she's got the others on a short leash, though,' Ruth said.

Helen grimaced. 'Her daddy had Lia and Jake on three-month rental contracts – which ran out in December – and *nobody* wants the hassle of a move in the middle of their finals.'

Ruth looked around the room, wondering if Kara had been on the same contract. She really needed to speak to these kids out of Angela's hearing.

Kara must have hoicked a ton of flat-pack furniture up the stairs, judging by the quantity of shelving in the place, some of which was set at right angles to the walls, creating reading niches. A beanbag served as a reading chair. Books on drama theory, critical studies, set design, texts on movement and voice were stacked two deep on the shelves, and the tops of the bookcases were cluttered with files, folders, books and photocopied sheets. A team had already sifted through this lot, extracting anything that might provide names to follow up, but Ruth flicked through them anyway.

'Did Kara seem different in any way, in the lead-up to her disappearance?' she asked.

'No,' Helen said. 'But I was working nights, and I didn't see much of her, apart from the night of her performance in *Macbeth* – I agreed to work Christmas Day so I could be there.'

'Was it worth it?'

'She was stunning. Like I told her she would be.'

Ruth looked up from a text on cultural context in theatre. 'Did she need telling?'

'She'd had a bad experience a few weeks before; it knocked her confidence a bit.'

'Oh?' Ruth said, inviting further explanation.

'She didn't want to talk about it,' Helen said. 'All she'd say was it was a life lesson she wouldn't forget.'

Ruth guessed that whatever the others were hiding, it had something to do with that 'life lesson'.

She moved on to the wardrobe; it yielded nothing of more interest than a preference for black clothing. A three-shelf bookcase tucked under one of the sash windows caught her eye. A collection of biographies: Laurence Olivier, Judi Dench, Sheila Hancock, Benedict Cumberbatch, Barbara Streisand, Hayden Panettierre – and many more, all bristling with stick-it notes.

'This is what you call devotion to the art,' she murmured, picking up one of the books to sift through it. The text was heavily marked, too: passages pencil-underlined or highlighted in bright colours; marginal notes in a tiny, neat hand. Questions, observations, exclamations.

Kara was focused, obsessed, even – but she had a friend who would give up Christmas Day to support her through a crisis, peers who described her as a genius and tutors who spoke of her as though she were already on her way to becoming a great actor. She picked up the next book, and the next, and discovered an additional row of books behind them. Texts on mediums and cold reading, one entitled, *How To Become A Psychic*.

'Did you know she was into all this?' she asked.

Helen frowned. 'She didn't seem the type. Maybe it was research for a role?'

'Maybe.'

Ruth skimmed through a couple of the biographies. Kara's notes and jottings – even the sections she had highlighted – emanated a warmth of spirit. Here was a way into Kara's true character.

Her excitement must have showed, because Helen said, 'Have you found something?'

Ruth slipped her phone from her pocket. 'Not yet, but I think this may be exactly what I was looking for.'

She fast-dialled John Hughes.

'John, could you arrange to have some books from Kara's place logged in to evidence and delivered to my desk?'

'Which ones?' he said. 'The guys I sent round there said the place was better stocked than the British Library.'

She smiled. 'I'll send you a list.'

Half an hour later, she paused on the steps of the Georgian terrace and took a breath of clean, fresh air. She felt for Kara even more, having heard what her housemates had to say. Kara must have felt terribly isolated in that place – admired and resented in equal measure.

As a female detective in what was still, despite all protestations to the contrary, very much a man's world, Ruth knew what it was like to be an outsider. Over the years, she had managed by creating an aura of mystery about herself; was that what Kara had tried to do? If so, she had miscalculated: in her world, expressiveness and emotional intensity were tools of the trade, and Kara's quiet reserve had made her somewhat suspect – at least among her peers. Ruth had learned precious little from them, but one thing was certain: Kara's housemates were definitely holding back.

## 13

Ruth Lake approached her car, keys at the ready. Her mobile rang, and she checked the screen: it was Emma.

'Ruth?' She sounded choked.

'Emma, is everything okay?'

'I thought you'd want to know.'

*He's dead.* A suffocating tightness gripped Ruth's chest. 'Is he—?'

'He's awake.'

The pressure eased. 'So soon?' It was only five days since he'd been shot.

'I know – I never thought . . .'

The critical care team at the hospital had reduced the level of anaesthesia as the swelling in Carver's brain had subsided, but they said it could be weeks before he came round.

'He's responsive?'

'Not just *responsive* – he's properly awake.'

Ruth felt a cold sharp pain just below her breastbone. She flashed to the moment she had crouched in front of Carver with the gun still in her hand, and the horror she'd felt seeing that flicker of movement in his eyelid. *What does he know? His eyes were open, he must have seen all of it.*

'They've removed the breathing tube,' Emma was saying. 'He *spoke* to me, Ruth.' Emma gave a gasp of laughter that ended in a sob.

*Oh, God.* 'What did he say?'

'He said he was sorry. He said he loved me.'

'That's . . . that's good, Emma,' she managed, hearing the strain in her voice, cursing herself for her wooden response. *'Good'? You should be ecstatic he hasn't pointed the finger at you.*

'I – I'm coming in.'

'Good. He said he wanted to see you.'

Another thud of dread. Ruth leaned on the car bonnet, trying to catch her breath. After a second or two, she managed to say, 'Why?'

*Stupid, stupid question.*

'I told him it was you that found him, got him to the hospital,' Emma said. 'God, Ruth. If you hadn't been there . . .'

Ruth felt sick with guilt. *You don't know what I did.* 'I really need to get going,' she said.

'I know – you'll want to see him as soon as possible. I told them you'd be in. I'm going home to shower and change, catch a few hours sleep,' Emma said. 'It'll be good for him to see a familiar face – they're only allowing family, and he doesn't really have any, as you know. Apart from me, I suppose. And you.'

Ruth experienced a second wave of nausea. 'Emma—'

'I know,' Emma said, with another shaky laugh. 'I'm babbling – I can't help it. Ruth he's *awake*. A few days ago, the neurosurgeon told me not to give up hope. How could I *give up*, when I'd never *dared* hope? I'd prepared myself for . . . for something far worse. Now they're saying he could make a full recovery.'

Ruth concentrated on her breathing, letting the other woman's words wash over her, and slowly she became more calm.

When she tuned in again Emma was saying, 'I'll be back this afternoon.'

'I'm on my way right now,' Ruth said. 'I'll be there in half an hour.'

DS Ruth Lake is watched from a parked car as she leaves Kara's place. She stands in the cold air as if it is a welcome respite from the atmosphere inside the house.

She doesn't give much away – after all, she's had years of police work to polish that outer shell of hers, to make it hard and reflective. But trotting down the steps, she does seem to be more buoyant than when she went in. What does she think she's discovered in that cuckoo's nest of petty privilege and small-minded jealousy?

The detective carries on down the street, and as she passes the open window of the car, her phone rings. She is close enough to touch, and it takes an effort of will not to call out, to ask her something, pass a comment that will make her turn and look.

'Emma,' Ruth says, 'is everything okay?'

The urgency in her voice arrests any further urge to make direct contact. This is far more entertaining. Greg Carver's wife must be delivering the good news that DCI Carver has regained consciousness. In the last fifteen minutes, it has been broadcast on local and national radio, and shared and tweeted so many times on social media that it's become a trending topic. But standing there, keys in hand, it seems that Ruth is only hearing it now, for the first time.

Strange that she looks so distressed.

She moves on to her car. Much of her one-sided conversation is carried away on the wind, or drowned out by traffic noise, but then she says, 'He's responsive?' Sharply, almost in a tone of command — which is odd.

A few more exchanges, then she crumples suddenly.

*Now, why is that? I seem to be taking the news rather better than you, Sergeant.*

She really is *very* striking – dark-haired, thirtyish, attractive. Perhaps a little more athletic than the ideal, but there are compensatory factors. Chief among these is the simple fact that she is continuing the investigation. For now, she is a more than satisfactory surrogate for Chief Inspector Carver.

For the last five days, at a discreet distance, the Thorn Killer has been watching Ruth Lake travel from her home to Carver's bedside, from there to the police HQ; calling in at academic offices, bouncing back and forth to student flats, onward to performances, trying to catch the more elusive of Kara's peers. Throughout this time, the sergeant has looked purposeful, in control, despite the additional burden Carver's shooting has placed on her. Yet now, in the face of the excellent news that Carver is much improved, she seems . . . what does she seem? *Anxious?* Possibly. Certainly wounded in some way.

Women who harbour secrets are peculiarly thrilling.

*Ah, she's on the move.*

Ruth Lake slides behind the wheel of her car. It is parked parallel to the kerb, two cars away, facing the killer's own. The distance and the obscuring effect of the two car windscreens and rear windows mean she's hard to make out. For a few moments she sits there. Her hands show white through the gloom of the car interior; she is gripping the steering wheel. Finally, she starts the engine and she's off.

Knowing where she is headed, the killer waits until Ruth is a block away before performing a leisurely U-turn and, seeing no reason to stay close, keeps a distance of two or three cars between them.

In the early days, learning that Carver had a reputation for clearing difficult cases was flattering. It was sometimes a challenge staying ahead of the game, and that gave the cat-and-mouse with the detective a frisson. He also came with a certain notoriety as a flouter of rules, and that is always worth closer examination: it suggests a possible narcissistic streak – even psychopathic leanings. Carver had fulfilled his promise, breaking a few of those rules in the course of the investigation into Tali Tredwin's death. If anything, the pattern escalated with each of the women that followed, but he had stalled the game in the last week.

Kara, so carefully crafted, entirely for Carver's benefit, had been wasted. Carver has been silent for *five days*, and under those circumstances it's difficult not to feel thwarted.

This feeling is typical of the empty disappointment that follows in the weeks after a kill. But this time, the desire to find a new quarry has come sooner and with greater force. The instinct to hunt is urgent, compelling.

And as if the gods have seen a need and made provision, here is Sergeant Lake. Watching her car dodge in and out of the traffic, the killer senses a shift; not the tectonic shift you might expect after an earthquake, when the rumbling has stopped and the ground that seemed to turn to liquid has solidified to rock and earth again. No – this shift is more subtle: Ruth Lake is cool, fragrant air after a rainstorm. She plays the role of serious investigator, friend, protector, but she *is* concealing something, and it weighs heavily on her conscience.

The hysterical narcissism packaged as 'honesty' in this new confessional age nauseates the killer. But those who lock their secrets within themselves, carrying them silently, thoughtfully, with discretion, are fascinating. Gaining such a woman's confidence, discovering her secrets, is an intense and intimate privilege. Like prising open an oyster shell and finding a pearl.

## 14

Shadows. Shapes, like smoke. Like ghosts . . . pain. A flash of light.

*You've screwed up the timeline, pal. That's not how it happened. The flash came before the shadows. Before the pain.*

Greg Carver opened his eyes.

Ruth Lake was standing by his bedside.

'Hey.' His voice came out as a croak.

Startled, she turned to him, and he saw that she had the framed photograph of Emma in her hands. Their honeymoon photograph.

'Greg, hi.' She placed the photo on the night stand. 'You were out of it when I came in.'

'Did I oversleep?'

'You need your rest, Greg,' she said.

'What are you talking about? Ruth, what are you doing here?'

She gazed at him, her brown eyes calm, unaffected by his own agitation. 'Where do you think you are?'

Trick question – he'd been asked this before – got it wrong last time, he seemed to remember. He looked around: four beds in open-fronted bays. Bodies, barely recognisable as people, all on drips, three on respirators; the astringent smell of antiseptic gel and a constant noise of electronic monitoring kit.

*Not at home, that's for sure.*

'Let me take a wild guess,' he said. 'Hospital?' *That must have been one hell of a bender you went on, old son.* He started coughing and she handed him a cup – the type with a lid and a built-in straw. *So it's come to this – sucking from a granny cup.* Humiliated, he took the cup but couldn't hold it steady, and Ruth caught it and held it for him. He tapped her hand when he'd had enough.

For once, he was grateful for the impenetrable calm of her poker face – at least he could be sure he wouldn't read any pity in it.

'Which hospital?' he asked.

'The Aintree Neurosciences Centre.'

*The head injury unit.*

'Do you know what happened?' she asked.

Another trick question. 'Why does everyone keep asking me that?'

'Do they?'

'That, and the name of the current prime minister.'

Her eyebrows twitched. 'Which is?'

'Google it,' he said. He couldn't remember the PM, but the rest was coming back to him. Flashes of the last two days, as seen through a mist, fading in and out of focus. Voices, first – disembodied – like a conversation heard on a radio. Then faces – was Emma's among them? And over and over, the questions: 'Can you grip my hand/ open your eyes/ feel this, Greg? Do you know where you are? Can you remember what happened?'

It all seemed like a recurring dream in which, half-awake, he would be quizzed on a test he hadn't prepared for.

Ruth was still watching him, with that mildly curious, dispassionate expression, not wanting anything in particular; simply interested to hear what he would say next.

'I fell and banged my head.'

'What?' Ruth said.

'That's what happened.' A reasonable assumption, given he was in a specialist head injuries unit – and he hated to appear incompetent – especially to Ruth.

She drew up a chair and sat, looking straight into his eyes.

He saw a shadow, a figure flitting about his apartment. Ruth, peering into his face, her eyes dark.

'Were *you* there?' he asked.

'When?'

'When it happened.'

She withdrew slightly, but held his gaze.

'I called it in.' She searched his face. 'You don't remember?'

*Jesus, why does everything feel like a test?* He closed his eyes and sank back into the pillows. 'No, Ruth, I don't.'

'You were shot, Greg.'

His eyes flew open. He lifted a hand to his head, tested for signs of tenderness, and found a dressing. 'In the head?'

She was watching him closely. 'In the chest.'

'Then, what's this? ' He fingered the dressing.

'You also had a concussion.' She jerked her chin. '*That* was to remove the fluid build-up. The doctors say your head injury may have happened hours before you were shot. So, you remember falling?'

He shook his head. 'I don't even know that I fell,' he admitted.

She waited.

He took a breath and exhaled slowly. 'I was working on the files. I cracked open a bottle of malt – must've got completely tanked.' She didn't comment, and he went on: 'Then . . . nothing.'

'You really don't remember anything after that?'

*She doesn't believe me.* 'No, Ruth, I really don't. Did you catch the shooter?'

'No.'

'D'you have a suspect?'

'DCI Jansen is looking into the possibility it was the Thorn Killer.'

She seemed to be waiting for him to say something. 'What do *you* think?' he said.

'TK didn't shoot you.'

'How can you be so sure?'

'You know why, Greg.'

'Ruth, I've got a bullet in my chest; I've been knocked on the head and shot full of drugs. Humour me.'

She lifted one shoulder, let it fall. 'Because our guy takes his time,' Ruth said. 'He considers himself an artist. He put Kara in a grotto and sprinkled fairy dust on her eyelashes. The Thorn Killer would *never* do something like this. It's too . . . ugly.'

'So tell me what did happen.'

'I can't do that,' Ruth said. 'I can only tell you what happened after.'

'Then that'll have to do,' Carver said, thinking that was an odd response.

Ruth took him through finding him in his sitting room, shot, calling emergency services.

'My files?'

'Gone.'

Why had she left that part out till he'd asked?

'Forensic evidence?'

'The only fingerprints in your flat are mine, and yours.'

93

'No fibres, footwear marks, signs of forced entry?'

'A footwear-mark.'

Ruth was never apt to give more information than necessary, but this was as painful as pulling teeth.

'What about the gun?'

She hesitated. 'A small calibre pistol – .22 maybe.'

'Don't they know?'

'The bullet is still inside you, Greg,' she said.

His hand went to his chest. 'And they didn't find the gun?'

'No.'

'Look, what is this, Ruth?'

'I don't know what you mean.'

'That mask of yours – I can't read it any better than the rest, but I do know when you're being evasive.'

'I'm being as honest as I can be, Greg.'

'Did you mess up at the scene – is that it? Jeez, Ruth, you'd just found me shot; I don't give a shit if you messed it up.'

'I was a CSI for five years, Greg; a CSM for two. I know how to manage a scene.'

'There you go again. It's like you're talking in code, and I'm just not getting it.'

'Who did you meet at the Old Bank Hotel?' she asked.

'What?' His heart began to thud.

'You spent two hours there the night you were shot.'

The air around her seemed to darken and for a moment he thought he might pass out. Then the darkness lifted and he saw an orange glow around her.

'I told you, I don't remember what happened that night.'

'That's understandable. But you're known there, Greg – the staff recognised you. So why were you there on those *other* occasions?'

His head began to throb in pace with the pulse of blood in his arteries. 'I don't remember.'

The orange glow around her intensified. 'You were seen heading towards the lifts. Were you visiting someone?'

The machine to his right began a jangling alarm signal.

'I don't know.'

She glanced to the array of screens. 'That heart monitor says different.'

He closed his eyes and concentrated on his breathing until the monitor returned to a regular *blipblipblip*.

'Who did you meet at the hotel?'

He looked at her and tried to mirror the quiet curiosity in her eyes.

'Was it an informant?'

He didn't answer.

'You need to understand something,' Ruth said. 'Jansen's only going through the motions, investigating a Thorn Killer connection. He doesn't believe it any more than I do. This is all to keep Superintendent Wilshire off his back – Wilshire's being bugged by the press, and he wants our guy ruled out. What Jansen is *really* interested in is *you*, Greg.'

'Me? Why?'

'He doesn't like you. I know, he's a dickhead – but he's good at the job. So, is there anything I should know?'

'Like what?'

'If I knew *that* I wouldn't have to ask, now, would I?' she said, and her eyes showed a rare flash of anger.

*What does she know?* Carver listened to the steady blip of the monitor and willed it to stay that way.

She took out her notebook. 'Jansen's team found an untraceable number on your mobile,' she said.

The monitor picked up pace and he covered by saying, 'Why have they got my phone?'

'You were found concussed and shot, Greg.'

She held the notebook up for him to read. 'This number appears on your phone log over two dozen times.'

He just kept breathing.

'You called it the night you were shot. Then you went to the hotel, after parking your car a good fifteen-minute walk away. Who is it, Greg? Who did you meet?'

'I don't know.'

'I don't believe you.'

She wasn't playing fair, reading him while he was so messed up.

'I'm tired.' That was a lie: he was nauseous and weak, but his mind was jangling like a dozen alarm bells.

Ruth wrote something on a fresh page of her notebook and tore it out. 'Okay, it's not my case – DCI Jansen is investigating the shooting, not me. He will want answers, and he won't be as sympathetic.' She slapped the slip of paper onto the bedspread. 'The number – in case you forget.' This was as angry as he'd ever seen her.

He closed his eyes against the fierce glow around her.

*I'm losing my mind,* he thought.

He sensed her hovering for a moment or two longer.

'Greg,' she murmured. 'I'm trying to help you.'

When he was sure she'd gone, he picked the paper up and clenched it in his fist.

## 15

*Day* 7

Five books lay open on Ruth Lake's office desk, another pile was stacked next to it. Kara's marginal notes were cryptic; she needed help to understand what all this background reading was for, so she rang the student's academic tutor.

'At least ten books on psychics, mediums, premonitions, cold reading . . .' she explained. 'Was she preparing for a presentation?'

'All of her cohort *should* be, of course, with showcases coming up in February and March,' he said. 'But Kara was planning to use a scene from *Antony & Cleopatra* and something from *Educating Rita* as a contrast piece.'

'So this psychic stuff can't be about her coursework?'

'I doubt it – you see, she would have to've run it past me to get it approved, and this is all news to me.' He paused. 'Of course, she could've been preparing for an audition.'

'Paid work? Wouldn't she have mentioned that to you?'

'It gets *insane* around here – especially as the final semester rolls round,' he said. 'Students can get paranoid about losing an opportunity – they'll use all kinds of tactics to improve their chances at an audition. '

Ruth finished the call and dialled Crime Scene Manager John Hughes.

'How's it going, Ruth?' he asked. 'You get anything from those books I sent you?'

'That's why I'm calling,' she said. 'The psychic texts Kara squirrelled away behind the biographies – I think she might've been reading up for a role. It's possible she had an acting job in the offing.'

'Okay – so we'll need to look for emails from theatres, TV and film—'

'And theatrical agents,' Ruth said. 'Oh, and can you run a search for anything with "audition" in the subject line?'

'I'll get someone on to it.'

'Thanks.' She was about to hang up when he spoke again.

'How's Greg?' he asked.

She'd been dreading the question. 'Emma says he's doing well.'

'You haven't seen him?'

'Not in a couple of days,' she said.

'Oh.' He sounded shocked. 'Well, I suppose he's in good hands . . .'

'Yeah,' Ruth said, refusing to feel guilty for the neglect. In fact she'd stayed away from the hospital since she'd confronted him about the hotel and the burner phone number on his mobile phone log. Until Carver decided to be honest with her, he could stew. Her mobile rang, and she said, 'I've got to go, John. Thanks for this.'

She hung up the landline and checked her mobile. It was Darshan Singh, the toxicologist who was working on skin samples from Kara. They had worked together on a few cases when Ruth was still a CSI, and he had done a rush job on Kara's tox analysis as a favour.

'Ruth,' Singh said, 'I have those results for you, and your theory was correct – the poison *was* mixed with the tattoo ink.'

'You've identified the poison?'

He cleared his throat and in her mind's eye she saw his prominent Adam's apple bobbing.

'It was tricky,' he said. 'It had been significantly diluted before it was mixed with the pigment to make the ink. Added to that, we had only a small patch of freshly inked skin to work with – the older tattoos did not retain the toxin.'

'Darshan.'

'Yes, Ruth?'

'Did you identify it?'

'Of course,' he said, more in apology for digressing than out of pride. 'It's an alkaloid.'

'Alkaloid,' she said. 'Like you'd get in potatoes, or deadly nightshade?'

'And the opium poppy, and tobacco – and about four thousand other plant species.'

'Well, that doesn't exactly narrow it down, does it?' Ruth felt her shoulders slump. 'Okay, thanks, Darshan – it was worth a try.'

'Wait,' he said. 'You haven't heard the good part. It *is* alkaloid, but we found three distinct peaks on HPLC analysis.'

That sounded more promising – High Pressure Liquid Chromatography was a biochemist's go-to kit for anything from pharmaceuticals to organic chemicals to TNT. Three distinct peaks meant Darshan had identified three specific types of alkaloid, and that brought them three steps nearer to knowing the name of the poison.

'Go ahead,' Ruth said, picking up a pen, ready to jot down the list.

'Mesaconitine, hypaconitine and aconitine,' the toxicologist said.

'It's aconite?'

'Yes,' he said, like a man bitterly disappointed to have been beaten to his punchline. 'I've emailed my full report; if you have any questions, you know where to find me.' He sounded hurt, and Ruth felt the need to make it up to him.

'No, wait,' she said. 'I'll take a look now, if you can spare ten minutes to talk me through it?'

'All right . . .'

Of all the lab specialisms, toxicology was the least glamorous, and rarely got its share of the credit. Tox results usually came through long after the first flush of excitement in an investigation had faded. Added to this, toxicologists rarely got out into the field – they were very much laboratory creatures, often isolated even in that setting as cerebral and a bit stand-offish.

'Okay, I'm opening the file now,' she said, adding, 'Aconite is a garden plant, isn't it?' although she already knew the answer.

'Common names: wolfbane, monkshood or mousebane. There are many subspecies, and it's unlikely we will identify the exact source – too many variables – but alkaloids of aconite are both *neuro* and *cardio*toxic.'

'Nerves and heart . . .' she murmured. 'And is skin contact enough to poison you?'

'Even picking the plant leaves with bare hands can be dangerous,' he said, warming to his theme. 'I found a paper from the *Journal of Analytical Toxicology*. Let me quote you: "Tingling starts at the point of absorption and extends up the arm to the shoulder, after which the heart will start to be affected." Imagine how much worse it might be if the skin has been broken – or punctured.' He was sounding pleased with himself and she was pleased for him.

She read from the report, 'Symptoms of aconite poisoning involving skin contact alone include numbness of the skin, weakness of muscles, tachycardia, atrial fibrillation . . . bradycardia.'

'Yes, he said – it can *speed* the heart rate *or* slow it down.'

'And if it slows down—'

'It could cause asphyxia,' he finished, and she could almost *see* him nodding enthusiastically at the other end of the line. 'There is one small dipteran in the emollient, however – I mean—'

'Fly in the ointment. Yeah, I got it.' Ruth didn't mind smoothing ruffled feathers, but she refused to be patronised. 'And the dipteran is . . .?'

'The relatively low concentration of aconitine – Kara really wasn't exposed to very much of it.'

'So how much would it take to kill a person?'

'About two milligrams of the pure stuff is enough to kill a healthy man. But take a look at the chromatograph.'

There were two smaller peaks, like minor pulses in a cardiograph.

'The stuff wasn't pure,' she said.

'Exactly,' he agreed. 'Added to that, the effects of aconitine are unpredictable – some people seem to have a natural tolerance.'

'And others succumb more easily.' She was thinking about Tali Tredwin, their first victim, killed within ten days of disappearing, her tattoos incomplete. 'It would take no more than a pinch to finish off the average person, though?' she asked.

'There, or thereabouts.'

'How much was Kara given?'

'It's impossible to even estimate the original concentration – but it would be very low, and the dye itself is likely to have affected the way the toxin worked. We haven't identified the black dye he used on Kara, but he used woad, a natural indigo dye, on all the others. It's slightly alkaline, and high pH weakens the effect of the aconitine.'

'Could the effect be cumulative?' she asked. 'We know the killer subjected the victims to this stuff over a period of weeks. Could it have – I don't know – weakened their hearts over time?'

'That's more a pathologist-type question,' he said with regret.

Her next question wasn't really one for Darshan, either, so she thanked him and hung up, ran off a copy of his report and went in search of DCI Parsons.

Parsons skimmed the details and set the report aside.

'Where are you with re-interviewing witnesses?' he asked.

'Almost done,' she said, not ready to share the details with him yet.

'Well, it's useful to know the poison, I suppose,' he said, with a glance at the printout in front of him. 'For future reference, I mean.'

She got the feeling that he'd ticked this box and was ready to move on.

'I think we can use it now, sir,' she said, keeping her voice light and non-confrontational.

Parsons blinked. 'How, exactly?'

'The killer chooses his victims carefully and he keeps them for an extended period. He used a natural plant tool – the fire-thorn – to create elaborate tattoos on their bodies. In the first four victims he used a herbal dye, and today we discover that Kara was injected with a neurotoxin that could explain cause of death, and it's *also* a herbal extract – taken from a plant so dangerous that just handling it could kill you.'

She waited for her boss to join the dots.

Parsons frowned. 'Safely extracting poison from a plant like that must take specialist knowledge,' he said.

'I'm thinking, who would have that kind of knowledge?' Ruth said. 'A herbalist? A toxicologist – anthropologist, even?'

'You're asking me to bring in an independent forensic adviser?'

She shrugged. 'Can't hurt.'

## 16

'I have the results of your CT scan.' The neurosurgeon stood by the side of Greg Carver's bed in the rehabilitation unit, an e-tablet in his hand.

'Okay . . .'

'You look uncertain. Do you remember having the scan?'

A huge creamy-white machine, the constant exhalation of cooling fans. Then the whooshing drone of a jet engine. Red laser cross hairs had lit his body as he rolled into the vast drum, and he couldn't get the thought of gunsights out of his head.

'I remember the scan,' Carver said. Since he'd woken up in this hospital, people were always asking questions like this. Sometimes he lied that he remembered, and sometimes he lied that he didn't. This time, searching the face of the grey-haired, besuited man by his bed, he answered truthfully: 'I just don't remember *you*.'

'I wasn't there for the scan, of course,' the doctor said. 'But we have spoken several times . . .' He seemed to be waiting for a eureka moment from Carver which never came.

The consultant smiled. 'Well, you do have a rather large team managing your treatment.' He introduced himself again. Carver immediately forgot his name. 'Your brain swelling has normalised,' the doctor went on. 'But we will need to monitor you.'

Carver nodded, trying to commit the facts to memory.

'So, have you had any unusual feelings or sensations?'

'Like what?'

'Smells that seem out of place – the smell of burning, or a strong perfume, for instance? Seeing things that aren't there?'

He means hallucinations.

Carver said, 'No,' thinking of the shadows that haunted his waking moments, the flash of light, the *presence* that he knew wished him evil, but that he could not visualise.

The doctor kept his faded blue eyes on Carver for a long five seconds, but seemed to decide it wasn't worth forcing the issue. He turned the tablet to show Carver a biological diagram of a human spine outlined in black; the heart and its blood vessels coloured red.

'The bullet is still lodged behind the descending aorta.' He pointed to a thick blood vessel that looped over the heart and backwards to the spinal column. 'It's trapped between the aorta and these two vertebrae – T4 and T5 – in the thoracic region of your spinal column.' He turned, indicating with his thumb a position on his own back between his shoulder blades.

'Can you get it out?'

'We could, but we won't – not if we can avoid it,' the doctor said.

*Is he telling me I'm going to be an invalid*? That would invite a yes or no answer, and Carver could not deal with a yes, right now, so he said, instead: 'Doctor, I need to work.'

'You need to focus on getting well, Mr Carver.'

'How can I do that with a bullet inside me?'

'Nine times out of ten, surgery to remove bullets usually does more harm than good,' the doctor explained. 'Infection, damage to surrounding tissues as we seek out the foreign object – to say nothing of the risks involved in opening your chest. Because we *would* have to do that to get at this little bugger.'

He swiped the screen of the tablet and a new image appeared. 'This is the actual scan.'

It looked like a slightly fuzzy greyscale photograph, and Carver could see the bullet as a bright slug, nestled between the artery and the bone. The thought of this alien object lodged near his heart made his chest constrict and his stomach turn to liquid.

'The bullet's position means there's a risk of damaging the aorta itself – *the* major blood vessel supplying blood to the chest and the lower part of your body,' the doctor went on. 'Nerves pass out from the spinal column in this region which control the upper chest, mid-back and abdomen, as well as the lower limbs. Damage could result in anything from breathing problems to paraplegia.'

'But if it's left in there, surely it could cause the same damage?' Carver resisted the compulsion to press a hand to his chest.

'Your tests so far have been very positive,' the doctor said. 'No muscle weakness, tingling or numbness in the lower limbs. And the physio team say they had you up and walking earlier today – only a week after you were brought here in a coma. The signs are good.'

But Carver couldn't shake the panicky feeling that one sudden movement could cripple him, that he would end up in a wheelchair for life. 'What if it shifts?' he said. 'Injures my spine anyway?'

'We will monitor you closely as you rebuild your strength,' the doctor said. 'If we see any worrying changes, we can re-evaluate the risks of surgery against the benefits. For the moment, my biggest concern is the head trauma. You have no idea how it happened, or when?'

'No.'

'The reason I ask is because, if treatment of concussion is delayed, it can cause long-term problems,' the consultant said. 'And you *do* seem to be having difficulty remembering things.'

'I'm fine,' Carver said.

'Can you tell me my name?'

Carver didn't answer; he couldn't.

The doctor didn't comment but after a moment he went on: 'The nurses and physiotherapists have also noticed that you have problems with concentration. Which you would expect in someone who has just woken from a coma.' He paused. 'But there are complicating factors in your case.'

Carver glanced up: complicating factors were always a bad thing.

'Concussion is only part of the picture,' the doctor said. 'You also suffered serious bodily trauma when you were shot, and even before that happened, you were suffering from acute alcoholic poisoning.'

Carver bowed his head.

'Would you describe yourself as a heavy drinker in general?' The doctor waited until Carver established eye contact with him. 'I'm not judging you, Mr Carver – it just helps to give a more accurate prognosis if we have good information.'

Carver passed a hand over his face. 'Since this case started I've been having trouble sleeping,' he said, approaching the question crabwise.

'How much trouble?'

'Two, maybe three hours on a good night.' Once or twice, he had even experienced hallucinations.

'Okay . . . sleep deprivation could be another factor affecting your brain function. And you've been drinking to help you sleep?'

'Yeah.'

'And waking at three in the morning in a cold sweat, I should think.'

Carver nodded. He had lost count of the number of times he'd woken halfway through the night, with a burning thirst and racing heart, having drunk himself into a stupor only a few hours earlier.

'The *good* news is that, although your liver function tests are elevated, your liver seems relatively healthy,' the doctor said. 'And it will recover with time. But long-term alcohol abuse can affect memory. So we're still looking at a complex picture here.' The doctor set his tablet down on the bedside table and took a seat, turning the chair to face Carver. 'Medicine is very much like a police investigation,' he said. 'The more intelligence you can gather, the clearer the picture becomes. Medics, like detectives, follow the evidence to identify the culprit – but too often people aren't honest about what they know. That slows things down, and can even result in greater harm.'

Carver exhaled.

The doctor waited for him and slowly, as though cranking the truth up from a deep well, Carver began. 'You asked about hallucinations,' Carver said. 'I keep smelling gunsmoke, and I get an acrid, metallic taste in my mouth. Sometimes I wake up and I see . . . shadows.' He looked for the doctor's reaction, but the surgeon only cocked his head to show he was listening.

'It feels like –' Carver swallowed '– Like there's someone in the room, and I *know* they're there, but I can't see them. They're there but *not* there. And – this is really weird – when my colleague, Ruth, is talking, I see coloured lights around her. I know, it's crazy.' He stopped talking.

'The smell of gunsmoke could be a flashback to the night you were injured,' the neurosurgeon said. 'As for the rest, you're describing "auras" – a common side effect of neurological damage, usually associated with headaches. Some patients have auditory disturbances, too – hearing sounds or voices – but visual disturbances are more typical.'

'What's causing them?' Carver said, trying to recall if the lights were linked with headaches.

'The brain misfiring,' the doctor said. 'Making odd connections as it reroutes information through undamaged tissues. So you smell something that isn't there, see odd lights, experience strange sensations – like the shadow that is, but isn't. It can be disturbing, but it is part of the recovery process.'

'So it *will* get better?'

'It might. Just to be sure, I'll ask for a new panel of tests. We'll do repeat CAT and MRI scans, and an EEG to check the electrical activity in your brain. I've asked a neuropsychologist to come and have a chat with you, too, so that you can discuss the way forward.'

'But I *will* be able to work?'

'It's a real help that you've been open with me,' the surgeon said. 'As I said earlier, the signs are positive, but I'm afraid it's too early to make that call.'

Carver wondered if the doctor would think the signs were as positive if he knew that the shadows had paid a visit just before his arrival. This time, one of the shadows had flickered and coalesced into something – *someone* – he recognised. It exploded in a supernova of light an instant later, but left an afterimage in his mind of Ruth, and she was holding a gun.

## 17

DS Ruth Lake was sitting at her office desk, watching a 'psychic' perform on YouTube. John Hughes had been quick to get back to her – Kara Grogan *had* signed up with an acting agent – there was a history going back to the beginning of the previous November. And she *did* have an audition – timed for four-thirty that very afternoon, at a studio in London.

Ruth had tried the agent's number a couple of times, unsuccessfully; she had left messages but was still waiting for a reply. It was now four o'clock.

Kara had also downloaded or bookmarked a lot of programmes, both reality TV and drama, onto her DVR, and did a lot of online searches on mediums, psychics and cold reading. Hughes had sent Ruth a number of links to search items cached on Kara's computer, and she had already trawled through a few of them. Printouts of documents from Kara's computer files entitled 'Mentalism', 'Non-Verbal Cues' and 'Body Language' lay on her desk. The websites Kara had accessed included blogs and YouTube presentations tagged: 'How To Spot A Liar', 'Reading Body Language', 'Cold Reading Techniques' and 'Tricks of the Psychic Trade' – that one was an article in *Psychology Today*.

Good to know that Kara was looking at both sides of psychic phenomena, Ruth thought. It was just a pity all that knowledge didn't save her. It did mean, though, that Kara would probably have been more on her guard than most. The killer had to be a good liar. For a microsecond, Ruth felt a spark of optimism, but when you came right down to it, all that told them was what they already knew: they were looking for a psychopath – a flat-out, natural born liar.

She sighed, made a note and moved on to the next video.

Partway through a James Randi exposé of a yet another fake, she got a call from John Hughes.

'Kara just got a stinking email from a theatrical agent, ripped her to shreds for missing an audition.'

Ruth checked her watch; it was after five p.m. 'And she isn't returning my calls. How could she *not* know what happened to Kara?'

'Beats me,' he said. 'Anyway, she says she's taken Kara off her client list, tells her not to bother getting in touch. I've just forwarded it to you.'

Ruth checked her inbox. 'Okay,' she said. 'I've got it.'

The subject line read, 'Audition No Show – are you effing *kidding* me?'

She skimmed the body of the text.

'I stuck my neck out. A student, not even graduated, given a chance in something that could give her a rocket-powered ride to stardom and you *don't show up*? Get this in your head: you are the bottom of a very big sugar mountain of potential talent, and you just blew the best chance you will have this year – possibly in your entire fricking *career*. So, buckle up, baby, you are in for a bumpy ride, and you're going to have to do it without this agent holding your sweaty little hand.'

'She's *really* pissed off,' Ruth said. 'Thanks, John – I'll get onto it.'

She copied the agent's email address and pasted it into the 'to' line of a new email and began composing, keeping the tone neutral, merely stating that she needed to speak with Ms Frinton about her client, Kara Grogan. This done, she phoned the agent's office again. The first two times, the line was engaged; the third time, she heard the tell-tale change of ring tone that said her call was being re-routed, and she was put through to Hayley, Ms Frinton's assistant.

'Ms Frinton is away,' a young voice told her.

'Away, where?'

'All over – she's interviewing new talent.'

'Well, Hayley, tell her to call me – urgently.' Ruth gave her contact details without much hope of a return call.

She barely had time to take her hand off the receiver when her phone rang again.

It was Carver. 'Ruth,' he said. 'We need to talk.'

'About what?' she said, keeping her tone even.

'The lies I've told you.'

'Okay . . .' she said. 'I'm listening.'

'Not over the phone,' Carver said. 'I want to talk face to face; you need to come here.'

Angry as she was with Carver, she was bound to him by the year they had worked together, and by her own actions in his apartment that terrible night.

She checked her inbox one last time to be sure there was nothing from Kara's agent. 'All right,' she said. 'I'll be there in thirty minutes.'

## 18

Carver was working through a memory exercise on an e-tablet, and trying not to panic that a task that would have been child's play a few weeks ago was taking all his concentration. He had been moved to the rehab unit, a block a short distance across the hospital campus, and was allocated a private room – a relief, as it shielded him from curious looks from visitors to the unit.

'Greg.'

He looked up. Ruth Lake was standing in the doorway, her right hand grazing the seam of her trouser leg. For a splinter of time, the light changed to bitter orange, and it looked like she was holding something hard and metallic loosely in her grip.

Then a sharp whiff of gunsmoke, and the light shifted back to the cold white of the low-energy LEDs.

She looked tired. Carver knew DCI Parsons as a box-ticker and approval-seeker, so he guessed that Ruth would be carrying most of the weight in the ongoing investigation.

'You seem a lot better,' she said.

Carver was sitting on a chair at the side of his bed; Emma had brought him a pair of pyjamas and a dressing gown, which at least allowed him the illusion of a return to normality.

'I am – much better, thanks.' He set aside the tablet and took a breath. 'Look, I don't like the way we left it last time.'

'You said you wanted to talk about the lies you told me.'

As usual, her tone didn't give away much, but a faint after-glow of orange seemed to shimmer around her and he thought, *She's angry.*

'The lies, yes.' He didn't add, 'And the lies you've been telling me,' but maybe he would get to that later.

'So . . .' she said.

'DCI Jansen came in to see me – I should say "to question me". You were right, he really doesn't like me.' He tried a smile, but Ruth remained neutral.

'What did you tell him?'

'What I told you.'

'You told me nothing.'

'I told you I don't remember.'

'Which was a lie.'

He felt her close scrutiny as a bright light. The orange glow came and went, blurring her features a little. He hesitated before admitting, 'It was partly true.'

'And partly a lie.' He saw a flicker of a smile, but there was no humour in it.

'Don't be such a smart arse, Ruth. I remember *some* of what happened, but I don't know what's real, and what is . . . I don't know – a dream? A fantasy?'

He thought he saw something – nothing so visible as a wince or a frown; this was something far more subtle, as though a grey membrane had slipped across her corneas. He had seen her do this a few times before, in interviews with particularly thuggish criminals, and also when she was lying to the senior ranks.

'For instance?' she said.

'Shadows,' he said. 'A smell, like gunsmoke – hallucinations, the doctor calls them – but . . . they do seem real.'

'So, what are these shadows?' she asked.

'People,' he said, looking straight at her. 'A person. I want to look at them – I can't move, but I know they're there.'

A flash of purple around her eyes, there and gone in less than a second, but unmistakable.

'You . . . don't know who . . .?'

'It's still fuzzy.'

'Well, can you remember the start of the day?' she said. 'Getting up, going to work and so on?' It felt like she was changing the subject.

'I had a meeting with you, talked about Kara. I said I didn't think she was meant as a threat to me, or Emma. You agreed.'

She nodded. 'That's how it went. Which is good, isn't it – that you're getting clear on that?'

He didn't comment, wanting to keep his own lies to a minimum.

'So, when do things start to get fuzzy?'

'Uh, around the time I left the office.' That was an outright lie.

He saw a fizz of orange light around her again. *Angry,* he thought. *It means she's angry.*

'You left the office at around eight p.m.,' she said, her voice hardening, and he knew he was right about the anger. 'That would be just after you'd called the mystery burner phone number on your mobile.'

Well, he wasn't the only one who was lying. He pushed back: 'One of the shadows is holding a gun.'

The angry flare of colour faded.

'Who?' she said.

'I don't know. Like I said, it was a shadow.'

She stared at him and she was just Ruth again, no pyrotechnics, no lights, and completely unreadable.

'Where are my files?' he asked.

'Don't you remember? I told you, they're gone.'

'Gone where?'

'The only signs they were ever in your apartment are a few Blu-tack stains on the walls of your bedroom, and a box-shaped imprint in the carpet.'

He was tiring now, but he thought he caught a gleam of green light from the corner of his eye.

'You're being evasive again,' he said.

'Back atcha,' she said.

'What happened to the gun?' He asked the question with no expectation of a straight answer, just to see her reaction.

'The most likely explanation is the shooter took it with him.' The air around her seemed to luminesce green.

'You said you don't believe the Thorn Killer shot me.'

'I don't.'

'Then who? And who would take my files?' Carver said, circling back to the earlier question, testing her. 'Why would they be of any interest to anyone other than the Thorn Killer?'

She went on the offensive. 'I thought you asked me here to tell me the truth.'

'I can't understand why you're so sure it wasn't the Thorn Killer who shot me,' he countered. 'There must be something in the files – otherwise, why did he take them?'

She groaned. 'What makes you so sure *he* did anything? *You* could've hidden them somewhere – or burned them.' She hardened her voice. 'Or put them back where they belonged – under lock and key with the rest of the case notes.'

'Great theories,' he said, 'Except I was reading those files at home the night I was shot.'

'I'm surprised you're so sure,' she said. 'Have you been holding out on me all along?'

'If the Thorn Killer didn't steal the files, then who did?' he countered.

'Whoever shot you.' The purple swirl of colour returned.

'I've been focused on this case for a year – *who else* but the Thorn Killer would hate me enough to take a gun and shoot me?'

'I don't know,' she said, and the purple colour morphed to bile-green luminescence.

*The colour of lies*, he thought.

'You *do* know,' he said, feeling sick and weak with exhaustion, 'or you think you do.'

'What are you, now?' she said, going on the attack again. 'Some kind of mentalist?'

'I know a lie when I see one.'

'You mean when you *hear* one.'

'Non-verbal cues,' he said. 'There's something you're not telling me.'

She shrugged. 'Looks like we're both keeping secrets, doesn't it, Greg?'

After she'd gone, Carver slumped in his chair.

*'Non-verbal cues'? I can't believe you fed Ruth that crap.* She of all people deserved honesty. But he couldn't shake the memory he'd had when the neurologist last spoke to him: the supernova of light; the afterimage of Ruth, holding a gun. Ruth standing at the entrance to his hospital room, the dull gleam of something metallic held loosely in her hand. Was this another example of his healing brain misfiring? Nerve impulses zigging when they should be zagging, making connections

that were never there, trying to make sense of what happened and ending up with the equivalent of a circuit meltdown? Maybe. But he couldn't deny the lights, auras – or whatever he should call them – when she spoke. He had seen it as plainly as if she had confessed it: Ruth was lying to him.

## 19

Back at HQ, Ruth Lake drove past a cluster of reporters loitering near the front entrance and continued around to the car park, letting herself in the back way to avoid questions. Inside, she ran up four flights of stairs, partly to run off some of her anger, and partly to bypass DCI Parsons, who was stepping into one of the lifts as she entered the building.

She yanked the fire door open on the second floor as DC Ivey pushed it from the other side. He tipped forward, but righted himself with nifty agility.

'Sorry, Sarge,' he said, standing back to let her through.

'My fault,' she said. 'Tom, isn't it?'

He nodded, flushing slightly. His delicate complexion must make it hell for him in the dating stakes.

'How's it going?' she asked.

'No joy on the hotel meeting,' he said. 'Or with the throw-away mobie.'

*Tell me about it.*

'How's DCI Carver?' the young detective asked.

'He's . . . *fine.*' She had only just managed to avoid saying, 'He's *full* of it', which was what was really in her mind. 'Getting there, anyway.'

'From what the boss says, his memory's still off,' Ivey said.

'Only to be expected,' she said, clamping down, remembering who Tom Ivey's boss was.

'How's your case going?'

'Slow,' she said. 'Thanks for asking, though.'

Leaving it at that, she walked back to her own Major Incident Room feeling a little calmer. It was getting late, and most of the detectives on the case had gone home, but Ruth was still too fired up to think about packing up for the night. She checked her emails and voicemail; there was still nothing from Kara's agent.

There must be something online about these interviews or showcases, or whatever they called them, she reasoned, and she began by typing the agent's name and 'acting agent'. She was in fact listed under 'talent agent', and the trade press rated Wendy Frinton Talent Agency one of the top twenty in London. There was no list of events, other than those of her impressive list of actors, and there was nothing on the website about showcases or interviews. As far as Ruth could make out, the website acted as a kind of buffer or firewall between Frinton and the hordes of wannabes clamouring for her attention.

Further down the Google search list, Ruth found links to dozens of YouTube videos; Wendy Frinton had her own channel. She skimmed the list, flicking back to a title that stood out from the 'How to' clips. A link with the tagline: 'OMFG you've GOT to see Wendy Frinton RANT!!!' It was date-stamped at just forty minutes earlier. She clicked on the link and found herself looking at a thumbnail image of the woman herself, mid-rant, judging by the twist of her mouth. Ruth clicked the 'play' icon.

Wendy Frinton buzzed onto the screen like a hornet on caffeine. Her hair was bright yellow, and stood up in tufts from constant tousling. A vivid yellow and black top completed the look. She was seated at a white melamine table; behind her, what looked like a hastily erected screen made from a swatch of curtain fabric. She gripped the table edges as if ready to tear a piece off and hurl it at the computer screen. Ms Frinton introduced herself at breakneck speed, but slowed down long enough to enunciate the name of her agency clearly.

'Okay, it's five-fifteen in the evening, UK time,' she began. 'And I am in the middle of schlepping up and down the country interviewing actors, slogging through about a *million* showcases (no exaggeration), trying to find the stars of tomorrow. So, if I look frazzled, it's because I freaking *am*.'

She gazed with a baleful eye into her laptop camera. 'You know I love you guys, and I want you to be the best you can be, but I am NOT your fricking MOTHER. So, I'm going to ask you some questions you should already have asked yourselves and, by the way, you should ask yourselves *every time* you get the teeniest, tiniest whiff of an opportunity. You might want to snatch up a pen and paper and write this down. Okay? Ready?' She paused for breath. 'Here goes: One – are you prepared? Two – did you rehearse your audition piece ten different ways to Christmas before setting out today? Three – if it's a blind audition, have you practised blind readings?' She raised a finger and pointed at the screen. 'Do *not* tell me you can't rehearse a blind reading – YES, YOU CAN – because every time you read something, *anything*, blind, you will get more *confident* at reading blind.'

She slumped back in her seat for a second, as though exhausted by the need to tell her protégés what she deemed obvious.

'Where was I up to?' she murmured, glancing down at something off-screen. 'Three. Okay, so this is four: when it's your turn, do you step onto your spot with a big smile? Five:

Did you greet the casting director? As an aside, because I really, *really* shouldn't have to say this: *before* you got there, did you check him/her out of Google?' Her eyes bugged as if someone had said something outrageous to her from the other side of the screen.

'Come *on* – you're Generation Y, the "Millennials", you're supposed to be online, connected, twenty-four seven. You were *brought up* on this stuff. So get connected – do your *research*, guys!' She jutted her jaw out and blew enough air to lift the hair off her forehead. 'Which I guess brings us to number six, *banner* headline: "BE PROFESSIONAL". Seven: Did you show up on time? Did you show up *at all*?

'Oh, God, you've *got* to show up. Don't *ever* fail to show up for an audition.' She stopped, and clamped a hand over her mouth. For a second it looked like she would terminate the video; she even reached forward as if to do just that. But at the last moment, she snapped her hand back, and drummed both hands on the table top.

'Look,' she went on in a slightly more subdued vein, 'I'm going to share this with you because it pissed me off *so much* and I do NOT want you to make the same mistake. Brief story: I arranged an audition for a client. This is a young actor – not even out of college, yet. But talented – I mean REALLY . . .' She sighed. 'So I got her this audition, it's with a *big* TV production company. *Major* opportunity for her – I mean *huge*.' She looked away from the screen for a second, and Ruth could see she was struggling for control.

'I get a call this afternoon – she didn't show up.' She slapped a hand to her forehead as if she had just got the call, a look of horror and disbelief on her face. 'She missed the freaking *audition*.'

Ruth leaned closer to the screen. Was she talking about Kara?

'Believe me, budding starlets,' Frinton said. 'Chances – I mean *annnn-y* chances *at all*, but *especially* chances like this, do NOT. Grow. On trees.' She stared wrathfully into the laptop camera. 'I called her. She didn't get back to me. I emailed her. Nothing.'

She grabbed two handfuls of hair and dragged her fingers through the already tangled mass. 'What am I supposed to *do* with that? I'll tell you, my talented friends. The next email I sent, I fired her.'

*She is – she's talking about Kara.* Ruth reached for her desk phone and punched in Ms Frinton's office number.

'You cannot *not* show up for an audition,' Frinton went on. 'Nobody owes you *anything* in this world.' She pinched a little smidgen of nothing between her forefinger and thumb to emphasise her point. 'And if you think the world out there is a tough place, it's a bowl of fricking *cherries* compared with the acting profession. *No*-body even owes you a *chance* in this business. If you're *offered* a chance and you blow it off . . . do not expect a second go-around.' She took a breath. 'Sorry if that sounds harsh,' she said, sounding anything but. 'It's just the way it is.'

Someone spoke, and she glanced over her shoulder.

'Okay, my assistant says I gotta go. Think on that, little ones. Make sure you're ready when the call comes, and I wish you all a wonderful showcase season.' She blew a couple of stage kisses, and the video ended.

The agency's landline gave up ringing and went through a reroute procedure to a mobile phone. A moment later, Ruth was talking to Hayley, the assistant.

'Detective Sergeant Lake again,' Ruth said. 'Remember me?'

'I'm afraid Ms Frinton—'

'I know, she's schlepping up and down the country. I've just watched her video. But I asked for an urgent call back on police business, and since I gather she's had time enough to post to YouTube, she can make time for me.'

'I'm sorry, she's in the middle of—'

'Showcases, yes, and I'm in the middle of a murder investigation, so listen to me very carefully, Hayley. You will put her on the line, or I will charge you, and possibly the god-like Ms Frinton, with obstructing a murder inquiry. Have I made myself clear?'

Within two minutes, Wendy Frinton herself was on the line.

'Listen, Sergeant. I don't care who you are – you can't just threaten my assistant—'

'Nice YouTube tutorial,' Ruth interrupted, speaking over her. 'The talented actor who didn't show for the audition was Kara Grogan, wasn't it?'

'I didn't name any names. And anyway . . .' her voice trailed off and Ruth imagined her making the connection between Kara Grogan's name, and a cop investigating a murder. 'You're not saying that Kara . . .'

'Great excuse for a no-show,' Ruth said, deliberately brutal. 'Being dead.'

She heard a faint echo as Ms Frinton whispered 'dead'.

'Murdered.'

'God, I feel like shit for calling her the way I did. How did it – I mean, what were the circumstances?'

'Don't you read the news, Ms Frinton?'

'This time of year, I read *The Stage*, *Entertainment Weekly*, *Spotlight* – and nothing at all in the last few days. You see it's—'

'Showcase season, I know. But Kara was murdered nearly *two weeks* ago.'

'Oh.' She sounded chastened.

'We think she was abducted by a serial murderer.'

'The Thorn Killer?'

'So you *do* watch the news.'

'I may live in a theatrical bubble, but it's tethered to planet earth,' Ms Frinton said.

Ruth heard voices off and the agent responded with a gruff, 'Tell them to *wait*.' Then, 'Okay – what d'you want to know?'

'You assumed Kara had blown off the audition, but her peers and her tutors say she was one of the most conscientious and driven people in her class.'

'I thought it was that damn phobia of hers.'

'What phobia?'

'Stage fright. I thought she'd chickened out.'

'That doesn't make sense,' Ruth said. 'I watched her on YouTube; she was brilliant.'

'That doesn't mean a thing. A good actor can be a puking, mindless, shaking *mess* a minute before they step on stage, and give the performance of their life as soon as they hit the spotlight. *Everyone* gets stage fright. The *best* actors get the *worst* stage fright because they will not accept anything less than perfection of themselves. I told her. I gave her a list of the best of the best who all had to learn to deal with going on stage despite the frickin' monster of stage fright on their backs. Told her to read their biographies, then ask herself why she should be any different.'

'Did "the best of the best" include Laurence Olivier, Judi Dench, Sheila Hancock, Benedict Cumberbatch, Barbara Streisand?' Ruth reeled the names off from memory.

'Yeah, those and a few more . . .' There was a question in the agent's tone.

'She bought the biographies, Ms Frinton. She read them cover to cover, made notes in the margins.'

'I should have known,' the agent sounded sick. 'The kid was well prepared. Said she was getting help, too.'

'What kind of help?'

'Therapy, I assumed.'

They had found no record of Kara seeing a therapist. But the skin on Ruth's scalp prickled, and she knew she was on to something.

'She didn't tell you *who* she was seeing – or where?'

'Sorry, I don't usually get into personal stuff with my clients.'

'What was she like – as a client?'

'Star material. I liked Kara; she *had* something, and she was willing to put in the work, too. She put stuff online, she had a range of roles prepped – she showcased her talents, when so many of these kids just want to get "discovered".' She groaned 'I *really* should've known . . . this wasn't like her. But I was embarrassed and angry she didn't show up for the audition.'

'It's unusual to have an agent before you've even graduated, isn't it? Ruth asked.

'You saw her on YouTube. Like I said, Kara was talented.'

'Yet she didn't want her housemates to know she'd signed with you . . .'

'Of course she didn't – you don't want to piss off the people you'll have to act with on your final presentations.'

'Is it possible her peers didn't know about the stage fright?'

'Who can say? We all cover up. Who wants to appear weak or vulnerable?'

'I can identify with that,' Ruth said with unusual candour. 'But isn't acting all about exposing your emotions and vulnerabilities?'

'Touché,' Ms Frinton said. 'But I'm afraid you'll have to talk to her peers about that.'

'Not even her tutors knew about the audition.'

'Here's how it works,' the agent said, clicking into YouTube mode. 'Only two per cent of drama school students end up in the West End. And the choice parts go to the likes of RADA and LAMDA actors. The rest are lucky to get *any* kind of acting job in the first six months after they graduate. The truth is, most of these starry-eyed lovelies will abandon drama as a career in less than a year, and even if they stick at it, they'll probably earn less than ten thou' per annum. But there's another, far more important reason Kara wouldn't have told anyone. She was under embargo.'

'She couldn't tell anyone she had an *audition*?'

'I was approached because, despite my somewhat mouthy persona, the casting director knows I don't blab. This is, "I'd tell you but I'd have to kill you", stuff. This is *Star Wars, the Force Awakens* level of secrecy. Y'see, they've lined up an A-list star for the lead and they're keeping a tight embargo till . . . and there I go again, running off at the mouth. You really don't need to know all this,' she said. 'Sorry.'

'She was researching mediums, psychics, that sort of thing.'

'For the role,' Ms Frinton said, then muttered, 'Shit. Do *not* tell anyone I told you that.'

'It really was a big opportunity, then,' Ruth said.

'Hugh-frickin'-*mongous*.' Ms Frinton sighed. 'I'm gutted for the kid – she would have been good – maybe even great.'

Another muffled interruption, and the agent said, 'Sorry, I can't hold them off any longer. Anything else you need?'

'Yeah,' Ruth said. 'You might want to take the YouTube rant down.'

# 20

Ruth Lake hung up the phone, pushed her chair back from her desk and stared at the ceiling. A smoke alarm was positioned a few metres away, and she focused on the periodic flashes of its LED.

Competitiveness, jealousy, secrecy . . . those words just kept coming up, and now 'stage fright' was a new piece in the human jigsaw that was Kara Grogan.

Kara's housemates were lying to her, she was certain. Did they know about the murdered girl's terror of going on stage? Would they be willing to exploit that terror to gain an advantage? Her academic tutor had said the competition could get ugly, and Ruth wondered just how ugly. Did it even matter? After all, it wasn't Kara's *friends* who had murdered her. But the revelation that Kara suffered from stage fright was new, and it was different. It was Ruth's duty to investigate further, but she also *needed* to know.

It could be that Kara confided in Helen, the housemate who had helped her with line rehearsals. It might even follow that Helen knew who was helping Kara to deal with her stage fright.

Ruth checked her watch. It was after seven p.m. – she might just catch the housemates at home.

Angela answered the door. She was carrying a steaming mug in one hand and had a sandwich stuffed in her mouth, presumably to free up her other hand to open the door. She gave an inarticulate squawk of displeasure, ripped the sandwich from her mouth and opened her arms wide.

'Sergeant Lake!' A quantity of her hot drink overtopped the rim of her mug and sloshed onto the floor tiles, but she ignored it. 'What a surprise!' She stood back to let her through.

Helen came trotting down the stairs a few seconds later. 'Is there news?' she asked.

'A few questions,' Ruth said. 'If you have a minute?'

Helen was dressed ready for going out in a parka jacket and scarf, and she had a shoulder bag strapped messenger-style across her chest.

'I'm on my way to work,' she said. 'Late shift. But, sure – anything to help.'

Angela's mouth twisted into a mocking smirk. She turned and led the way to the sitting room.

It was empty, and Ruth noticed the two cards she'd left still lying on the coffee table, gathering dust.

'Can you call Jake and Lia downstairs?' she asked.

'They're out,' Angela said, taking a seat on one of the sofas. She spoke with a finality that said she did not intend to be helpful.

'Okay . . . Did any of you know that Kara was preparing for an important audition?' Ruth asked.

Angela's expression hardened for a microsecond, and Ruth thought, *There it is again: jealousy, the green-eyed monster.*

'Clamshell Kara share her good fortune with the rest of us? Not a chance,' Angela said. She swivelled in her seat. 'You're very quiet, Helen,' she said, peeping over the rim of her mug as she took a sip.

Helen gave her housemate a cold, hard look. 'That's because I've got nothing to say.'

'What do you know about Kara suffering from stage fright?' Ruth asked.

Helen looked concerned, but Angela set her face into an unresponsive mask. 'Why should we know anything?'

*Interesting, that – answering a question with a question.* Ruth chose to answer with another question of her own.

'Is it possible that Kara was seeing a therapist about it?'

'Anything is *possible*,' Angela said. 'But it's not like she would tell *us*.'

'I'm afraid she didn't mention anything to me, either,' Helen said, with a quick glance at her watch. 'And I've really got to go . . .'

'Okay, but if you think of anything . . .' Ruth scooped up one of her business cards from the coffee table and handed it to Helen.

'No problem,' she said, jamming the card into her pocket.

Ruth left five minutes later, convinced that Angela was lying: she knew about the stage fright. Her car was parked half a block away, and as she reached it, her mobile buzzed. It was a text message.

'Meet me at the Quarter in Falkner Street – Helen.'

It was less than five minutes' walk, but Ruth drove, thinking that Angela might be watching.

In her early years on the force, Falkner Street was synonymous with sleaze. Back then, this area of town had been on her beat, and sex workers had plied their trade on every corner between Falkner Square and Hope Street. A woman could not walk a hundred yards from her home to a bus stop without being propositioned by a kerb crawler – or worse – a pimp looking to recruit new girls. Now those same streets were part of the trendy Hope Quarter, synonymous with five star restaurants, bistros, cafes and boutique hotels.

Ruth squeezed into a spot on Hope Street and walked the last few yards. The place she was looking for stood mid-row of a cluster of restaurants in a Georgian terrace, fronted in heritage-style colours. The cobbled road and York stone pavement lit by the warm glow of faux Victorian streetlamps completed the atmosphere of chic. It was freezing cold, and little patches of snow still clung, soot-blackened, in the shelter of the lemon-coloured sandstone wall enclosing the grounds of Blackburne House, opposite.

The restaurant was packed, but Helen had bagged a table outside. 'Sorry,' she said. 'Best I could do.'

'No problem.' Ruth dipped in her pocket for an e-cigarette. 'At least it'll give me the chance to suck on one of these.'

Helen smiled sheepishly, lifting three fingers of her gloved hand to reveal her own vape. 'You'd think I would know better, doing what I do for a living – but what can I say? It's an addiction.'

'Oh, it is that,' Ruth said, taking a gentle draw on her e-cig.

A moment later, a server appeared with two tall glasses.

'I ordered coffee,' Helen said. 'I hope you don't mind?'

'You're kidding?' Ruth said, reaching for her glass with a smile of thanks. She took her first, welcome sip. 'So, are you really heading to work, or was that just an excuse to get out of the house?'

'No, I'm on my way in – I heard your voice in the hall and hit upon a plan to waylay you.' Helen took a breath. 'Angela is lying through her teeth.'

'I won't argue with you on that. I'd like to speak to Lia and Jake – I get the feeling they would be more . . . amenable. I don't suppose you'd happen to know where they are?'

Helen smiled. 'Why d'you think I lured you here? They're guiding a 'Haunted Liverpool' tour around the Georgian Quarter. They should finish at St James's Cemetery at eight.'

Ruth checked her watch. 'Which gives me fifteen minutes to enjoy my coffee and a nicotine hit before I sprint over there.'

It was almost a year to the day since the last time Ruth had visited St James's Cemetery, and as she approached the Cathedral concourse she slowed, remembering how they had found the body of Tali Tredwin on a table tomb at the base of the old quarry wall.

The entrance to the cemetery lay on the left side of the cathedral concourse at the end of the spiked railings that protected the oratory building – a Greek temple in miniature. At the top of the escarpment, an access tunnel to the old quarry had been hewn out of the sandstone. Lined with gravestones lifted from the cemetery below, the tunnel curved left, sloping gently down into darkness. A faint light shimmered on the tunnel walls, and Ruth shivered but kept going, her footsteps echoing dully from the stone floor. As she reached the sunken cemetery, she heard voices.

The air was even colder at the bottom of the sandstone cliff, and a mist swirled around the exit, clinging to the ground, merging with pockets of snow. A short distance away the light source was revealed as a hurricane lamp, hanging from a lantern pole that was jammed into the ground. A group of around ten people huddled around its light.

A clear, male voice declaimed in portentous Shakespearean tones: 'For two hundred and fifty years, the rock was hewn from these ancient walls. Chronicles of those gone-by times speak of fairies, sprites and hobgoblins, which nightly, and in divers ways did perform their unseemly vigils on this very spot, to the great terror of every schoolboy and nursery-maid who had the temerity to venture through this darksome way.' The narrator paused.

Could this be Jake? It didn't sound like the mumbling, inarticulate youth Ruth had spoken to at the shared house, but she couldn't see past the crowd of listeners.

'But nought in this world is everlasting, and by 1825 the quarry was exhausted,' he went on. 'The city corporation sought a new use for it, and the cemetery in which you stand this evening was consecrated in 1829. Since then, fifty-seven thousand souls have been laid to rest in this place.' Here, he lowered his voice, but it carried well on the thin night air.

An owl screeched suddenly and, pale and luminous, swept low over their heads.

Someone said, 'Oh, my god!'

The speaker waited for the muttered exclamations and suppressed laughter to die down.

'It is not owls alone that haunt these darkling paths,' he said. 'Only a year after the cemetery opened, The Right Honourable William Huskisson, MP, attending the official opening of the Liverpool and Manchester Railway line, fell under the wheels of Mr Stephenson's steam engine, *The Rocket*, and died of his wounds, earning him the dubious honour of being the first person to be killed by a train. His remains are buried in the grand mausoleum yonder.'

Here, the speaker turned, raising one arm, and the group broke the circle to look towards the domed building at the centre of the cemetery. Light from the hurricane lamp fell on one side of his face, and Ruth recognised the brooding features: it was indeed Jake – Kara's housemate. He wore a dark frock-coat and top hat, and looked confident and poised.

'But Mr Huskisson's soul does not lie easy. And oftentimes in the dead of night he is seen limping and groaning around the foundations of his monument.'

A murmur of disconcerted delight rippled through the audience. Then a second person spoke: 'Another spirit said to haunt this place is that of a Victorian lady, dressed all in black, who is seen gliding along the paths of the cemetery.'

This was the nervous little waif, Lia; a tall wig constructed of elaborate curls was piled on top of her head. Pinned to her coiffure, a small, feathered hat. She was shivering in silk crinoline skirts and a velvet jacket. Her voice, high and piping, lacked the strength to carry far in the open.

'The lady's tomb was ransacked by grave robbers and it is said that she weeps as she searches the paths for her lost jewels. Often, she will move frantically from one end of the cemetery to the other, before vanishing in the tunnel, whence we, too, must make our way, for now our journey is ended.' She raised her forearm to the horizontal and swept it wide, turning one-eighty degrees to point towards the tunnel entrance, where Ruth stood.

Lia gasped, seeing Ruth, and several of the group gave little yelps of frightened surprise. Laughter quickly followed, and the audience dispersed, couples clinging to one another, others talking excitedly, smiling at Ruth as they passed.

Only the two actors remained. They were not smiling.

'What are you doing here?' Jake asked. 'How did you—'

'I just called in at the house,' she said, leaving them to assume that Angela had told her where to find them. 'I have a few more questions.'

'What's the *matter* with you? We don't *know* anything,' Lia burst out. The feather in her cap quivered with indignation.

'Something new has come to light,' Ruth said.

She told them about the audition and Lia's shoulders slumped as though she felt another opportunity had slipped past her. Jake closed his eyes for a second as though he felt a physical pain.

'The audition was today,' Ruth said. 'Her agent was furious that she didn't turn up.'

Jake's anguished expression told Ruth that he wanted to come clean, but Lia refused to meet her eye.

'Let's find somewhere where we can talk,' Ruth said.

'I don't *want* to talk to you.' Lia all but stamped her foot. 'I *won't*.'

'Come on, Lia,' Ruth said. 'It's just a chat.'

'*No.*' Lia lifted the hem of her dress and swept past Ruth. 'I'm cold,' she said. 'I'm going home.'

She bustled off through the tunnel, her skirts whispering against the gravestones as she fled.

'So, it's just you and me,' Ruth said. 'Nice performance, by the way.'

'It was crap. Lia doesn't *own* the part. "It is said that she weeps". Seriously?' He gave a dismissive snort. 'If *she* doesn't believe it, why should the audience? "She will move frantically" – what the hell does that even *mean*?'

Suddenly, Ruth understood. 'This was yours and Kara's tour, wasn't it?'

He frowned, seemed about to deny it, but changed his mind.

'Kara had the punters looking over their shoulders, jumping at shadows,' he said. 'I should never have carried on after . . . It's – I dunno – it feels disrespectful.'

'Well, at least you didn't mention that Tali Tredwin was discovered here.'

He sucked air through his teeth. 'Angela's bagged that. She's planning a Thorn Killer Murder Walk, visiting all the sites where victims were found.'

'And how do you feel about that?'

'Fucking horrible. Okay?'

In fairness, he did look sick.

Without another word, he unhooked the hurricane lamp and dragged the hook out of the ground. He made to walk past her, but she sidestepped, blocking him.

'Okay, you feel terrible – good for you. But what're you going to do about it?'

'What *can* I do? It's a free country.'

'You could tell Angela what you think.'

'And if I kick up a stink, she'll call Daddy and tell him I'm being "beastly". I could end up on the streets, trying to find new digs during finals. I can't *handle* that.' His voice broke, and in the lamplight, she saw that his eyes were filled with tears.

'What are you hiding from me?' she said.

'Nothing.'

'No,' she said. 'It's something. It's like a parcel you pass between you: you and Lia and Angela. You did something – you and the others.'

His forehead creased, and she knew she was getting through.

'Look, I know you're not proud of it, and I'm pretty sure that given a second chance you would do things differently.'

He peered into her face and she saw how tortured he was.

'Kara is gone – I'll never be able to make it up to her,' he said.

'But you can help find her killer.'

'I don't see how,' he said, and it sounded like a howl of anguish.

'I need to understand what was going on in Kara's life at that time. If something upset her – knocked her off her normal equilibrium – she might do something out of character, take a risk she wouldn't usually take.' She could see that he was listening. 'Knowing Kara's state of mind could help us to uncover what she was doing in the last few days and hours before she vanished, and *that* could lead us to the person who killed her.'

For a full ten seconds he looked past her into the mist and the shadows. Then he sighed. 'All right,' he said. 'All right. I'll tell you. But not here.'

They ended up at the Roscoe Head, only a short walk away, but where Jake was unlikely to be seen by fellow students. Ruth settled the student in a quiet corner and went to the bar. She knew the landlady, Carol Ross, from her days on the beat.

'On duty or off?' Carol asked.

'On,' Ruth said, with a wince of regret. Off duty, she would have a half of whatever guest beer Carol recommended. On duty, it was always tonic water, with ice and lemon.

'What about Lord Snooty?'

'Rum and Dr Pepper.' Carol rolled her eyes and Ruth said, 'I try not to judge.' She looked over her shoulder at the scowling youth and added, 'Better make that rum a double.'

She sat at forty-five degrees to the student, which gave her the dual advantage of being able to read his face without making the interview feel confrontational.

'Kara could be a bit full of herself,' he said.

'Bragging?'

'No . . . just . . . she knew she was good.'

Ruth couldn't equate the two, but she didn't let it show in her face.

'She was *super*-organised. I mean, pretty anal about it, actually.'

Kara's agent seemed to think she was doing what they should all be doing, but Ruth kept her eyes wide, and her body language interested and sympathetic, leaning in to him slightly, and nodding every now and then in encouragement.

'When I first moved into Angela's place, everyone got on fine,' Jake said. 'It was good – the parties were fantastic . . .'

'Until . . .' Ruth prompted.

The corners of his mouth turned down for a fraction of a second. Sour taste, bitter memories.

He sighed. 'One time, we were playing "Truth or Dare" with vodka shots. We all got totally wasted. Kara went for a "truth".' He shook his head, staring into his drink as he remembered. 'She told us she had terrible nightmares the night before a performance. Standard stuff – like going on stage and you haven't learned your lines, or you don't even know what *play* it is. That would've satisfied the rest of them, but she wasn't used to drinking, and she said more than she should.'

Ruth waited.

'She should've just shut up,' he said. It sounded like a justification.

'Was it so bad, what she told you?'

'Not bad, just . . . dangerous.'

He paused, and when she didn't comment further, he sighed, and his shoulders slumped.

'She said she would go looking for her rehearsal script – this is in her dream – and when she found it, her blocking-notes, pencil marks, script analysis, highlighting – it was all gone.'

He glanced quickly into Ruth's face, and she realised the notion terrified him.

'You saw the notes she made – how she marked everything up?'

Ruth nodded.

'Angela thought it would be a laugh to get hold of Kara's script, change the order, replace it with an unmarked script.'

'Tapping into Kara's worst fears,' Ruth said.

'Then they pretended they didn't know what she was talking about.'

'"They" being . . .?'

'Angela and Lia.'

No surprises there. She recalled her first visit to the house; Angela had wished her luck in gaining entry to Kara's room.

'So Angela lied when she told me she didn't have a key?' If she had, it could mean that she had tampered with evidence – and that could have serious repercussions.

'No – by the time you came, only Kara had a key – I'm getting to that.'

He took a deep breath, letting it go slowly, and Ruth knew that this was the part he'd been building up to.

'We do a lot of community theatre on one of the modules,' he said. 'We're supposed to show we can do stuff on our own – you know, organise a production, take it out to schools and community projects. Create our own "revenue streams" if we can't find proper acting jobs.'

He sounded contemptuous, and Ruth guessed that he had his sights set much higher.

'One of the challenges was to devise, improvise, script and rehearse a piece all in one week, then perform it in a community setting – school, church hall, day care unit – whatever. It was all about teamwork – you know, the camaraderie of the touring companies of old – *Nicholas Nickleby*, "The Crummles Troupe" and all that bollocks.'

'Sounds like you didn't think much of it,' Ruth said.

'I didn't think I would, but –' he shrugged '– it was good – you know, fun. Kara was brilliant – as usual. We knew she would outshine us all, and I guess we were envious.' He gave a slight shake of his head, remembering, and she saw regret and self-disgust in his face.

'So, on the last day of rehearsals, while Kara wasn't around, Angela said she'd decided to change the script – not all of it – just one page. Kara wasn't to be told. I didn't want to, but the others said we're *supposed* to throw challenges at each other, learn how to improvise when someone misses a cue, or skips a line, or dries in a performance.'

'So you went along with it.'

'I didn't *like* it. But it was only a page – I mean about a *minute* of performance time – then we would go back to the script. It was a community fill-in, no big deal; it wasn't even worth that many course credits. She could've just stood there, said nothing, picked up the next cue, nobody would've noticed. It was how she made *us* feel a lot of the time. You know – a bit useless, out of our depth. But when we started saying the new lines, taking up new positions – I thought she would have a heart attack. She started shaking, couldn't breathe. We were at this place for kids in care. The audience was weirded out, one of the support workers asked Kara if she was all right. I went over and touched her shoulder, and she jumped like I'd burned her. She looked at me. I mean *right into* me.' He sighed. 'Then she turned and walked out.'

'What did you do?'

'Well, we couldn't just *leave*. We finished the performance – by the end of it, the audience thought it was part of the drama.

She didn't come home that night. When she did show up the next day, she changed the locks on her door, didn't speak to any of us. Angela didn't even dare complain to her dad.'

'From what you said earlier, I would've expected Angela to tell her father.'

He shrugged. 'Kara could have made things very difficult for us if she'd reported what we did, but she didn't. In some ways that made it worse. If she'd been angry, at least I could've reacted. But she blanked us. Didn't eat meals with us, go out with us, wouldn't watch TV with us . . . I tried to apologise, she said, "It's okay, Jake. I've learned a valuable lesson." It was like she decided she was on her own, and she was going to deal with it, no matter what it took. She changed workshop groups, started going out at night on her own. The only person she would even talk to was Helen.'

'And Helen was the only person who didn't know what was going on.' Ruth kept any judgement out of her tone. 'Those nights she went out – do you have any idea where she was going?'

'No. Is it important?'

'Her agent thinks she was seeing someone to help her with stage fright.'

Jake loosened his scarf and opened his coat, his skin flushed with emotion. 'We did that to her. Jesus – I am such a fucking *shit*.' He stopped, the colour drained from his face, the self-pity and self-justification replaced by a look of horror.

'Do you think we shoved her into the path of the psycho who killed her?'

## 21

*Day 8*

The next morning, directly after the briefing, Ruth Lake drove to the university's anthropology museum, where she had arranged to meet with Doctor Lyall Gaines, their new forensic adviser. The museum was housed in a Georgian terrace on Abercromby Square. Most of the square was pedestrian access only, and the roadway near the museum only accessible via card-access barriers. She circled for ten minutes, then gave up and parked down the hill on Mount Pleasant.

The city's two universities, a further education college and the Institute of the Performing Arts all had buildings in this square mile of the city, and the streets were thronged with students making their way to early morning lectures. Ruth dodged past the slow-moving groups, cutting right at the corner of Abercromby Gardens, arriving just a few minutes late.

The receptionist buzzed her in and pointed her towards the east staircase. 'All the way to the top,' she said, handing Ruth a visitor pass.

The hallway and stairs were covered with utilitarian grey vinyl, but the cornices and mahogany stair rail were still in place. The museum was housed on the ground and first floors, the offices on the second floor. Dr Gaines's office was tucked away through a fire door at the end of a narrow, creaking landing.

She knocked and felt the floorboards under her feet vibrate as he crossed to open the door.

Dr Gaines was probably in his late forties, but dressed much younger in khaki combat trousers and a sweatshirt hoodie. He wore the sleeves pushed up to reveal a collection of bracelets on both wrists: silicone bands, stone beaded, leather and fibre braids, and one that looked disturbingly like plaited human hair. His own hair was collar-length and shaggy, greying in streaks that looked suspiciously even in colour.

He smiled, swinging the door wide. 'Welcome to my domain.'

The room was large by modern academic standards, and Gaines had hung it with African and South American masks. On his desk were piles of exam papers and essays.

'Marking,' Gaines said with a grimace.

'It's good of you to take the time to look at this,' she said.

'Not at all. This –' he waved dismissively at the papers on his desk '– is merely how I earn a living.' He lifted a pile of photographs from the chair in front of his desk, and Ruth caught a glimpse of a post mortem image of Kara Grogan; he had requested the images prior to their meeting. '*This* is why I come to work every day,' he finished.

He moved to a sofa which was shoved against a bookcase on one side of the room. 'Come. Sit.'

On a low table set in front of the sofa, Ruth saw four more piles of photographs, one for each of the Thorn Killer's victims. She glanced up and caught him watching her with his pale blue eyes.

She sat at the far end and he took the centre, closer than was strictly necessary, or polite.

'Beautiful, aren't they?' he said, staring at the tattoo markings on the victims.

'You think they're beautiful?' she said, keeping her tone neutral.

'Primitive, admittedly. But beautiful nevertheless.'

He looked away, then quickly towards her again, his hard, blue eyes sharp, alert, as if trying to catch her in an unguarded moment.

'Tattoos are a rite of passage in many cultures.' He thrust an e-tablet into her hand. He had compiled a set of photographs, all women, mainly of African origin, their faces scarified or inked. 'They can be a mark of status and of beauty, drawing attention to a person's best features. Eyes, teeth, labia, cheek-bones, all enhanced or highlighted by the markings.'

He swiped left and a new set appeared. These showed girls and women in the process of being inked or cut, their faces bloody and swollen.

'They're fully conscious,' he said. 'It's a test of their bravery and fortitude that they can endure the pain.'

Ruth felt his close scrutiny. She turned her eyes on him and handed the device back with a cool, level gaze.

'Our man doesn't mark their faces,' she said.

'Hm . . . that *is* interesting, isn't it? Probably something you will want to put to your tame forensic psychologist.'

Interesting that he knew this, yet saw fit to show her these images. Interesting, too, that although their 'tame forensic psychologist' had recommended Gaines for this job, Gaines didn't have the courtesy to name him.

'I'll certainly mention it to Dr Yi,' she said, maintaining a neutral tone. 'He said you might know something about the killer's use of thorns.'

'Mm,' Gaines said. 'It's odd. Thorns are most commonly used for scarification, these days, but your chap seems to be hand-tapping – and with a single thorn. It's the oldest method, very slow, and *extremely* painful.'

'If it's old, is it possible our man is from a particular ethnic group?'

'The method *is* still practised by the Kalinga in the Philippines . . .' He played with the bands around his wrist as he thought. 'But there are very few practitioners still living, and Kalinga tattoos are sophisticated, intricate, highly stylised. Comparing your Thorn Killer's efforts with Kalinga tattoos is like setting a child's crayon drawing next to a Rembrandt and calling it art.'

She nodded. 'Is there anything you can tell us about the symbolism in the tattoos?'

He nodded slowly. 'Early days, but the eyes tattooed on victim one's body are reminiscent of early representations of the Eye of Providence.'

'Tali Tredwin,' Ruth supplied automatically.

He blinked at the interruption.

'The first victim – that's her name – Tali.'

He quirked an eyebrow. 'The Eye of Providence is a symbol of God's watchfulness over the faithful,' he said, as though she hadn't spoken. 'But they also bear some resemblance to the eye of Horus. In ancient Egyptian culture, the eye of Horus is a symbol of protection and healing.'

'Didn't do much for Tali, did they?' Ruth observed.

He chuckled as though she'd made a joke. 'You're right. With each new embellishment of her skin, the symbols of healing brought Tali closer and closer to death.' Again, Gaines let his gaze drop, then glanced quickly up.

Those quick, sharp, piercing looks had an almost percussive effect on Ruth as he switched his attention from her eyes, to her forehead, to her mouth, sweeping down to check what her hands were doing, then back up to her face. His obvious attempt to read her was apparently supposed to make her self-conscious, put her off her stride.

'The tattoos on Kara's body are black,' she said, sticking to the case, refusing to be provoked. 'The forensic chemists think he's changed to a different dye. Any thoughts on why he might do that?'

'Do they know what the new stuff is?'

Ruth shook her head. 'We're waiting on the biochemical analysis.'

'You already know that the indigo he used on victims one to four is not ideal. Woad is corrosive; skin reactions can get messy – it's in your report. So perhaps he changed to something less likely to cause tissue damage? Victim five is much better executed.' His eyes gleamed.

'Kara,' she said, thinking, *Don't let him get to you*. 'The fifth victim is Kara.'

## 22

Emma was sitting in the chair next to Carver's bed, staring at the honeymoon photograph when Carver opened his eyes. Morning sunshine lit her hair a lemon-yellow and softened her features.

'Hey,' he said, smiling, feeling warm and soft with sleep. He checked the time; it was ten forty-five. 'You should have woken me.'

'The doctors say you need your rest,' she said.

'I'm *fine*,' he said. 'The physio was brutal this morning, that's all.'

'Your balance is improving, they say.'

He'd had some problems with weakness and uneven gait at the start of the rehab sessions.

'Yeah. The concussion knocked me about a bit, but I'm . . .' He trailed off, distracted by the muddy brown aura around her. 'Emma, are you all right?'

She turned her gaze on him and he saw such pain and confusion that he couldn't bear to look at her and, instead, stared at his hands. They felt slightly numb, and sometimes, when he saw them lying inert on the white bed sheets, he had the surreal feeling that they did not belong to him. The knuckles seemed too bony, the fingers too long. At first, the medics were concerned that the bullet might have moved, might be pressing on his spine, causing more damage, but a scan proved that it had stayed put. It could be a hangover from the concussion, they told him; it would likely disappear with time. But he hadn't told them that he'd had the numbness before he'd ended up in hospital. He'd looked it up when the symptoms first appeared, so he knew that tingling and numbness in the hands was one of the signs of alcoholism – a hangover that might never go away. He'd kept it to himself because they would tell Emma, and he was shamed enough in her eyes.

'I'm sorry, Emma,' he said.

'What?' She cocked her head as if she hadn't heard him right.

'I'm sorry – for everything that happened. For everything I've done.'

Her face seemed to darken – not figuratively, but in a real, tangible way – as though a deep shadow had fallen across it, making it impossible to see her eyes, her mouth, her expression.

She touched the frame of the photograph lightly with the tips of her fingers. 'Did you ever think we would end up like this?'

'None of it was your fault,' he said.

'It takes two to make a marriage, Greg,' she said, and it sounded like the kind of answer a counsellor would give – logical, sensible, but lacking the emotion that went with actually having lived through that marriage.

'Only one to break it,' he said, recognising the scrabbling flutter in his chest as panic. 'And I *am* sorry.'

'I know,' she said, barely audibly.

'Emma, I . . . I want to try again.' She didn't answer, and he said, 'Can we do that?'

Her face emerged from the shadows for an instant, and he was sure she would say no. Then the muddy aura swirled around her again, shot through with inky blue, now; like petrol on water, it shifted and reflected the light, so that he could not read her.

'Now isn't the time,' she said. 'You need to focus on getting better.'

'Is that a no?' he asked, his heart thudding hard in his chest. He hardly dared look at her for fear of what he would see. But she waited, and he did look, and he saw that same confused swirl of colour and darkness, but with one or two bright spots of light.

'It's not a no,' she said. 'But it's too soon to think about the future, Greg. My feelings are mixed up in the . . .' He thought she was going to say 'the shooting', but she changed course, avoiding any direct reference to it. 'In *what happened* to you,' she said. 'You were in such a terrible state when they brought you here. For days, we didn't know—'

She broke off, and he saw a shaft of sharp blue light, and he knew he was seeing her pain, a manifestation of it, and he realised for the first time just how hard all of this must have been for Emma.

He wanted to apologise again, but she seemed to anticipate it, and raised a hand as if to forestall him.

'You can ask me again, when you're up and about,' she said.

'I *was* up. I just needed—'

Again, she stopped him. 'You were having a mid-morning *nap* when I got here,' she said, softening the blow a little with a rueful quirk of her lips.

He gave a half-smile and sank back on the pillows.

'I won't come back to you because I feel sorry for you, Greg. If I *do* come back, it won't be as your nurse, and I *will not* go back to the way we were.' She spoke quietly, and without anger. 'You need to take control of your life: the drinking, the obsession with this horrible case. Then we can talk.'

She kissed him on the forehead and he almost reached to grasp her hand as she straightened up. But he knew that if he tried she would pull away, disengage, and he was afraid it would only deepen the distance between them.

She turned at the door and gave him a small wave before leaving.

His legs felt heavy as he swung them over the side of the bed, and the room tilted so steeply that the pull of gravity felt like he was in freefall. When the room settled to a slow spin, he reached gingerly for the photograph, trying to keep his head steady. She *did* look happy, then, certain of a good life with him. Had things changed so very much in the years since?

It hurt too much to look at her trusting expression, knowing how much it had hardened in the years that followed, because Carver knew that he was the cause. So he placed the picture face down on the cabinet and asked a health care assistant for a phone trolley. He dialled the mobile number on the slip of paper Ruth had given him – the number for the pay-as-you-go phone he had rung so many times in the month before he was shot. He had hidden the scrunched-up scrap of paper in the drawer of his bedside cabinet, but he didn't need to look at it: he knew it by heart.

As the phone rang out, the sounds around him faded, and the light dimmed. He heard raised voices – his, and a woman's. Then, breaking glass. A scream.

Darkness. The taste of whisky in his mouth, the stench of it on his skin and clothes. He felt a rush of violent nausea and hung up before the line connected.

For a half minute, he sat at the edge of the bed, his hand clamped over the phone receiver, holding it down, holding down the roiling sickness in his stomach, huffing air out of his nostrils to purge the stench of whisky.

Then breathing. Just breathing.

## 23

Ruth Lake typed up her notes on her meeting with Dr Gaines. She had dealt with enough forensic experts over the years to accept a level of arrogance from them. Many were too ready to assume ignorance in anyone who was not in their field; the narrower the field, the bigger the ego in her experience. It didn't bother her particularly, and sometimes she had fun playing verbal tennis, allowing them a few easy lobs before smashing them out of court with some arcane scientific detail of her own. Gaines had the worst features of the worst of them, and he was sleazy with it. It was not the sort of thing she could put in her notes, but she had been with the police for long enough to trust her instincts.

Job done, she called the forensic psychologist who had put Gaines's name forward. He wasn't picking up, so she left a message for him to call her when he had a moment. Then she set to work on a report detailing Jake's confession, together with the new information from Kara's agent.

She sent it through to DCI Parsons, as well as printing a copy off to deliver personally. She thought of handing the thing off to one of the admin staff, but decided that would be pathetic, and went instead to his office. The place was empty and clean – tidier than she had ever seen it when Greg was the occupant. She added her report to one of the neat stacks on his desk, conveniently labelled 'REPORTS', with an orange stick-it note to help it stand out among all the other buff folders.

Back at the incident room, she checked on her emails. John Hughes had sent a set of bookmarked links the IT techs had found on Kara Grogan's computer, and she worked through them for a couple of hours, looking for patterns of use. As expected, there were a lot of links to mediums, clairvoyants and the like, and a similar number to sceptics and myth-buster type websites.

Among the mediums was a set of UK-based psychics. Ruth grouped these in one file and discovered that there were a few duplicates – the same website listed twice, sometimes three times. A closer look told her that Kara had bookmarked the events pages of a few of the psychics as well as their homepages. Ruth printed these off, and picked up a highlighter pen. Six of the psychics on the list had given 'readings' in Liverpool in early November – around the time Kara had disappeared. Had Kara attended those events as part of her research for the audition?

Ruth made a note of the psychics and their contact details, together with the dates and the venues where they had performed. Some 'intuitive readers' even offered readings by phone or Skype. Ruth was no psychic, but she did consider herself an intuitive reader of people, and in her experience, it was always harder to hide a lie face to face. So she checked out their events pages for January and found that three of the six were returning to Liverpool in the next few days.

The start of a new year must be a busy time: all those sad people desperate to get in touch with those they'd lost. Then there would be another fat wodge of overspent, turkey-stuffed folk with post-Christmas blues, devastated that the turn of the year hadn't turned their lives around.

She tapped details into her mobile phone calendar, and as she finished, a group of officers in uniform trooped past the incident room door. A team had been sent out mid-morning with photos of Kara. They were tasked with stopping and questioning motorists and joggers around Sefton Park, and had just finished a four-hour stint. House-to-House and this team were sharing one of the larger seminar rooms down the corridor. They still didn't know exactly when Kara's body had been left at the Fairy Glen, but after TV and media appeals, a couple had come forward. The guy had proposed to his girlfriend in the snow by the frozen waterfall; they had been there around midnight, and they had seen nothing untoward. Ruth hoped the macabre discovery a few hours later hadn't made the young lovers feel jinxed.

The clump of boots and murmur of conversation faded and the police sergeant leading the canvassers paused at the door of the incident room.

'Anything?' Ruth asked.

He grimaced, shaking his head.

'Maybe the second shift'll catch something.' A smaller team was scheduled to set up at midnight; they would stick at it until the early-morning joggers had come and gone.

'Let's hope,' he said, and trudged on.

Ruth's mobile phone rang.

'Ruth, it's Greg. I know you're busy, but . . .' He broke off, sounding choked.

'What's happened?'

'It's Emma – I thought she was . . . I thought we had a chance, but . . . oh, shit, I'm sorry – I know I shouldn't be bothering you with this.'

She checked her watch; it was well past lunchtime, and she hadn't even taken a coffee break, yet. She could zip over to the hospital, be back in time for the afternoon debrief.

\*     \*     \*

He was sitting in an armchair by his bed, dressed in lounge-wear pyjamas – a long-sleeved tee and jogging bottoms – and he was squeezing a green gel ball, switching it from his right to his left hand every few seconds in some kind of physio exercise. The wound where they'd inserted the drain into his skull was healing in a purplish stripe, and a fuzz of hair had started to grow over it. He looked gaunt, hollowed out.

Ruth pulled up a chair and sat facing him. 'Give her time,' she said. 'She's been frantic – she's probably too exhausted to think straight.'

He lifted his eyes to hers. The hazel irises, flecked with gold, usually danced with intelligence. But right now they were faded, almost colourless.

'No,' he said. 'She's seeing things exactly as they are.'

'She said she's definitely leaving you?'

'I told her I wanted to try again. She said now was not the time.'

'So she didn't say no . . .'

'She said I could ask her again – when I had "things" under control.'

'Meaning the drinking?'

'That, and the case.'

Ruth didn't know what to say; she wouldn't lie to him, but she wanted to comfort him somehow.

'Well, you haven't had a drink in over a week. But the case – now, that's a *real* addiction . . .' She twitched her eyebrows to show she was joking, and he smiled weakly.

'Look,' he said. 'I was thinking – maybe an anthropologist might make some sense of the tattoos.'

Ruth said, 'Have you been quizzing someone at the office?'

He looked mystified, but then his eyes suddenly brightened as if light had flooded the room, pouring colour and life into them. 'You mean you've already spoken to an anthropologist? What did he say?'

For a moment, she stared at him. 'Why did you call me here?' she said.

'I don't follow.'

'Is it really because you're worried about losing Emma?'

'You know it is.' He looked hurt.

'I know you said you needed someone to talk to – I *assumed* that meant about you and Emma. But now I'm here, all you seem to want to talk about is the case.'

'Ruth—'

She shook her head, impatient with his excuses and rationalisations. 'You're losing her all over again because of your obsession with the Thorn Killer. Greg, you *have* to let it go.'

'It's *my case*,' he said.

'And it nearly killed you.'

'Yeah, well I'm not dead, yet.'

'You're unbelievable. Don't you know how close you came?'

'I'm just trying to do my job, Ruth.'

She threw up her hands with a snort of exasperation.

'Hear me out,' he said. 'Just one more time, then I'll – I'll leave it alone.'

She didn't believe him for one second. She let him talk, but this was the last time – the very last – that she would fall for his bullshit about concern for his wife, or his marriage.

'I've been trying to reconstruct the files in my head, to crystallise in my mind what I was thinking just before I was shot. I think I'd made a link between the victims.'

She was curious, despite herself.

'Which was . . .?'

'I – can't remember,' he said with a shrug. 'But he took the file – why would he do that unless it's important?'

'You're wrong.'

'No, I'm not. The answer is in the files, Ruth. I'm sure of it.'

She stood up, pacing away from him, then spun on her heel to face him again. 'Listen to yourself: "Why did he take the files?", "I'm reconstructing the files." It isn't all about the bloody *files*, Greg.'

'It *is*. It must be. Otherwise why'd he take them?'

*He didn't take them; he didn't take them; he DIDN'T take them.* It took every ounce of self-control to keep her mouth shut, when all she really wanted to do was voice the screaming in her head.

She took a breath, let it go. 'Leave it, Greg. For your marriage, for the sake of your sanity, you *have* to stop.'

'So you're my self-appointed marriage guidance counsellor, now?'

Stung, she said, '*You* rang *me*, remember?'

He closed his eyes and dropped his chin to his chest. 'I know. I'm sorry – I just feel so . . . frustrated, stuck in here.'

Ruth stared at the healing scar on his scalp. 'You're off the case. If you can accept that, then maybe you and Emma have a chance – but you *have* to stop this.'

'I can't,' he said. 'Not with this bullet inside me as a constant reminder that somebody wants me dead.' He jabbed his chest at a spot just about where the wound dressing would be, and she winced.

'Who would hate you enough to want you dead, Greg?'

'I don't know,' he admitted.

'You just said the Thorn Killer took the files,' she countered. 'D'you think it was him?'

'I don't—'

He stopped, staring past her in such a peculiar way that she thought someone must have walked into the room.

She glanced over her shoulder. 'What?' she said.

'Your colours are all wrong.'

She looked down at her black jacket, trousers and shoes.

'Forget it,' he said. 'I get muddied – I mean, muddled. You seem . . . sad.'

'You have no idea.'

He seemed to shake himself out of it. 'So I was thinking – if I could get access to the official case files—'

'Jesus, Greg!' Ruth paced to the window and stared out onto a patch of sodden grass and a single, dripping tree. *He's never going to let this go.* She came to a decision, and finally turned back to him.

'How much do you remember about that evening?' she asked.

'Almost nothing.'

'Almost?' she repeated, convinced he was lying.

He shrugged.

*Okay. Fine. Let's see how you deal with the truth.* She said, 'I found you sitting upright in your armchair with a bullet hole in your chest.'

He frowned, dismissive. 'I already know that.'

She nodded. 'What you pretend *not* to know is that there was a gun on the floor beside you.'

'No,' he said. 'There was no gun.'

'You were shot,' she said. 'There must have been a gun.'

'Don't be a smart arse,' he growled. 'Whoever shot me took the gun with them.'

'*Somebody* certainly did.' She watched his face for signs of anxiety, slowly putting on her own unreadable mask.

He seemed perplexed, rather than anxious. His brow cleared as he made sense of what she said, and when the full realisation hit him, his eyes widened.

'Oh, no. Ruth. *You* took it?'

'The files, the box, the gun.'

'It really *was* you in the shadows?'

'Like I keep telling you.'

He wiped a hand over his face. 'What were you *thinking*?'

'What do *you* think?'

Her mask must have slipped for a second, because a horrible realisation seemed to slowly surface through the foggy workings of his brain and he looked at her in horror. 'You think I shot my*self*?'

The ground seemed to shift under her feet. 'You were depressed. The case was driving you crazy.'

'And you thought I'd put a gun to my chest and pulled the trigger? For God's sake, Ruth! Why would I do that?'

She stared at him. She couldn't have got it so wrong. 'You blamed yourself for Kara Grogan,' she said. 'Even before that, you'd been drinking yourself stupid for months.'

'I was drinking hard,' he said. 'But . . .'

'Really? Are you *still* trying to kid yourself you were in control?' She put her head back and gazed at the ceiling for a moment. 'D'you think I didn't notice the tremors in your hands when you reached for your first cup of coffee in the morning?'

He looked away. 'I was tired.'

'Sure,' she said. 'You were *tired* every day of the week – you positively *reeked* of exhaustion towards the end.'

He began to protest, but she spoke over him. 'D'you know the real reason I went to your flat that night?'

'I told you, I don't remember.'

'You rang me, depressed, rat-arsed drunk, not making any kind of sense.'

He blinked and Ruth thought he was making an effort to remember. 'I came over to tell you to find yourself an AA meeting and take some sick leave or I would report you.' She watched him closely: 'There was an empty whisky bottle by your chair. You stank of it – your whole apartment did – I wouldn't have lit a naked flame within a block of you that night.'

He stared at his hands in his lap, and began digging his nails into the gel ball. 'I don't remember,' he murmured.

'That's the point, Greg,' she said, more gently. 'It was a pattern. You knew it – we both did – we just didn't talk about it.'

He rubbed his hand hard over his chin. 'So,' he said. 'You took the file, you took the gun; you compromised the scene. Why, Ruth? Why would you do something so stupid?'

How could she even begin to explain the horror of seeing him slumped in the chair? The panic when she'd realised – *thought* she'd realised – what he'd done. And the guilt she'd grappled with ever since.

Tears sprang to her eyes. She hated showing weakness, and tried to cover it with anger. 'See this?' She picked up the honeymoon picture from the night stand. 'I found it in your kitchen with the crime scene photos, along with all those images of Kara. If I *hadn't* taken the gun, you know what people would say? That the Thorn Killer's mind games got to you. That you couldn't take the pressure.'

He shook his head, slowly.

'You know what they would have *seen*? A sad drunk. A coward who tried to take the easy way out, shot by his own hand – dying alone in his empty flat.'

He stared at her, his face grey. 'Oh, Ruth . . . I thought you knew me better than that.' He sucked in some air, and for a few moments the only sounds were his shuddering breath and the distant chatter of staff and patients on the other side of the door. 'I may be an idiot,' he said at last. 'I *know* I'm a drunk. But I'm no coward – how could you even think that?'

Looking into his face, she knew he was telling the truth. *Oh god, Ruth . . . What have you done?*

'What else was I supposed to think?' she said, and her voice sounded weak and defensive to her ears.

'What everyone else did,' he said. 'That I was about to break the case – that this was the Thorn Killer, covering his tracks.'

'Except we both know he would never do something like this, don't we?' she said softly.

He hesitated, but finally he nodded. After another short pause he said, 'Okay . . . What's the damage?'

Ruth returned to the chair opposite and took a few breaths before she began. He watched her intently, and she had that odd feeling that he was looking at a third person in the room again.

'The only fingermarks we have from your flat are mine because *I* wiped the place down.' She swore softly. 'I cleared up after the shooter.'

Her hands were shaking and she clasped them between her knees.

'Ruth,' he said.

She couldn't look at him at first, but he dipped his head, trying to catch her eye, and eventually she looked up.

'The shooter probably cleared up before you arrived.'

'Yeah,' she said. 'I'll keep telling myself that. Doesn't make what I did any better though, does it?' Her phone buzzed and she checked the screen.

'Urgent briefing,' the text read. 'Thirty-five mins.'

'I've got to go,' she said.

'But you will come back?'

'I will,' she said. 'Of course I will.'

## 24

Carver watched Ruth go with a looming sense of dread, and not only because he had no memory of calling her the night he was shot. It wasn't as if it was the first night he'd got blind drunk, but if he couldn't remember the simple fact of making a phone call to her, what else had he done that night?

The argument he'd got into filled his head in a blast of light and noise: screaming, breaking glass.

He stopped. Before the argument, he'd had sex – he remembered that, now. But he couldn't push past that moment, couldn't remember what happened after the fight, the screams, the sound of breaking glass.

*Had* it been a fight – had he got physical? Would he use force against a woman? *Did* he?

The day she threw him out, Emma had said, 'I don't even *know* you when you're drunk, Greg. You're a different person – it isn't safe to be around you when you're like that.'

He wiped sweat from his brow. His skin was cold and clammy, and his hands were shaking. DTs or terror? It was hard to tell the two apart. Harder still to pinpoint the exact moment when his heavy drinking became binge drinking, and slid into dependency.

A nip of whisky had become a part of his daily ritual after he and Emma split up. A takeaway meal, a splash of whisky to dull the edge while he read over the team's reports for the day, compared details of the killings, looking for a pattern that would help them crack the case. But a splash of whisky became a slug, and as the months crawled by and the Thorn Killer took another victim, and another, he'd lost the knack of sleeping. So he would pour a drink – *just one* – he told himself, stoppering the bottle firmly. Yet, a half hour later he would be on his feet again, ready for a top-up, and a little later, topping up again, drinking steadily for hours, poring over his files, waiting to pass out so that he could get some rest. But he would wake with a clang in the early hours, his mind grinding over the same questions, carrying the same sense of failure that he hadn't prevented another murder.

The night he'd got the message to go and look for Kara – a text from a burner phone giving him the location, signed off as TK – he was already a quarter of the way down a new bottle of Scotch. He had laid off the booze while he'd called in the CSIs and briefed Superintendent Wilshire, and spoken to his team. He drank coffee while he talked to Ruth Lake about prioritising tasks and briefing the press office, and later, speaking to the Home Office Pathologist, he was stone cold sober – juiced on nothing stronger than caffeine and adrenaline. But when the day's work was done, he had downed the rest of that Scotch.

No, it wasn't the first night, nor even the tenth that he had drunk himself unconscious, and it wasn't the first that he had blanked out the stupid, destructive, shameful things he'd done. The rows, the insults, the maudlin phone calls to Emma. How many times had he conducted morning briefings with a headache that felt like someone had taken a sharpened pencil and jammed it into his eye socket?

In the months since he and Emma had broken up, a pain seemed to centre around his heart. At first, he thought it was an ulcer, that stress, caffeine, bad food and hard drinking had burned a hole in his gut, but now he saw it as a physical expression of his self-disgust. He had thought he couldn't go any lower after Emma kicked him out, but now he could see that Kara's murder had sent him on a final downward spiral that landed him in a coma, with Ruth believing he had attempted suicide.

Ruth Lake had covered for him dozens of times in the last few months. Consoled him, and calmed him too, with her quiet, undemonstrative presence. What an arrogant prick he was, berating her for thinking he could attempt suicide. He had been killing himself for months – only more slowly, with booze.

## 25

Ruth Lake rang DCI Parsons on his landline and his mobile. He wasn't answering, so she tried John Hughes.

'Have you been called to this emergency briefing?' she asked.

'Yes,' he said.

'Any idea what it's about?'

'My guess would be the new body, just turned up at Beetham Tower.'

She said, 'Is it one of ours?' *It can't be. Not so soon after Kara.*

Someone spoke off-mic and the Crime Scene Manager said, 'I'll be right there.' Then, 'Sorry, Ruth. I've got to go.'

She hung up and ran to her car. It was headline news on the radio: a woman's body found at Beetham Tower. The block was only half the height of the iconic Manchester skyscraper, but still tall enough to dominate the Mersey waterfront. Less than a mile along Strand Street from the Merseyside Police headquarters, it was among the priciest property locations in the city.

The cluster of press and media had vanished from the station entrance when Ruth Lake returned to HQ. A police constable on guard was stamping his feet and blowing steam into the freezing air on the steps outside. Ruth could imagine the scramble when the news came in: reporters and photographers and social media snappers dashing for taxis to take them to the scene, hoping for another Thorn Killer victim.

She hurried up to the Major Incident Room. The place was empty, but further down the corridor she could hear a buzz of chatter from the larger seminar room. The place was packed. DCI Parsons stood at the front, notes on a clipboard, set square against one of the corners of the desk; several more stacks of papers laid out next to it; whiteboard markers arrayed in a row between two of the stacks.

Ruth sidled up to John Hughes. 'The Beetham Tower murder,' she said softly, keeping her gaze on Parsons and her face free of any emotion. 'Does it look like one of ours?'

'Adela Faraday,' Hughes said. 'A stockbroker. She was found on the terrace of her penthouse apartment.'

'Ah,' Ruth said, feeling some of her jittery nervous tension dissipate: the Thorn Killer's victims had all been found in public places. 'Cause of death?'

DCI Parsons rapped on the table to call them to order so she didn't get to hear the answer. He was wearing a charcoal-grey suit with a white shirt and dark blue tie today. He cleared his throat and smoothed his tie, and fixed them with his serious gaze.

'An hour ago, a woman's body was found in her apartment at Beetham Tower,' he said. 'Fifteen minutes later, these head-lines were appearing online.' He picked up a remote-control unit for the data projector and clicked on a link. One tabloid newspaper's website had run an image of Beetham Tower with the headline, 'Slain Businesswoman Thorn Killer Victim?' A second link led to the more lurid headline: 'Was Shooting Victim Tattooed?'

'As you can see, the media are not inclined to wait for the true facts of the case to emerge. However, I sincerely hope that nobody in this investigation is fuelling their flights of fancy. Because discussing the case with anyone outside of the investigation would be completely unacceptable.' He clicked again, calling up the next headline, this time from the *Daily Mail*: 'Adela Faraday Death "A Mystery", Police Source Says'.

They had her name just an hour after she was found – and from 'a police source', too. No wonder Parsons looked so grim.

'Let me be clear,' he said, scanning their faces. '*Anyone* found leaking information to the press *will* face disciplinary measures.'

Nobody moved, but Ruth felt the heightened tension in the room, most resenting the implication that anyone on their team might be responsible, a few perhaps wondering if a careless comment of their own had been quoted as the source.

'Someone close the door.' When the order had been carried out, Parsons shut down the screen and swept his gaze over the team. 'What I am about to say is for your ears only,' he said. 'It is most unlikely that Ms Faraday was in any way linked to this investigation. She does not fit the killer's preferred "type". In fact there are no significant points of similarity between this lady and the confirmed victims. She was found at home – it looks like she'd been there a week or more – and there are *no* tattoos.'

A murmur went around the room: the lack of tattoos had settled any doubts they might have had on that subject.

Parsons waited for the noise to subside before going on: 'I would expect all of you to discourage conjecture of any kind.' He looked around the room. 'So . . . if you are approached, you will respond: "Talk to the Press Office, they will provide regular updates." Do *not* tell them this isn't your case – because they will interpret your words to suit the headline of the day. Your answer to *any* question should be: "Talk to the Press

Office, they will provide regular updates." I don't care if they ask you for *the time of day* – that will be your standard answer. Is that clear?'

A few nods, a muttered, 'Yes, Boss,' from others.

He paused, breathing hard through his nostrils for a few seconds before shuffling his papers and starting again in a more measured tone: 'All right. Coming back to Kara Grogan: we have house-to-house, motorist canvassing, and the re-interviewing of Kara's housemates and tutors. Who wants to go first?'

Ruth listened with half an ear to team reports all saying the same thing: the killer had not been seen leaving Kara's body in the park. Parsons didn't seem to think it necessary to comment on the findings, and heads were drooping.

Ruth spoke up: 'You know the drill, folks – it's not easy with a victim who's gone missing a while before it's reported. We all need to stay alert, keep asking questions – and listen carefully to the answers.'

Parsons looked peeved that she'd taken it upon herself to give the pep talk he should have given himself. 'You've been off asking questions of your own, over the last few days, DS Lake,' he said. His tone implied that she'd been playing truant. 'Anything you'd care to share on that?'

'Sir.' Ruth Lake had already moved to a more central spot, so she had a good view of the two detectives who had conducted the original interviews with Kara's peers. Neither looked at her, but she felt their ill-will.

'Kara cut herself off from her peers in the weeks before she disappeared,' Ruth said. 'All that stuff about her being "reserved" was a lot of guff. She had shared some very personal fears with her project group, who were also her housemates. She had a phobia about freezing on stage, forgetting her lines. They set up a nasty prank that made her look like she had done just that in front of a live audience.' She paused and the two aggrieved detectives looked uncomfortable.

'That destroyed her confidence for a bit. But she was a plucky lass, and showed more promise than most, according to her tutors. So she changed study groups, insulated herself from the instigators, became more secretive. She was preparing for an audition for a prestigious role.' She nodded to John Hughes. 'We have the computer techs to thank for that information.'

'And that is significant because . . .' Parsons said.

'Kara's housemates said she went off in the evenings – they don't know where – but the techs identified websites she had been accessing a lot – psychics and the like . . .'

'Research for her audition,' Parsons said, lightly fingering the report she'd placed on his desk earlier in the day. He still seemed unsure how this might be relevant, but didn't want to appear foolish.

'I think she might have gone to some of the readings,' Ruth said.

Parsons nodded, and thanked her, then checked something on his order of business, and she realised that he was about to move to the next topic.

'I'd like to talk to the psychics who appeared in Liverpool around the time of her abduction,' Ruth added, and he frowned, still not getting it.

'It might help to fill in the gaps in her timeline,' she said, as though she was continuing her theme – it wouldn't help to put Parsons on the defensive. 'Provide more insight into her state of mind in the days before she disappeared.'

One of the detectives who had first interviewed the house-mates piped up: 'Think they'll contact her in the spirit world, Sarge?'

'If you had done your job first time round, we might've had this information at the start,' Parsons snapped, cutting off the laughter before it really got started. A hush descended over the meeting as a good number of the team upgraded Parsons from pen-pusher to someone who shouldn't be underestimated.

Ruth went on as if nothing had been said: 'I've read Kara's research; it seems these psychics are expert cold readers. Her housemates don't have a clue what Kara was up to – but if she contacted some of the psychics on her list—'

'You're not suggesting we *consult* these . . . people?' Parsons looked alarmed.

'No, sir – I want to interview them. Kara was vulnerable. Maybe that nudged her into making bad choices. Maybe one of the psychics noticed her with someone, or maybe she told them something during the performance that might help us . . .' She lifted one shoulder as if to say, 'Worth a try?'

Parsons stared at his clipboard for a few seconds. 'All right,' he said. 'But I don't want to wake up tomorrow to the head-line: "Thorn Killer Cop Consults Psychics". Understood?'

She nodded.

'I need to hear it, Sergeant Lake.'

'Understood,' Ruth said.

## 26

Towards evening Ruth Lake was trawling 'what's on' sites for Liverpool to make sure she hadn't missed any of the psychics that Kara had been interested in.

The online newsfeeds were full of Adela Faraday's murder, most of them with thumbnail images of crime-scene tape and police at the exclusive apartments where she'd lived. One tabloid said that Merseyside Police 'were not treating Ms Faraday's death as linked to the "Thorn Killer" murders'. They even quoted 'a police source' who said that there was no evidence of the serial killer's 'trademark tattoos' on Adela's body. Parsons would not be happy. Curiosity piqued, Ruth clicked through a few links, eventually landing on the *Liverpool Echo* website. They had got hold of a photo of the murdered woman at what looked like a business event. She looked familiar.

Ruth clicked the image to enlarge it.

Adela Faraday was tall, slim and blonde, expensively clothed in a black dress, and wearing what looked like a diamond bracelet on her wrist. She wore red lipstick and carried what the paper described as a Birken crocodile handbag. Apparently, a Birken bag cost around six thousand pounds new. Adela was looking over her shoulder, one eyebrow raised, and looked on the point of laughter.

*I know that face.*

Ruth flashed to the CCTV footage of Carver walking into the Old Bank Hotel the evening he was shot.

\*　　　\*　　　\*

An hour later she was zipping through the CCTV recordings in DCI Jansen's Major Incident Room. It had taken all that time to catch the room empty, and with a computer still logged into the system. That was her only way in, since her own ID would not have given her access to the files she was interested in: the investigation into Greg Carver's shooting was, at least officially, none of her business. She was seated at DC Tom Ivey's desk – had watched him nip out thirty seconds earlier. If she was caught, Ivey would be in almost as much trouble for leaving his computer vulnerable as she would be for accessing the investigation files without permission. But she had to find out if she was right, and if she was quick and careful nobody need ever know that anything was amiss.

On high alert for signs of DC Ivey's return, she glanced towards the door, thinking she heard footsteps in the corridor, and almost missed Greg Carver on the screen, walking up a snowy street towards The Old Bank Hotel. She let the recording run on for five minutes then rewound, leaning close to the screen, her eyes darting right and left in her eagerness to take it all in.

There was Greg, stepping backwards out of the hotel foyer, vanishing from sight as he went out of range of the camera. She skipped back to ten minutes before he had arrived, took a breath, then set the controls to fast-forward.

Five minutes in, she found what she was looking for: a woman hurrying along the street, her collar turned up, one hand holding her coat lapels closed at the neck.

'Turn around,' Ruth muttered. 'Let's see you.'

As if in response, the woman glanced over her shoulder, and Ruth's heart stopped. She rewound again, played it forward

174

and hit the pause button as the woman looked towards the CCTV camera. Ruth exhaled in a whoosh of breath. 'Greg . . .' she murmured. 'Oh, God, Greg – tell me it isn't true.'

But she rarely got a face wrong. She opened her own laptop, setting it next to DC Ivey's computer, and clicked through to the *Liverpool Echo* photograph of the murdered woman.

The woman was Adela Faraday. She had arrived at the Old Bank Hotel only minutes before Greg Carver.

Ruth printed a still image of Adela from the CCTV recording as well as the image of her from the *Liverpool Echo*. Heart hammering, she jammed a memory stick into one of the USB ports on Ivey's computer and performed an illegal download before leaving the office. DC Ivey was heading up the corridor in the opposite direction.

She said, 'Hi, Tom,' and carried on walking, barely glancing at him.

'Did you want something, Sarge?' he asked.

Ruth slowed her pace and stopped, turning to greet the younger detective. 'Just wondered how things were going with the investigation. Looks like they've gone home for the night – all except you.' She'd found that flattery could be a good deflecting tactic.

'D'you still want to know?' he asked, 'I could tell you over coffee.' He made it sound tentative, a question, not wanting to seem pushy.

She returned his gaze with a cool, steady look, and he blushed.

'I – I mean just as a – I didn't mean—' He was glowing from the neck up by now. 'Um, sorry, Sarge . . .'

'Tom, it's fine,' she said, easing up now that he wasn't focusing on the oddness of her visit. 'Normally, I'd be glad to, but it's late, and I should pop over to the hospital on my way home, see how Greg is.'

It wasn't until she was on the concrete fire escape stairwell that she thrust her clenched fist into her pocket and let the thumb drive slip from her sweat-slicked hand.

Accessing DC Ivey's computer could get her a wrist slap, but performing that download could get her arrested. When her heart had stopped trying to batter its way out of her ribcage, she returned to her office, grabbed her shoulder bag and jammed her laptop into it.

Then she headed straight to the hospital.

An uneaten plate of food lay on the trolley next to his bed, and Carver was standing at the window, staring into the dark. He turned slowly as she came into the room, grazing the window ledge with the tips of his fingers, and she realised he must be having problems with his balance.

She said, 'You okay?'

He smiled. 'Better for seeing you.'

'Got a moment to look at something?'

He gestured with his free hand to the empty room. 'I'm not exactly snowed under.'

She dipped into her bag for her laptop and cleared a space for it on his bed trolley, then pulled the thumb drive out of her coat pocket.

Carver said, 'What is it?'

'CCTV.'

'From the case?'

She tilted her head, letting him think what he wanted to think as she set up the video, then let it run, watching his reaction. He froze when he saw the woman hurrying towards the hotel.

'You know her?' she said.

He said nothing, and his silence made her doubt him all over again.

She jumped forward to the moment he walked down the street.

'Well, you must recognise *this* character.'

A fractional hesitation, then he said quietly, 'You know that's me.'

She paused the video and placed two printouts in front of him: Adela Faraday in the *Liverpool Echo*, and Adela Faraday from the CCTV recording at the Old Bank.

'This woman was found murdered today in her apartment on the waterfront. And there she is, walking into a hotel, minutes before you, on the night you were shot. Does that strike you as . . . odd?'

'Coincidental, maybe.'

'You don't know her?'

'I can't be sure.'

'Is that you covering your backside in case I find proof that you did?'

He didn't answer.

'She'd been dead a while, Greg. Maybe even as long as you've been in hospital.'

She saw something, a slight drawing together of his brows.

'Was this your doing? Did *you* do this to her, Greg?'

He looked wounded by the question, but still he didn't speak.

'I've been beating myself up, thinking I should never have doubted you. But now I'm thinking maybe I was right after all – about the lies, about the booze you tried to drown yourself in that night. About the gun I found by your chair.'

He began to shake his head.

'Then explain it to me. Tell me why I should—' She tried to take a breath, but her chest constricted and she felt a sharp pain below her ribcage. She slammed her laptop closed and scooped up the two images.

'Ruth,' he said.

She held up a hand to stop him. 'You need—' Her lungs failed her and she saw dark blurring at the edges of her vision. She bent double, hands on her knees and Carver took a step towards her. This seemed to release the locked muscles of her diaphragm and she waved him away, whooping in air.

'You need to start being honest with me,' she said at last.

Alone in his hospital room, Carver sat in his armchair and flicked the on-switch of the TV remote. BBC News 24 was playing a loop of the main stories of the day; he had been watching it moments before Ruth arrived. The instant he had seen her picture on the TV screen he'd known it was Adela Faraday. She had gone under a different name, but it was her all right. He turned the TV off but the events of that night continued to play out as if projected onto the screen.

He remembered full well following her into the hotel – hadn't he watched her from the lobby, lurking in the background as she signed in, brushing past her, stepping into the lift ahead of her so that he could stand behind her, stroking the wool of her coat lightly with his fingertips, drinking in her scent? She drew away, gathering her coat skirt, moving closer to the door.

She got out on the second floor and he rode the elevator to the third, returning by the fire escape, seeing her fumble the swipe card in her hurry to get into the room. He'd held back just long enough for her to push the door wide. The lights flicked on and she let the door swing to. He ran, thinking he'd left it too late, heart tripping, ears straining to hear the double click as the lock engaged. But he made it, catching it just in time. She turned, her coat already shucked off her shoulders; her eyes widened, and the lust he'd felt at that moment was animal, violent.

They had sex. He remembered an argument, and that Adela was frightened. He couldn't remember her leaving, and that frightened him, didn't remember phoning Ruth afterwards – didn't even remember how he'd got home – but he did remember vividly a gun flash, a sharp, sulphurous reek of smoke. Then everything faded to shadows.

'How are you, Greg?'

A man's voice. Carver turned from the blank TV screen. The man's face looked grey and washed out under the hospital lights. Purples and yellows and greys swirled around him, and then dispersed.

Abruptly the man's eye magnified, turning dark brown, the edges blood-red. It spun like a circular saw, and the features seemed to break into sections. His right jaw slid down and his cheekbones splintered, shattering into a thousand silvery shards.

Carver braced himself for the grating crash of glass, for the splash of blood.

'Greg, can you hear me?'

For an instant the man's voice distorted, then the image – memory? hallucination? – faded and Carver recognised his neurologist.

The doctor reached for the tumbler on the night table and crouched next to Carver's chair. 'Here,' he said, 'take a sip.'

Carver wanted to dash the glass from his hand, thinking *poison*. But he had no strength, couldn't even raise his hands, and the doctor was gently insistent. He took a sip, and it was only water.

'Hallucination?' the doctor said. 'A flashback?'

Carver shook his head, unsure of what he'd seen, unable to speak, his tongue thick in his mouth.

'Are you in pain?'

'No.' He took another sip of water.

'So, no headache?'

'Hallucination, I think – like a bad trip.'

'I'm sorry it's taken a while to get you that referral to a neuropsychologist.'

'But you said the scan was normal.' The doctor didn't answer at first and Carver thought he'd made a mistake. 'Didn't you?'

'Yes. Yes, I did,' he said. 'The EEGs are normal – you are not suffering epileptic seizures. The MRIs and CT scans show good recovery from the concussion. But even MRIs can't always identify subtle nerve damage. If it were visual disturbance alone – lights and flashes, say – I would suggest migraine as the cause.'

'I don't have headaches after the auras. In fact, I haven't had many headaches at all since my first week here.'

'It's fairly common to have migraine auras without headache,' the doctor said. 'Think of them as an electrical disturbance, passing like a wave over the visual part of the brain – it's common after head trauma. But most people see lights and patterns – you are seeing people and things that aren't there, which is . . . unusual.'

The neurologist was unshakably calm, as always, and the halo of colours around him were pastel-pale, but for a moment they intensified and Carver saw clashing colours of puce and lemon shimmer at the edges of the doctor's face.

'It's bad, isn't it?' Carver said.

'You've made a good recovery,' the doctor reassured him. 'But you have been subjected to psychological as well as physical trauma. So, we need to consider the possibility that this is a psychosomatic response.'

Carver felt a spike of fear. 'You're talking about PTSD, aren't you?'

'I'm saying it could be related to stress – you say these auras are related to emotion, after all. But we're just exploring possibilities.'

*Oh, God . . .*

'Look,' the doctor said. 'I'll make a few calls, see if I can hurry things along with the referral.'

Carver nodded. 'Thanks,' he managed. He'd known a few people on the job who had suffered Post Traumatic Stress. None of them returned to work after the diagnosis.

## 27

Ruth sat in the hospital car park for ten minutes before even starting the car. She hadn't lost control like that in years. Why now? *Because you compromised a crime scene, stole evidence, put your career at risk for Carver*, she rationalised. And in repayment, he had lied and lied and lied. But it wasn't betrayal that had knocked the air out of her lungs; it wasn't his lies. She had read enough on trauma to know the true answer: finding Carver – a man she cared about deeply – apparently having attempted suicide, had triggered other traumatic memories. A therapist had once told her, 'You can't ignore the effects of trauma. They're like the living dead. You can lock them down tight and bury them deep, but someday they will claw their way out and come after you.'

It was eight-thirty p.m., and the Carver Major Incident Room was empty when she got back to the office. Only Tom Ivey remained at his desk, peering at his computer screen as though staring through a smeared window, his expression intent. He looked up as she came in.

'What did you get up to on my terminal?'

She walked around to his side of the desk. As she'd expected, he was working through the CCTV recording; the digital clock said he had missed the crucial moment.

'You haven't found it, yet?'

'I will,' he said, his mouth set in a grim line.

She understood. A cop using another cop's log-in was never up to anything good. More likely they were doing something illegal. Added to which, DC Ivey was a relative newbie, and as a detective sergeant, her word would carry far more weight than a lowly constable if the nefarious activity ever came to light.

'You need to rewind eight minutes,' she said.

He glared at her and Ruth said: 'You've every right to be pissed off. But I'm not playing games – you need to rewind.'

He caught it that time. 'That's . . .'

'Adela Faraday,' Ruth said.

He swivelled to face her so fast that she had to take a step back to avoid a collision with the top of his head. 'You recognised her and didn't *say* anything?' He stared at her, and she could see he was trying to work out just how deep she was mired in Carver's shit, and who he should call first. 'The boss showed you this *days* ago.'

'I know,' she said, hoping the detective constable's instinct for self-preservation would make him hold off making that call – after all, he was in trouble himself for his lapse in security protocols. It made sense to hear her out, if only to work out his best plan of attack. 'But I didn't recognise her then.'

'So – what – it suddenly came back to you in a flash of inspiration?'

'No,' Ruth said, noting the sarcasm, thinking, *Well good for you, newbie*. DC Ivey might be diffident, but he was no pushover. 'I've never met her. But Adela Faraday's picture is all over the Web.' She raised her chin, indicating the image on his computer screen. 'I realised she looked familiar, and—'

'It suddenly kind of . . . clicked?' He gave a short laugh. 'D'you really expect me to believe that?'

'I lied to you about why I was in your office,' she said quietly. 'I used your terminal without authorisation. So, no, Tom – I don't expect you to believe me.' She paused. 'But it *is* true.'

'She was on the CCTV for what – five seconds? So excuse me, Sarge, if I tell you that's, just—'

'A load of bollocks?' she finished for him. 'I know it seems that way. But it's a thing with me,' she went on. 'You know how some people say they never forget a face? With me, it's literally true.'

He shook his head, and reached for his phone.

'Don't,' she said. 'Look – have you heard of something called "face blindness"? It can be caused by brain damage. People can't recognise faces, even family, children, their spouse—'

He nodded reluctantly. 'My aunty had it, after she had a stroke.'

'Well, it's got an opposite twin – a few people at the other end of the scale – "super-recognisers". We can recognise a face we've seen just once, sometimes even years before.'

He didn't look completely convinced, but for now he'd left his phone where it was.

'There's a Harvard study on it,' she said. 'The Met's even got a special unit – Google it.'

He picked up his mobile phone, still doubtful.

'Go ahead,' she said. 'I'll wait.'

After a minute or two scrolling through the text, he glanced up at her, confusion and wonder on his face. 'You're not lying.'

'No, I'm not.'

'Says here there's a test you can do,' he said.

'I aced it.'

'So, why aren't you doing this full time?'

'Because I'd like to stay sane.' In fact, when she'd transferred to CID she'd had to resist pressure from above to keep her at a computer screen. 'Anyway, investigation is a *lot* more fun.'

He considered her answer, and after a moment he nodded.

'So, did Carver admit to knowing Adela? That *is* why you were in such a rush to get to the hospital, isn't it?'

'Yeah.' She admired his ability to assimilate and accept information that most men found freakish.

'And?'

Ruth dipped her head. 'He says he can't remember.'

Ivey scoffed.

'I know,' she said. 'Look, maybe Carver is lying. Or maybe it's just a bizarre coincidence.'

'A coincidence that they went to the same hotel on the night Carver was shot? Possibly the night that Adela was murdered?'

'Wow, sounds bad when you put it like that.'

'It's not funny.'

'No,' she said, and meant it. 'No, it's not. Which is why I'm going to shake the tree, see what falls out. Do you want to come along?'

He gripped the armrests as though he half expected her to haul him to his feet. 'I should call my boss right now,' he said.

'Sure. If that's what you think you should do.' She made eye contact, fairly certain that he wouldn't be able to pass up an opportunity to shine. But he took out his phone and started scrolling through his contacts.

'Of course, if there *is* anything to this, you would have to take the credit,' she added.

He looked up from his smartphone, amused outrage on his face. 'Well, that's generous.'

'I'm all about the giving.'

'Don't give me that,' he said. 'This is you covering your back.'

She smiled. 'You got me.'

She watched, breathing slowly and trying not to fidget, while for a good thirty seconds he stared at the phone in his hand as though he was reading Tarot cards. Then abruptly he pocketed it.

'What did you have in mind?' he said.

The receptionist at the Old Bank was male, dark-haired, handsome. Standing behind a mahogany counter that might once have formed part of the bank's furniture, he looked almost as polished and gleaming as the woodwork.

He recognised Adela from the photo Ruth handed him, and he knew that she was the businesswoman found murdered in her apartment. But he hadn't known her by that name.

'She registered as Anna Flynn.'

'You know that without having to look it up?' Ruth said.

'She always ordered good champagne – and she tipped well.'

'*Always*?' Ruth repeated. 'So this was a regular thing?'

'Two or three times a month for the past six months. One night only.'

Ruth exchanged a look with Tom Ivey: she could think of a few reasons why a woman living a mile up the road might book one night in a hotel, at least two of which involved sex.

'Did she share this "good champagne"?' Ruth asked.

'I never *saw* her with anyone,' the receptionist said. 'But she always requested two champagne flutes and sometimes she ordered a room service meal for two.'

'She never came down to the dining room?'

'I think she was too busy having fun.' The receptionist looked past her to DC Ivey, though not for the usual reasons. Men often assumed in a male-female detective combo that the man held seniority, but this guy was ignoring her because he liked the look of Tom Ivey more.

'Do you have CCTV at reception?'

He grimaced at the suggestion.

'In the lifts?' she said, already knowing the answer.

He inclined his head in gentle reproof. 'The Old Bank prides itself on its exclusivity and its discretion,' he said, still eyeing Tom. Something passed between them and the young detective flushed.

*Oh*, she thought, *how did I miss that?* The brushed brass nameplate on the receptionist's lapel read 'Lucien Lloyd, Reception Manager'.

'All right, Lucien,' she said, rapping the counter to drag his attention away from DC Ivey. 'When did Ms Faraday last check in?'

His fingers rustled over the keys of his computer terminal positioned under an overhang of the counter, safe from prying eyes. Sure enough, Adela Faraday, aka Anna Flynn, had booked a room at the hotel eight days ago, on the night Carver was shot.

'Did anything unusual happen that night?' she asked.

'This is a celebrity-favoured hotel,' he said. 'Define "unusual".'

She stared at him, showing no signs of the annoyance she felt, knowing that she could outwait him.

After a few moments, he gave an irritated shrug. 'Well, your partner isn't much fun, is she?' he said, with an accusing glance at Tom.

'She's my boss,' Tom said, putting just enough edge into his voice. 'And you need to answer the question.'

The receptionist suppressed a sigh. 'There was a disturbance – a guest in the adjoining room complained, I had to call security.'

'What was the nature of the disturbance?' Ruth asked.

'Something and nothing.' He rolled his eyes. 'A bit of shouting. A mirror was broken.'

She nodded, thinking *forensics, trace evidence*. 'Well, you must keep a record of repairs and maintenance.'

'We do.'

'I'd like a printout. And we'll need access to that room.'

'I'm afraid that's out of the question,' the receptionist said. 'A guest has just checked in.'

A man approached the counter from her left, and Ruth turned to him and flashed her warrant card. 'Police business, sir, if you wouldn't mind waiting over there.' She pointed to a cluster of chairs about fifteen feet from the desk and the guest looked put out, but also a little concerned. It had the desired effect on the receptionist; he was shaken.

She kept her warrant card in her hand, tapping and rotating it between her fingers. With the young detective hovering nervously in the background, she said, 'I'm going to offer you a choice, Lucien. On the one hand, you could have a small, quiet team of CSIs who will tiptoe in through the service entrance and conduct their search without most of your guests even noticing they're here. On the other hand, I could trudge back to HQ, organise a warrant, and a whole *squad* of detectives and CSIs will descend with enough crime-scene tape to tie a big yellow bow around the entire hotel.'

She stared past him to a spot just above his head as if thinking it through. 'Of course, they'll want to talk to staff, maybe even canvas guests. Oh, and the press have been camped out on our doorstep for almost two weeks. If they get wind that Adela Faraday was up to who knows *what* at your bijou little gem two or three times a month . . .'

188

She raised her shoulders and let them drop, leaving him to develop that scenario in his own head.

On the surface, the receptionist remained calm, but behind the eyes she saw a man calculating the risks like it was a long and complex mathematical problem.

In fact, if the CSIs found any evidence pointing back to Carver's shooting it would get messy with or without the hotel's cooperation, but the quicker they got to work on that room the better.

Apparently, the problem was above the Reception Manager's pay grade; he called the Front of House Manager, who had the guest currently occupying Adela Faraday's room quietly upgraded to a suite. Ruth and Ivey headed upstairs, leaving a relieved reception manager to soothe the guest they had kept waiting.

Ten minutes later, Ruth stood with DC Ivey at the entrance of the lift on the second floor, twenty-five paces from the room where Adela Faraday had stayed, but with a clear view of it. She would leave him to finish organising what followed. The hotel room represented a possible crossover between Carver's shooting and Adela Faraday's murder, so Ruth had resisted the impulse to have a nosey: she didn't want to be accused of compromising the scene.

*Ironic*, she thought, *given what you did at Carver's flat*.

Keeping an eye on the door to 214 she said, 'Any questions?'

'No, I think I can handle it.' Even so, Ivey fiddled nervously with his smartphone.

'You know what they say about the only stupid question being the one you don't ask? It's true.'

'I'm not sure what we can gain from this,' he said. 'We know Carver was here, but it doesn't prove anything.'

'You're right,' she said. 'But the more information we have, the more we can make connections, fill in the timeline.'

He nodded, but still seemed unsure.

'Look,' she said. 'We know that Carver was in the hotel at the same time as Adela Faraday. But we *don't* know that he was in her room – and if he *was*, we don't know if he was involved in the disturbance. We don't even know, yet, if Adela left the hotel safely.'

The constable's eyes widened. 'Are you saying that DCI Carver—'

'I'm saying we need to find out what went on in that room.'

'Yeah. But without CCTV . . .'

Ivey was new, and she liked him, so she indulged him, falling into CSI training mode. 'The CSIs will look for trace evidence, such as . . .'

'DNA?' He turned the corners of his mouth down. 'That room's been cleaned loads of times since she was there.'

'Right. But a ten-minute clean and a change of bedding doesn't wipe away every trace,' she said. 'The CSIs will also look for traces of the broken mirror glass in the room.'

'I don't see how that helps.'

'That's because you're not thinking like a detective. Remember, every contact leaves a trace, and DCI Carver's clothing would have been taken as forensic evidence.'

'Oh,' he said. 'They'll look for the same glass on his clothing?'

'Now you're getting it,' she said. 'If they find a match, that would put him in the room, though it wouldn't necessarily mean he was involved in the fight – he might have gone into the room after the event, for instance. So they'll need to look for Adela's hair on his clothes – which would put him in close contact with her.'

He frowned at the screen of his phone, looking puzzled.

'Question?' she said, her reserves of patience running low.

'Just . . .' He shrugged. 'I thought you were on Carver's side.'

Ruth Lake wasn't easily shocked, but that rocked her on her feet. 'A woman has been murdered, DC Ivey. This isn't like covering for your mate who's pulled a sickie to go and watch the match.'

'Sorry, Sarge.'

'You follow the evidence where it leads, not where you would *like* it to take you.'

He nodded, chastened.

She held his gaze a moment longer, knowing he would not be able to read in her eyes just how sick she felt at the thought that Carver might be guilty.

'Okay,' she said. 'I'm heading downstairs, but I'll stick around till the SIO arrives. Make your calls. Do not let *anyone* in or out till the crime scene guys get here. And you log anyone who goes through that door. Clear?'

'Clear,' he said.

She pressed the call button for the lift.

As it reached the floor below them, Tom Ivey shuffled his feet and cleared his throat.

'Um, that – thing,' he said, his voice low, 'with the reception manager.'

'What?' she said. 'My little white lie about bringing in a squad? Don't worry about it.'

'No . . .' He glanced over his shoulder. 'The other thing.'

'The *look*, you mean? Relax, Tom, he was just flirting.'

The detective constable looked like a man who was terrified to speak in case he said the wrong thing.

'You're not "out"?' Ruth said.

'I'm out – just not at work.'

'Okay.'

'So . . .'

There was a question in his tone, and that *did* offend her.

'Oh,' she said, and 'You're asking if *I* intend to out you?'

'No,' he said, immediately flustered. 'I mean – I just wouldn't want it to become common knowledge.'

'Your personal life is your own business.' The doors slid open and she stepped inside the lift. 'Ask around – I'm not known for idle chit-chat.'

'I know,' he said, with a little smile that told her there was *plenty* of idle chit-chat about her. It didn't bother her – and even if it did, she would never have let it show.

She hit the button. 'Make those calls,' she said.

On the ground floor, Ruth made her way through the foyer and found the fire escape stairs that opened onto the courtyard at the back of the building. The management had agreed to disable the door alarm to allow the crime scene guys unobtrusive access. She made a quick recce of the stairs to check there were no obstacles to get around, and poked her head out at the second floor to establish which way they would have to turn to get to Adela Faraday's room. Ivey was standing outside room 214. He had his back to her, but she could read tension in every muscle of his spine.

As she ghosted down the fire escape on her way back downstairs, a member of the housekeeping team came through the door on the first floor. She looked startled, and Ruth said, 'It's okay, I'm just avoiding someone.'

The girl smiled. 'I know this feeling.'

She should have left it at that, but couldn't help herself. 'I'm police,' she said, adding at the girl's look of alarm, 'We're just checking out one of the rooms.'

'Oh,' the girl said. 'Is problem?'

Her English was heavily accented, eastern European.

'Not for you,' Ruth said, and the chambermaid relaxed a little.

'This woman . . .' Ruth took the photo of Adela out and handed it to the girl. 'Do you recognise her?'

She nodded, 'Anna.'

Ruth took out her mobile phone and scrolled through to an image of Carver.

'Yes,' the maid said. 'Him – with her.' She held up the picture of Adela.

'They were here together?' Another nod. 'When?'

The girl shrugged. 'Five, six times?'

Ruth took a couple of slow breaths before asking. 'Which room?'

'Two-one-four. Always same.' The room number where the CSIs would soon be making themselves busy. 'Last time. Big argument.'

'You saw them?'

The girl held up the photograph. 'She is very angry.' She mimed a throwing action.

'She threw something at him?'

'Shoe. Coat. Shirt. His things.' The girl mimed again.

'She threw them on the floor?'

'Outside room.'

Ruth began to feel a little better. He left. They had argued, but Greg left.

'Then he go . . .'

'He left?' Ruth said, wanting to be absolutely certain.

The girl frowned. 'No, he *went* – back in room.'

Ruth's ears boomed. The girl smiled nervously and she realised she must have been staring. She hesitated, not sure if she
wanted to know the answer to her next question. Still, it had to
be asked: 'What happened then?'

'Security come.' The girl shrugged. 'I go.'

When the first of the CSIs arrived, Ruth should have left them
to it. Her job was done. DC Ivey would explain how he'd seen
Adela on the CCTV recording and decided to ask a few questions at the hotel. The last thing Ruth needed was DCI Jansen
asking awkward questions about why she was hanging around.
But standing at the bottom of the fire escape, her hands in her
pockets and the cold seeping into her bones, she felt she had to
do more. She needed straight answers from Carver, and she
wasn't going to get them unless she knew enough to work the
detective's bluff: a suspect would generally meet you halfway if
you had a few key facts and spoke with confidence.

*A suspect? Is that what Greg is now?*

He certainly wasn't blameless, and remembered a hell of a
lot more than he was saying. She was sure he knew Adela, but
Carver knew every trick in the interrogation book, so it
wouldn't be easy, getting him to admit what he remembered
– and she would need a lot more than she had right now to
work the bluff.

CSM John Hughes had attended Carver's flat after the
shooting, so he would probably stay away, manage the CSIs at
this new scene from his office. Which meant that he wouldn't be
around for her to sidle alongside and wheedle information out of.

A CSI, suited but not yet booted, approached from the car
park. He was fairly new, and she'd never supervised him as a

Crime Scene Manager herself, but he recognised her, and nodded in thanks as she held the fire escape door for him while he hefted his crime scene bag and a UV 'darklight' into the stairwell.

'Looks like I'm doorwoman for the night,' she said, with a self-mocking smile.

'We can't have you mucking up the scene, Sarge,' he said, with a grin that said he knew he was being cheeky.

'How's the Faraday scene-processing going?' she asked. A different team would be working on Adela Faraday's apartment, but a scene like that, word got around.

'Looks like the killer dragged her out onto the terrace after he did her in,' the CSI said. 'So it's not a smelly one.'

The body wasn't in an advanced state of decomposition – that could be good news for Greg Carver.

'She'd been buried in the snow,' he went on. 'But when that started to melt, the seagulls got at her. Eyes were gone.' He shuddered. 'God, I hate it when the eyes are gone.'

Ruth felt a pulse throbbing in her neck: no decomp, and little predation by gulls. Adela can't have been out there for long before the snowfall – and they'd had no fresh snow since the night she'd found Carver. Adela Faraday was probably murdered the same night.

She listened to the CSI labouring up the stairwell with his heavy kit, and suddenly she couldn't stand to be near the place any longer. She walked back to her car, parked in a bay on the main road, her limbs jerky, teeth chattering, sick with dread.

## 28

It was late by the time DS Lake walked through the doors into the hospital, and the ward doors were locked. She pressed the buzzer, but nobody came. She pressed again. The third time, the intercom clicked, and a voice that sounded fifty miles away asked her to explain her business. The nurse listened to Ruth's request in silent disapproval.

Mr Carver was resting, she said. She should come back in the morning.

'He'll see me,' she said.

'Not tonight,' the disembodied voice said.

'I know he's there,' Ruth said. 'Tell him he'll see me, or he'll see Detective Chief Inspector Jansen. His choice.'

Seconds later, Greg Carver made his way unsteadily into the common area and looked at her through the reinforced glass of the ward doors. He said something; it was muffled by the thickness of the doors, but it sounded like, 'Orange.'

'I'll see her,' he said.

A nurse appeared from a room off to the left. 'Patients are trying to rest,' the nurse said. 'We can't allow this disruption.'

'It's all right,' Carver said. 'We're going through to the family room.'

The nurse sucked her teeth, eyeing Ruth with dislike, but Carver walked past her and pressed the door release, coming through the ward doors into the corridor.

'Five minutes,' the nurse said.

Ruth kept her eyes on Greg Carver. 'If that.'

He led the way to a room off the main corridor. He seemed to be making an effort to lift and place his feet, as if he was walking on uneven cobblestones, and when he gripped the door handle, he used it to steady himself. 'Definitely your angry colour,' he murmured, glancing into her face.

'What?'

'Orange,' he said. 'It's your angry colour.' He opened the door and went ahead of her.

A photographic print of cherry blossom covered a third of one wall. A few armchairs were placed around a coffee table. An empty sandwich wrapper, two coffee cups and a box of tissues lay on its surface. The room smelled of bad digestion and stale coffee.

'CSIs are processing room 214 at the Old Bank Hotel,' Ruth said.

Carver was lowering himself into a chair as she said this and he didn't look at her, but she thought she saw a slight jolt run though him. He eased himself back in the chair and gestured towards the one opposite, but Ruth remained standing.

'Two-one-four,' she said again. 'That's the room Adela Faraday was booked into on the night you were shot.'

He didn't reply.

'It's a crime scene, Greg – possibly even a murder scene. The CSIs will be thorough. Are they going to find your DNA?'

'I don't know.'

'I'm giving you a chance here, Greg.'

He said nothing.

'I spoke to one of the staff. She saw you in Adela's room.'

He shrugged.

She stood in front of him. 'Still playing the amnesia card?' He wouldn't look at her and she shook her head in disgust. 'I'm sick of your lies.'

'I'm not lying—'

'Jesus, Greg – will you *stop*?'

He gripped one hand with the other, perhaps to steady a tremor, and stared at the fists clamped in his lap.

'Look at me.'

Reluctantly, he raised his eyes to her.

'I *know* you were screwing Adela Faraday. I know about the argument – I know she dumped your stuff out on the corridor, kicked you out. I know that you went back in. A mirror was smashed in her room that night.'

Something flickered in Carver's face, but he was hard to read.

'Is Adela's blood in the room?' She waited. 'Is yours?'

He took a breath, hesitated.

'Fine,' she said. 'You don't want to talk. But DCI Jansen already knows you were at that hotel on the same night as Adela. It took me less than an hour to find someone who saw you in her room; it won't take Jansen much longer – and believe me when I say you *really* shouldn't expect any second chances from that quarter.'

Carver remained stubbornly silent, and with a gasp of exasperation she grabbed the door handle and swung the door wide.

'Ruth, wait.'

She was so angry with him, she almost kept walking.

'We were dating,' he said.

Ruth took a few seconds to steady herself before turning back to him. 'Dating,' she said.

'Sex.' A finger went to his eyebrow, a sure sign of embarrassment. 'I didn't even know her real name – her choice,' he added, as though it actually mattered to him what she thought. 'She – Adela – said she wanted a "no strings" relationship.'

Ruth watched him closely. She believed him. It was hurting him too much for it to be a lie.

'We made a pact never to talk about ourselves, only about ideas,' he went on. '"Only small people talk about other people," she said.'

'Ms Faraday was quite the philosopher . . .'

'Don't Ruth, please.'

She folded her arms. 'All right, I'm listening.'

'We had good conversation, great sex, and none of the responsibilities of a conventional relationship. I didn't feel . . . I don't know – compelled to talk about the Thorn Killer, and I never had to explain or apologise for my absences.'

She stared at him and he said, 'What?'

'All those times you were with Adela – how many was it?' She already knew the answer, but wondered if he would be straight with her.

'Five,' he said. 'Maybe six.'

He'd passed that test, but it didn't make up for the rest of his lies.

'Five or six times,' she said. 'Did you even think how Emma was feeling?'

'I wasn't really thinking of anyone but myself back then,' he said.

She gave a short bark of laughter.

'I'm trying to be honest, Ruth.'

'It never used to be an effort, Greg.'

He bowed his head.

'Didn't you think we should know about this woman? That she might have had something to do with what happened to you?'

'No,' he said. 'We broke up the night of the argument.'

So, he was admitting that, too.

'It was a "no strings" relationship. Why did it get ugly – why didn't you just walk away?'

'She was in a rage, screaming at me,' he said. 'I . . . said some things.'

'They had to call *security*, Greg – that's more than an exchange of words.'

'Push came to shove, I suppose.'

'You *hit* her?'

'I . . .' He frowned, and she could see him struggling to remember. 'I . . .' He stopped again, and this time he looked frightened. 'Ruth, I truly don't remember.'

'So, when Adela – whatever she called herself – didn't get back in touch, didn't come and see you after you were shot – what did you think?'

'She'd said she never wanted to see me again.' He shrugged. 'I thought she was just being as good as her word.'

'Well, now you know different,' Ruth said quietly.

He looked at her. 'I should have told you earlier. But there's so much I can't make sense of.'

'I want to help you,' Ruth said. 'But you need to be honest with me.'

He sighed. 'Okay.'

He didn't begin immediately, but she sensed this was not the time to rush him, so she waited, and after a while he began.

'I keep having flashbacks to that night. There's . . . a shadow – a darkness – it's in my dreams. Sometimes . . .' He seemed to struggle for a moment. 'Sometimes it's there when I'm awake, too.'

She moved to the chair opposite him and sat down. 'We talked about this,' she said. 'That was *me*.'

'I don't think so,' Carver said. 'I do remember you being there. But this other presence. It felt . . . I don't know how to describe it. It felt like it wanted to destroy me. I know that sounds over-dramatic.'

'You'd just been shot, Greg, a bit of drama is allowable. But look – I was there, and I was beyond angry. I thought you'd tried to kill yourself – I was *furious* with you. Maybe you picked up on that . . .'

He shook his head, staring into a darkness she couldn't see.

'If not me, then who? Adela?'

'Not Adela. It feels too strong. Powerful . . . Like . . . ' He cast about as if trying to see the word that evaded him. 'Like . . .' He gave up. 'I don't know.'

'Okay,' she said. 'Take me through what you do remember about that night.'

'It's confused,' Carver said. 'I remember calling her, setting up the date. I hung around reception when she checked in, followed her into the lift. She got out at the second floor, I went up to the next floor, came down the fire escape. It was a game we played – if I got to the room before her door closed, we were on for the night. If I didn't – well, it depended on her mood.' He couldn't meet her eye.

'How did it go that night?'

'I got there in time. We had sex, a few drinks. I went to the bathroom to shower, and when I got back, she was watching the news on TV. Saw me, talking about the murders. She said I should have told her, but our entire relationship was built on *neither* of us knowing anything about the other's life. I said she was being unreasonable. We argued. She threw me out.'

He stopped, and it seemed like he was trying to conjure up an image. 'But I don't remember leaving. I don't remember going back into the room.' His eyes darted left and right. 'And I don't remember breaking the mirror. I swear that's the truth.'

Ruth felt something loosen in her chest, like a spiral of tightly wound wire had released its hold and she could breathe freely again. Finally, he was telling her the truth – as much as he remembered of it.

Distracted by the sound of footsteps and voices in the corridor outside, Ruth delayed answering. Through the glass panel of the door, she got a fleeting glimpse of DCI Jansen.

'You have visitors,' she said softly, and a moment later Jansen backtracked and opened the door into the family room without knocking.

'Well, this saves me the trouble of trying to get past the gate-keepers on the ward.' He stepped into the room, revealing that the man with him was DC Tom Ivey.

It was as well Jansen had his back to the young detective: Ivey looked a bit wild-eyed at finding her with Carver.

'I'll get out of your way, sir,' Ruth said.

'Don't leave on our account, Sergeant,' Jansen said.

He was blocking the way out, anyway, and didn't look willing to move, so Ruth calmed herself and waited.

'We're here to share some news about DCI Carver's whereabouts on the night he was shot,' Jansen said, his tone cool, his tall, imposing presence an implied threat.

Ruth arranged her features into a look of quiet interest.

'Does the name Adela Faraday mean anything to you, Chief Inspector?' Jansen asked.

'She's been on the news all evening,' Carver said.

*Evasive tactics.*

'Doesn't answer the question,' Jansen said. But Carver maintained a weary, slightly muddled look, watching the other man's face as though trying to read his lips. Ruth recognised it as one of her own tricks.

'You shared a room with her.' Jansen paused. 'Not ringing any bells?'

Carver shook his head slowly, faking an effort to remember.

'That night's still hazy,' he said, again avoiding an outright lie. *Why doesn't he tell them?* Ruth glared at him, but he ignored her.

'So you didn't arrange to meet her?'

Carver raised his shoulders and let them fall, a look of hopeless confusion on his face.

'You don't remember having an argument with Ms Faraday?' Jansen said. 'A broken mirror? Security being called?'

'I wish I could . . .'

He'd just told them an outright lie.

Furious that she'd allowed herself to be dragged into his mess, Ruth took a step towards the door. 'Look, it's been a hell of a long day,' she said. 'I need to get some sleep.'

She slipped out of the unit as the ward sister came in search of her patient.

Parked at the kerb across the street, the Thorn Killer watches Ruth Lake emerge from the rehabilitation unit.

*So, now you know* . . . about Carver's sex dates with the Faraday woman, about his tryst with her the night he was shot. About the lies. His betrayal of Emma.

*How do you feel about that, Sergeant Lake?* Disgusted? Do *you* feel betrayed? It's hard to tell. Three visits to Carver's hospital bed in one day had to be significant, though. Right now, she looks thoughtful. She hides a lot behind that thoughtful look. But Sergeant Lake's cool facade is like ice on a river: fragile – even brittle – and beneath it the waters are turbulent.

## 29

Ruth Lake could not sleep. Tempting as it was to chug half a bottle of wine and suck on e-cigs till she passed out, she left the vape in her coat pocket and played 'Stellaris' on her laptop. Ruth had been a gamer since her mid-teens: it helped her to relax, and it had given her confidence that order could be created from chaos at a time when her life seemed to be falling apart. But tonight her thoughts kept circling back to what Carver had told her that evening. His relationship with Adela could well be the reason he was shot, and the weapon she had secreted in her spare room might hold definitive proof of that fact – maybe even of the identity of the shooter. But she couldn't introduce the gun into evidence without ending her career – perhaps even facing criminal charges.

What it came down to was could she trust Greg Carver? She really didn't know. She thought he was telling the truth about not remembering the detail of what had happened at the hotel while he did remember being there. But why had he lied to Jansen? She groaned, trying again and again to keep her mind on the game. But Stellaris was a game of strategy; every move she made to influence events in its imaginary universe only reminded her that her real-life strategic decisions the night Carver was shot had been disastrous.

Finally, she gave up, took her laptop to the kitchen and checked her email while she brewed coffee. Lyall Gaines had sent something at just after midnight; the subject line was,

'Written on the Skin.' Did that pass for humour in Gaines's world? she wondered.

She didn't acknowledge receipt, but she did follow the links the anthropologist had provided, trying not to think too much about the man who had sent them. Gaines thought that the stylised flowers and vines inked on the victims' skins looked similar to those seen in embroidered or cross-stitched samplers. He had provided a selection for her to look at, but as far as she could make out, they were only similar in the way that stylised trees and fruit and people *always* looked similar – because they had been stripped down to their most recognisable parts.

After an hour or two trawling the Web, the intricate needle-work began to merge into one – until, browsing off-piste, a piece caught her eye that had no images, only small, neatly worked print. She clicked on the image to enlarge it and discovered what was described by the website as a 'confessional' sampler.

The silk cloth it was embroidered on had yellowed and was spotted here and there with faint water stains, the embroidered red lettering fading to the colour of old blood. But every word neatly picked out with needle and thread was still clearly legible after nearly two hundred years.

The sampler told the story of Elizabeth Parker, a virtuous girl placed in service. At the age of thirteen she had refused the sexual advances of the master of the house and was thrown downstairs for her obstinacy. She fled her cruel master, but 'being young and foolish' she said, she did not tell her friends what had happened to her. In her new post, she became sullen and moody and had tried to commit suicide. The sampler was her confession, and atonement for her attempt at 'that great sin of self destruction'.

Ruth considered her own foolishness at a similar age when she had cut through the alley at the back of their house and witnessed that fatal stabbing. It could just as easily have been a violent attack or a sexual assault she herself had been subjected to. And she recalled that she too had become moody and withdrawn after witnessing the killing.

The clock over the kitchen sink read five past two, and the night stretched ahead like a long and tedious journey. Ruth yawned, ruffling her fingers through her hair, then crossed to the kettle to make a fresh mug of coffee. Five minutes later she was back at her task. During their meeting at the university, Dr Gaines had focused on the eye motifs the killer had tattooed on both Tali and Kara.

'Early representations of the Eye of Providence,' was how he had described them.

The kitchen was cold and rain spattered against the window. Slipping out for a crafty vape was out of the question, and she knew that if she started using the thing indoors, she'd be back on the equivalent of a pack a day in no time at all. She considered turning on the heating, but inertia kept her at the table. The latest link she'd clicked on had taken her to a webpage with a series of images: line drawings, woodcuts, book illustrations, stained glass windows – even a United States dollar bill. All depicted some version of the 'Eye of Providence'. Some with clouds, some not, most bounded by a triangle – a symbol of the Holy Trinity, according to Dr Gaines – and every one of them showed rays of light beaming from the eye. She went upstairs to the wardrobe in the spare bedroom and hefted down the box of files she had stolen from Greg Carver's flat.

Back in the kitchen, she dug through the manila folders, lifting out Tali Tredwin's and Kara Grogan's. Carver's duplicate files included numbered post mortem photographs. She selected a few close-ups of the tattoo details, setting the prints down on the kitchen table so that she could compare them with the images on her computer screen. She saw no rays of light, no triangles. She had never really examined the markings in any great detail before. If she was honest, she found the killer's deliberate scarring of his victims harder to stomach than some of the bloodied murder victims she had seen in her former career as a CSI. But focusing on this one, small element in the pattern allowed her to gain the scientific objectivity she needed.

The eyes scored on Tali's body were closed, or half-closed. But those tattooed on Kara stared out of the picture like something from a horror movie, wide open. They had an exotic shape – Egyptian, or even Indian, maybe. Looking again at the tattoos on Kara's body, the shape of the eyes reminded Ruth of depictions of the third eye of the Hindu god, Shiva. She looked it up, skimming the webpages for the meaning of the third eye. In Hindu culture, she learned, Shiva was the possessor of all knowledge. 'When his inner eye, or "chakra" opens,' one blogger wrote, 'it will destroy all that it sees.'

That seemed to fit with the end game the Thorn Killer had devised for his victims. Literal destruction.

Ruth scattered papers and photographs, finding her mobile phone under one of the folders, and thumbed through her contacts to Dr Gaines. Waiting for the connection to complete, she glanced up at the clock over the kitchen sink; it was four-thirty. Cursing, she ended the call before the first peal had finished. This was exactly the sort of thing she had criticised Carver for when the case had really got its hooks into him.

A second later she was startled by her phone vibrating in her hand. It rang out, and she checked the screen. Dr Gaines. Almost like he'd been waiting for her call.

'Glad I'm not the only one burning the midnight oil.' He sounded almost jaunty. 'Do you have the tattoo photographs to hand?'

'I do,' she said.

'I've been working on my theory that the inking has a protective role,' he said. 'Look for TT three-five.'

Each post mortem photograph was individually labelled; TT35 was one of the close-ups of Tali Tredwin. It was still in the folder, and she had to sift through to find it. 'Okay,' she said. 'I have it.'

'See the repeated circular images? They're rather blurred, but you can make out that the lines are intertwined. The tattoo-ists thought it was a crude attempt at some kind of snake. It isn't – it's a Celtic knot. Every *Braveheart* fan and new-age hippie knows them from their use in Celtic jewellery. But these knots go back to the fifth century, and possibly earlier.' He sounded excited.

'Okay . . .'

'Look closer. Can you see that it's impossible to see a beginning or end to the knot?'

'It's a symbol of the eternal cycle, and how everything is interconnected,' Ruth said, dredging up the fact from her hours of online research into symbolism.

'Not bad,' Gaines said. 'But it can also represent an uninterrupted cycle of life – effectively warding off sickness or bad luck. Remember what I said about the Eye of Providence in our first meeting?'

'It's protective,' she said.

'Precisely. Now look at the latest victim. Image KG five-seven.'

Ruth found it in Kara's file

'You see the circle in the bottom left of the picture?'

'With four thorns pointing inwards?' she said.

'Those aren't thorns, ' he said. 'They're *swords*. Poorly drawn, admittedly. Which is why it's been difficult for your previous consultants to establish their significance.'

But not a problem for the great Dr Gaines.

Aloud Ruth said, 'And that significance is?'

'It's a symbol used widely across many cultures – the swords may represent the four directions, guardian angels, spirit clans. And they're protective. In fact, I've identified five symbols which are used in sigils to banish evil spirits – and that's aside from the repeated use of the eye of Horus and the Eye of Providence in the tattoos.'

'I've been looking at the eye tattoos as well,' Ruth said.

'*Have* you?' He sounded simultaneously indulgent and patronising.

'It's the reason I called you. In Hindu culture, when the third eye opens, it destroys everything, yes?'

She heard a sharp sound at the other end of the line – a cough, or maybe a stifled laugh.

'And you infer . . . what, exactly, from that?' Gaines asked.

'Well, these women did end up dead. So, I wondered – could the tattoos be some kind of punishment?'

'Oh, my dear . . .' He stifled a laugh. 'I'm afraid you've taken a rather – forgive me – unsophisticated reading of the word "destruction". You see, the third eye, or "chakra" is a symbol of *knowledge*, so when it opens, it destroys ignorance. The destruction you describe is symbolic. It leads to a higher consciousness

– an uncovering of hidden truths.' He paused. 'Are you with me?'

Ruth had her own Zen-like ability to distance herself from insults. This was about the doctor's need to assert his authority rather than a shaming indictment of her own ignorance.

'Hidden truths? That's really helpful, Doctor,' she said, and meant it.

'I'm very pleased to hear it,' Gaines said, sounding equally sincere, which confirmed Ruth's assessment that flattery always went a long way with men like Dr Gaines. 'I can come over, talk you through my findings?' he added with disconcerting eagerness.

'Why don't you put it in your report,' she said, with that instinctual queasiness she'd felt in her encounter with the anthropologist the previous day. 'I'll present it to the team just as soon as I have it in my inbox.'

'Or I could jot down a few notes, trot over to your head-quarters and give the investigative team the broad brushstrokes at your morning briefing.'

*He just won't take no for an answer.* 'Best to have it in writing.' She hung up, simultaneously reaching for her laptop.

She found the confessional sampler, thinking about what Dr Gaines had said about hidden truths.

The pathologist at Tali Tredwin's post mortem had noted signs of oesophageal damage typical of bulimia. Evidence of bone breakages which they initially thought might be signs of spousal abuse were eventually put down to early-onset osteoporosis, which could be linked back to earlier anorexia. He had requested her full medical records, which revealed that she had a history of body dysmorphia. At the age of fifteen, Tali – known as Natalie back then – had overdosed on a cocktail of aspirin and vodka. She had never told her ex-husband or her children about the suicide bid.

'Hidden truths,' Ruth murmured. She dipped into Carver's box. 'Where are you, Jo . . .?'

She extracted Jo Raincliffe's file. Her husband had lost his job as a corporate accountant in the second wave of mass redundancies, three years after the 2008 banking crash. The Raincliffes had two children, both under six, and with the bank threatening to foreclose on the mortgage, Jo started a frantic search for jobs. Before she'd had the kids, she'd been in charge of four staff in the history department at the local Roman Catholic high school, and had supervised Confirmation classes for the girls, but despite her qualifications and experience, she'd struggled to find work. At a time when councils were putting teaching assistants in charge of classes, the unspoken message was that she was too expensive to employ. She finally managed to secure a learning support post at a city centre community college, and supplemented her earnings teaching evening classes in family history research. At least that was what she'd told her husband.

But Jo had massively over-inflated the hours she worked. In fact, she did ten hours as a learning support assistant and two hours of actual teaching. But she left the house at five every evening, five days a week, and didn't return home some nights until after eleven. Her bank account statements, kept under lock and key, provided the clue: she'd made monthly payments to an upmarket agency providing a shopfront to venues looking to hire exotic dancers. The agency was helpful: in exchange for a monthly fee from their clients, they vetted venues and provided photos to events organisers. Jo's portfolio was only circulated to people looking to hire, it couldn't be accessed freely online, which at least partly explained why she'd been able to keep the truth from her family for so long. For years, Jo – stage name 'Joline' – had been a regular at strip clubs and 'secret parties' in Liverpool, Wigan and Manchester. The cash payments she earned from stripping were undocumented, but the mortgage had been paid on time every month, and there was always food on the table.

Evie Dodd and Hayley Evans didn't seem to have any buried secrets or hidden shame, but then neither had Kara Grogan, until Ruth had started digging deeper into her circumstances and found out about her secret audition – and, of course, her stage fright.

Ruth picked up one of the PM photos of Kara and looked again at the open eyes tattooed on the young woman's flesh. They stared out of the picture like something from a horror movie, eyes wide open. A symbol of wakefulness – awareness, maybe. Is the killer demonstrating that he sees her as she really is? Or could it symbolise Kara's awakening – that she saw others as *they* really were?

What had Kara said to Jake? 'I've learned a valuable lesson.'

Shiva's third eye stared back at Ruth from the photo. The chakra, symbol of knowledge; destroyer of ignorance. But what kind of knowledge? That you couldn't trust *anyone* – not even your friends? Knowledge of that kind didn't just destroy ignorance, it shattered faith in the goodness of others and ground hope to dust.

## 30

*Day 9*

Early next morning, Greg Carver was watching the TV news. The leader of the council hurried across the cobbles of Exchange Flags towards the rear of the Town Hall in the rain. A reporter followed him, asking him for a comment on the murder of Adela Faraday. He scuttled on, his coat collar turned up, rain driven by the wind off the Mersey battering his hair flat. Another journo joined the first, thrusting a microphone under his nose. Two more appeared in shot, and now the councillor was beginning to look beleaguered as he pushed through the cluster of bodies and cameras. Finally, he stopped, raised his hands in a placatory gesture and said, 'I'll give you a statement – in ten minutes. But first I must address my colleagues in the chamber.'

Nice touch, Carver thought – putting the concerns of the Council Chamber before the needs of the press.

The broadcast returned to the studio, and the presenter rehashed the story of the discovery of Adela Faraday's body, her background in finance, the fact that she hadn't been seen since just before New Year. 'Mr Hill emerged fifteen minutes later to make a statement,' he finished.

The footage switched back to outside broadcast; Exchange Flags again, the cobbles shimmering with rainwater. Mr Hill had shed his overcoat, appearing in a charcoal grey suit, white shirt and dusty pink silk tie. His hair looked freshly styled: thick and black and glossy. He strode out to a podium, placed to use the north face of the Town Hall and the grey stone of Nelson's monument as a backdrop. The rain had stopped, and sunshine sparkled on the four figures in chains arranged around the base of the monument.

Councillor Hill approached the podium like an elder statesman and waited for silence. Reporters clustered around him: local press, cable TV and radio, BBC and ITV news, as well as reporters from Channels 4 and 5.

The council leader was in his mid-forties, an energetic poster-boy for the new guard seeking imaginative ways to generate income for a cash-strapped city. Councillor Hill, businessman and entrepreneur, had brought some hope to a city that in the words of its former mayor had been 'staring into the abyss' after seeing its government grants cut by two-thirds since the recession. But Hill had made enemies, particularly on the left.

'I'll keep this brief, ladies and gentlemen,' he said. 'First, let me extend my condolences, and those of all council members, to Ms Faraday's family and friends. Our thoughts and prayers are with them at this difficult time.' He left a respectful pause. 'Ms Faraday was a highly valued adviser to the council and we are shocked and horrified to hear of her death. Naturally, we will do everything in our power to assist the police in bringing the guilty party to justice.'

A voice from the crowd asked, 'Why has it taken so long to respond to the news of Ms Faraday's murder?'

The leader of the council glanced down at his notes.

'The Christmas holidays, and the freelance nature of her work meant that Adela, um, Ms Faraday – ah, that nobody missed Ms Faraday,' Hill said, fumbling his answer.

Carver saw a definite tint of mustard yellow and bile green around the man, and he wondered if this was the colour of lies for Councillor Hill.

You should take a look in the mirror sometime, Carver, he told himself. See the colours you shine on.

'Miss Faraday's appointment to the council was controversial, wasn't it, Councillor?' a local reporter asked.

Councillor Hill fixed the young reporter with a glassy eye. 'She wasn't "appointed", she was an advisor, John,' he said. 'And this isn't the time to be making political points. For the national press: Ms Faraday advised on investments – and in an extended period of belt-tightening and government cuts, Liverpool City Council has sought innovative approaches to the challenges we've faced,' he went on, slipping easily into political rhetoric. 'Decisions, I might add, that have brought significant benefits to the people of Liverpool and the wider Merseyside region.'

'Do you have a message for the person who killed Ms Faraday?' the ITV reporter asked, bringing him back to the subject.

'Yes.' Hill seemed to prepare himself, like an actor shrugging on an overcoat to get into character. When he was ready, he looked straight into the camera. 'What you did was an act of cowardice. The decent thing – the courageous thing – would be to give yourself up.' He shook his head. 'But I don't suppose you will. To others who may have noticed odd behaviour in somebody close to you – a spouse or friend acting out of character, perhaps: if you have any suspicions – any information *at all* that might help in this investigation – come forward, take responsibility. Speak to the police.'

The air around the council leader again seemed to swirl

mustard yellow, like sulphur gas in a test tube, and Carver thought he caught a whiff of its acrid stink.

He clicked off the switch and tossed the remote control onto the bed just as the door to his room opened, and Emma came in. She was pale, and her eyes looked a little puffy.

He felt a thud. She knew.

'Emma . . .'

'Don't.' She raised one finger. 'Don't say a word.'

He eased himself onto the arm of his chair, ready to take whatever she had to say.

'The police came to my home,' Emma said. 'They asked did I know Adela Faraday? Well, naturally, I knew the name – she's been all over the news since last night. But did I know that you were *seeing* her?' She snorted. '"Seeing her" – nice euphemism. How *could* I know? How could I suspect that while you were so busy killing yourself with booze, you still found time to betray me.' Her face twisted with pain. 'You lied to my face that you were working late. Month after month, you lied. You wouldn't even *touch* me, while you were—'

'No. Emma, I didn't even meet up with Adela until after we split up.'

'You expect me to believe that? You've lied and lied and *lied*. I don't think you know what the truth *is* any more.'

What could he say? There comes a point when you have to stop believing anything a liar tells you, if only to protect yourself.

Emma was speaking, now, and he made an effort to concentrate. 'They think you murdered her, don't they?' she said.

He hesitated.

'I know they questioned you, Greg.'

'Who told you that?'

'Unlike you, I still have friends on the force. So, tell me it isn't true.'

He said nothing.

'I thought so.'

'Do *you* think I did it?'

'You don't get to ask those questions any more,' she said, quietly.

He looked at her, and saw hatred and cold rage in the maelstrom of colour that swirled around her.

He gritted his teeth. 'Was it Ruth?'

'You think I'd *tell* you?' she demanded, the colours coalescing, breaking, reforming as she spoke. 'Do you think you're *entitled* to that righteous anger?'

He looked away because the colours spinning around her hurt his eyes. 'No,' he said. 'I don't.'

She snuffed air through her nose. 'Ruth Lake may be the one friend you have left. You might at least try keep her on your side.'

He closed his eyes. *Too late*, he thought. When he opened them again, Emma was staring at the honeymoon photograph.

'I still love you, Emma,' he said.

She turned her gaze on him.

'Part of me hopes that you really mean it.' She sounded cool and in control, except for the colours that poisoned the air around her. She must have read the incredulity in his face, because she added, 'No, really. Because then you would feel a tiny slice of the torture you've put me through.'

'I know, and I—'

'I've had it with your apologies,' she broke in. 'I'm finished with you, Greg.'

An icy chip of the disease that had racked him for the past year pricked his heart and he stood, snatched up the framed photograph and shoved it at her.

'You can take that with you – I don't know why you brought it in the first place.'

She took a step back, her hands by her sides. 'You think *I* brought it? Don't flatter yourself.'

For a second longer he held the picture out to her on the palm of his hand.

'Keep the damn thing,' she spat. 'I've no use for it.' She walked out, closing door after her.


Carver held himself in check for a few seconds, then hurled the photograph at the door. In that split second it opened. The frame smashed on the leading edge of the door and glass splintered and shattered on the floor.

'Oh, god . . .' Carver took a step forward, staggered and bumped his hip against the bedframe. Gripping the rail for support, he righted himself, his heart pounding. He tried again to reach the door, but his legs wouldn't support him. 'I'm sorry,' he called out. 'Are you all right?'

Silence.

A second later a hand appeared, waving a paper tissue. A woman's face followed a moment later. 'Is it safe?' she asked.

'I'm so sorry,' he said. 'Come in. I'm harmless.'

'And I'm Laura Pendinning,' she said solemnly, though there was a twinkle of humour in her eye. 'How d'you do?'

She was in her mid-thirties, small, which made her seem younger; dark and pretty, though she wore no makeup and her hair was pulled back from her face in a rather severe ponytail.

'Was I expecting you?' he said, with a spurt of anxiety that he'd forgotten something.

'About three days ago. I'm afraid I got sidetracked.' He frowned and she added: 'I'm a clinical psychologist – your neurosurgeon asked me to drop by?'

Carver remembered having a conversation with a grey-haired man in a suit, something about the weird hallucinations he'd been experiencing, but he couldn't recall the name of the surgeon, or when they'd spoken. He nodded, trying not to look too clueless.

The psychologist smiled. 'Sorry it's taken a while.'

'Cutbacks,' Carver said.

She tilted her head. 'Something like that.' She remained in the corridor, peering into the room from beyond the door-frame. 'Can we talk?'

The rush of adrenaline from his row with Emma had sent cold chills through Carver's limbs, leaving him feeling shaky and weak.

'It's not the best time,' Carver said.

'Really?' The woman looked drolly at the shattered glass at her feet. 'I don't think I could have come at a more auspicious moment.'

A nurse appeared behind the doctor. 'It's all right,' Pendinning said.

'That needs to be cleared up before someone gets hurt,' the nurse said.

'It'll wait.' Pendinning sounded firm. 'We're just going to have a brief chat first.'

The nurse retreated, and Carver found himself under the scrutiny of the psychologist.

'Look,' he said. 'I don't want to be rude, but . . .'

She chuckled. 'Oh, I think we're way past polite exchanges.' She crouched to extract the photo from what was left of its frame.

'Be careful,' Carver said.

She carried on, gently shaking glass from the paper onto the floor.

'I don't want it. It doesn't matter,' Carver said of the honeymoon photograph that had stood on the dresser in their shared flat, then in their family home and more recently on his bedside table in the apartment he'd taken after Emma threw him out. For fifteen years, wherever he set up home, he kept that picture close by, as a reminder of what they had been to each other, and a warning of what he stood to lose. Had lost.

The psychologist offered him the photo, and he couldn't stop himself making the comparison: Emma on their honeymoon; Kara, dead. Kara Grogan, the victim who looked just like Emma.

Dr Pendinning quietly placed the photo at the foot of his bed, then ran her hands over her skirt, straightening it. 'Sometimes it's good to be reminded of what matters to us,' she said, as if she'd read his mind. 'Even if it doesn't *seem* to matter any more. Even if it causes us pain.'

## 31

'Hi Tom.'

DC Tom Ivey jumped like a cat, spinning to face Ruth Lake.

'Where the hell did you spring from?'

'My mother's loins,' she said, just to see him blush.

'Look, Sarge . . .' He glanced over her shoulder.

'We do work in the same building,' she added in mitigation.

Ivey had just parked his car at HQ, and in truth she'd been inside the rear entrance, waiting to pounce. She had seen the news, and there was something very off in Councillor Hill's responses. Carver had lied – to Emma, to her, to Jansen – but angry as she was with him, she was certain that he'd been telling the truth about having no memory of leaving Adela Faraday's hotel room, and her mind kept going back to that broken mirror.

'So, how did it go last night?' she asked.

'I shouldn't even be talking to you,' he hissed.

'Come on . . . it was a good call at the hotel, wasn't it?'

He shuffled a bit, and she saw the slight shoulder-lift that said it was more than merely 'good'.

'DCI Jansen appreciative, was he?'

DC Ivey gave a reluctant nod, still looking past her. 'And suspicious.'

'Yeah, well, that's his nature.'

'Sarge, I've got to go.'

'I know – DCI Jansen called you in to attend Adela's PM with him. You're practically his protégé.' He was still avoiding her gaze, and she shifted her stance to make that impossible. 'Quid pro quo, Tom.'

He closed his eyes for a second, then his shoulders sagged, and she knew he'd tell her what she needed to know as long as she didn't push him too hard. So she gave him a moment, and finally he sighed.

'Okay . . .' he said. 'Carver's still hiding behind the amnesia.'

'Your opinion, or Jansen's?'

His face hardened. 'I can think for myself. And I know when a man is lying.'

'Really? I don't – not always.' She could have added, 'Certainly not where Carver is concerned.'

He scowled, shoving his hands in his coat pockets, and she added, 'But if there's *evidence* one way or the other . . .'

She waited, looking patiently into the young detective's face. He clenched his teeth, every muscle in his neck and shoulders tense, and she realised it was up to her to break the impasse.

'Let me help you,' she said. 'The CSIs working on Adela Faraday's apartment discovered a second phone – unregistered, pay-as-you-go. It has three numbers on it, and one of them is Carver's.'

His hands came out of his pockets. 'That's confidential to the inquiry, how did you—?'

'I will *never* tell. Which is why you can be sure that whatever you tell me now is safe with me. Now I'm guessing that Carver says he doesn't know anything about the burner phone, either.'

He hesitated, but only for a second, then he began, talking softly, barely opening his mouth to get the words out. 'DCI Jansen requested a DNA sample but Carver refused. He said he has no memory of that night, so if he gave a sample, and we found something that incriminated him, he wouldn't be able to explain it – and he won't leave himself wide open in that way.' He paused. 'Seems a weird response from an innocent man, don't you think?'

'It does,' Ruth said. 'But if I've learned anything in life, it's to keep an open mind. So, you're trying to trace the other two numbers in the phone?'

He looked over her shoulder again. 'Mm.'

'And Adela? She's quite the woman of mystery, isn't she?'

'What do you know?' he demanded.

She let her mouth curl into the ghost of a smile. 'What do *you* know?'

He sucked his teeth. 'Where's your car?'

She lifted her chin, indicating a section of the car park off to the right. 'Behind one of the Matrix vans.'

He glanced towards the chequered, bumblebee-yellow battle buses of the city's Serious and Organised Crime Squad.

'I'll follow you.'

She went ahead, sliding behind the wheel, thirty seconds before he opened the passenger door and sat beside her.

'She was mega-rich.'

'Riverfront apartment,' Ruth said. 'It's a no-brainer.'

'Not just the apartment – she had *millions* in assets: bonds, stocks, commercial and residential properties. If she kept paper records, we haven't found them, and her computer's encrypted, so we're having to go via her bank accounts. There could be a hell of a lot more.'

'Who stands to inherit?'

'We haven't found a will, yet. We're looking for any family she might have. Thing is, she was secretive. She went freelance seven months before she died, moved from a five-bed house in Calderstones to the dockside apartment, but it was one of thirty in her residential property portfolio. It was listed with the concierge as empty and she didn't even have the landline connected.'

'Mobile phone?' Ruth said. 'The official one, that is.'

'There's masses of contacts on it, but they all seem legit: rich business clients mostly, but a few key names on the Liverpool City Council.'

'And?'

'And what?' he said

'Well, you must have interviewed them . . .'

He stared at her. 'You just never stop, do you?'

'It's one of my more endearing qualities, when you get to know me.'

His mouth twitched as he fought the impulse to smile.

'Ms Faraday had a reputation for risk-taking,' he said. 'But she was clever – "brilliant", according to them – always bang on the money when it came to investment opportunities.'

'Hm,' Ruth said. 'I stopped believing in investors with the Midas touch in 2008.'

'We'll be looking into the possibility of dodgy deals as soon as we get access to her financial records.'

She nodded. 'Well, I shouldn't hold you up, Tom. Thanks.'

'Not so fast,' he said. 'Quid pro quo, remember? Now it's your turn.'

She really was beginning to like Tom Ivey. 'When Carver was admitted, did they find particles of glass in his hair?'

'That's your quid pro quo – another question?'

'Check with the A&E doctors, and the surgeon who operated on him,' she said.

'Because . . .?'

'The head injury.'.

'What about it?'

'Nobody seems to know how or when it happened. But when you walk back through the timeline . . .' She raised an eyebrow, waiting for him to get it, and he stared through the windscreen at the car parked in the next row.

'The broken mirror in Adela's room?' he said at last.

'It's possible, isn't it? The medical staff haven't found any other explanation for Greg's concussion.'

He frowned. 'So . . . Adela assaulted *Carver*?'

'Or he fell, or someone else shoved him. But we're speculating before the evidence.'

'I'll talk to the medics.' He opened the car door and got out. 'And Tom?'

He ducked to keep her in his line of sight.

'You should talk to your friend on the reception desk at the Old Bank, too – ask for times and dates Adela booked a room over the past month, then haul in the street CCTV. If she met other men, you might just catch them like we caught Greg.'

'What makes you think she was seeing other men?'

'Three numbers on her throwaway, only one of them belonging to Greg Carver.'

He tapped the roof of the car with his free hand. 'He told you something, didn't he?'

'Let's say I get the feeling Adela wasn't a one-man kind of gal,' she said.

## 32

Sitting at her desk with office buzz going on around her, Ruth Lake reflected on the frustrations of the morning briefing. The house-to-house enquiries were a bust. The Sefton Park canvas hadn't brought in even a scrap of new intel. She couldn't present Doctor Gaines's theory on the significance of the tattoos because he hadn't delivered his report. Maybe she should have been more conciliatory, but sleepless nights and the daily graft involved in presenting an armour-plated front to the alpha males who would have her job given the chance wearied her beyond exhaustion.

As their most recent victim, Kara was still their closest known connection to the Thorn Killer. If they knew what she had been doing in the evenings immediately prior to her disappearance it might just lead them to TK's door. But the young actress had covered her tracks well. She was single minded and determined, had shucked off her old friends like clothing she had outgrown. That thought seemed to muffle the office chatter for a second.

In a sense, Kara *had* outgrown her student peers: hadn't she been on the cusp of a new and brilliant career? Her house-mates, her tutor and her agent had all said that she was completely focused on her acting. Which in the short term meant her audition.

With a guilty pang, Ruth remembered that she'd intended to check out the list of psychics whose performances Kara may have attended around the time she disappeared – they still didn't have a definitive date. Cursing mildly, Ruth grabbed the mouse and clicked through her files. She had street addresses for two of the psychics. She scribbled them into her notebook, shut down her computer, snatched up her mobile and was out of the office in under a minute.

Wilson Daventry ran a gift shop on the Albert Dock. His website offered psychic insights, crystal therapy, Reiki and Tarot card readings. His shop supplied a range of New Age paraphernalia, from crystals and Celtic jewellery to angel figurines and yoga mats.

A girl with blue hair, sleeve tattoos and facial piercings fronted the place, but when Ruth asked for the boss by name, he shimmied from the back of the shop through the crystal-beaded curtain in a rainbow of refracted light.

He took Ruth's hand between both of his and stared deep into her eyes. With a look of intense compassion, he nodded, his hand tightening fractionally as he said, 'I sense a dark presence near you.'

'Oh,' Ruth said, giving him nothing.

She had read enough of Kara's research to know that the way these people worked was to unsettle. And as a cop, she knew that people who are unsettled often reveal more than they intend to. So she controlled the urge to try to liberate her hand, and stared back into his eyes, summoning her most fathomless gaze.

'I'm also sensing resistance,' he said, with a sad smile.

She flashed her warrant card, and Daventry let her hand slip from his.

'Is there somewhere we can talk?'

He held back the bead curtain and ushered her through to his consultation room. It was simply laid out, with two chairs either side of a Tarot card table draped with purple velveteen. Judging by the cards fanned out on the table, Daventry had been practising when she arrived. Beyond his chair was a large window with a view across the inner dock. Light dazzled in myriad colours from crystals hung by fine threads in the windows and over the table. Daventry moved around to the far side of the table, turned and paused, his fingertips just grazing the velveteen.

Before he could fully take control of the situation, Ruth took a print of Kara from her pocket and offered it to him.

'Do you know this woman?' she asked.

He studied it. 'I don't believe we've met.'

'She may have been at your reading last November – the one at the Unity Theatre.'

He shook his head, doubtful. 'I wish I could help.' He took the picture. 'Tragic, what happened.'

'Is this you sensing things again?'

He handed the photo back. 'This is me keeping up with current affairs,' he said, with the slightest hint of a self-deprecating smile. 'I watch the news.'

Second on Ruth's list was Mrs Jasmine Hart. She lived in a Victorian red-brick mid-terrace near Newsham Park, east of the city centre. It was larger than Ruth's own home, but not grand by any means, so Mrs Hart clearly wasn't making a fortune from her spiritual insights.

She invited Ruth into the front sitting room and went off to brew coffee.

Two plain rectangular sofas were set either side of a dark wood coffee table with a box of tissues and a silver business card stand set dead centre of it. A single wingback armchair stood to one side of the fireplace and a fire burned in the hearth – living flame, but the tiles and surround looked authentic Victorian. The mantel was covered with 'thank you' cards – the only sign of clutter in the room. Ruth took a squint at a few – all from grateful clients, thanking Jasmine for giving them solace, or advice.

A rattle of crockery warned of Mrs Hart's return, and Ruth opened the door wide to let her through.

'Sit yourself down, Sergeant.' Jasmine Hart was a short, dumpy woman in her mid-forties; her accent was broad Lancashire, but she spoke in gentle tones she had obviously worked hard to perfect. 'It's warmest by the fire.' She nodded to the armchair close to the fireplace.

*Old-fashioned courtesy*, Ruth thought.

Mrs Hart set down the tray of coffee on the table, nudging the box of tissues out of the way and moving the silver business card stand off to one side.

Ruth explained the reason for her visit as Mrs Hart poured the coffee, and she responded in a quiet, sympathetic manner. She wore her mid-brown hair loose to her shoulders, and occasionally tucked it carefully behind her ears when she needed to give herself time to think. The left hand bore no wedding ring, but Ruth guessed that married status was desirable in female psychics. She handed Mrs Hart the photograph of Kara, and the woman took it with no hint of drama.

'Yes, I *do* remember her,' she said. 'Last November. I did a Psychic Night at the Epstein Theatre. A young lass was causing bother, tinkering with an e-tablet.' She stared at the photograph. 'Seeing this, I realise now it was Kara. That's when she went missing – November?'

Ruth nodded. 'What sort of bother?'

Mrs Hart paused, a frown creasing three parallel lines between her eyebrows.

'She said she was making notes, but it was causing . . . problems.'

'Members of the audience complained?' Ruth said.

Mrs Hart tucked a stray lock behind one ear. 'Not as such . . .'

Ruth tilted her head, waiting patiently.

'You see—' The psychic broke off, and when she spoke again it was in low tones, imparting a confidence. 'Electromagnetic sources can interfere with the spirit messages, and I was pretty sure Kara was secretly recording the session.'

Ruth held back from asking if Mrs Hart had experienced any psychic 'interference' from the radio mics she must have used at her gig, and instead made a note to have the techs search for the recording on Kara's tablet.

She widened her eyes. 'What did you do?'

'I asked her to leave. Thing is, love, some folk in the audience are in a very vulnerable state when they attend a reading. I have to consider their feelings —respect their privacy.'

'Of course . . .' Ruth sympathised. 'And Kara was alone?'

'She was. You'll want to know if I saw the poor lass speaking to anyone afterwards.' She gave a regretful grimace. 'I'm afraid I didn't. See, the session ended at ten, and Kara was long gone by then.'

'Do you remember *when* she was asked to leave?'

Another wince of regret. 'Sorry, love. But you could ask Harry – my manager.' She slid a business card from the holder on the coffee table and handed it to Ruth. 'It was just before the interval, so probably around eight-ish. I lose track of time during the sessions.'

The card listed a mobile number and website address for Mrs Hart, and an email address for Harry Rollinson.

'How are you doing with the investigation?' Mrs Hart asked.

*Here we go* . . . 'I'm afraid I can't discuss that,' Ruth said.

'Oh, of course not, love. Confidences – I understand that. But you're doing all right, are you? It *was* your colleague was attacked, wasn't it?'

'As I said—'

'Shot, wasn't he?'

Ruth said, 'I'll give your manager –' she glanced at the business card, although she remembered his name perfectly well '– Mr Rollinson, a bell.'

*You're letting her rattle you, Ruth.*

Mrs Hart raised her hand, palm down, hovering around the crown of her own head. 'I'm getting . . . pain,' she said.

'He *has* been recovering at a specialist head injuries unit,' Ruth said.

Mrs Hart's hand dropped to her lap, and she tilted her head, as if listening to something far off. After a moment she said, 'Oh,' an astonished look on her face. 'He wasn't shot in the *head*, was he love?'

They had kept that out of the news bulletins. Ruth wasn't sure what had betrayed her – muscle tension? Something in her tone of voice? As a person who habitually read others' body language it wasn't a very pleasant feeling *being* read.

'I *am* sorry, love,' the woman said. 'I've made you uncomfortable, haven't I?'

*And there she goes again.* 'Of course not,' Ruth said. 'But I am pushed for time, so . . .'

She left a minute later.

\*　　\*　　\*

Back at headquarters, she searched the web for Jasmine Hart's audio and video podcasts, and was surprised to find that Jasmine Hart had her very own YouTube channel. Ruth ran a few of the recordings – mostly short clips from her shows, and mainly poorly disguised adverts for Mrs Hart's business.

But a link further down the Google search results caught her eye.

'Jasmine Hart – FAKE.' was the main title. The description read: 'See the other side of Jasmine Hart's contacts with the "Other Side".'

Ruth clicked the link to a YouTube channel calling itself 'Psychic Tricksters', and found a recording of Jasmine's run-in with Kara. Far from 'asking her to leave', Kara had been physically bundled out of the place by an older man. Was this Rollinson? He tried to grab Kara's e-tablet, but she held on to the device, clasping it to her chest, while he pushed, prodded and shoved her down the centre aisle of the theatre to the exit, amid gasps of shock and disapproval from the audience.

A Google search for Harry Rollinson trawled up a couple of teenagers and twenty-somethings on Facebook – all way too young to be the man in the video. Rollinson was listed on Jasmine's website, but there were no photographs. Which was not suspicious in itself, but the fact that the man apparently had no web presence, and only one client – Jasmine Hart – *was* odd.

She played the video again and watched the big bear of a man bully and shove a frightened-looking Kara out of the theatre. A man with a temper like that – a man willing to lay hands on a woman – would likely have form, she reasoned, so she checked the Police National Computer Names File. There were several Henry Rollinsons – two of whom were too old to be her guy – as well as a Henry Rollinson, aka Brian Rollinson, aka Brian Henry Rollinson, aged sixty-seven. About the right age, judging by the video, and the multi-aliased Mr Rollinson had convictions for common assault, assault and battery, and fraud.

The Names File on the PNC provided links to fingerprints and DNA records, but it didn't carry digital information like photos. So she put in a request for photographs and closed the database, returning to Jasmine's website to check out her events page. Mrs Hart had a psychic reading back at the Epstein Theatre in the centre of the city that night. Ruth intended to be there.

The final psychic on Kara's list was an act calling himself 'Shadowman'. His website and Facebook pages showed a man photographed, predictably enough, in shadow, and his website made a huge deal of telling people not to bring phones or cameras to the gigs. 'Bags will be searched and phones confiscated until after the performance,' the booking terms warned.

Shadowman had no events upcoming, and although the testimonials page on his website referred to events in named towns, there were no named venues. *Publicity hype*, Ruth decided – probably all invented. An invitation on the homepage to complete a questionnaire entitled 'How psychic are you?' intrigued her, though. *Click bait*.

'Okay,' she murmured. 'I'll bite.' She clicked the link.

But before she could get to the questions, she was required to submit her email address. Ruth closed the questionnaire, preferring to have their first encounter on her own terms, which meant not giving him the opportunity to research her. Shadowman's contacts page gave an email address for punters and events organisers together with a landline number. She dialled the landline and was put through to an answerphone service based at a business centre in north Liverpool. She left a message asking for a return call on her mobile number, without mentioning that she was police.

She was about to head off to the briefing room when her mobile buzzed. A text message from DC Ivey. 'Meet me at Cow & Co. caff, 5 mins.'

She took a short cut through the car park and was there in under three. It was five p.m., already dark, and her breath steamed in the freezing air. The café was in a quiet square near the red-brick facade of Chancery House, another of the city's turnaround stories – what had once been a refuge for the destitute was now a luxury apartment complex beyond the financial reach of most Liverpudlians.

She ducked inside the tiny café and saw Tom Ivey skulking in a corner. He pointed to the two cups on the table and she went straight over, shrugging off her coat.

Ruth sipped her cappuccino with her back to the door, while DC Ivey talked her through Adela Faraday's post mortem results. The approximate time of death had been determined by Adela's last known sighting, which was at the Old Bank hotel, the night Greg Carver was shot. The snow covering her body confirmed TOD that same night. Adela had had rough, but possibly consensual, sex around time of death.

Ruth swallowed down a wave of nausea. 'Cause of death?'

'She was beaten and shot,' he said. 'It was the bullet killed her.'

She set her cup down, careful that it didn't clatter against the saucer rim. 'What calibre of bullet?' she said.

'The slug was a bit mashed up, but it's probably a .22.' She felt his eyes on her. 'Recovered from her heart.'

It was hot in the confined space of the café, but Ruth felt suddenly cold. She nodded, her mind racing, but she kept her expression impassive.

'I can't help you any more,' Ivey said.

She looked him in the eye 'Why?' she said, thinking about the bullet lodged in Carver's back, feeling a ripple of contraction in the muscles around her mouth, and hoping Ivey hadn't seen it.

'Adela Faraday was shot; so was Carver,' he said, clearly surprised he needed to explain. 'Two people who know each other, shot in the chest, by a small calibre pistol. Probably around the same time. What are the odds of it being a coincidence?'

*Vanishingly small*, she thought.

'Did you trace the other numbers on Adela's burner phone?'

He leaned forward, his shoulders hunched. He was so close she could see a tiny crystal of sugar caught on his upper lip. 'I can't *help* you,' he repeated.

She pinched his jacket lapel between her thumb and forefinger and leaned in, closing the gap. 'Then why are you here?' she whispered.

He flushed, sat back. 'I just . . . I didn't want you to hear it from Jansen.'

'Have you questioned Carver?'

'*Sarge*—'

'Hey,' she interrupted. 'You wouldn't have the link to Carver if it wasn't for me.' She saw him begin to waver, and added, 'You *know* you can trust me.'

'Jesus, Sarge, you're *killing* me.' He rubbed his right eye with the pad of his thumb, and she realised he was soothing a tremor in the eyelid.

She held still, keeping her eyes on his face. 'Tom . . .'

He sighed. 'It'll be on the news anyway,' he said, half to himself. He took another breath. 'But you didn't get this from me.'

She widened her eyes as if to say, *Goes without saying*.

Again, he hesitated, but then blurted out, 'One of the phone numbers belongs to Councillor Hill.'

'The leader of the *council*?' She felt a tiny glimmer of hope.

He nodded. 'Jansen asked him to come in, but he refused.'

'And?' A pulse throbbed behind her eyes.

'He's about to be arrested.'

## 33

DCI Parsons wanted an explanation for Ruth's late arrival at the evening briefing. She made an excuse of her interviews with the psychics, earning a few Brownie points when she pulled up the YouTube video of Kara's altercation with Rollinson at Jasmine Hart's psychic performance.

'Okay, bring him in,' Parsons said.

'Mrs Hart is performing tonight,' Ruth said. 'I'd like to see for myself how he operates – get some more out of them before we make things official.'

Parsons thought about it. 'All right. But I want him formally interviewed – here at the station – tomorrow morning.'

'Absolutely,' she said.

The remainder of the debrief was more nothing: nothing from the canvas, nothing from the TV appeals, nothing from the stop and question.

They were about ready to go home for the night when Parsons said, 'One piece of good news . . .'

Heads came up, eager for something other than disappointment to pack up and lug home from the day's graft.

'The Adela Faraday MIT have made an arrest.'

Murmurs of surprise, a few sly glances in Ruth's direction, half the team thinking it must be Carver. She stayed calm and affected polite interest, waiting for the DCI to tell them that the suspect was Councillor Hill. Hearing the Councillor's name, the more loyal detectives on the team exchanged satisfied nods; John Hughes, her old friend from the Crime Scene Unit, smiled over at her; a few of the younger members of the team were already thumbing their smartphones, trawling for news reports. Ruth made eye contact with Parsons and lifted her chin in a gesture of thanks. With Carver off the list of suspects, the team had the boost it needed to start the next day with renewed purpose.

She only wished she could be as sure that Greg Carver was innocent.

Parsons called her over as the room emptied.

'Good work on the psychic connection,' he said. 'You were right – it does narrow down the time frame.'

'Thank you, sir.'

'I'd like you to take someone with you this evening, though.'

'I want to keep a low profile, observe, rather than participate,' she said. 'On my own, I'll be just another face in the crowd.'

His brows drew down, and she thought he was about to order her to take someone with her. Then his shoulders twitched in a micro-shrug and she realised he'd given his tacit consent.

'DC Ivey,' he said.

He knew something. But Ruth was far too experienced in interrogation techniques to fall for his clumsy attempt to use her guilty conscience to leverage an unguarded response. 'You want me to take DC Ivey?' she said. 'Isn't he on the Faraday investigation?'

'You know he is,' Parsons said, displeased.

She looked guilelessly into his face, as though waiting for him to explain.

'Whatever you've been up to, DCI Jansen has noticed. Stay away from Ivey – Carver's shooting is none of your affair.'

In one very important way, it was, but she said, 'Okay . . .' with just enough upward inflexion to sound puzzled.

He snorted. 'Clear off, Sergeant – and remember what I said – I don't want any tabloid headlines linking this investigation with psychics.'

Ruth went home to change into jeans and a sweater before heading back into town, aiming to blend in. She swapped her overcoat for a parka, let her hair down, then tied it back again – not that she was vain, but Ruth knew that her brown curls could turn heads. She screwed the ponytail tight and tucked it under a peaked corduroy cap.

At the theatre, she bought her ticket just before the curtain went up, spoke to no one, and slumped low in her seat as the audience murmur died down.

Jasmine Hart was dressed in a gleaming white skirt suit. She cast a benign eye over the audience, spread her arms, and said, 'Welcome.' Her pitch and tone conveyed the same warmth and kindness Ruth had experienced earlier: you might believe she was chatting with a few pals in her own sitting room – her voice implied a friendly intimacy. But that was down to a good sound system – and the psychic's practised and carefully modulated tones.

In the days since she started seeking out video recordings of psychic performers, Ruth had seen fast-talking conmen who dazzled their marks, denying them any chance of rational thought. She had seen homely grannies who cosily invited the dead to come forward and chat. She'd seen the solemn and the serene; the smiling and excitable; psychics who spoke aloud to their 'spirits' and those who seemed to listen intently, only nodding to show that they were in communication.

Mrs Hart was a talker.

'I've got a young man coming through,' she would say, or: 'I'm hearing someone called Sally – does that mean anything to anyone?' After a series of miss-hits, she lowered her chin to her chest, let her hands fall to her sides, and was silent for ten seconds.

Just as the audience became restless, she turned her head the slightest fraction, as though sneaking a look from the corner of her eye. 'Don't be shy, love.'

A murmur of anticipation rippled through auditorium.

'Shhhh . . .' Mrs Hart soothed. The sleek radio mic headset was almost invisible from the audience, so it seemed that she was in conversation with someone just beyond their sight. 'Don't mind them,' she said. 'They'll not harm you.'

She twitched the fingers of her right hand, gesturing as if someone stood to her side and she was encouraging them to come forward. 'Come on then,' she said. 'You can hold my hand, if you like.' Her right hand closed as if a hand had indeed tentatively slipped into hers.

She closed her eyes. 'So cold . . .'

Someone in the audience behind Ruth sobbed and she turned slowly, not wanting to attract attention. A woman two rows back had a hand to her mouth. She was shaking. Another woman sitting beside her rubbed her arm. Rollinson was already making his way down the aisle towards her with the roving mic.

Jasmine Hart opened her eyes. 'I'm getting a child,' she said.

There was no visible shake of the head, and the woman didn't speak, but Ruth sensed a stiffening, a withdrawal.

'*Our kid*, maybe . . .' the psychic went on as if she hadn't noticed.

The woman gasped.

'Does that mean something to you, love?'

This was Liverpool – it was a safe bet half the audience referred to a brother or sister as 'our kid'.

The punter nodded. 'My brother,' she said. 'Our M—'

'No, don't tell me. Let him speak for himself. He's been waiting a long time to say this.'

Ruth saw a slight crease between the woman's brows.

'At least it *seems* a long time, he says,' Mrs Hart corrected. Another good recovery. Then, as an aside: 'You're not coming through clear, love.' Focusing again on the woman in the audience, Mrs Hart said, 'I'm getting Mark . . . no . . . Mike?'

The emotion on the woman's face told her she'd guessed right second time.

'Mike tells me he's not long passed over.'

'Three months,' the woman said.

'That's right.'

Ruth knew that when she recalled it, the bereaved woman would swear that Jasmine Hart had specified the three months.

'It was quick,' Mrs Hart said.

The woman pressed her lips together, tears streaming down her face, the flutter of the mic in her shaking hands sounding like the irregular stutter of her heart. Rollinson was standing at the end of the row, and Ruth chanced a glimpse at him from under the peak of her cap. He was big and heavy, with hands like a butcher. He searched the audience like a bodyguard on a high-security detail, but it was possibilities he was looking for, not threats.

'Is he . . . is he all right?' the woman asked.

'He is.' With her left hand, Mrs Hart patted the imaginary hand in her right. 'There's so much he wants to tell you.' A momentary cloud passed over her face. 'He *is* cold though . . .' she added with a little shiver.

'Oh, God . . .' the woman choked out. 'He kept saying that, when he—'

'What's that, love?' Mrs Hart interrupted, talking to her imaginary companion. She laughed. 'I don't know if this makes sense, but he says they've got footie on the other side.'

The woman laughed into her hand, wiping snot and tears from her face. 'He was mad for it – said if they didn't have footie on the other side, he'd come back and haunt Anfield.'

Laughs of recognition and empathy from the audience.

Mrs Hart smiled with them, her head cocked as if trying to hear a distant voice above the laughter. 'Oh,' she said, and her face fell. 'Okay, love. He's going . . . says he's tired.'

The woman stretched out her hand, brought her fingers trembling to her lips.

'What's that, love?' Mrs Hart turned, looking to her right. 'Right-oh.' She focused on the woman. 'He says he has a private message for you. But he's fading – his first time, see – and he's a bit shy talking in front of all these people.'

The woman levered herself out of the seat. 'But how can I . . .?'

'If you'd like to see me after the group reading, I'll see if I can coax him. Not to worry, love, we'll sort you out.'

The joy and anxiety on the woman's face was pitiful.

Mrs Hart opened her hand, as though gently releasing the 'spirit' from her grasp. She swayed for a moment.

'There's another voice coming through . . .' She held her hand out indicating the front rows, and while Mrs Hart started a new riff on a small woman with a name like a flower, Ruth watched Rollinson take the radio mic from the first woman and send a notebook and pen down the row for her to write down her details.

The second spirit was called Rose, and on a lighter note, Mrs Hart joked about her being thorny. The punter, a sixty-something who looked like she'd been around the block a few times, laughed with the rest. Rose was an elderly aunt, she said, prickly as a hedgehog. Mrs Hart wowed them with the revelation that Aunty Rose was pleased she'd found the ring.

The woman obligingly stood and held up her left hand to show the audience the ruby ring her aunt had left her, but which had been so well hidden they hadn't found it for almost a year after her death.

Many of the 'messages' Mrs Hart received were of such a broad nature that half a dozen hands would go up, begging to be chosen. The psychic would punctuate her insights with, 'Do you understand?' or 'Does that make sense?' and occasionally, when it clearly didn't, she would say firmly, 'It might be something that hasn't happened, yet. But it *will* make sense in the future.'

Jasmine Hart took a break halfway through and Ruth saw Harry Rollinson approach Mike's sister and guide her to the steps at the side of the stage, where Mrs Hart was waiting. The psychic took the woman's hands in her own, and led her backstage.

Ruth mingled with the audience in the bar, listening to exclamations at the extraordinary accuracy of the reading, telling stories of their own. She saw that Harry Rollinson had stayed front of house, too, moving from group to group, hovering at the edge of little clusters. She scanned the crowd, wondering if any of these people had been there on the night Kara was physically ejected from the theatre, and on her second sweep, her eye snagged on a familiar face.

*Lyall Gaines?*

He started to turn away, and it looked like he would try to duck out, but he must have realised he'd been rumbled, because he turned back and sauntered over, pasting a cocky smile on his face. 'You look surprised to see me,' he said.

'I'm surprised to see you at a psychic show—'

'Reading,' he interrupted. 'It's "a reading".'

'I'm surprised to see you at a *psychic show*,' she began again, 'when I'm still waiting for a report on those tattoos eleven hours after you said you'd deliver it.'

'I think I actually said I could give it to you *orally* in time for the morning briefing.' He paused. 'The written word is a far more demanding task mistress, isn't she?' he added, nipping the pink tip of his tongue between his upper and lower incisors.

'When can I expect it?' she asked, reflecting on how he managed to oil all his exchanges with innuendo.

He smiled. 'Relax. You'll have it by lunchtime tomorrow.'

'And the reason you're here?' Ruth asked.

'Are you interrogating me, Sergeant?'

'If that's what you want to call it.'

She kept her eyes on him, and after a moment, he shrugged.

'It's work. As an anthropologist, I have a professional interest in psychics. The human craving for a spiritual afterlife that transcends this mundane existence is cross-cultural. This –' he glanced around at the knots of people '– or versions of it, exist in every corner of the world . . .'

She let Gaines burble on while she kept an eye on Rollinson. He had his back to a small group: two women, two men and a teenage boy – family, judging by the resemblance.

'The shamans of ancient cultures from Alaska to Taiwan worked via supernatural channels,' Gaines went on. 'And shamans were often tattoo masters.'

She glanced at him and his eyes brightened.

'I thought you would find that interesting. Tattoos, supernatural insights, religion and ritual are bound up in human history and our psyche. The shamans of ancient cultures derived their power from the ancestral spirits they communicated with in dreams or visions. They have a *lot* in common with modern mediums, clairvoyants and psychics.'

'You think?'

He followed her gaze. Rollinson was staring at his smartphone, and occasionally thumbing in a few words, but he was listening so hard to the family group his ears were practically flapping.

'Shamans or charlatans. It's all about belief, Sergeant.'

Gaines watched her watching Rollinson for a while; she could feel his steady scrutiny.

'Got Mrs Hart and her "assistant" worked out, yet?' he asked.

'He's more than just the mic man,' Ruth said. 'He's watching the audience like a dog on point. I think they have some kind of code, too – and she's pretty good at cold reading.'

'Well, *you* would know.'

'Meaning?' she asked pleasantly.

'Never mind.'

She lifted her chin, indicating Rollinson. 'He's probably sending texts to Jasmine right now, feeding her a few choice facts about the bereaved family over there.'

Gaines's eyes gleamed. 'Are you disappointed?'

'I'd have to've believed in "psychic phenomena" in the first place.'

'There are more things in heaven and earth . . .'

'Yeah, more bullshit, too.'

He laughed. 'They *are* quite the double act. Daddy also haunts the bar before curtain up, gleaning little snippets they can use during the night.'

'Rollinson is Jasmine's father?'

Gaines nodded. 'Her real name is plain Jane Rollinson.'

It seemed Rollinson *père* wasn't the only family member who favoured aliases.

'I saw Jasmine take Mike's sister off for a quiet word,' Ruth said, thinking about Kara.

'Common practice,' he said. 'A punter reacts strongly to mention of someone "passing over" suddenly or violently. They hone in and extract info that the "spirit" died by suicide, a tragic accident, murder – whatever.' He eyed her, curiosity and devilment in his look. 'What do *you* think happened to Mike?'

'He kept saying he felt cold,' Ruth said. 'And they had time to talk about whether there was football in heaven. My guess is he got sick.'

'That's how I would have read it,' Gaines said.

'The charade with the hand-holding was a neat trick.'

'These people are masters of manipulation,' he agreed. 'Cynical atheist that I am, their quiet chit-chat with the dead while they stare into the grieving relative's eyes sent shivers up and down my spine. When the punter is on the point of breaking down, they'll say that the deceased has a lot to communicate, but they feel it should be done in private; or the punter's loved one is "drifting away"; or there are other voices shouting them down. Classic pressure sales tactics. They exchange details, set up a session, one session becomes two, and . . .' He spread his hands.

Ruth said, 'Do they always focus on bereavement, the dead? Or do they sometimes tap into other aspects of people's lives?'

Gaines narrowed his eyes. 'What are you thinking?'

She was thinking that Kara might have confided her fear of freezing on stage, might even have arranged a private reading, but she wasn't about to tell Gaines that.

'Could they pick up on some insecurity or trauma the person had gone through?' she asked.

'It's their stock in trade,' he said. 'Self-awareness makes the naked ape lonelier than any other on the planet. Nobody really "gets" us. And yet, here is someone who seems to read our thoughts, empathises with our pain . . . It's heady stuff.'

The bell for the second half of the performance sounded and Ruth headed towards the auditorium. Gaines shadowed her, and she glanced over her shoulder at him. 'Was there something else?'

'Where are you sitting? I could slide alongside, give you some quick and dirty tips. We could go for a drink after – compare notes.'

She smiled. 'I'm fine, thanks,' she said. 'But I'd really appreciate it if you could get that report to me by tomorrow.'

## 34

At the end of the show DS Lake flashed her ID to gain back-stage access.

Mrs Hart was seated at the mirror in her dressing room, her back to the door, while Rollinson sprawled on an armchair in a corner. As Ruth entered, he gripped the armrests and boosted himself out of the chair, blocking her view of the psychic. He seemed even taller standing so close – bulkier, too.

'Help you, love?' he said. He spoke with the same Lanca-shire accent as Jasmine, and his tone was affable, but Ruth sensed an undercurrent of violence.

'Maybe.' Ruth didn't explain further, and his smile hard-ened.

'Jasmine's just about tapped out for the night, but I can take your details,' he said. 'She'll give you a bell tomorrow – how's that?'

'As a matter of fact, it's you I wanted to see, Mr Rollinson.'

'I don't get *that* too often, now do I, Jasmine?'

Ruth watched him in silence, interested to see how he would react.

He spread his hands, the smile rigid on his face. 'Well, here I am, love.'

Still she didn't speak.

'Shall I do a twirl?'

Mrs Hart peered around her father's solid back. 'Oh – ' she said. 'Harry . . .'

He ignored her.

Ruth watched those hands, thinking how Rollinson had manhandled Kara out of the theatre. He wore a ring on the little finger of his left hand; there was something etched on the face, but she couldn't make it out.

'Nice ring,' she said, knowing he would automatically turn it over to look at it. 'A Celtic knot – symbol of the eternal cycle, isn't it?'

'What d'you want?' he demanded, the smile gone. 'Some kind of journo, are you?'

'*Harry.*' Mrs Hart tugged at his sleeve. 'Wind your neck in. This is the *police* lady who came to see me. Now shift yourself – I'm getting claustrophobic.'

He moved out of the way and Jasmine Hart stood, looking a little flustered. Normally, Ruth would let Mrs Hart's introduction stand, but she wanted to see how Rollinson responded when he was caught off-balance, so she took out her ID and formally introduced herself.

'So, what do I call you – Harry? Brian? Or is it Henry?'

His mouth twitched. Now he knew that she'd looked into his criminal past he was probably scrolling back through his recent misdemeanours to try to establish which had caught him out – but he was too good a conman to show it.

'Harry's fine,' he said. 'Now, what did you want to see me about, Sergeant?'

'Kara Grogan,' she said.

He looked blank. 'You'll have to give me a clue, love.'

She showed him the photo of Kara and he took it, frowning,

'The lass I told you about,' Mrs Hart said quietly, and there was a warning in her tone.

But it seemed Rollinson wasn't in the mood to be

cooperative; he thrust the photo back into Ruth's hand. 'You're better at faces than me, Jaz,' he said.

'Kara Grogan – the one that died,' Mrs Hart said.

'The one that was murdered,' Ruth corrected.

Mrs Hart reacted to the harshness in Ruth's tone with a melting look of sympathy, but Rollinson stiffened.

'Give us another squint at that,' he said.

She handed over the photograph again, and as he stared at the image she saw him consciously relax every muscle that had tensed at the word 'murder'. That in itself told her something: she just wasn't sure what.

'Aye,' he said after a few seconds. 'I do remember.'

'I told the sergeant you'd had to put her out of the theatre, on account of the electromagnetic interference,' Mrs Hart added, reminding him of the script they'd no doubt agreed to. 'You wanted to know what time that'd be – is that right, Sergeant?'

'That's right.'

Ruth kept her eyes on Rollinson.

'Just before the interval,' he said. 'Eight-thirty, eight forty-five – summat like that. She was very understanding. Nice lass – terrible what happened to her.'

'That's not what the video says.'

'What video would that be?'

'The one that ended up on YouTube.' Ruth took out her phone. 'I'm surprised you didn't pick up on the electromagnetic interference.'

'Oh, you're funny,' Rollinson said. His jaw was tight enough to crack a molar. 'You should be on telly, you're that funny.'

Ruth had the video ready to play, and while Rollinson viewed it, she said, 'That's Kara. Recognise her now?'

His eyes darkened.

'Doesn't look to me like she's being "understanding", Mr Rollinson,' she said, glancing at the action on-screen. 'In fact, she looks frightened.'

He chuckled, which wasn't the reaction she'd expected.

'All right, I overreacted,' he said. 'I'm under a lot of pressure at a group reading – audience expectations, Jasmine relying on me to pick up the cues and pass them on without breaking her concentration. I realised I'd gone a bit over the top, apologised to the girl. Refunded the price of her ticket. Even gave her one of Jasmine's cards – she said she wanted a private reading.'

'About what?'

'Didn't ask,' he said, cockiness firmly back in place, now. 'Didn't like to pry.'

Ruth turned to Mrs Hart.

'*Did* she come and see you?'

The woman glanced quickly at Rollinson – looking for cues, no doubt. Ruth would be sure to separate them as soon as they came to the station for interview the next day. She tilted her head, waiting for an answer.

'I don't know what you mean,' Mrs Hart said. 'Surely you don't think I had anything to do with . . .'

'Her disappearance? Why would you think that, Mrs Hart?'

She flushed. 'I thought – I mean, didn't you say she disappeared that night?'

'No,' Ruth said. 'I didn't.' Though she found it interesting that the psychic had made that assumption. 'Now, can you answer the question?'

'No. No – she never did call.'

'It's not unusual,' Rollinson said, settling comfortably again into his role as Jasmine Hart's facilitator. 'Folk get cold feet, change their minds.'

'So,' Ruth said, returning her attention to him. 'Which way did she head?'

'How d'you mean?'

'Into town, towards the docks?'

'We had a reading on,' he said. 'I didn't hang about.'

The doorman let her out of the building at ten-thirty, and Ruth stood on the step for a few minutes, watching the traffic pass. The flow went in pulses, owing to a set of traffic lights thirty yards down the road. Twice in five minutes a queue of stationary vehicles built up in front of the theatre. If Rollinson was telling the truth about throwing Kara out at around eight-thirty, it would put the student on Hanover Street at a time when traffic was even heavier as people headed into the city for a night out. There were two pubs almost opposite the theatre and a bar restaurant next door – surely someone would have seen Rollinson manhandling Kara out of the theatre? Admittedly it *was* a while ago, and minor scuffles in the city centre at that time of night weren't exactly rare, but it might be worth canvassing for witnesses. They should track down the person who had posted the video online, too.

The way home for Kara would be up the hill towards the cathedrals, the obvious route being Wood Street or Fleet Street – either of which would have taken her past bars, restaurants and clubs. More canvassing to do. But home was no haven for Kara, and from what her housemates had said, she'd become pretty much unreadable in the weeks prior to her abduction. Wouldn't she want to walk off her agitation after her set-to with Rollinson, rather than risk showing any signs of weakness back at her digs?

Ruth turned right out of the theatre into School Lane as a fine rain began to fall. The lane at this end was barely wide enough for single-file traffic, and there were double yellows all the way. It widened at Bluecoat Chambers, but that section was pedestrianised, with vehicle access controlled by rising bollards.

She pulled up the hood of her parka jacket and walked past the Old Post Office pub. The city centre had undergone a major redevelopment in 2008, but the Old Post Office had survived unchanged. It squatted opposite the sheer brick face of the Quakers' Meeting House. At the end of the pub, the road took a sharp right into an alley. The building opposite was occupied by Primark, its corners protected by zinc plating, its high walls topped with razor wire.

Ruth walked on, and discovered a set of delivery bays on the left. The filthy alley continued right, looping back on itself till it wound on Hanover Street, only a few yards along from the theatre entrance. There was no reason why Kara would come this way – more likely she would keep to the relatively well-lit lane, heading down to Paradise Street.

Retracing her steps, Ruth rounded the corner of the alley as a figure loomed out of the darkness. A man. She sidestepped, but he reached out to grab her arm. Ruth swept her right arm up to bat the hand away, simultaneously stepping forward, straight-arming him with her left, striking his chest hard with the heel of her left hand. He stumbled back two paces, twisted his ankle in a pothole and went down, bouncing off a wheelie bin on the way.

'Bloody hell, Sergeant!' It was Lyall Gaines.

'What the hell d'you think you're doing?' Ruth demanded, still on the balls of her feet, adrenaline fizzing in her veins.

'I wanted to make sure you got out of there in one piece,' he said, picking dirt from his skinned palms. 'It seems my concern was misplaced.'

Another man rounded the corner and Ruth turned to face him, keeping one eye on Gaines. *'Police!'* she yelled. *'Stay back!'*

The man held up his hands. 'I work in the pub,' he said. 'Seen you were having some bother – come to see if you needed help.'

The walls on both corners were windowless, but Ruth glanced up and spotted a security camera attached to the side of the pub. 'Thanks,' she said. 'I'm fine.'

'I can see that.' The man chuckled. 'I'll leave you to it, then.'

She hauled Gaines to his feet, walked him to the end of the alley and pointed him in the direction of Hanover Street.

'Go home,' she said. 'Do what we're paying you to do. Follow me again, and next time, I won't be so gentle.'

Ruth waited until he'd limped around the corner and disappeared from sight before she turned to gaze thoughtfully at the camera dome attached to the pub wall. School Lane reverted to open vehicle access and widened at the far end, with parking as well as passing places for delivery trucks, so it was just possible that Kara had been picked up by her abductor at that end of the lane. Walking the length of it from Hanover Street to Paradise Street, a distance of around 350 yards, she counted twelve CCTV cameras. Smiling, she fast-dialled the CSM, John Hughes. If Kara *had* been abducted on this street, it was almost certainly on camera.

## 35

*Day 10*

At six a.m. the next day, Ruth Lake was staring at the post mortem photograph of Kara Grogan. The close-up focused on a detail of one of the tattoos. It looked a lot like the Celtic knot etched on Harry Rollinson's signet ring. She needed to talk to Gaines, but not until he'd sent in his report. A man like that would always try to take the upper hand if he snouted a weakness in the opposition. A quick browse through her favoured sources on symbolism confirmed what Gaines had already said – that the symbol often had a protective role. But she also found references to 'clarity', 'understanding', 'longevity'. It appeared these mythologies could be used to say just about anything you wanted them to.

Frustrated, she gave up and went to shower. By the time she'd finished, Gaines's report had arrived in her inbox with a formal note: 'Report on symbolism in victim tattoos, per your request.'

It rehashed what they had discussed over the phone: the symbols in his view were protective icons. There was no mention of her own suggestion that the tattoos might hint at secrets the victims had kept from those close to them. She didn't mind that – better that she had time to work on her theory.

Right now, she had Kara hiding the truth about her big film break and her fear of performing, Tali Tredwin's secret eating disorder and Jo Raincliffe's lies that she was teaching at night school when she was making a good living from stripping. It was a start, but Ruth would need a lot more than that to argue the case.

She typed a reply to Gaines, thanking him for the report, and adding a request for his thoughts on the Celtic knot on the face of Rollinson's signet ring.

By seven, she was dressed and ready to go, a cup of tea in one hand and a round of toast in the other. She turned on the radio for the breakfast news as she boxed up the case files and snapped her laptop closed.

The reporter recited the morning litany of unrest in the Middle East, government reassurances on the economy and councils rebelling against underfunding. The sport report would be up next. As she reached for the off-switch, the presenter said: 'We're just receiving news that police investigating the murder of Merseyside businesswoman Adela Faraday have arrested a thirty-seven-year-old man at the Aintree Neurosciences Centre. The man remains at the hospital under police guard. Merseyside Police have declined to comment, but we are expecting a press briefing in the next hour. Stay tuned for regular updates.'

Her hand trembled as she flicked the 'off' switch. Who else could it be but Carver?

DC Ivey's phone went straight to voicemail. She closed the call and rang John Hughes.

'I just heard it on the news,' he said, before she had the chance to speak.

'Can you find out what's going on?'

'I'll make a few inquiries, get back to you,' he said. 'Oh – and you might want to draft in a few uniforms to work on that CCTV footage you asked for – there's going to be a lot of it.'

Her heart sank for a moment – if Hughes thought *that* would be a big job, how much more work would it be tracking Kara's movements if she'd actually made it out of School Lane? She shook the gloom off. This was an opportunity: she would get the job done.

But first, she needed to see Greg Carver.

She made it to the hospital in under thirty minutes, traffic being light. The staff were quick to buzz her in, for once, and Ruth was greeted by the sour-faced nurse who had given her a hard time over her late call to the unit two nights before.

'This isn't necessary,' she said.

Ruth followed her line of sight to the police constable guarding Carver's door. 'I know. How is he?'

The nurse frowned. 'Not great.'

Ruth took a moment to use the antiseptic gel dispenser, sizing the young constable up as she rubbed her hands. He was in his early twenties, soft-featured, half asleep, slumped in his seat; the newspaper he was reading covered his lap like a rug.

She went straight to Carver's door, feeling the nurse's eyes at her back.

The constable jerked upright. 'Excuse me,' he said.

She gripped the door handle and turned it.

He stood, cascading the newssheets to the floor. 'Hey!'

Behind her, the nurse shushed, and he raised both hands, apologising, then resumed in a whisper: 'What are you *doing*?'

'Visiting my friend,' Ruth answered, keeping her voice low and reasonable.

'He's not allowed visitors.'

'Oh,' she said, still pleasant. 'Doctor's orders?'

'It's a police matter.'

She looked around her. 'But this is a hospital.'

'Look, *madam*, he's under arrest.'

'My understanding is he was released on court bail,' she said. John Hughes had got back to her with some useful information on the drive over. 'Which means he's not in custody. Under the terms of the Bail Act, 1976, he's free to see who he likes – provided that doesn't breach the conditions of his bail.' She paused, looked into his face. 'Do you happen to know the conditions of his bail, Constable?'

The young officer blinked rapidly, but before he could gather his wits to speak, she launched a new attack.

'Of course, under the terms of the Police and Criminal Evidence Act 1984, any person arrested may not be held under police detention for more than twenty-four hours without being charged. So, it's fairly important that we're clear on whether Detective Chief Inspector Carver is detained pending further inquiries, under arrest or has been released on bail. Because if he's still under arrest, and he *hasn't* been charged, the PACE clock is ticking.'

The constable drew himself to his full height and attempted a sneer. 'What are you, then, his lawyer?' he said.

She took out her warrant card and held it next to her face so he could get a good look. 'Like I said – he's a friend.'

'Oh.' He flushed. 'Sorry, Sarge. He *was* released on bail, but I'm under orders not to let anyone except medical staff past.'

She pinned him with a look. 'Check the bail conditions,' she said. 'I'll wait.'

He hesitated and she tapped her watch. 'Tick-tock, Constable.'

He looked torn. 'You know I can't use mobile or radio comms in here,' he said, sounding injured.

The nurse appeared at his elbow. 'You can use the landline at the nurses' station,' she said.

'I think I'll just stay here till my shift changeover,' he said, eyeing them both as if he suspected them of collusion.

'Your call,' Ruth said. 'But I'm clocking every minute you refuse me access, which will mean a minute less of interview time for the grownups when they come to ask their questions.'

He stood square in front of her, but his feet were angled at forty-five degrees the other way: in his head, he was already halfway over to the nurses' station.

She jerked a thumb over her shoulder, indicating the room behind her. 'And if he gets it into his head to sue, it could kick up a shit storm that will follow you like a bad smell for the next ten years of your career.'

He sucked his teeth, keeping his eyes on Ruth, but after a few seconds his shoulders drooped a fraction. 'Where's that phone?' he said.

Carver was sitting in the armchair. He looked up when she came in, and Ruth saw pain and disbelief in his eyes.

'We need to make this fast,' she said. 'I don't know how long I've got.'

'DCI Jansen made the arrest,' he said. 'He said they found evidence of me in Adela's flat.'

'Where?' she asked.

'On a toothbrush, hairs in the plughole.'

'Did they take buccal swabs, fingerprints?' she asked. The arrest would have given police the right to take a confirmatory DNA sample from Carver.

He nodded. 'Both. There was a fingerprint on a whisky glass.'

He stared at his hands, turning them over as if he didn't recognise them. 'How did they get my DNA?' he said, half to himself.

Carver had refused to give a voluntary sample for comparison earlier in the investigation, and Ruth thought he meant that.

'There was *plenty* of DNA to be had in your flat,' she said, picturing the armchair, soaked with his blood. 'CSIs collected samples. And as soon as you were linked to Adela Faraday, your shooting and Adela's became a joint investigation. Didn't they explain this to you?'

'Ruth, I've had a knock on the head, but I still know the rules of evidence,' he said with some of his old fire. 'What I *don't* know is how my DNA was in Adela Faraday's flat in the first place. I was never there.'

She raised an eyebrow, and Carver said, 'I swear I'm telling you the truth.'

'How can you be sure? You've admitted you can't remember what happened after Adela kicked you out of her hotel room that night.'

'I didn't know who Adela Faraday *was*, much less where she lived – how would I even find her?'

'You argue, she throws you out, you hang around the bar getting drunker and meaner. You see her leave, follow her home . . .'

He shook his head. 'No. No . . .'

'There are *hours* unaccounted for on your timeline.'

'I know,' he said. 'But look – those flashbacks I told you about? I keep having them. I'm in my sitting room. There's a figure – a shadow—'

'I told you, that was *me*,' she said.

'Just consider it seriously for a moment,' he said. 'What if someone else *was* in the room? What if it was *someone else* who held a gun on me, shot me?'

'Then I destroyed evidence that might have led them to the shooter,' she said. She was tormented by the thought; but even more by the possibility that Carver had shot Adela and then turned the gun on himself.

'Where's the gun?' he said, as if he'd read her thoughts.

'The gun?' she repeated, giving herself time to collect her thoughts.

'You said you found a gun by my chair. You kept it, didn't you?'

She didn't answer.

'I know you did. Where is it now?'

*He wants me to get rid of it.* 'What if I said it was at the bottom of the Mersey?'

He smiled. 'Once a CSI, Ruth . . .' At first, she thought he was reading her body language, but then she realised he was looking at the air around her.

When she still refused to answer, he said: 'I think you kept it. I think you did your best to preserve any evidence there might be on that weapon.'

'It's safe,' she conceded. A part of her would always be a CSI – he was right about that much. And being a good one, she had wrapped the pistol in printer paper to preserve the evidence, and she had sealed it up in a new evidence box the first chance she got. She lifted her chin, challenging him. 'Forensically safe,' she added, challenging him, letting him know that although she had lied for him, she would not cover up a murder.

262

'You need to run forensics on it,' Carver said.

Ruth blinked; she hadn't expected that. 'Because . . .'

'Whoever shot me might have left some trace on the weapon. And even if they didn't, it might be registered – or ballistics could lead us to the shooter.'

'What d'you expect me to do? Drop the weapon off at DCI Parsons's office and tell him, "I'm afraid I forgot to log this"?' She threw her hands wide and let them drop to her side. 'I've already put my career on the line for you – why would I dig an even deeper hole to bury myself in?'

'You don't need to implicate yourself,' he insisted. 'You're resourceful – you could find a way to—'

'To *what*? "Discover" evidence I stole from a crime scene?'

'I know it's asking a lot, but . . .' He rubbed a hand over his face. 'What if . . .' He closed his eyes, briefly and started again. 'What if I did kill her? What if it *was* me? Would you want to protect me?'

'No,' she said without hesitation.

'So find a way. *Please*, Ruth – I can't live with myself, not knowing.'

The police constable put his head around the door few moments after Ruth left.

'Where is she?' he said.

'Who?'

His police guard swore under his breath, but retreated, closing the door after him, and Carver slumped back in his chair, exhausted. Faking confusion had become easier over time, but he wasn't sure if he'd got better with practice, or if his mind was really slipping.

263

The door opened briskly, and he braced himself for the constable's reappearance.

It was his physiotherapist.

'I'm sorry,' he said. 'I can't do this now.'

She tried to persuade him, telling him that it was important to work on his problem areas.

'I'll get better anyway,' he said. 'You said so yourself.'

'*Eventually*,' she said. 'But not as fast, and not as strong.'

He took a breath, but she held up her hand to forestall him. 'I know you want to return to work. You're at the stage when your muscles are mending, but if the fibres don't heal in alignment, you could experience weakness. The scar tissue—'

'I know,' Carver interrupted. 'I appreciate what you're doing, but I just . . . I can't. Not now.'

She regarded him quietly for a few moments, but seemed to make up her mind that it wasn't worth pushing, and left him, promising that she would try again later.

Five minutes after that, Dr Pendinning appeared at his door.

'Look,' Carver said. 'I've heard all the arguments – I know she's right, but I'm not in the mood to co-operate right now. Okay?'

'Fine with me,' she said, adding after a pause, 'Whatever you're talking about. It's fine.'

'Oh. I just turned the physio away,' Carver said. 'I thought you were—'

'Did you throw anything at her?'

He glanced up, but the smile in her eyes made it impossible to be angry. 'Only words,' he said.

'Well, I'd call that progress.'

He suppressed a smile. 'So, why *are* you here?'

The psychologist came into the room and dragged a chair away from the wall to sit next to him. 'I heard a police delegation had been in to see you,' she said, adding with a tiny lift of one shoulder, 'And I saw the news . . .'

He closed his eyes with a sigh.

' . . . And thought you might want to talk.'

She didn't say anything after that, but Carver sensed her quietly waiting, ready to listen, and after a while he realised he was talking.

He admitted that he was about as low as he'd been since the night of the shooting. That the few instances he did remember were disjointed and confused.

'The hallucinations,' she said.

'That's just it . . .'

' . . . You don't know if they *are* hallucinations.'

He opened his eyes. She always seemed to know what he was thinking.

She didn't speak for a long while, and to Carver it seemed she was struggling to come to a decision.

At last she said, 'I want you to try something. Settle back in your chair and close your eyes again.'

He did as he was asked.

'What do you see?'

'Eyes,' he said.

'Whose?'

'They're tattoos – on the victims.'

'The victims?'

'I was looking at the post mortem photographs before I was shot.'

'How soon before?' Her voice was soft, no more than a murmur.

He shook his head. 'I can't remember. I couldn't bring myself to look at Kara Grogan's file.'

Carver recalled he'd reached for it, and for a few seconds, he was there, in the grotto. Kara's body, glittering in the frost. Eyes staring out from her flesh. *Emma*, he thought and his heart rate kicked up a notch. *It wasn't Emma. You know it wasn't.* Even so, he couldn't open the file. Remembered thinking. *No, not yet.*

'I looked through the other files, made notes. Kept going back to Kara's, but I couldn't . . . I just couldn't . . .' He forced himself to breathe slowly.

'All right, she said. 'Did you pause, make some fresh coffee, perhaps?'

'I needed a drink,' he said. 'Poured a whisky, brought it back to the kitchen.'

'But you were in the sitting room when you were shot,' she said.

'How did I get there?'

Silence.

He remembered going to the sitting room. The curtains stood open and he saw in the pale glow of the streetlights that it was snowing again. He drew the curtains and crossed to the cupboard squeezed into the niche on one side of the fireplace, reached inside to take out a new bottle of Jura single malt and one of the two good whisky glasses he owned. He cracked open the bottle, poured himself a large drink, and set it back in the cupboard, taking his first swallow of whisky, savouring the burn. He paused a moment, wanting more, trying to reason with himself.

*You don't need this – you don't need to get rat-arsed.* But it had been a bad night; he was frustrated with the case and angry with Adela – Anna, as he knew her then.

So he opened the cupboard again and grabbed the bottle. The framed photo of Emma stood on top of the cupboard, next to a few Christmas cards. He switched the bottle and glass to his right hand, scooped up the photograph with the other, and carried the lot through to the kitchen.

'I took the bottle with me,' he said at last. 'There was no reason to go back in the sitting room . . . you see, I usually passed out over the files.' He feels no shame telling her this. It's an exploration, without judgement or shame attached to it. 'But for some reason I *was* there.'

'Okay,' she said. 'You're in the sitting room. What do you see?'

'Nothing. It's dark. I can smell . . .' He takes a breath, exhales through his mouth to control the roiling sickness in his gut; the stench of whisky is nauseating. 'I see shadows?' He hears the question in his tone.

'Look into the shadow. There's light from the streetlamp outside. Find the shadow, and look into it,' she says.

He hears a buzz – a *zzzzzzz-ip!* of sound. He can't move. His breath comes in short gasps.

'You're safe,' she says.

*I'm paralysed.*

Adela's face looms out of the shadows. Afraid. *No – that was at the hotel.*

*Did I make her afraid?*

'Can you tell me what you see?'

A flash. A burst of pain. *Can't move. Can't speak.*

'You're safe. Tell me what you see.'

He sees Ruth, her face close to his. She looks into his eyes and he sees recognition there. She swears softly and his muscles are released, free to move again.

\*    \*    \*

Carver opened his eyes. He took a huge, agonised breath, the inrush of air tearing the back of this throat.

'You're safe,' Dr Pendinning said again. 'Tell me what you saw.'

'Adela. She was afraid. I couldn't move. Couldn't breathe. Then Ruth came.'

'You remember Ruth coming into your apartment?'

He thought about it. 'No.'

'Was Adela in your apartment?'

'No.' He felt sure of that. 'Only the shadow.'

'Did you look into the shadow?'

He nodded.

'What did you see?'

'Nothing. Only darkness.'

'And this is what you see when you have the hallucinations?'

'No, they're . . .' He wanted to say terrifying, but pride made him change it to, 'disturbing.'

She gave him a comical look. 'And the shadow, the paralysis, the feeling of suffocation *aren't* disturbing?'

He gave a weak smile, despite himself. A sudden thought struck him and he stared at the doctor. 'I just realised something,' he said.

She said nothing, but maintained an expression of quiet interest.

'They are two different things: the pictures that keep replaying in my head are *memories* – flashbacks, whatever. The hallucinations are a reaction to what happened to me – but they're not real – at least, not in the usual meaning of the word.'

'And what you see in the flashbacks *is* real?'

'I think . . .' *Ruth, her eyes dark, angry. The shadow, ghosting through the room. A flash, like a punch to his chest.* 'Yes. I think so.'

'Does it help to know that?'

*I can't stop them, and I can't shut them out. But I can't make sense of them, either. Does it help to distinguish one kind of mental torment from another?*

'I don't know,' he admitted with a helpless shrug. 'The neurologist told me the auras I see around people are part of my recovery.'

'I think he probably meant auras in a different sense,' she said. 'Smells, visual disturbances such as patches of grey or sparkles of light, buzzing sounds, maybe. But you say you see them around *people*?'

Carver nodded.

'Um, okay . . . Do they change, or does everyone have a particular colour?'

'I think it depends on their mood. Ruth's is orange most of the time – she's angry with me.'

She put her hand to her lips and he had the sense she was controlling excited laughter. 'You might just be describing a form of synaesthesia,' she said.

'What, like seeing music as colours?'

'That's one form.'

'Did the head trauma cause it?'

'Possibly. Though it's very rare. You knew what I meant by synaesthesia – did you experience it as a child, perhaps?'

'No.' But as he said it, Carver had a vague memory of getting muddled about numbers and colours in junior school. He still thought of yellow when he saw the word Wednesday.

She opened the door into the corridor. 'Do any of the people out there have an aura?'

He watched for a second. 'The nurse over at the desk. She's purple.'

'Do you know what that means?'

He shook his head.

'Will it go away?'

She smiled. 'Why would you want it to?' Before he could frame an answer, she said, 'What colour is my aura?'

He peered at the light around her. She looked pale, more tired than usual, but her skin still retained a flawless, almost polished quality that made him want to reach out and touch it. *Inappropriate*, he told himself. The mood swings, the impulsivity, the inappropriate thoughts – his neurologist had told him that they were another consequence of either the concussion, or the oxygen deprivation his brain had suffered after he was shot. He concentrated for a good sixty seconds on the psychologist's face, but all he saw was white light reflected from the LEDs overhead.

'You don't have an aura,' he said.

She laughed. 'Well, you might break the news more gently.' Then in more serious humour: 'You think Ruth is angry with you?' She seemed to ask out of genuine curiosity.

'I know it.'

She watched him solemnly for a second. 'It's a rare and wonderful thing to know what another person is really thinking,' she said. 'Why is she angry?'

'Because she thinks I'm partly to blame for what happened.'

'Does it matter what she thinks?'

He nodded.

'Because . . .?'

'Because . . .' He sighed. 'She's right. Because she's a friend. Because she covered for me and protected me when I didn't deserve it.'

'Does she know you feel this way?'

He looked into her eyes. 'Is that a trick question?'

## 36

Ruth checked the time. The psychic calling himself 'Shadowman' still hadn't been in touch, and the business centre where his phone messages were being routed was at the north end of town. If she was quick, she could stop by on the way in and still make it to work in time for the morning briefing.

The receptionist was medium height, brown hair, dark eyes, in her mid-twenties. She wasn't keen to share clients' details, until Ruth explained that she was investigating Kara Grogan's murder. She called up the file immediately on her computer.

'Here you are . . . The account is registered to a Dr Lyall Gaines.'

*Gaines* was Shadowman?

The receptionist was looking at her as if she was waiting for an answer.

'What did you say?'

'His address,' she said. 'D'you want it?'

'Thanks, I've got it,' Ruth said.

'You don't think he's—'

'Thanks,' Ruth said again, cutting off the question. 'This is helpful.'

She waited until she was in the car before calling his mobile.

'Good morning,' she said. 'Am I speaking to Shadowman?'

A pause. 'Ah.'

At least he didn't bother denying it.

'You masquerade as a psychic?'

'I thought we'd agreed they all "masquerade" on some level.'

'So, the website is a sham.'

'Ye-es . . .' Apparently he found the question naive.

'I don't get it,' she said. 'What could you possibly hope to gain from this?'

'I told you last night, psychic belief is one of my areas of interest as an anthropologist. I hope to "gain" knowledge.'

She hated the way Gaines quoted her words back at her as though he found them funny, but she knew he did it to rattle her. *So calm down*.

'What I meant,' she said evenly, 'is how can you *use* your findings when your approach is ethically flawed?'

He didn't reply at first.

'Dr Gaines?'

She heard him take a breath. 'I suppose that in *your* limited sphere one would be required to take a rigid view of right and wrong.'

The stiffness of his tone told her that she had hit a nerve.

'The police are expected to obey the law, yes,' Ruth said, injecting a hint of a humour into her own tone.

'Quite,' he said. 'However, in the study of human behaviour, a degree of flexibility is required. In fact,' he added, 'many academics, like myself, feel that slavishly following ethical codes actually *stifles* research. I could cite half a dozen studies last year alone—'

'I think I can work out the difference between right and wrong without reading it in a journal,' Ruth said.

'Sarcasm, Sergeant Lake? I'd thought you were above that. You have to understand that sometimes you need to make compromises if you want to get the job done.'

'You mean engaging in dodgy practices – hiding your real purpose from unwitting subjects?'

'Nobody *made* them complete the form,' he said, his tone pitying. 'And the facts speak for themselves – in the space of just eight weeks, nearly *three thousand* people have completed the questionnaire. Can you imagine that happening if I'd complied with the narrow definition of "informed consent"? It would've killed this project. As it is, an astonishing *two-thirds* of respondents revealed personal details about themselves knowing – *knowing* – that they were talking to a so-called "psychic". People will share their darkest secrets with a *total stranger*, apparently in denial of the fact that this same person will later claim to have insight into their psyche and their lives. Why? Because they're convinced that the stranger who is asking them all these questions *already* knows their innermost thoughts and feelings. And they are convinced that this person – this "psychic" whom they have never met – can provide the peace and reassurance they crave, freeing them from questions and doubts that have tormented them for years.'

'All that proves is how desperate they are.'

He laughed, mocking the censure in her tone. '*That*, my dear lady, is ... the point. This entire field experiment was designed to demonstrate just how vulnerable people are to exploitation.'

'Demonstrating vulnerability by exploiting it. Doesn't that bother you?'

'It's research.' He sounded weary now. 'You have to divorce yourself from feelings.' He sighed. 'Well, I didn't expect you to understand. Not really ... Suffice to say it's legitimate, valid, replicable research, with persuasive results. I'll send you a copy, when it's published.'

'Can't wait.' Ruth ended the call, wondering if Kara Grogan had completed his questionnaire. Wondering if he had been in the audience the night Kara attended Jasmine Hart's last session at the Epstein Theatre. Wondering if maybe Dr Gaines had followed Kara out of the theatre the night she vanished, to "make sure she got out in one piece".

## 37

DS Lake presented Gaines's findings at the morning briefing. As soon as she'd ended her call to the anthropologist she had emailed Doctor Yi, the forensic psychologist who put forward Gaines's name to the inquiry team, asking him to contact her urgently. She was tempted to bring up her own theory about the women keeping secrets, but decided to wait until she'd spoken to Harry Rollinson and Jasmine Hart. Before she'd left the theatre the previous night, she had asked them to come to police headquarters to make a formal statement, and they were scheduled to come in at nine-thirty.

Parsons was distracted and distant, the team subdued, but they cheered up when she told them about the CCTV footage from around the theatre, and DCI Parsons even managed a 'well done', though it seemed grudging.

He paused on his way out at the end of the session. 'My office,' he said quietly. 'Five minutes.'

*He's heard about my visit to Carver.* She nodded, but carried on gathering up her presentation material, only sneaking a look at him as he walked through the door. He looked more thoughtful than angry.

DCI Jansen was waiting with Parsons in his office when she arrived.

'Would you like to account for your behaviour at the hospital earlier this morning?' Parsons asked.

She responded with a bland, 'Sir?'

Jansen butted in. 'DCI Parsons is referring to your cosy little chat with Carver.'

She gave him the puzzled-but-helpful look. 'I've been visiting DCI Carver most days since he was shot, sir,' she said.

'On *this* occasion, he had a police guard whom *you* gave orders to stand down,' Jansen said.

'No, sir,' she said. 'I drew the constable's attention to the Bail Act, 1976 and Police And Criminal Evidence Act 1984, and since he was unsure of the terms of bail, I advised him to seek clarification.'

'You sneaked into the room while he was on the phone.'

'If I breached DCI Carver's bail conditions, I apologise, sir,' she said.

Jansen's face darkened. 'You should have asked permission,' he said through clenched teeth.

'I wasn't aware I needed it sir.'

'That'll *do*, DS Lake,' Parsons said.

She bowed her head, accepting the chastisement.

'If Carver made an admission of guilt, you are obliged to say,' Jansen warned.

She thought about it, and decided it wouldn't hurt to give him a few details. 'He said he couldn't understand how you found his DNA at Adela's flat, since he was never there.'

Jansen scoffed, but Ruth continued. 'He also said that until he saw it on the news, he didn't even know Adela's real name.'

'You expect me to believe that DCI Carver – the man who at the time was leading one of the UK's most high-profile inquiries – didn't do a background check on the woman he was shagging?'

She looked squarely at Jansen. 'You don't know him, sir. So, no, I don't expect you to believe it. But I *do* know him, and I know he wouldn't misuse police resources to look into a woman he was having casual sex with.'

Jansen laughed. 'This is priceless. Is this the same Greg Carver who had a duplicate file on the Thorn Killer victims? I say "had" because that's gone. And *where* has it gone?'

Ruth's mind flashed to the box stashed in her spare bedroom. *He's not accusing you – wait him out.* She lowered her gaze and said nothing.

'I'll say it for you, shall I?' Jansen said. 'The Thorn Killer took it.'

'I'm not sure that's the case, sir,' she said, careful not to let her relief show.

He spread his hands. 'If not the Thorn Killer, then who?'

'Whoever shot DCI Carver.'

Jansen stared at her. 'You're saying the shooter *wasn't* the Thorn Killer?'

'I'm sure of it.'

'Based on what evidence?'

'It's not his MO,' she said.

'Oh,' said Jansen, 'Based on a negative, then.'

'That's pretty thin, DS Lake,' Parsons said. 'Do you have anything more substantial to support your claim?'

He seemed to be on her side, which only made things more difficult, because she had the gun – the best evidence they were likely to find. She couldn't think of a way to give it to them without implicating herself.

'No, sir,' she said at last. 'But . . .'

She pictured Carver's flat when she'd found him. The whisky bottle dropped and rolled. The gun. The stench of whisky and blood and gunsmoke. The sense of something not being quite right . . . Suddenly, she had it.

'There was no glass.'

'What?'

'The whisky glass you found at the Faraday murder scene,' she said. 'Is it Waterford crystal, cut glass?'

'What the hell has that got to do with anything?' Jansen said.

'I think it might have been taken from Carver's flat.'

'This is a diversionary tactic,' Jansen said.

'Maybe so,' Parsons said. 'But I want to hear it.'

'When I found DCI Carver, there was an empty bottle, but no whisky glass by his chair.'

'He'd downed the best part of a bottle of Scotch,' Jansen said. 'D'you think he'd be particular about swilling it from his favourite crystal, for God's sake?'

'I do, sir.' She appealed to Parsons. 'Look, it's true that DCI Carver had been drinking hard since Kara Grogan's body came to light—'

'*And the rest*,' Jansen said.

'But whenever I saw him drinking at home,' she forged on, 'he *always* drank from one of two Waterford crystal glasses. They were his father's – a family heirloom.'

She stared at Parsons, willing him to believe her, but he seemed doubtful. She couldn't blame him: she herself had been so convinced Carver had tried to kill himself that she hadn't properly assessed the scene.

'Ruth,' Parsons said, 'I know you want to help Carver, but—'

'Did you find his prints anywhere else in the flat?'

'His DNA was all over the place,' Jansen said.

'But only one fingermark,' she said, 'on an item that could have been brought in from outside.'

Jansen seemed frankly incredulous. 'You think he was *framed*?'

279

'Is one of the glasses missing from his flat?' she demanded.

'Even if it were, that wouldn't prove a thing,' he said.

'It would be suggestive,' she countered. 'And a forensic analysis of any residue in Adela's glass could identify the whisky.'

'Which Ms Faraday, along with thousands of other house-holders, probably kept in her drinks cabinet.'

'*Probably*. But you don't *know* that, do you?'

'Detective Sergeant *Lake*.' Parsons was glaring at her and she realised she'd raised her voice.

'I'm sorry, sir. But isn't it worth considering that whoever murdered Adela tried to put Carver in the frame for it?'

'That being the case, why didn't your mystery man leave the gun at Carver's flat?' He cocked his head. 'No brilliant insights, Sergeant?'

She couldn't answer.

'If Carver is innocent, why is he refusing to cooperate with my inquiry?' he demanded.

'He's confused,' she said. 'His memory for that night is beginning to come back, but it's patchy; he can't make sense of it. He thinks you've already made your mind up, and he's worried you'll fit the facts to your theory.'

'While you're entirely impartial,' Jansen sneered.

'I'm just trying to get to the truth,' she said, trying hard to ignore the voice in her head that said, *You hypocrite. You damned lying hypocrite. You'll get to the truth as long as it doesn't involve admitting you took the gun.*

## 38

The corridor was busy with people heading out on jobs by the time Ruth made her way to the interview suite. Harry Rollinson and Jasmine Hart should have arrived by now.

DC Ivey had just come out of the Carver/Faraday Major Incident Room, and when he saw her, she expected him to duck straight back inside, but he gave her a steady look and glanced across to the fire exit. She nodded, letting him go ahead of her, making a quick diversion to her own MIR to pick up her list of questions for the interview.

The stairwell was emptying, but a few people lingered, exchanging gossip. She slowed her pace to allow the laggers to find their way out, then continued down the stairs, but there was no sign of the detective constable, and it wasn't till she started back up that she realised he'd headed up to the floor above the incident rooms.

'I spoke to the surgeon who operated on DCI Carver,' he said. 'There was no glass in his hair. But he said the A&E team at the Royal had checked for head wounds on arrival, so I had a word with the charge nurse on duty the night he was brought in. There was no obvious head wound, but the CT scan showed up a concussion, so she took another look and found what she described as a fine "glittery particulate" in his hair.'

'Mirror shards,' Ruth said. 'Why wasn't this in their report when they shipped him out to Aintree? I mean, don't they have a handover procedure?'

He lifted one shoulder. 'Christmas and New Year, "glittery particulates" means "party glitter". She said she didn't think that much about it. It was a bad night at A&E, what with all the snow, and . . .' He shrugged. 'She forgot.'

'So there's no physical evidence and no written record that DCI Carver was assaulted prior to the shooting.'

He dipped his head. 'Sorry.'

'No, I appreciate you telling me,' she said. 'Does DCI Jansen know?'

'I was on my way to tell him when I saw you.'

'Thanks for the heads-up, Tom.'

'No problem. He's *really* pissed off with you, by the way.'

'Boy, do I know it.'


Rollinson was a different man to the one who had tried to intimidate her the previous night. He interlinked his fingers on the table top and smiled warmly as she came through the door. The ring was missing from his pinkie finger.

She looked into his face as she cautioned him and explained that the interview would be recorded.

'Right-oh,' he beamed. 'Let's get on with it, shall we?'

Ruth smiled. 'Well, you're in a good mood. I wouldn't have suspected you were a morning person, Mr Rollinson.'

Rollinson threw back his head and gave a booming laugh. 'Aye, sorry about that, Sergeant. I can be a bit grumpy after a show,' he said. 'But I'm a cuddly teddy bear when you get to know me.'

She went through the questions she had asked the night before, and he answered them without deviation from his previous recitation. The only difference today was that he was positively *seething* with good humour.

Another detective was interviewing Jasmine Hart, guided by Ruth's prepared questions and warned of the psychic's cold-reading ability. She was in no doubt that when she compared the interview recordings later, father and daughter would speak with one voice. Harry Rollinson's protestations that he didn't know what had happened to Kara after the gig would be echoed by Jasmine, and each would alibi the other for the hours up to midnight on the night in question.

Looking into Rollinson's jolly, jowly face smiling for the videocam, it would be easy to mistake him for an avuncular fellow. Ruth knew that he was a crook because she had read his PNC file. Rollinson had successfully conned scores of victims out of money on scam investments, dealt fake cheques, claimed Social Security benefits he wasn't entitled to – in effect, made a dishonest living in whatever way he could. She also knew that he was dangerous and violent, because he had served twelve months of an eighteen-month sentence for ABH. The complainant, a female reporter investigating one of his scams, had quit journalism, installed video intruder alarms at her home and rarely went out after dark.

Hearing him express concern for Kara Grogan ('poor lass'), seeing him shake his head sadly at the cruelty in the world, anyone who didn't have access to the facts – a juror, say – might conclude that although his lifestyle was unorthodox, here was a genuine man who helped his daughter to help the bereaved. But when Ruth looked into his smiling eyes, she saw the bruised and bloody face of the journalist Rollinson had left broken and traumatised.

'Sorry you've wasted your time, love,' he said. 'But like I said, when Kara left the theatre, she was in good health. What befell her afterwards, well . . .' He stared into her eyes. 'You know how it is: let your guard down for one split second –' he snapped his fingers '– your life changes for ever.'

The hairs on the back of Ruth's neck prickled. He'd put a slight emphasis on the word, 'you', and a chip of flint gleamed dully in his eye for a moment so brief she wondered if she'd actually seen it: '*You* know . . . one split second . . .' Ruth had first-hand experience of split-second decisions and the disasters that followed. She knew that a second was all it took, and she wondered how much Rollinson knew.

Playing the video recording back later, he would appear affable, if a little bluff. You had to be in the room with him to feel the implied threat in his words.

John Hughes was waiting for her in the Major Incident Room after she'd wrapped up and sent Rollinson and his daughter on their way.

'I wasn't expecting to see you,' she said.

He handed her a set of DVDs, each individually evidence-labelled and sealed inside a jewel case. 'The first of the CCTV recordings from School Lane. Those were the easy ones. We're going to have to clone some of the DVR hard drives, so it'll take a bit longer to transfer the data onto portable media. Looks like we've got a few we won't be able to download, so we'll have to seize the original equipment. There's a hell of a lot, Ruth.'

She saw where he was heading: 'Parsons has asked for additional bodies to handle the work,' she said.

'When?'

'It might take a day or two.'

'You're going to do it yourself, aren't you?'

She raised one shoulder and let it drop. 'I can make a start.'

'You'd better have a bottle of eye drops to hand, then.'

'I'll do that,' she said, knowing he wasn't a joking.

'Oh, and we tracked down the guy who uploaded the video of Kara at Mrs Hart's psychic performance.' He paused and she knew that this was the real reason for his visit.

'Well, don't keep me in suspense,' she said, for once not caring if her excitement showed.

'He said would we like the full recording?'

She grinned. '*Would* we?'

'I've arranged for a computer tech to go over to his house later this morning, to be sure there's no chance of any quibbles over the data retrieval,' he said. 'I'll send it to you as soon as it's ready.'

Ruth cracked the first evidence box and settled down to watch the nightlife of Liverpool pass under the all-seeing eye of the cameras. She skipped through to six p.m. on the night of the psychic reading. City centre workers and shoppers were heading home, but the numbers thinned rapidly, followed by an influx towards seven p.m. of people heading into town for the night. Some were dressed soberly in dark overcoats – couples and small groups of adults she guessed would be headed for Jasmine's psychic performance at the theatre. Kara was not among them.

Back when she was a newbie, Ruth hated getting stuck with this kind of duty. The ability to pick out a suspect from a blurry CCTV recording of a crowd was a useful asset, and her conviction rate was impressive, but spotting scrotes in the Saturday shopping crowds soon became a dull and repetitive game of 'Where's Wally?' Identifying people was a talent, a neurological quirk; reading people was where she really got her kicks,

285

and it was a relief when she found a DCI who was willing to listen, and had put her back on investigative work.

Right now, though, she was grateful that she could let the video evidence slide by, knowing that she wouldn't miss a familiar face while she mulled over her situation.

The 'glittery particles' the A&E charge nurse had seen in Carver's hair might well have been mirror fragments. Carver was a big guy. Could Adela Faraday have slammed him into a hotel mirror so hard that it smashed? Carver had held out at first, but Ruth believed him when he said that his recall of that night was confused and shifting. Was it possible that the shadowy figure he claimed to have seen in his apartment had actually shown up at the hotel? Had the fight been between Carver and the unknown man, and not between Carver and Adela? The missing whisky glass certainly pointed in that direction. Forensic checks on the gun might well complete that part of the puzzle, but she still couldn't see a way to introduce it into evidence.

Something caught her eye and she sat up, her hand going to the rewind icon on the monitor. *Kara?* The image was blurred and smeary, but it was Kara – she was sure of it. Walking west down School Lane, towards Paradise Street. She called John Hughes, gave him the evidence number, and directed him to the relevant section.

'Can the techs enhance it?' she asked.

'Just a minute.' She heard him tapping at his keyboard. 'I've got a note from the CSI who collected the recordings that this one had a lot of grime on the camera lens,' he said. 'We might be able to tweak it, but it'd only show a marginal improvement.'

Ruth rolled the DVD on, but there was nobody else with the student, and it didn't look like Kara had been followed – on this section of the street, at any rate. 'Leave it for now,' she said. 'I'll do a screen grab. If we need it cleaned up for cross-referencing, I'll get back to you.' She hung up and made a note, adding the time and position on the recording: it was 8:33 p.m. So Rollinson hadn't lied about that. She let the recording roll on in case Kara came back the same way, but she didn't.

An hour later, she switched to another disk. Different angles, different technologies; each camera would tell its own story, and maybe that would build to a narrative of what had happened to Kara that night. Time – and grainy photography – would tell. This camera was set higher than the last, on a building close to Bluecoat Chambers. The images were better quality, but the best shots were at a distance; anything closer than five yards of the thing was likely to be a clear shot of the top of a head. Clubbers, pub-goers, drunks, as well as the occasional rat, passed in three-shot bursts. Kara appeared a few seconds after 8:33 p.m., hesitated at Church Alley, then continued on, disappearing out of camera range.

Again, Ruth let the recording play on, but Kara was on her own, and she seemed fine. Ruth scrolled back to take a screen grab, still mulling over the pistol sealed in an evidence box at her home. Carver was right – she could never have tossed it – her CSI training and instincts were too strong for her to seriously contemplate destroying evidence.

*You did, when you wiped down Carver's flat*, she told herself. But destroying fingerprints was on a whole different scale to dumping a firearm into the river.

In truth, she'd regretted tampering with the scene with the first lie she'd had to tell. It was the night of the shooting; CSM John Hughes had asked how she'd gained access to Carver's, and she'd told him the place was 'wide open'. Lie had followed lie since then – and each lie, evasion or diversionary tactic had compounded her guilt.

The pistol she'd stolen from the crime scene could be the evidence they needed to solve both Carver's shooting and Adela's murder. She couldn't destroy it, and she couldn't hand it over without incriminating herself.

Twenty minutes on, as she watched the images flit across her vision, she realised that there *was* something she could do without landing herself neck-deep in trouble. DC Ivey had said that the bullet that killed Adela was a .22. But it didn't match anything on the ballistics database, which meant the gun hadn't been used in any previous recorded crime.

She was a bit rusty on firearms legislation, but she knew that the requirements for owning small arms in the UK had changed dramatically with the 1997 amendment to the Fire-arms Act. It was brought into British Law after the Dunblane massacre, when sixteen five- and six-year-old children and a teacher had been shot dead by a lone gunman. Automatic weapons had been banned entirely under the rules of the amendment, as was any weapon with a barrel less than thirty centimetres long.

Added to which, the regs said the overall length of the weapon should be no less than *sixty* centimetres; most gun enthusiasts agreed that the 1997 amendment effectively banned handguns. So, the neat little shooter she'd found at Carver's place was illegal by definition.

Of course, it *could* have started out as a UK-legal modified pistol and been *de*-modified back to its original state. Legal guns got stolen all the time, and a proportion inevitably found their way to crime scenes. But those were usually shotguns with barrels sawn down, or rifle stocks hacked down to stubs.

The handgun that Ruth had stowed in a box in her house was clean and neat; it seemed untouched. Even the serial number was intact.

So, could the gun have *belonged* to Adela? It was a well-recognised statistic that women who armed themselves with guns were more likely to be shot with their own weapons than to use them successfully in self-defence. If it was Adela's, there were two possibilities: either she had bought a 'clean' illegal weapon, or she'd had a UK-legal weapon de-modified.

Ruth took a break from the CCTV recordings and used her mobile phone to search for UK-legal handguns.

Gun clubs had come up with a novel solution to the 'sixty centimetre overall length' requirement: the pistols she found for sale as 'UK-legal' had a barrel extender at one end which you could mistake for a silencer, and an extension rod/counter-weight at the other that looked like a chunky radio aerial sticking out of the base of the grip. Which was nothing like the gun she'd found at Carver's place.

If the gun *had* been registered legally, the serial number would lead her straight to the legal owner. But she would have to log into the Police National Computer to make the search – and the electronic trail would lead straight back to her. She needed some other way to identify the owner.

A de-modification that made it seem the weapon *hadn't* been modified would take skill – and that meant contacts and money. Adela had the money, so where would she find someone who had the skills?

She picked up her smartphone again and searched for local shooting clubs, found five on Merseyside and made a note of their phone numbers.

The incident room was almost empty; even so, she moved to a distant corner to make sure she wasn't overheard placing the calls. On the fifth, she struck lucky: Ms Faraday *was* on their books, and the membership secretary she spoke to was ex-police. He knew Adela had been murdered, and was keen to help.

'Did she have any weapons registered with you?' Ruth asked. It was possible she'd used the club's guns.

'Give me a minute, I'll pull up her registration docs,' he said. 'Okay . . . I've got her with an Iver Johnson Low Mill nineteen-eleven Long Barrel Pistol – are you familiar with it?'

'Can't say I am,' she said.

'It's regulation standard,' he said. 'Twelve-inch barrel, minimum twenty-four for the overall length of the weapon – that's sixty centimetres in new money.'

The pistol Ruth had taken from Carver's flat was no more than fifteen centimetres, barrel, grip and all.

'Do you have a copy of the Firearms Certificate to hand?' she asked, keeping her tone business-like.

'Sure – I could email you a PDF, if you'd like?' he said.

'That's okay – just give me the serial number for the weapon. If we need the documentation, I'll come over and pick it up myself.'

She hung up and checked the room. Most people were out on jobs and it was almost lunchtime; she wouldn't be missed for an hour or so.

At home, Ruth double-gloved, suited and masked up. In the spare bedroom she cleaned the top of the chest of drawers using distilled water and sterile lint, then placed a sheet of white paper over the surface before taking the sealed evidence box down from the wardrobe and lowering it gently onto the paper.

*Here goes . . .*

With a scalpel, she sliced through the Sellotape seal on three sides of the box, the slight tremor in her hands vanishing after the initial incision. The weapon had a standard five-inch barrel, and an old-fashioned wood grip with an owl logo carved in the centre. The frame was stamped with the maker's name and the number '1911'. Which all looked right for Adela's gun, but the gun Adela had actually registered was technically classed as a carbine. This was no carbine.

After a few moments to catch her breath, Ruth lifted the weapon and, with infinite care, not knowing if it was loaded, gently turned it over. There was a smudge of what looked like polished aluminium on the butt of the grip, where the extension rod should be. She could see the serial number clearly stamped on the frame, just below the barrel.

It matched. No question. The gun she'd lifted from Carver's flat was Adela's.

She lowered the pistol back into the box, took another deep breath and let it go slowly.

Why was Adela's gun in Carver's apartment? Did he take it with him after he'd shot Adela? Or was Adela shot by the shadowy figure Carver claimed to have seen in his flat? Was it possible that Carver himself was shot because of his involvement with Adela?

Ten minutes later, the evidence secreted away, Ruth stood in her back yard vaping on an e-cig. Carver and Adela were both shot with a small-calibre weapon. The stats predicted that Adela been shot with her own gun, but the only way to find out was to run ballistics on the weapon – and that was not going to happen.

She breathed vapour into the cold January air. She could nudge DC Ivey towards the gun club – tell him she had just followed a hunch. But the Faraday team might already have checked if she was a gun owner. And what good would it do anyway? They needed the serial number for a definitive match, and that brought Ruth full circle back to the fact that she was in possession of vital evidence she could not release to the investigation.

Her phone buzzed on the kitchen work surface, startling her.

'Where the hell are you?' It was DCI Parsons.

'Lunch break, sir.'

'Well, isn't that nice for you?'

'What's up?' she said, damned if she would apologise for taking an hour's break in a twelve-hour day.

'Gaines just rang,' he said. 'He says that he's found a hidden message in the tattoos.'

Hope fizzed in her blood, and she headed inside, locking the back door and hurrying towards the front of the house.

'A symbol, he says, which is common to many cultures, and is used to represent secrets,' Parsons went on.

She slowed as she stepped out onto the street. 'Let me guess: the Eye of Horus, Eye of Providence.'

'He *said* he'd discussed it with you – why you didn't bring it to my attention at the briefing?'

*All credit to you, Gaines*, she thought. *You blindsided me with this little manoeuvre.*

'He didn't think it was worth pursuing when we discussed it,' she said, feeling it was pointless getting into an argument over who had come up with the idea.

'Well, he does now. And so do I. We need to look at the victims again, see if there's anything they might have been hiding. The ex-teacher was working as a stripper, wasn't she?'

'Jo Raincliffe, sir. Yes,' Ruth said. 'And Tali Tredwin hid an eating disorder from her family. Kara—'

'You've been investigating this, and didn't see fit to mention it to me?'

She picked up her car keys and slipped the latch on the front door. 'Just looking over the files, trying to see connections, sir.'

'This isn't a TV quiz show, it's a major investigation, Sergeant Lake,' he growled. 'I want you back at the office, and I want everything you've got on this lead.'

'Sir.'

'*Everything*,' he repeated.

The killer watches as DS Ruth Lake leaves her house. She is in the process of finishing a call, and as she slips her phone into the pocket of her overcoat, she is deep in thought – swathed in it, *layered* in it.

*I would relish the chance to peel back those layers, uncover the truths you hide.*

The detective passes by without so much as a second glance. *Don't you feel my eyes on you?*

Thirty minutes before, the detective had appeared at her front bedroom window. As she reached to draw the curtains, she was wearing pale blue nitrile gloves. What could she have in her home that would warrant crime scene get-up?

*Secrets, Ruth. So many secrets.*

Now, minus the gloves, the detective sits in her car. Minutes tick by. When she finally turns on the ignition, she executes a quick turn and guns the engine.

Quandary: follow DS Lake, or discover what she's hiding? Torn, the killer watches her drive away. The tail lights of her car flash like Morse code as she brakes hard at the junction. The phone call seems to have rattled her. Lake revs the engine aggressively, and the decision is made: anything that breaks through Ruth Lake's armour-plated veneer of imperturbability is too tempting to miss. Her house will still be there in an hour, or two, or three, and anyway, it will be easier to gain access under cover of darkness.

## 39

Dr Lyall Gaines owned a big Victorian house at the re-gentri-
fied end of Ullet Road, not far from Sefton Park. Set well back
from the street, the house was hidden behind a four-foot sandstone wall topped by a smartly clipped beech hedge. Ruth
parked her car on the street and walked through two massive
wooden gates onto the driveway.

Many of these grand houses had fallen into near dereliction
in the 1980s and '90s, but the new millennium had brought the
wealthy middle class back into the area in search of restoration
projects they could reinvent as homes with 'character'. This
place had it in spades, with a steeply angled roof and ornate
finials, bay windows, a gothic-style front door, and what looked
like genuine antique tiles on the top step; all it lacked was a
turret.

A BMW saloon was parked in the drive next to a Lexus
SUV, and the sweet aroma of burning wood wafted from the
back garden. She rang the doorbell, half-expecting Westmin-
ster chimes to ring out through the house, surprised to hear
what sounded like an old-fashioned electric bell.

After a minute, she rang again, and went around to the side
of the house. The way through to the back garden was gated
and locked. She rattled the gate, and called Gaines's name, but
no one answered. It was one-thirty, and DCI Parsons was
waiting. She turned away and was almost through the driveway
gates when she heard Gaines call her name.

He was dressed in his usual khaki combats and a sweatshirt hoodie; no jacket despite the cold. He dusted off his hands, eyeing her speculatively. 'Well, this is an honour,' he said.

'I came to congratulate you. I hear you've made a breakthrough with the symbolic meaning in the tattoos. Something about hidden truths?'

He combed soot-blackened fingers through his hair and she saw a hint of defiance in the lift of his chin. 'Yes, we discussed it, if you remember.'

'Oh, I do,' she said.

He jammed his hands in the pockets of his hoodie and, realising that they were still begrimed, pulled out a rag and began carefully wiping his hands.

'I'd had the "hidden secret" scenario in mind almost from the off.' He sounded defensive, now. 'I *told* Parsons we'd discussed it.'

Was this his idea of giving credit where it was due? She gave a mental shrug – if he had something new to say, she needed to hear it.

'Okay. But it wasn't in your report.'

He stared at her blankly.

'I meant something must've happened to change your mind – otherwise, why would you phone DCI Parsons to talk to him about it?'

'Oh,' he said. 'Yes, I see what you're driving at. But it was nothing, really – I just didn't want to risk your lot missing something important.'

So there was nothing new; this was just Gaines building his reputation on others' ideas. She nodded, keeping her eyes on him, and finally he shifted uncomfortably. 'Well, if I'd known you were going to be so possessive about it I'd have spoken to you first. Anyway, there's something else – something far more significant.'

'Oh?' she said.

'Look, it's freezing out here – let's go inside – warm our toes in front of the fire.'

He was through the side gate before she could stop him. She followed, just in time to see him vanish through a pair of French doors. Glancing right, she saw that the garden was sizeable – thirty metres long, at least. A tree at the far end had been taken down, leaving only the wide, flat plane of its stump; a giant stack of logs was piled to one side. On the bare earth caused by the old tree's shadow stood a large oil barrel, mounted on two strips of bricks. Flames licked the top of the barrel and the fire crackled. There wasn't much smoke, so she guessed it must be burning fairly hot.

'Well, come along,' Gaines said, returning to the door.

He showed her through a heritage-meets-modern kitchen to a sitting room overlooking the garden. A fire burned in the hearth, the alcoves either side of which were built floor to ceiling with bookshelves. Those to the left of the fireplace were dedicated to books on psychics, mediums, mentalism and cold reading. Ruth recognised some of the texts Kara Grogan had in her collection. The right side was filled with books on anthropology, history, archaeology, cultural and sociological texts, while the walls were hung with grouped sketches of tattooed men and women, and photographs of ritually scari-fied Africans, with raised keloid scars in elaborate patterns on their skin.

'Fascinating, aren't they?' Gaines said. 'In order to create the desired shape of scar, the wounds might be packed with clay or ash – or held open by stretching the skin.'

'It must be incredibly painful.'

'Intensely.' His eyes widened and his nostrils flared for the briefest moment. 'But rites of passage are rarely pleasant or easy. Blood and pain feature in so many traditions – to acquire status, beauty, desirability, one must endure.'

She nodded, finding it difficult to attune to the notion that scarring could be a sign of beauty.

He was watching her closely. 'I can assure you, the feel of scarified skin under the fingertips is a powerfully sensual tactile experience – highly sexually charged. I myself have a set of keloid scars – here.' He placed both hands over his abdomen, fingers splayed and pointing inwards towards the pelvic bone. 'Want to see?' His eyes gleamed with mischief.

Ruth gave him a cool look.

'Oh, you're *shy* . . .' His eyes roved over her body. 'Surely, you have at least one tattoo – testament to your rebellious youth?'

She let her gaze slide past him to the herbal illustrations hung in matching frames on the wall, many of which she knew as poisonous plants. 'You said there was something significant.'

He didn't answer and she forced herself to meet his gaze, giving him absolutely nothing. His eyes went dead, and he visibly clicked into a different mindset.

'Take a seat,' he said.

She didn't move, and he indicated a sofa in a curiously chivalrous gesture. 'Please,' he said.

Ruth sat on a sofa in front of a table arrayed with more research: poisons, tattoos, fetishes, shamanism. He waited for her to be seated before turning to a chair near the fireplace. A text on Celtic symbolism lay open on the seat cushion, and a newspaper article entitled 'Britain's Ten Deadliest Plants' was draped over the arm of the chair, the monks' hoods of aconite shining like sapphires from the page.

'Research,' he explained, clearing them to the bookcase before sitting down. 'I take it you still haven't identified the source of the woad used to make the tattoo dye?'

The inquiry team had contacted the main British manufacturer of natural woad, a small firm based in Birmingham. They had provided a list of customers: crafters, crofters and artists, mostly, but also a few fabric designers, and a film studio, none of whom looked suspicious. The Birmingham firm suggested the names of a few back-garden woad-makers, but nothing had come of that, either.

'I'll take your silence as a no,' he said. 'So-ooo . . . I'm thinking he made his own. Do you know how difficult that is? It takes a kilo of woad leaves to make one-to-four grams of dye. It has to be extracted from the plant in several stages. Soda ash is added to give the required pH, then it's filtered, concentrated and dried – which requires knowhow, and a sizeable quantity of the herb.'

'What's your point?'

The gleam lit his eye again. 'Doesn't it seem odd to you that he switched from blue woad to black dye when he tattooed Kara?'

Kara Grogan was the girl who didn't fit the MO; it was hard to find logic in that.

Ruth began to shake her head.

'Come *on* . . . He's making his own woad because he didn't want to attract police scrutiny by buying it in from a traceable source. Why would he switch?'

Ruth stared through the window onto the winter garden, its borders soggy, black and empty. 'He ran out of dye.'

Gaines smiled; the first genuine smile she'd seen on the man. 'And you need fresh leaves to make woad,' he said.

'So he couldn't make more.' Ruth thought back to her meeting with the botanist last August; the killer had changed from berberis thorns to pyracantha because the pyracantha was a better tool.

'It makes sense,' she said. 'He's pragmatic, adapts to circumstances. He would still want to stay under the radar, so the black dye has to be something he can make himself.' The breeze carried a whiff of wood smoke into the room and her eyes snapped to Gaines's.

'You believe he's making ink from soot?'

'Charcoal,' he corrected.

She glanced at Gaines's grimy hands. 'Is that what you were doing just now? Making charcoal?'

'I favour an immersive approach to my research.'

The false modesty in his expression was hiding something else. 'Does it work?' she asked.

He laughed. 'I'm still working on the process. Ask me again in a few days. Meanwhile, there's this.' He scooped up a netbook from beside his chair and, coming around the table, sat next to her.

She smelled the wood smoke on him, and felt the pressure of his thigh along the length of hers. For a second, she thought that he was pushing his luck again, but when he glanced across, she saw excitement of a purely scientific kind.

The image on-screen showed an arm. Brown, tanned in the way leather is tanned, but dried like hard tack. At the wrist, three parallel black lines.

'Meet Ötzi,' he said. 'He's 5,300 years old, although he was in his forties when he died. He has *many* tattoos, all of which were made by rubbing charcoal into scratched skin wounds. There's some disagreement about how the skin was prepared to receive the ink, but one theory is that they used thorns.'

## 40

Carver sat in his armchair and watched the sun lowering in the sky. It flared briefly through the bare branches of the tree outside the window and then disappeared behind a cloud. DCI Jansen hadn't been near since his arrest, but Carver was in no doubt that the chief inspector would be out there, meticulously building a case against him.

If he could just remember the sequence of events on the night at the hotel – but it was still a confusion of images and sounds. He remembered following Adela into the place; the nearness of her – exciting, tormenting. He remembered the sex, and after that, Adela screaming . . . But what he remembered most was the sex, the smell of her, the softness of her breast under his lips, her hunger for him, the way she rose to meet him with every thrust.

'*Jesus*, Greg . . .' he murmured. Emma was right to leave.

Disgusted with himself, he stood. Tried to. The room shifted sharply left and he ended up sprawled in the chair.

He consciously aligned his feet, legs and arms in a way that had never been necessary before his injuries. Except maybe when he was drunk. He pushed up using the arms of the chair and waited a moment. He'd found that stress affected his balance, and today had had more than a fair measure of that. He seemed to be stable, so he focused on a spot on the wall beyond the open door of his room, letting his fingertips play over the arms of the chair for a half-second longer before taking his first step. That worked okay, so he took another, pleased to find that he made it from the chair to the bedside cabinet on the far side of the bed without needing any further support.

He'd come for the photograph. It had lain in the drawer since Dr Pendinning had rescued it from the tangled mess of smashed glass and twisted frame the day before.

He traced the contours of Emma's face with his finger, feeling a physical pain deep in his chest. She didn't deserve this – any of it.

After a while – he wasn't sure how long – he became aware that he was being observed and turned his head, expecting to see the uniformed constable staring at him, but it was Dr Pendinning. She had the vaguely amused expression on her face that he'd come to think of as an antidote to his own grim self-absorption.

She slipped into the room and closed the door behind her. 'That picture means a lot to you,' she said.

'I took it on our honeymoon.' Carver placed it face down on the cabinet.

'It hurts to look at it?'

'Almost kills me,' he admitted. 'Seeing her as she was then; knowing how we are now.'

'And you blame yourself?'

'Who else can I blame?'

'It takes two to make a marriage, Greg.'

He snuffed air through his nose. 'Emma said that. But the problem was, there was always a third party in our marriage: the job – and the job always came first. That's down to me.'

'Did Emma walk out of your marriage because of the job, or because you were having an affair?'

'I tried, over the years, to build a barrier to protect Emma – to keep her innocent of all I saw and heard and did in this job – but I just built a wall between the two of us. I finally told her that, the day she left.' He sighed. 'She said, "But you never told me why you were building it. And you forgot to make a door, so I could come and visit."'

She had smiled so sweetly when she said that, it nearly broke his heart.

'I betrayed her,' he said. '*I* created the circumstances that allowed all of this to happen. If I hadn't obsessed over the Thorn Killer, I would never have been shot.'

'Do you believe it was the Thorn Killer who shot you?'

'No.' He bit back the urge to add, 'Not since Ruth told me she stole the files.'

'What about Sergeant Lake?'

For a second he was alarmed – had he spoken aloud, after all? 'What do you mean?' he stammered.

'Does she believe the Thorn Killer shot you?'

'She never did,' he said.

Pendinning tilted her head. 'Why not?'

'She thinks it lacks subtlety.' He frowned, distracted. *What was that?*

'Have you remembered something?' she asked.

'No – I just thought I saw . . .' He peered at the thin layer of air around her.

'I *do* have an aura, after all.' She sounded delighted.

'Maybe a glimmer.'

'What colour?'

He shook his head. 'I don't know, it's gone now.'

She seemed to regret her levity. 'I've been looking into synaesthesia. There's a lot of hokum on the psychic forums, of course, but some scientific papers suggest that clairvoyants who see auras around people may actually be synaesthetic. They are reading mood or emotion and the brain transposes them to colour and light.'

'Could my brain injury have caused it?'

'I've only found a few documented cases brought on by brain injury, and none of those experienced your form of synaesthesia. Hallucinations, on the other hand, are fairly common. Have you had any more flashbacks or hallucinations since we tried the relaxation exercise?'

'Nothing,' he said.

'When we worked on this earlier, you said there was a smell. Do you remember what that was?'

'Whisky.' Immediately he was hit with a roiling wave of nausea, and swallowed convulsively.

'You were drinking whisky when you were reading the files.'

'They tell me I downed a bottle of it that night, but . . .'

'The head injury caused amnesia.'

'That, or the alcohol.'

'Hm,' she said. 'The alcohol. Are you familiar with cognitive interviewing?'

'Of course.' Most police forces across the UK found it useful in drawing out details from witnesses. Carver himself had received some training in the technique.

'So, we try to put you back in the environment in which the event happened, using context, emotions, relaxation, starting the narrative from a different place, maybe from another person's perspective.'

'Let's do it,' he said.

'But it can be tough, emotionally – even physically.'

Carver had seen people break down and sob uncontrollably, remembering awful details of an attack. But he also knew that people remembered twice as much as they would in a normal interview, and that had to be better than the nothing he'd managed to dredge up so far.

'I need to do this,' he said.

She got him into the chair and talked him into a relaxed state.

'Tell me about the weather that day,' she said.

'It was cold. Cold enough for snow.'

'But not snowing, yet.'

'That was later.'

She walked him through the earlier part of the day, leaving work at eight in the evening, calling Adela.

'Let's skip to when you left the hotel,' she said. 'You're walking back to your car. How are you feeling?'

A quiver ran through his chest and arms. 'Shaky,' he said. 'Sick.' He brought his fingers to the back of his head. 'I – I think I broke a mirror.'

'Do you remember how?'

He frowned, trying hard to think. He remembered Adela screaming. Was she afraid? His breath came sharper, faster.

'Relax,' Pendinning said. 'We can come back to that. Let's take you home.'

The stuttering anxiety abated, and Carver took a breath of cold air. 'I'm at the car. God, I'm too drunk to drive.'

'Not to worry. You get home safely. Do you go directly in?'

'No.' The answer surprised him. 'I think I must have passed out. I wake up . . .'

'What colour is the clock on the dash?'

'Green.' Then, without thinking: 'It's five minutes after

306

eleven.' That was new – he hadn't remembered anything about arriving home before. 'I'm cramped and cold. I have a crick in my neck.'

'Okay, so you go inside. Is your flat warm, or cold?'

'It's freezing – it's just started to snow. I turn on the central heating, go to the kitchen and brew a pot of coffee. I'm looking at the files, but I can't make sense of them.'

'Because your head hurts?'

'No, the paracetamol took care of that.' Excitement rises in his gut: he's remembering more and more details. 'I . . . I can't bring myself to look at Kara's file, which is stupid, because Kara is the one person that will lead me to the Thorn Killer.'

'Why do you say that?'

'Kara was personal for the Thorn Killer.' He said it without thinking, but now he had, it seemed true.

'Personal?' Pendinning said. 'Like a grudge?'

He shook his head. 'Like a gift.' He sensed her close attention.

'A gift to her killer?'

'To me.' He swallowed.

'How do you feel about that?'

'I don't want it. I don't want to be responsible for Kara's death.'

'You feel responsible.'

'She would be alive now, if it weren't for me.'

'But another girl would be dead.'

He opened his eyes.

'You find that thought shocking?' she asked.

He considered that. 'No. If he hadn't taken Kara, he would have chosen someone else.'

'But not with you in mind?'

Carver nodded.

'Close your eyes again,' she said. 'You're doing well. You're in your kitchen. You smell coffee. Fresh brewed?'

'Cold.'

'So you're avoiding opening that one file . . .'

'I go to the cupboard in the sitting room where I keep the whisky. Open a new bottle.' He opened his eyes again. 'It *was* a new bottle. I went straight to the hotel from work. I don't — didn't — drink during work hours. I'd had a glass of champagne, with Adela. Maybe two, but it hardly touched me. How come was I drunk coming out of the hotel?'

She didn't answer, leaving him to think it through.

'I *wasn't* drunk,' he said at last. 'I felt sick because I hit my head.' He felt an instant of euphoria, quickly succeeded by dark oppression. 'Why can't I remember leaving Adela's room?'

'We'll come back to that,' she said. 'Your blood alcohol was dangerously high when you were brought here for surgery. You'd opened a new bottle of Scotch that night. Do you remember drinking it?'

He shook his head slowly. 'I poured a slug. Put the bottle back, changed my mind and took it through to the kitchen. After that . . .' He sighed, frustrated.

'You're doing well,' Pendinning said, her voice calm, reassuring. 'When Ruth came into your flat, what do you think she saw?'

'A pathetic drunk, passed out in his chair.' He said it without bitterness.

'Do you think she had compassion for you?'

'It doesn't matter,' he said. 'I didn't deserve compassion.'

'You're hard on yourself,' she said. Then, 'Are you ready to look into the shadow again?'

'Yes.'

'All right. I have a whisky miniature with me. The sense of smell is more closely bound with memory than any of the other senses,' she said.

'I know.' Didn't everyone? The odour of suntan oil on a hot day, the scent of a lover's perfume – it was the closest thing to time travel most people would ever experience.

'It's also highly emotive,' she said. 'It may well unlock your memories, but you have to consider that you are still recovering from serious trauma. You may not be ready to face those memories just yet.'

'I'm ready,' he said.

'Okay.'

He heard the metallic *crack* as she broke the seal on the whisky bottle.

He couldn't help himself – he opened his eyes. It was Jura, his favourite malt. Carver's heart thudded in his chest and he heard the blood roar in his ears.

'We can stop right now,' she said. 'If you're not comfortable with this, you just have to say.'

'No,' he said. 'I want to. I need to know.'

She brought the bottle up to his nose and he braced himself. His stomach rolled at the familiar smell of the malt, but he swallowed hard, said, 'I'll take a taste.'

'I'm not sure that's a good idea,' she said.

'I'm not going back now.'

He reached for the bottle; she kept hold of it, but allowed him to guide it to his lips.

*Fear. A flash. A roar of light. Sound and light become one. Darkness penetrates the light, overpowers it. He feels his breath tear through his chest, and suddenly he can't breathe at all. Bzzz-*

*zzzzziiip!*

*Can't move.*

*Ruth looms, her face distorted, amoeboid. The scream of a kettle whistle – her face splits in two. Ruth is holding a gun. The reek of whisky is nauseating. He is drowning in a lake of flame.*

*Fear. Terrible FEAR.*

*Ruth's face shatters, falls in shards, light scattering facets of her to the ground. Behind her a shadow. He has to warn her.*

'Greg. *Greg Carver* . . .'

He opened his eyes. Dr Pendinning was bending over him. She held a glass to his lips and he panicked, pushing her away.

'It's water,' she said. 'Just water.'

He took a cautious sip, then another.

'You're all right,' said. 'You blacked out, but you're all right.'

Her face blurred and he saw again a smudge of light around her head.

'What did you see?' she asked.

He tried to recall the terrible images just before he'd blacked out, but all he could remember was the fear, the feeling that he was drowning in fire, and a terrible dread that was somehow linked to Ruth Lake.

## 41

Under strict instructions from DCI Parsons, Ruth Lake spent the afternoon typing up her notes on Tali Tredwin, Jo Raincliffe and Kara Grogan. Parsons had tasked detectives to re-interview the family and friends of Evie Dodd and Hayley Evans, the other two victims, aiming to uncover their secrets.

Parsons had worked up such a head of steam it was pointless trying to explain why she hadn't included her suspicions about the women during the morning briefing. The fact that Gaines had given them something to follow up on Kara's tattoos had confirmed his usefulness in Parsons's eyes. Ruth had checked with the pathologist – things were backed up at the lab and they hadn't yet done the electron microscope scans, but preliminary analysis did indicate the presence of crystalline carbon in the skin samples they had taken from Kara, and Ruth was willing to bet it was charcoal.

The reports completed and delivered, she returned to the tedious process of working through the CCTV recordings of School Lane on the night Kara disappeared. The next camera in the sequence picked up the street action just after Bluecoat Chambers. A minute or so after the time on the last recording, Kara continued on her journey down the lane and encountered another woman. They stopped and exchanged a few words.

*Asking for directions*? No. There was familiarity in their stance – not what Ruth would call intimacy. Acquaintances, maybe? *A lecturer?* Possibly, but they had interviewed everyone who had direct contact with Kara at the drama school. The two women exchanged a few words, then carried on their separate ways. Kara continued on a little further, and disappeared from the camera's field of view. Ruth wound the recording back, following the woman, having to switch disks twice to track her all the way. She eventually turned left at the top of School Lane and out of view.

Ruth took a screen grab and made a note to check LIPA staff records, and to ask Kara's friends if they recognised her. It was just possible that Kara told the woman where she was going.

She was about to make a start on the next recording when one of John Hughes's team came into the office with the uncut recording of Jasmine Hart's reading from the psychic-debunking blogger. Ruth signed the continuity forms, eager to make a start, and was quickly immersed in the action. The blogger began by panning 360 degrees, taking in the entire auditorium. The theatre was almost full. She recognised some of the faces she'd seen on the street CCTV recordings: a few sombrely dressed groups; a young couple she'd pegged as lovers out for a night on the town.

She would run through the entire performance later, but for now, she skipped through to a few minutes before the confrontation between Rollinson and Kara, scouting for anyone who took an undue interest in the student – maybe even followed her out of the auditorium.

The blogger was focused on Jasmine, making heavy weather of a communication from a "spirit" called Alf, who didn't seem to have anyone in the audience willing to acknowledge him. The camera whipped round fast, blurring faces and colours, finally settling on Rollinson. He stormed up the aisle, one hand raised, and came to a halt at the end of a row. Judging by the angle and the number of rows visible, the blogger was on the other side of the aisle, four or five rows back. Kara turned and looked up at Rollinson as he held out his hand. His voice was muffled, but he was clearly demanding that she hand something over. Then he reached down and yanked Kara out of her seat. She clung grimly to her e-tablet, refusing to relinquish it as Rollinson half dragged, half shoved her towards the exit.

The clip the blogger posted online had finished the moment Rollinson and Kara disappeared through the doors, but the extended version rolled on, scoping the audience for their reaction. Jasmine was trying to reclaim the audience's attention, her voice, amplified by the sound system, was clearly audible as she began a pseudo-scientific explanation of the damaging effects of electromagnetic interference in psychic readings, adding that spirits were often shy of being recorded.

All the while, the camera roved restlessly, picking up on a woman who looked upset by the incident, stopping for a few seconds at a group of three women who tutted and shook their heads, apparently disapproving of Kara. It moved on, immediately coming to rest on a face Ruth recognised.

She reached for the phone, furious. Her call was answered instantaneously.

'Twice in one day, Sergeant – people will talk.'

Ruth took a breath and let it go, along with some of the anger. 'I'm looking at a video of Jasmine Hart giving a psychic performance at the Epstein Theatre on the night Kara was last seen,' she said. 'Kara is in the audience – or was, for about an hour. You know who else is there?'

'I'm guessing, by your confrontational tone, that it's me,' Dr Gaines said. 'As I am growing rather tired of telling you, I have a special interest in psychics and mediums.'

'How many times have we spoken, and yet you didn't think to mention this to me?'

'Why would I?'

'Kara was in the audience,' she said.

'Along with another four hundred people.'

'There was an unpleasant altercation between Kara and Rollinson,' Ruth interrupted. 'Is that ringing any bells?'

'Come to think of it, I do remember a bit of a scuffle,' he said. 'But I was taking notes.'

He was just too damn glib for his own good.

'In fact, you seemed to be making notes *about* the scuffle. Funny you don't remember that.'

'Look . . .' he said, his voice syrupy and wheedling, now. 'I thought it'd look bad, my—'

'Being there the night Kara was last seen? Yes,' she said. 'It looks bad.'

'I was *in the audience*,' he said, as if that made all the difference.

'What makes it look worse,' Ruth went on, 'is you not mentioning this to me or anyone else.'

'This was what – six, seven weeks ago? I didn't make the connection.'

'You didn't make the connection, or you thought it would look bad – which is it?'

He didn't answer immediately, and when he did, it was with stiff formality: 'Since you need me to spell it out for you, I didn't make the connection initially, and when I did, I thought you would overreact – as, indeed, you have. Anyway, it's irrelevant, since I had *nothing* to do with her disappearance.'

'It's not for you to decide what is or isn't relevant to this inquiry.'

In the few seconds of silence that followed, Ruth felt his hostility, his impotent rage.

'You need to come in and make a formal statement,' she said. 'Today.'

'I can't possibly – I'm . . . about to go into a meeting.'

Probably another lie. But Gaines was a leading academic in his field, a Merseyside Police-appointed consultant. He'd been vetted and approved – and recommended for this particular job by a psychologist Ruth herself knew and respected. She could only push so far.

'Tomorrow, then,' she said, keeping a lid on her temper.

'I think I might be able to find time late morning.'

'Eleven-fifteen,' she said. 'Don't be late.'

Parsons listened sympathetically to Ruth's account of what had just passed between her and Gaines, came around his desk and offered her a seat – even made a few notes as she spoke. But the DCI was inclined to give the anthropologist the benefit of the doubt: he was a busy man, *and* an academic, and entitled to a little eccentricity. Surely things slipped Ruth's mind on occasions?

'He lied, sir,' she said. 'I want to know why.'

He seemed to disapprove of her bluntness. 'I'll put it to him that he could have been more frank with you,' he said.

'*You* will?' She shook her head. 'Thanks for the offer, sir, but I can do that myself.'

'I'm sure you could,' he said. 'But it might be counter-productive, given your feelings about the man.'

She raised an eyebrow. 'My "feelings"?'

'Now, Sergeant, don't take it that way,' he said. 'I'm simply suggesting that there seems to be some . . . animus between you.'

'There is,' she said evenly. 'Because . . . he *lied* to me.'

Parsons frowned. '*Lie* is a strong word.'

'He denied having seen Kara, and only finally admitted it when I confronted him with video evidence. I don't know what else to call it.'

'And yet he *has* proved helpful. The significance of the tattoos, for instance . . .'

Ruth sucked her teeth, wishing she'd handled that one better.

'And the pathologist *does* believe that the killer used charcoal to create Kara's tattoos . . .' Parsons went on.

'Which is no more help than knowing he used woad on the other victims.'

'I don't follow.'

'He probably made the stuff himself,' Ruth said. 'He made the woad dye – and that's a lot harder.'

'Surely charcoal-making is a factory process?' Parsons said.

She shook her head. 'Doesn't have to be. Dr Gaines was cooking up a batch in his back garden when I went to see him earlier. I looked it up online: all it takes is wood and a couple of steel drums.'

His shoulders slumped. He'd probably been planning to task some poor sod with phoning around charcoal makers and retailers for customer lists. Then the incongruity of what she'd said seemed to strike him. 'Why was Dr Gaines making *charcoal* in his garden?'

'That's something I'd like to ask him, sir. I'd also like to see the notes he made at the psychic event. And I'd *love* to know if

Kara responded to a questionnaire he's been touting on a fake website for the past two months.'

Parsons's eyebrows shot up. 'A fake website?'

She told him about Gaines's psychic persona, 'Shadowman', and the fact he'd collected personal data from unsuspecting punters.

'Did he explain why he would dupe people in that way?' Parsons asked.

'He calls it research,' Ruth said.

'I see.'

By the worried expression on his face, she thought he was beginning to.

'But there could be a perfectly innocent explanation for all of this,' Parsons added.

'If there is, I'd like to hear it.'

Parsons considered her for a long moment. Finally, he said: 'I don't know you very well, Sergeant Lake. My *impression* is that you're usually a cool customer, yet Dr Gaines seems to have well and truly rattled your cage.' He paused. 'You need to ask yourself why.'

'He's manipulative,' she said. 'And I don't like being lied to. But what really rattles me is that he has withheld key information, possibly hampering the progress of this inquiry.' She might add that he was an arrogant, patronising, sexist wanker, but that would only confirm what Parsons had already said. He had a point: Ruth had been subjected to enough sly sexual comments in her work to know that some men regarded it as innocent banter – even deluding themselves that women found their innuendo flattering. And senior officers and peers alike had taken credit for her work at one time or another. But if there was one thing every man and woman in the job hated, it was a whiner. It would take more than a gut feeling and a few off-colour remarks to tempt her to confide in Parsons.

So instead, she finished with, 'He's slippery and untrustworthy, and I'll say it again – he's a liar.'

Parsons pursed his lips, his expression grave. 'Well, yes, you *do* seem to've caught him in a lie,' he conceded.

She watched him think through the options, keeping her gaze steady and cool, knowing that he'd come up with a compromise before he even opened his mouth.

'All right,' he said. 'You can take the lead at interview. But I will be in the room, and you will take a respectful tone.'

'Thank you sir,' she said. 'I will.'

*As respectful as the toerag deserves, anyway.*

## 42

The evening briefing was mercifully short, but Parsons wanted a written update on her interactions with Dr Gaines, so it was after seven by the time Ruth walked out into a clear, cold night.

She couldn't stop thinking about Adela's gun, and she knew that the problem would gnaw at her until she did something about it, but she kept coming back to the impossibility of getting the weapon to the murder team without admitting her own guilt in stealing it. Adela's flat had been thoroughly processed, as had Carver's, so smuggling it into evidence that way was not an option.

She eased herself behind the wheel feeling about a hundred, and turned right, intending to scoot immediate left along Wapping towards home. Traffic was heavy, and she crept forwards, sitting through three changes of lights at the T-junction. Across the roadway, the squat buildings of Albert Dock glowed in the spotlights, reflecting bronze and blue and white off the glassy-black waters of the dock. The Wheel of Liverpool, ghostly white on its southerly edge, rotated inch by inch, reflecting the slow circling of her own thoughts. Why had Carver been targeted? How could she have been so stupid as to steal the gun from his apartment?

Squeezing at last onto the main arterial road, a new, more helpful question popped into her head. *Why did Adela feel the need to even own a gun?* She had been a financial advisor, and the 2008 crash had bankrupted a lot of people. But not Adela.

Could Adela have been threatened by a disgruntled client who saw her continuing to prosper when so many had failed? Had she bought the gun for personal protection?

Counter-intuitive though it was, the stats said that women had less to fear from strangers than from the men close to them. It followed that gun-owning women were more likely to have their guns turned on them by those same male partners and lovers. And Adela had plenty of those.

Ruth made a sharp left at the first available turn, looping back on herself, in a detour to Adela's gun club in the north of the city.

On the outskirts of Aintree, housed in a disused railway tunnel, Fenton Shooting Club boasted four ranges, each with eight firing points. The floodlit car park was almost full and the clubhouse busy. The friendly membership secretary she'd spoken to earlier in the day was unavailable, and Ruth was asked to wait in the bar-restaurant area while they called the manager in.

Adrian Garvey was a privately educated forty-something businessman. Tall, not overtly handsome, but with the charisma to draw appreciative looks from the female club members when he came through the door.

'I understand you want to talk about Adela Faraday,' he said, offering Ruth his hand. 'Terrible business.' He gestured to a table in a quiet corner of the room, and Ruth positioned herself to gain a good sweep of the place. Couples, groups of men and, incongruously, families, gathered around tables, eating their evening meals. A waitress came past carrying a tray of food, the tantalising aroma of steak pie and chips wafting in her wake, and Ruth realised she hadn't eaten since she'd snatched a round of toast at breakfast.

'Can I get you anything?' Garvey asked. 'A drink . . . ?' He glanced over to the bar, and Ruth caught the barman ogling her. He looked quickly away.

Ruth declined. 'I was wondering if you might answer a few questions about Adela,' she said.

'Whatever I can do to help.'

Ruth nodded her thanks. 'What reason did she give for wanting to own a firearm?' The law required a stated reason on the application form, and the majority used the catch-all 'sport'. Ruth expected the same of Adela, but she was curious to see the manager's reaction.

'This is a sport club,' he said. 'We do target shooting. A few are licensed to shoot vermin on their land, but members come here for the sport, and to socialise.'

He hadn't answered the question, she noticed, but she'd come back to that. 'What did Adela like best – the shooting, or socialising?'

He smiled. 'Adela was a party animal. Life and soul.'

'You knew her personally?'

'She was the sort of woman who could light up a room,' he said, fondly. 'But Adela was an excellent shot, too. Had one of the club's highest scores for a .22 multi-shot carbine.'

His admiration of the dead woman was obvious, and Ruth wondered how far that admiration went.

'She had her own pistol, I understand.'

'Yes, but she usually came direct from her office in Liverpool, so more often than not, she borrowed a club gun.'

Ruth lifted her chin in acknowledgment, thinking, *That's odd*, because Adela's riverside apartment was on the main route to the north of city; surely it would have been easy for her to stop off and pick up her own carbine.

'D'you have changing facilities here?' she asked.

He blinked. 'We have rest rooms – why do you ask?'

'Well, Adela being a financial adviser, I imagine she dressed business-smart. She must have changed before she went onto the range.'

'Oh,' he said. 'I suppose . . .'

Ruth felt eyes on her and glanced over at the bar again. The barman was slight, average height, grey-haired, with a neatly clipped beard. He looked panicked to have been caught, and turned sharply away.

*Now, what's got you so twitchy?*

'Could I change my mind about that drink?' she said. 'I could use a tonic water.'

'Of course.' Garvey called over to the barman and ordered drinks for both of them. The barman looked decidedly jittery at the prospect of bringing them over.

'So what kind of people do shooting for sport?' she asked, tracking the room.

'As you can see,' Garvey said, with an amused smile. 'All kinds.'

'Specifically?'

He glanced at the ceiling for inspiration. 'Historians, keen to fire their antique weapons, ex-police and armed forces – as you'd expect. Businessmen and women . . . a fair few engineers –'

'Engineers . . .' That surprised her, but thinking it through, it made sense. 'I suppose the mechanics of weaponry would be kind of in their line?'

It was a leading question, but it didn't put the manager on the defensive.

'I expect so,' he said. 'I hadn't really thought about it.' Garvey sat back, opening the conversation to the barman who had just arrived with their drinks. 'David would know.'

The barman looked alarmed at being put on the spot. 'Know what?' he said.

'You were an engineer before you retired, weren't you?' Garvey said. 'David's here most days – and nights – filling in for absences and so on. Detective Sergeant Lake was just wondering why we have so many engineers among the members.'

'Schoolboys who never grew up, I guess,' the barman said, with a weak laugh.

'You must have known Adela Faraday,' Ruth said.

The barman looked ready to deny it, but Mr Garvey said, 'You were friends, weren't you, David?'

The barman looked stricken. 'Shooting partners,' he corrected, but it didn't sound like a denial.

'Did Adela seem worried in the weeks before her death?' Ruth asked. 'Had she been threatened, or followed? Pestered by anyone?'

'We didn't really talk about personal stuff,' he said.

Carver had used more or less the same words. 'She didn't mention a name – someone she was having trouble with in her work?' Ruth asked.

David shook his head, avoiding her eye.

'Well, if you think of anything – anything at all – give me a call.' She offered him a business card. For a second he looked at it stupidly, and when he reached out for it, his fingers trembled slightly.

Garvey spoke in a low voice as the other man walked away: 'David has taken Adela's death quite hard.'

Ruth nodded, keeping her eyes on the engineer's retreating back.

Returning to Adela's reason for wanting a firearm, she asked Garvey for a copy of the registration documents, and he showed her to his office, a small, cluttered cubbyhole with brick walls painted cream and covered with photographs of firearms, shooting competitions and social events.

'There you go,' he said, stapling the sheets together and handing them to her. 'The nineteen-eleven Low Mill LBP is modified from an Iver Johnson pistol, which is itself based on a nineteen-eleven Colt.'

Ruth looked at him like she didn't have a clue what he was talking about, and he pointed out an image on a wall chart. It was the same make and model of gun that squatted like a malevolent toad in a box in her mother's wardrobe, at home. But the legal version had an extension barrel and grip added.

'As you can see on the form, Adela's reason for keeping a gun was target shooting.' He tapped the page at the appropriate box.

Ruth scanned the form. 'So it says. But working for the police, you get to know the meaning of box-ticking.'

He frowned. 'You really think she was being threatened?'

'Just making an observation,' she said. Mr Garvey had helpfully printed Adela Faraday's membership form along with her firearms certificate, and glancing down to the signature, Ruth noticed that Adela joined the club seven months ago. Which was exactly how long it had been since she had shut up her house and moved anonymously to an apartment in the city centre.

By the time Ruth returned to the bar to have a private chat with the barman he'd gone. One of the waitresses said he wasn't feeling well, had to get off home.

She hurried out to the car park, and spotted him carrying a rifle case and sports bag. He saw her as he opened the car boot, and for a second she thought he'd bolt, but instead he flung the sports bag inside, laid the rifle next to it, and stood there like a man waiting to be arrested.

'Adela's form says she needed a pistol for target shooting.'

He stared at her, his eyes dull, shoulders hunched, his arms folded defensively across his chest.

'So?'

'I half expected to see "pest control" on there.'

It may have been the light from the spots overhead, but for a second she thought she saw twin points of hard white light in his eyes.

He looked down. 'Why would that be? Adela lived in a nice apartment in an exclusive development.'

'Good question,' Ruth said, thinking he knew damn well she was talking about the kind of pest that walked on two legs and couldn't take no for an answer. And it occurred to her that David must be one of the very few people who knew that Adela had moved into her riverside apartment.

'Here's another one for you,' she added. 'Why would Adela use the club's firearms when she had her own pistol?'

He considered her, and after a moment turned to the open boot of his car. 'Look at this – ' He took out the rifle case and, opening it, drew out not a rifle, but a pistol. The freakishly long barrel at the business end and long, weighted rod at the butt end seemed even more incongruous in reality than in the photographs.

'These things will just about fit in a rifle case,' he said.

'Isn't that kind of the point?' she said. 'To make it a harder to wander about with a deadly weapon stuffed in your waistband?'

'*If* you follow the rules,' he said. 'But criminals aren't great respecters of the rules, are they? Your average scumbag criminal can get hold of a fully automatic pistol as easy as popping down to Tesco for a pint of milk. Decent, law-abiding citizens get *this* . . . abomination.' He stared in disgust at the chimera in his hands.

'I don't like guns,' Ruth said, thinking it was time to bring this down a notch. 'But I take your point: that's an ugly-arsed piece of kit.'

That startled a laugh from him. 'Sorry,' he said. 'Sorry. It's just . . . the bastard who did this to Adela is still out there.'

'She must have been a remarkable woman,' Ruth said.

He seemed offended. 'What would *you* know?'

She looked at him for a long moment. She was sure he wanted to help, but if he did, he could leave himself open to prosecution, and Ruth knew how that felt. If she wanted an honest answer from him, she needed to give him something to hold over her.

'I'm going to tell you something that could put me in real trouble.' She took a breath. 'This isn't my case.'

His eyes flicked to hers, confusion and curiosity in them.

'Then why are you . . .?'

'Just trying to help a friend,' she said. 'He's in a mess. He was in a . . . relationship with Adela.'

David gripped the weapon tightly, his eyes flashing. 'If you know something. If he *did* this—' He broke off, his eyes red, his face chalky under the bright white spotlights.

'He was shot with the same calibre of weapon Adela was.'

The barman stared at her, and she waited for him to make the connection. When he did his eyes widened.

'My God – it's that policeman, isn't it?'

She said nothing, but the shock and disbelief in his face convinced her that this man had nothing to do with shooting Greg Carver.

'Does it surprise you that she was seeing someone else?'

'No,' he said, still working through what she'd told him. 'Adela wasn't – she didn't have exclusive relationships.' He paused. 'D'you think whoever shot her came after your friend?'

Ruth raised one shoulder, let it drop. 'I'm just asking questions,' she said. 'Because whoever shot Adela and Greg Carver needs to be found and punished.'

Though he didn't speak, his eyes burned, and she thought the time was right to say, 'So – can I ask you a hypothetical question?'

His eyes hooded, but he gave a wary nod.

She glanced at the carbine, which he now held in one hand, the barrel in line with the seam of his trouser leg. 'Can an "abomination" like that one be converted back to something that looks like a regular pistol?'

Every muscle in his neck tensed and she had to tell herself that no self-respecting gun club member would ever carry a loaded gun in the boot of his car. Even so, she held his gaze, because she was half afraid that another glance at the weapon might make him think of using it. Perhaps he realised what she was thinking, because he turned away and shoved the weapon back into its case, then set it carefully in the boot well. As he straightened up, she heard the bones and sinews in his back and shoulders crackle with released tension. Then she saw a puff of vapour as he let his breath go with a gasp.

'You're asking me, *hypothetically* – as an engineer – if a nineteen-eleven rimfire carbine could be converted to a standard, nineteen-eleven rimfire Colt?' he said.

'Hypothetically.'

He gave a tight nod. 'It's not easy –' He coughed. '*Wouldn't* be easy, I mean. But, yes. It's absolutely – hypothetically – possible.'

'That's what I thought.'

He held her gaze, a frightened look on his face. 'Can I ask *you* a hypothetical question?'

'Of course.'

'If an engineer *did* de-modify her pistol, do you think he put it in the hands of the murdering scum who shot Adela?'

'I didn't say that. Look, David, the inquiry team hasn't even located the gun, yet,' she said, truthfully, adding less honestly, 'There's no way of knowing if Adela was shot with her own weapon.'

He seemed relieved to hear it.

'Even so,' he said. 'I wish I could take it back. I wish I'd never . . .' He seemed stricken.

'This man she needed protecting from – did she give you a name?' she asked.

'Chris,' he said.

'No surname?'

He shook his head.

'An ex-boyfriend, someone she worked with?'

'She wouldn't say – I only know this much because she let it slip one night. We'd been drinking, and . . .' He shrugged.

'Did she say *why* she was afraid of him?'

'Only that he was harassing her.'

Which would explain why Adela had sold her nice house in the suburbs and secretly moved herself to one of her investment properties. 'Did she report this harassment to the police?'

Another shake of the head. 'She said she could handle it.'

# 43

*Day 11*

Ruth fell into bed just after midnight, and dreamed of her father. He hadn't been around much after her fifteenth birthday and most of her memories of that time were of stormy exchanges and violent outbursts, but tonight, he was in mellow mood. He cracked some silly joke, and she laughed. He watched her, a look of affection on his face.

'I do love you,' he said. 'Never doubt that.'

Then Dad was gone, and Ruth was anxious because the lock on the front door was faulty. She went downstairs to investigate noises coming from her sitting room and found Harry Rollinson playing 'Hitman' on her Xbox, which seemed odd, because she didn't own the game. His thumbs twitched at the console, and on-screen, the hitman snapped an adversary's neck. Rollinson looked up and smiled.

'One split second,' he said. 'Your life changes for ever.'

She woke with a start, and lay awake, her mind churning over her interview with the man. 'One split second,' he'd said. 'You know how it is.' Thinking about it again, there had been a definite emphasis on 'you'. He could mean '*you* know because you're police', but the dead look in his eye made her think otherwise: there was a deeper message in what he'd said.

She went to the front bedroom and opened the wardrobe. Under a stack of shoeboxes was a blue leatherette scrapbook, the kind with self-adhesive pages and plastic protectors to hold papers in place. Ruth shone a torchlight over each shoebox as she lifted it out, checking for fingermarks or signs of disturbance. She hadn't moved them in months, and a fine patina of dust confirmed that neither had anyone else.

She knelt on the floor with the album clasped on her knees, building the courage to open it. After five minutes, she took a breath and turned the cover. It opened with a faint *crack*, and a whiff of age. The first eight pages held the usual stuff: family snaps; swimming certificates; a photo of Ruth and her brother, kitted out for an aikido competition. After that, the content got darker: newspaper cuttings and condolence cards, a pressed flower from a funeral wreath; Dad's note: 'I do love you. Never doubt that.'

She checked every page. Nothing was missing.

After a while, she closed the scrapbook and replaced it, carefully loading the boxes on top of it.

She didn't recognise Rollinson, and she never forgot a face. But he recognised her – she was sure of it.


Ruth arrived at the hospital just after seven a.m. as the nurses were in the process of doling out medications, and care staff were giving out breakfast. She sneaked in as a trolley of breakfast trays was wheeled through the door, and the nurse gave her a scolding look.

'What happened to his chaperone?' Ruth asked.

The nurse rolled her eyes. 'Maybe the powers that be saw sense and decided it was a waste of time.'

Ruth thought it was more likely that DCI Parsons had pulled in so many additional bodies to review the Thorn Killer victims that Jansen didn't have anyone to spare.

Carver was in bed. It was still dark, but Ruth knew they got most of the patients up and out of bed by six-thirty. Carver looked grey and weak, and she felt a stab of concern. He lifted a hand to wave her in, and let it drop to the bedsheets as if the effort was almost beyond his limits.

'Are you okay?' she asked. 'You look terrible.'

'I'm fine,' he said.

'Seriously, Greg, we can do this another time.'

'Don't you dare leave,' he said, struggling to get up. 'You've got news – you're *glowing* with it. I want to hear it.'

The whole aura thing was disconcerting. Logic and science told her that this was some kind of neurological anomaly, but she couldn't help glancing at her reflection in the darkened window. She saw only her deceptively calm face staring back at her.

'It's the Thorn Killer, isn't it?' he said, his voice weak and querulous. 'What do you know?' he struggled to get up. 'Tell me.'

'Will you calm *down*?' She pushed him gently back onto the pillows. 'I'm here to ask a question, that's all.'

Ruth felt bad about not filling him in, but the link between the victims was still tenuous at best, and Greg Carver had literally nearly killed himself over the Thorn Killer; she was not about to encourage him to rekindle his obsession with the case. Adela Faraday was another matter, she told herself; she needed to know what Carver knew.

He stared at her, his eyes huge as if, improbably, he'd lost weight since the night before.

'Ask the question,' he said.

'The handgun. Do you remember seeing it before the night you were shot?'

He frowned. 'Give me a minute.' He closed his eyes, but a second later he sat up, gasping, a sweat sheening his face.

'Greg?' She poured a tumbler of water and held it to his lips. He took a sip, then another. 'You really do look terrible,' she said. 'We can do this later – when you're feeling better.'

He shook his head, resting back on the pillows. 'No. I'm okay. I tried a cognitive interview with the psychologist yesterday, that's all. I'm a bit wrung out.'

'You can say that again.' She paused, then couldn't help asking, 'I take it you didn't remember anything useful?'

'There was something . . .' He stared past her for a few moments. 'It doesn't make sense, but I needed to warn you.'

'About . . .?'

He struggled, gave up in frustration. 'I don't know – *something*.'

'You couldn't vague that up a bit for me could you?'

The anxious look he gave her made her regret her flippancy.

'I'm sorry Ruth. I tried, but . . .' He wiped his face with an unsteady hand.

She hated seeing him so debilitated. 'Hey, I got the message, I'll be on the alert,' she said. 'If anything else comes back to you, you can ring me, okay?'

He took a few breaths and said calmly enough, 'You were about to tell me about the gun.'

'Okay, but don't freak out,' she said. 'It's Adela's.'

He didn't answer straight away, then: 'How sure are you?'

'Certain sure,' she said. 'The serial number's a match.'

'A *ma*—' His eyes bugged. 'Tell me you didn't search the PNC.'

'I wasn't born yesterday, Greg. Adela joined a shooting club. And what's even more interesting is a guy there thinks she was having trouble with an ex.'

332

'How does Jansen not *know* this?' Carver said.

'Adela was hiding out in an empty apartment for months,' Ruth said. 'The *concierge* didn't even know she was living there full time.' She tilted her head. 'Actually, when you think about it – all those nights she spent in hotels around the city – she *wasn't*.'

'I told you, I only saw her half a dozen times.' He sounded defensive.

'That maybe, but you weren't the only one,' she said dryly. 'There was Councillor Hill, the other unknown male on her burner phone – and I'd be willing to bet she was bonking at least two of the men at the club.'

He looked a little shocked.

'Don't take it too badly, Greg,' she said. 'It seems she didn't let anyone too close.'

'Or she did, and that's why she had to hide out for months,' Carver countered.

'That's the theory I'm working on,' she said, relieved to see some colour had returned to his face.

'I saw they'd arrested Hill.'

'To be fair, Jansen did give him the option of coming in for a friendly chat. He declined – so much for taking responsibility and coming forward with information. But he was abroad with his family over Christmas and New Year, so he's in the clear.'

'Then, what's your theory?'

'Adela's friend at the shooting club gave me a name – Chris – but that's all he knew.'

'It's not much to go on.'

'We already know that Adela walked out of a high-paid job and went freelance last June, which suggests a work romance

333

that went bad. The fact that she quit work, sold her house *and* moved into one of her rental properties around the same time is practically a smoking gun.'

He winced, and she apologised.

'If Adela *did* make a complaint to police, Jansen's team would know about it, and they'd have brought this "Chris" in for questioning at the very least. But as far as I know, the only two they've questioned so far are you and the leader of the council.'

He nodded. 'She didn't make a complaint.'

'That's my guess. The trouble is, I can't take this to Jansen's team without having to answer a lot of awkward questions. So . . . I'll just have to go and ask some of my own.'

'That's not a good idea, Ruth,' Carver said. 'You could end up having to answer a hell of a lot more questions further down the line.'

'Which is why God invented LinkedIn,' she said, with a smile. 'Adela's profile is comprehensive – although she only allowed people to get in touch via InMail – to keep her clingy ex at arm's length, I suppose. Her work history says her last job was at the Liverpool office of LC&K Assets – a London-based asset management company. I checked out their website and found this fine, grinning, lounge lizard of a man on the "Meet the Team" page.'

She handed Carver her mobile phone and he read the name beneath the photograph. 'Chris Barrington . . .'

Ruth could see him searching his memory, struggling to recall the face.

'You don't recognise him.'

'I don't *think* so.' He stared at the phone screen. 'I'm sorry, I wish I could be more help.'

'Okay, it was worth a try.'

'But you think Barrington is worth a second look?'

'Back in the nineties, Mr Barrington was taken to an employment tribunal by a female employee for sexual harassment,' she said. 'He made the problem go away with an undisclosed out-of-court settlement.'

'It's a big leap from sexual harassment to stalking and murder.'

'Depends what form the harassment took, surely? And some men do make that leap. Anyway, it won't hurt to ask a few questions.'

'You plan to go and see him?' Anxiety again flickered like a candle at the back of his eyes. 'Take someone with you,' he said.

'Parsons and Jansen both warned me off interfering; there's no one else I *can* tell.'

'Ruth . . .'

She checked her watch. 'I've got to head in for the team briefing, and I'm interviewing Gaines with DCI Parsons later this morning, but I should have enough time to sneak out for an hour to speak with Mr Barrington and be back in the office before anyone misses me.'

'Who's Gaines?' he asked.

'*Doctor* Gaines – an anthropologist we're consulting with,' she said, trying to sound offhand, cursing herself for letting it slip.

'Then why did you say you were *interviewing* him?'

He might be weak, but he was still sharp.

She moved to the door. 'I have to go.'

'What are you keeping from me?'

'*Everything*, okay? It's not your case any more.'

335

He stared at the air around her as if trying to focus on a mote of dust. 'There's something off about this Doctor Gaines, isn't there?'

'His credentials are good.'

He gave a choked laugh. 'You just *lit up*, Ruth.'

'I did *what*?'

'Fluorescent bile green – it's the colour of lies for you.'

'How attractive . . . You know we'll have a talk about this . . . thing with auras at some point,' she said. 'But all right: Gaines is a creep with a huge ego and a talent for being in the wrong place at the wrong time. I'm going to have a chat with him about that . . . and a few other things. Parsons is going to referee. Satisfied?'

'Nowhere near,' he said. 'But there's nothing I can do about it, stuck in here, is there?'

'Not a damn thing.'

'Well, can we at least exchange mobile numbers?'

'I thought you weren't allowed mobile devices in here.' Besides which, Ruth knew Carver's own smartphone was still logged in evidence

He gave a brief smile. 'Special dispensation – someone smuggled in a pay-as-you-go handset.'

She indulged him: it must be hell for him having to sit by and watch.

He gave her the number and Ruth pinged him a text: 'STOP WORRYING!'

He managed a smile at that.

She was almost through the door when Carver called her back. She would have left him to it, but the possibility of him getting out of bed and falling flat on his face made her turn back.

'*What?*' she said.

'This thing with Barrington,' he said. 'Be careful.'

'I'll be fine,' she said, unbuttoning her jacket to reveal a Casco baton holstered on her trouser belt. 'And if I'm not, you know where to send the cavalry.'

# 44

The morning briefing finally over with, Ruth left a spare jacket over the back of her office chair and stole out of the Major Incident Room. Her phone rang as she headed down the fire escape. It was Dr Yi, the forensic psychologist who had recommended Gaines to the investigation.

'Sorry it's taken so long to get back to you,' he said. 'You wanted some background on Lyall Gaines?'

'Just your general impression of him,' Ruth said.

'I don't know him personally,' Yi said. 'But he's respected in his field, and he has a solid publishing record. When he expressed an interest, I thought why not? He seemed to have a thorough knowledge of the case, and he was keen.'

Ruth slowed on the stairs. 'So, did you approach him, or did he approach you?'

'I put out a few feelers across social sciences and anthropology departments,' Yi said. 'Now I think of it, he wasn't on the original list. But he rang to say he would like to be considered.' He stopped. 'Is there a problem, Sergeant?'

'Honestly, Doctor? I don't know,' Ruth said. 'I'll be talking to him later – can I get back to you if I have any concerns?'

Yi promised he would do anything he could to help and she rang off. One more question to ask Gaines when she interviewed him.

She hoofed it the half mile up the road to Adela Faraday's previous place of work. The Liverpool office of LC&K Assets was based in a shiny new block near Mann Island. With the grand Port of Liverpool building and the Liver Buildings as neighbours, it was prime office space.

The building was clad in glass and black granite, giving a chequerboard effect from the street. Two sets of glass doors glided open with a discreet sigh, and a besuited receptionist greeted Ruth with just the right balance of warmth and professionalism. Ruth showed her warrant card and asked to speak to Mr Barrington.

The receptionist picked up the phone and moments later told her with a smile that Mr Barrington's PA would be down in just a few minutes, if she wouldn't mind signing in? Formalities completed and visitor's pass clipped to her lapel, Ruth turned to the lifts as her phone vibrated in her pocket. She checked the screen: it was Greg Carver. The lift doors opened a second later, and a man stepped out.

'Ms Lake,' he said.

'Detective Sergeant Lake,' she corrected, and saw something jump behind his eyes.

'Apologies,' he said, in that bland way men do when they think you're being a bitch but haven't the nerve to call you on it.

She declined Carver's call and followed the PA into the lift. Access to the fourth floor required a pass card and he flashed his at the near-field reader, then turned and stood next to her. He fidgeted all the way up, adjusting the card on the lanyard around his neck, tucking it inside his jacket, then tugging the jacket hem, front and back, and smoothing his tie. The lift doors slid open and he led her through a second set of obscured glass doors into the main office.

Mr Barrington's office was a partitioned section at the far end of an open-plan space. He rose and came around his desk to greet her. A big man, his suit well-tailored to hide a good five stones of excess weight, he had silver hair and sharp blue eyes, and wore a gold watch that probably cost more than she earned in six months.

'Sergeant Lake,' he said, with a falling inflection. He offered his hand as if to a recently bereaved relative. It was warm and soft, and well cushioned, like the rest of him.

She gripped it, hard, maintaining eye contact, and saw a slight tightening around the eyes and the tiniest hint of a down-turn of the corners of his mouth.

Mr Barrington released his grip before she did.

'Coffee, Sergeant?' he said. 'Water, perhaps?'

'No,' she said. 'Thank you.'

He nodded to his assistant, and the younger man left, closing the door after him.

Barrington waved her to an armchair in the corner. Normally, Ruth would opt for easy access to the door, but he was already wary of her and if it would get him to loosen up, she'd concede that much. He seated himself adjacent and leaned forward, forearms resting on his knees, hands lightly clasped in front of him. 'I expect this is about poor Adela?'

'It is.' Ruth looked past him to the PA's desk on the other side of the glass partition. He fussed over his paperwork the way he fussed with his clothing, straightening and tidying, without seeming to achieve very much.

'I spoke to one of your constables several days ago,' Barrington said. 'I'm not sure what I can add to that.'

That would be one of Jansen's team. She lifted her chin, acknowledging the information as though she knew all about the previous interview.

'We've had new information, and I was hoping you would be able to shed some light, sir,' she said.

'Of course – if I can. Bearing in mind Adela left the firm some seven months ago . . .' He opened his hands in a helpless gesture.

'This relates to something that actually *happened* seven months ago, sir,' she said, watching for his reaction.

His hands moved and she thought he was going to clasp them again, but he quickly diverted, resting them on the arms of the chair instead. He placed his feet wider apart and even slid one out so that it was almost touching her chair. If she wanted to get past, she'd have to climb over him.

Classic aggressive assertion.

He didn't speak, waiting for her to make the next move.

'A witness has said that he felt Adela was being harassed.'

'Really? How does one get an impression like that?'

'I was hoping you would tell me, sir. The witness said he thought it was an ex-boyfriend.'

'I'm afraid I wasn't privy to Ms Faraday's personal life.'

She noticed that he'd distanced himself from Adela, switching to her surname, and that he was leaning his chin on his cupped fist, his forefinger curled over his upper lip, to cover the lie.

*Oh, you were lovers all right,* she thought.

'She told the witness the name of her persecutor,' she said.

The tension in his body extended from his neck muscles to his arms, and the muscles in his thighs. She watched him, ready to act if he suddenly lashed out.

'His name was Chris,' she added.

Barrington stood abruptly, and she steeled herself.

He gestured to his PA to come in, and Ruth heard a clang as the younger man crashed his chair into his desk jumping to do the boss's bidding.

'You can see Sergeant Lake out,' Barrington said, when the PA put his head around the door.

Barrington didn't look at her, and Ruth read panic in the assistant's face when she didn't move from her chair. If this was how Barrington made his male staff feel, she could imagine that a woman might feel extremely intimidated.

'I didn't get to my question,' she said, standing smoothly, so that when he did turn around, they met eye to eye.

'The question,' he said, his jaw clamped tight, 'was implicit in the statement – and I *resent* the implication.'

'I kind of got that,' she said, pleasantly.

Blood darkened his face. 'Should you have any further questions regarding this fictitious "Chris" – or Ms Faraday, for that matter – you may ask them in the presence of my lawyer,' he said.

Ruth looked at him, thinking, *I most certainly will have more to ask you, Chris Barrington*. She wasn't about to go around him, so she waited and after a moment he seemed to rein in his temper, and turned away to his desk.

Ruth walked to the office doors in silence, the PA a pace behind, but she could feel the nervous energy crackling off him like static. He stood by her side at the lift, jangling the coins in his pockets.

'That didn't go well, did it?' she said, giving him a sidelong glance.

He cleared his throat, his Adam's apple bobbing, but didn't reply.

Something seemed to be holding up the lift, and she said, 'Did Adela have any problems with Mr Barrington?' He seemed to stop breathing, and she glanced over her shoulder. 'It's okay – no one can see us from here.'

He flushed. 'I really can't comment,' he said.

The assistant was in his late twenties, good-looking, if you didn't mind your men boyish, and the way he filled his suit, she wouldn't be surprised if he worked out. But his eyes were too watery, prone to dart away from direct contact, his fingers in a constant state of agitation, plucking and primping and tugging at his clothes.

'Be sure to hand your visitor's pass in at reception,' he said, as the lift doors finally slid open.

'You're not coming down to see me out?' she said.

'Just press the "zero" button. You don't need a pass to get out.'

She shrugged, and dug in her pocket for a business card. 'In case you want to talk,' she said. He didn't reach for it, and she tucked it in his breast pocket. He flinched as though she'd dug him in the ribs.

The man was badly scared.

Her phone buzzed and she checked it as she got into the lift. Carver again; his injuries seemed to've turned him into an old woman. As the lift's recorded voice intoned, 'Doors closing; going down', the PA stood square on to her for the first time, his jaw clamped tight as if he was afraid he'd blurt something out, but his fingers, traitorous and restless, spoke eloquently. They smoothed his lapels and snagged upon the ID card untidily trapped between this suit jacket and his tie. Ruth glanced at it, read the name: Chris Lomax.

*Chris.*

The doors began to slide across and Ruth stuck her hand in the safety beam. They juddered and opened again and she made a move to step out of the lift.

He slammed the heels of his hands into her chest and she bounced off the back of the box, her head booming from the

343

impact. He followed through with a punch to the side of her head and she buckled. Fighting a rising wave of nausea, she reached for her Casco baton even as she went down. He trapped her hand against her side, jabbed one of the buttons on the console, and punched her again. Light and pain exploded above her left eye, and then she felt nothing.

## 45

Just after midday, Greg Carver rang through to the police headquarters switchboard and asked to speak to DCI Parsons.

'Chief Inspector?' Parsons said, and Carver heard wariness in his tone.

'This is going to sound odd,' Carver said. 'But is Detective Sergeant Lake all right?'

He heard silence, and he knew it wasn't good.

'Why do you ask?' Parsons said.

'Because she's not answering her mobile, her home phone, or her desk phone, and I'm concerned,' he said.

'Do you have a reason for this "concern"?' Parsons asked.

Carver had dealt with the man before, and knew him as a prig, so he made an effort to slow his breathing and stay rational. 'Is she at her desk?'

More silence.

'Did she get back in time for her interview?' he asked, already knowing – dreading – the answer.

'How do you know about that?' Parsons said sharply. 'Has DS Lake been discussing the case with you?'

'For God's *sake*, man – will you get the rod out of your arse and *listen*? I've been ringing her all morning, but I can't raise her, and I think she's in danger.'

Parsons said, 'Dr Gaines postponed – but she would have missed the interview if he hadn't.'

'Have you tried her mobile?'

'She isn't answering,' Parsons admitted.

'You need to check with Chris Barrington, north west area manager at LC&K Assets. Ruth went to talk to him after the briefing – and, no, she wasn't discussing the Thorn Killer with me – she thought Barrington might know something about Adela Faraday's murder.'

He heard a muffled curse at the other end of the line. 'I'll send someone immediately,' Parsons said, surprising Carver with his business-like response. 'And I'll get someone to ping her phone.'

'Wait,' Carver urged. 'Tell me you'll get back to me – I need to know she's okay.'

Parsons hesitated. After an agonising moment, he said, 'All right. I'll call you as soon as I know anything.'

Carver waited fifty minutes for the call, refusing food and drink, sitting in the chair with the illicit phone in his hand between spells of pacing, staring at the screen, willing it to light up. He stood and looked out of the window, hoping to see Ruth cross the scrappy patch of grass below, on her way in to tell him what she'd found out from Barrington. He texted her. Tried her home number again. He even considered phoning Barrington himself but discounted that as a terrible idea.

He checked for the hundredth time, and saw DCI Parsons hurrying up the path towards the main entrance of the unit. DCI Jansen followed after him, with a younger man who looked familiar.

Carver felt a sudden cold weakness, and sat down heavily on the bed.

He heard a commotion in the corridor, a nurse's voice raised above those of Jansen and Parsons, and then his door burst open. Carver forced himself to his feet and turned to face Jansen.

'What the fuck have you been playing at?' Pale blue light danced like St Elmo's fire around Jansen's face.

Parsons got in front of the man and raised his hands, palm down. 'This isn't helping. DCI Carver, we need to know what Ruth told you. Why did she want to interview Mr Barrington?'

'Will someone for pity's sake tell me what's happened?'

'Ruth is missing,' Parsons said.

'Barrington?'

'Barrington is in custody. You need to tell us everything she told you.'

Carver felt cold and sick. He took a breath, hating this weakness, his inability to take action. 'She said she'd found a witness who said Adela had been harassed by someone named Chris—'

The two senior detectives exchanged a look. 'It is Barrington, isn't it?' Carver said. 'He's done something to Ruth.'

'What else did she tell you?'

'Nothing.'

'He's holding back,' Jansen said.

'I'm not,' Carver said, but he knew there was something else she'd told him. If he could just—

'Do you want to get her killed?' Jansen yelled.

Carver's heart beat fast and shallow; he couldn't think over the screaming in his head.

Then it stopped. For two whole seconds, the pounding in his chest ceased altogether, and then he felt a huge surge of pressure, as if a blockage had been forced out of an artery.

'No – wait. She said Adela was in a shooting club. That's where she got the intel. Adela told someone there that she was

347

being hassled, stalked – I don't know what. But the man who was bothering her was named Chris.'

'What was the name of this shooting club?' Jansen demanded. 'What was the name of her informant?'

Carver shook his head, 'I'm sorry, she wouldn't say.'

Jansen eyed him with contempt. 'You're a disgrace to the service. So is she.'

Carver leaned against the window, gripping the ledge hard, knowing that if he let go, he'd fall down. 'I may be,' he said with an effort. 'But know this: *everything* DS Lake has done is to find out the truth of what happened.'

Jansen turned away.

'DC Ivey –' Jansen pointed at Carver without looking at him '– watch him.'

Jansen was out of the door, Parsons close behind him.

Carver moved to the armchair, using the furniture to keep upright.

'Are you okay?' the younger man asked. 'Should I call a nurse?'

Carver shook his head. 'I could use some water.'

The detective poured him a beaker of lukewarm water from the jug on his bedside table, then took a respectful step back.

Feeling better after a couple of sips, Carver studied the young man. His pale skin and reddish hair, the keen, hungry look. Suddenly, he remembered.

'DC Ivey – you were with DCI Jansen when he came to question me the first time.'

He stood to attention. 'Yes, sir.'

'Do you know what happened, Ivey?'

He saw a flare of emotion, but Ivey said quietly, 'No one does, sir.'

'But you do know *something*.'

The younger man stared at his feet, and Carver watched a swirl of confused colours coalesce around his head and chest.

'You care about her.'

'We all do.'

'But you *know* her. I can tell by . . .' He changed what he was about to say to, 'By your reaction. You know Ruth Lake is a good person – a brilliant detective.'

Ivey nodded.

'Don't you want to help find her?' Carver didn't need to read the man's aura to see how desperately Ivey wanted it. 'Then tell me what you know.'

'She went to LC&K Assets, like you said,' Ivey began reluctantly. 'Chris Barrington said he had a few words with her, sent her off with his PA.'

'Can anyone corroborate that?'

'The staff we spoke to said she was only there a few minutes – they saw her walk out of the office with Barrington's PA. But she didn't sign out at reception.'

'What does the PA say?'

Ivey shifted his weight from one foot to the other.

'DC Ivey.'

'He's missing as well,' Ivey said.

'*He*? His name is Chris, isn't it?'

The young detective gave a curt nod.

The floor seemed to drop away, and Carver closed his eyes. 'Jesus, Ruth . . .'

'He's got no criminal record, nothing to mark him out, so maybe they just—'

'What?' Carver said. 'Went off for coffee and a *chat*?'

'I was gonna say . . .' Ivey bit his lip. 'Never mind what I was gonna say.'

Carver's thought processes were slow, as if every packet of information was having to be re-routed around the parts of his brain that had gone through the bruising experience with the psychologist the previous day. Now, a fresh realisation jostled to the forefront of his consciousness: he had a right to be questioned by someone of equal or senior rank, but that didn't explain why both Parsons *and* Jansen come all the way to the hospital.

'There's something else, isn't there?' he said.

A shimmer of green clung close to Ivey's silhouette.

'For pity's sake, man – she's my *friend*.'

The glow of light flared, changing to electric blue, as if all the contained energy of Ivey's emotional pain had gone beyond his control for a second. He rubbed his chin and nodded, twice, as though settling some internal dispute.

'Okay,' he said, 'You should know. I'm sorry, sir . . . there was blood in the lift.'

Carver wiped a hand over his face.

'They've sealed the building,' Ivey added quickly. 'A senior PolSA is advising on the search.'

Carver shook his head. 'I don't care *how* senior the Search Adviser is. They're wasting time, he's long gone. And so is Ruth.'

'It's possible,' Ivey agreed. 'But our lot's got every angle covered – all available personnel are looking for her – for both of them – sir. They've got people checking ANPR recordings around the city centre; there's an all-points warning out for Chris Lomax; a Matrix unit was on its way to his flat as we left HQ. If she's there, they'll find her.'

'Her phone?'

'Switched off, or destroyed,' the young detective said, looking sick. His own mobile phone rang and he jerked as if it had jolted forty thousand volts through him. He dragged it from his pocket, almost dropping it in his hurry to answer.

Carver watched as anxiety changed to confusion and despair. Ivey finished the call and turned a stricken gaze on him.

'They've found Lomax in his car – it was dumped within sight of Merseyside Police HQ.'

'Was Ruth with him? Is she all right?'

Ivey shook his head. 'Lomax was jammed in the boot – serious head injuries. He died at the scene.'

'And Ruth?' he said again.

'Her mobile phone was in the boot – wrecked. And . . .' He stared at Carver as if he couldn't make sense of what he'd been told.

'*What*?'

'They found a .22 pistol in the glove compartment.'

## 46

DC Ivey left the hospital shortly after the phone call, meaning Carver's only access to updates was BBC News 24. He watched, afraid to blink in case he missed something. The latest images showed a reporter talking from the edge of a police cordon. The mud-coloured block of Merseyside Police headquarters was visible in the distance, but as the camera focused in on the reporter, a grey Audi A3 saloon car came into view. The rear end of the car was shielded by a white forensic 'incitent'.

Carver recognised the reporter as one of the regulars from BBC News North West. He faced the camera and checked his earpiece before launching in.

'The body of a twenty-eight-year-old man was found in the boot of this car at two forty-five this afternoon,' he said, gesturing to the car behind him. 'Merseyside Police have named the man as Christopher Lomax. He was wanted for questioning in connection with the disappearance of Detective Sergeant Ruth Lake, who was last seen with Mr Lomax at the offices of LC&K Assets, a short distance from here.'

The presenter in the studio butted in: 'Now, Andy, Detective Sergeant Lake is a senior member of the team investigating the so-called "Thorn Killer" murders in Liverpool.'

'That's right,' the reporter said. 'But in a bizarre twist, police say that they do *not* believe Detective Sergeant Lake's disappearance is linked to the Thorn Killer inquiry, but instead, may be connected to the murder of a local businesswoman and the shooting of another Liverpool detective over the Christmas period. Detective Chief Inspector Simon Jansen, who is leading the inquiry into the murder of Adela Faraday, made a brief statement in the last few minutes.' He lowered the mic as the news bulletin switched to the interior of a briefing room at the headquarters at Canning Place. DCIs Jansen and Parsons sat at a table. On a screen behind them, the Merseyside Police logo.

An array of at least twenty microphones was set up in front of them, and cameras flashed as Jansen began: 'Detective Sergeant Ruth Lake spoke to a senior manager at the offices of LC&K Assets at nine-thirty this morning,' he said. 'She was last seen being escorted from the offices by this man – Christopher Lomax.' An image of a defensive-looking man in a business suit and tie appeared on the screen. The photographers went wild, and the room lit up for a few seconds.

When the activity died down, Jansen went on: 'We have no knowledge of events after that point, but we do have reason to believe that Detective Sergeant Lake may be injured.'

*The blood in the lift.*

The screen switched to an image of Ruth, and for a moment, Carver couldn't catch his breath.

'We would ask members of the public to look out for Sergeant Lake,' Jansen said, allowing time for the flurry of camera flashes to subside again. 'Please report any sightings to the hotline that has been set up for this purpose.' He gave the number, which simultaneously appeared on the news ticker at the bottom of the screen.

'We would stress that Sergeant Lake may be disorientated, so proceed with caution. Call the hotline number and wait for police and emergency medical support to arrive.'

What the hell was he implying – that Ruth bashed Lomax over the head and bundled him into the boot of his car?

Jansen was hit by a barrage of questions and as he waited for relative calm, Carver's mobile phone screen lit up.

Number withheld.

He slid the icon to 'answer'.

'Is this enough to get you back in the game?'

A chill ran through him. The caller was using a voice distorter, but he knew without question that he was speaking to the Thorn Killer, and that he had Ruth.

'What d'you want?' Carver said. These first few words had no power, and he forced some steel into his voice before he tried again. 'D'you want me? You can have me – just let her go.'

A soft chuckle. 'I thought I'd made myself clear. I don't want *you* – I want your attention. Do I have it?'

'One hundred per cent.'

'It's good to have you back.'

'Now, let her g—' Carver heard the tumbling notes of the disconnect before he even finished the word.

He rose to his feet, reached to the call button on the trolley by his bed, misjudged the distance and knocked the plastic beaker, the water jug and the TV remote control onto the floor.

The clatter brought a nurse running.

'I have to leave,' he said.

'Don't be stupid – you're not fit to go anywhere except back to bed.'

'I'm leaving,' he said, 'whether you like it or not.'

The nurse tried to ease him backwards to his chair, but he shook her off. A second nurse appeared at the door and she called over her shoulder: 'Get the ward doctor – we might need the neuro consultant, too – he's having an episode.'

'I'm not having an *episode*,' Carver said, 'I just want to *leave*.'

The nurse didn't try to force him into the chair, but she held her arms wide, moving left and right as he tried to pass, effectively corralling him.

'Can I help?'

Carver looked past the nurse and saw Dr Pendinning, looking with apparent surprise at the mess on the floor and the nurse trying to control her patient.

'You could talk some sense into him,' the nurse said, without turning around.

'Okay. Do you want to let me try?'

Pendinning remained where she was, a quiet calm presence in the midst of all the chaos, and Carver felt somewhat abashed; the nurse, too, it seemed, because she dropped her hands and straightened her uniform.

Carver felt suddenly exhausted; he staggered back a couple of steps to the window and leaned against the ledge for support.

'I don't know what the hell's got into him,' the nurse said.

'I expect he's been watching the news,' Pendinning said, glancing towards the screen.

The nurse followed her gaze, and gave a little wince of apology. She turned off the TV and after another silent exchange with the psychologist, walked out of the room, taking the remote wand with her.

Carver stared at his phone.

'There's nothing you can do, Greg,' Pendinning said. She sounded compassionate, but rational.

'Knowing it doesn't make it any easier.'

'I know.' She waited, and that pause – her taking the time to consider what he'd said – made him feel like she really did understand. Finally, she asked, 'What do you think you should do?'

'Get out of here and look for her.'

'You think that will help?'

He closed his eyes, exhaled in a long sigh. 'No.'

'So . . .'

He looked into her face. The last time he saw her, Pendinning looked tired, but today there was a slight flush to her cheeks, and he wondered if she was more disturbed by his behaviour that she was willing to admit. As always, her hair was pulled back into a ponytail, but the habitual twinkle of humour was gone from her eyes.

'They have squads of people looking for her,' Pendinning said. 'If she's wandering the streets they'll find her.'

'That's just it,' Carver said. 'I don't believe Ruth overpowered Lomax and just *wandered off*.'

She looked genuinely curious. 'What *do* you think?'

'The Thorn Killer has her.' He stated it as fact, and just saying it made him feel weak.

She took a breath. 'Why would you think that?'

'Because I just spoke to him.' He clenched his jaw to stop it trembling.

'My God . . .' Pendinning said, 'you have to tell someone.'

He hadn't thought of that. *What the hell is wrong with you?* He fumbled with his phone, got through to the Canning Place switchboard and was put through to Parsons.

'A crank call,' Parsons said. 'Must be.'

'No,' Carver said.

'The hotline has been inundated.'

'The call came through to my new smartphone. I've had it for less than a day. How would—'

356

'All right,' Parsons said. 'Give me the number, I'll have someone check where the call came from, get back to you.'

'Thank you,' Carver breathed.

He had felt Pendinning's gaze on him during the entire call, and when he closed the line, she said, 'Is there anything I can do?'

He flashed to the cognitive interview experiment the day before, though he couldn't say why. Whatever information lay buried in his subconscious about the night he was shot was buried too deep.

'Help me get out of here,' he said.

## 47

Darkness. A stillness in the air that feels familiar, oddly comforting. A whiff of dusty cobwebs and autumn woodland fills Ruth Lake with a warmth and peace the like of which she hasn't felt in almost twenty years. She realises she is in her grandfather's 'sanctuary', his secret place in a neighbourhood so crowded and oppressive he used to joke there wasn't room to have a private thought without asking someone to shove up a bit to make room for it.

Her grandparents' house is in a shabby Victorian terrace of two up, two down dwellings with shallow-pitched roofs of slate. Crouched in the shadow of Goodison Park football stadium, it is narrow and pinched, and smells faintly of damp. The front door opens to a tiny porch, and the parlour is screened off from the street by a red velvet curtain. To Ruth, coming in, it always feels like she might lift that curtain and step through a magical doorway into a strange and wonderful story. Sometimes, if Granddad is in yarn-spinning mood, those stories do unfold, and Ruth never tires of listening to his tales of adventure.

But that was years ago, she thinks. Granddad is long gone . . . *I must be asleep, dreaming. I need to wake up.*

For a few more seconds the feeling of comfort and warmth persists, then she hears a sound. A footstep.

Someone is moving around her, in the dark.

*You need to fight this.* But she can't move, can't even open her eyes.

She remembers the lift. The PA coming at her. Sees Lomax draw back his fist to punch her a second time. A splintering of light as he drives his fist into her face, sending shards of pain into her brain. Then the reek of oil and engine fumes. Lomax, forcing her into the boot of a car. Her heart is beating so fast it hurts. She grabs his wrist, but she has no strength; he shakes her off, pulls his fist back. She waits for the impact. Hears a soft thud. Lomax turns, shock on his face, his arm raised in defence, now. He's too slow. Ruth sees the killer blow, feels Lomax's blood spatter, warm on her face. He drops and she hears a dull, wet thud she knows is the sound of his head hitting the concrete.

She tries to boost herself out of the car and a strong hand reaches in to help her. But relief quickly turns to fear, as the hand shoves her back. She feels a hot needle of pain.

*Wake up!*

Ruth opens her eyes. Tries to make sense of where she is.

*So dark . . .*

She is parched; a metallic taste at the back of her mouth reminds her of a novocaine injection she once had for a dental procedure, and she realises she's been drugged.

She senses, rather than sees, a shadow off to her right, but can't turn her head to look. She tries to lift her hand; there is no feeling in it.

A searing flash. She closes her eyes, and when she opens them again, she sees the silhouette of a figure, magnified by the intense light and her blurred vision. It looms, huge and dark for a second. Then it vanishes and there is only the light, unbearable, blinding. She whimpers, squeezing her eyes shut against the pain, hears the clang of a metal door closing, and is plunged into darkness again.

## 48

By three fifteen, Carver was stepping out of a taxi outside Ruth Lake's house. Dr Pendinning had phoned Emma on his behalf, since she was blocking his calls, had even persuaded her to bring some clothing and the personal effects she'd been looking after since his hospital admission.

The sun was already setting, casting an angry red pall over the street, and his shadow fell long and alien on the grey pavement. The front door was secured and a quick recce revealed that the alley at the back of the row was barred by a steel gate which he was in no condition to climb.

His mobile rang. It was Parsons.

'Where are you?'

'Did you trace the call?' Carver said.

'Yes. I sent someone to talk to you at the hospital, but you weren't there.'

'Did you get a location?'

He heard a long exhalation at the other end of the line. 'It was made from a payphone at the hospital.'

Carver leaned against the side wall of the house.

'We've got people on site, now,' Parsons said.

'You won't find him. He rang from there to – '

'To what?' Parson said.

'To make a point. To get my attention.'

'Look, I agree with you. I think you may be on to something. But if he left a trace, we'll find it.'

'Yeah, well good luck with that.' Carver hung up, returned to the street and rang next door's bell. No answer. He tried the other side. Nothing. Across the street, a front door opened and a middle-aged Pakistani woman peeped out.

He smiled and started to cross the street, but she slammed the door shut. He dipped in his pocket for his wallet and fished out his warrant card. He knocked, announcing himself as police, but the door remained firmly shut. He couldn't blame her: a man with the unsteady gait of a drunk, his hair cropped unevenly, a scar still showing through the regrowth, peering in at the neighbours' windows.

He turned away, lost his balance and grabbed the gatepost to avoid a fall. He sat on the low wall for a few seconds, while the street did a slow three-sixty degree turn, heard hurried foot-steps, the sound of pram wheels.

'You all right, love?'

He looked up, saw not a young mother with a pram, but an elderly woman with a shopping trolley. She was as wide as she was tall, and wore a rainproof jacket buttoned tight across her middle.

'Just . . . had a bit of a dizzy spell,' Carver said.

She folded her hands across her middle and appraised him for a moment. 'Come on,' she said. 'I'll make you a cuppa.'

He gave her a quizzical look. 'Don't you think you should be careful who you invite into your home?'

'Go-waaay . . .' She grinned, showing a set of dentures that looked slightly too big for her mouth. 'Everyone knows you. You've been on the telly – you're Ruthie's boss.'

'*Ruthie?*' he said.

She turned her back on him, calling over her shoulder: 'Her mum and dad moved next door in nineteen seventy-five – just after they got married, that was.' She crossed the street, using the trolley like a rolling Zimmer frame. Still talking, she pulled a huge bunch of keys from her jacket pocket and sorted through them on the doorstep. 'She grew up here – played on this front step with my grandkids.' The old woman slotted a key in the Yale lock and looked him in the eye. 'Your Sergeant Lake'll always be Ruthie to me.'

He followed her down the hallway to a modern kitchen and she told him to pull up a chair while she brewed tea and made him a sandwich. He tried to decline, feeling a panicked sense that the more time he spent here, the more Ruth was in peril.

She wagged the bread knife at him like a scolding finger. 'When was the last time you ate?' she said, pronouncing it 'et'.

He admitted it was probably the night before, and she tutted. 'No wonder you're fainting in the street, then, is it?' She shook her head, muttering something about hospital food, and a few moments later, presented him with a mug of tea and a sandwich five inches thick.

'There y'are – proper docker's doorstep.'

He felt suddenly ravenous and took a huge bite.

She laughed. 'Does me good seeing a man with an appetite sitting at my table,' she said.

She sat opposite him and chatted, introducing herself as Peggy Connolly, mother to seven, grandmother to fifteen, great-grandmother to more than she cared to count. When he'd finished the sandwich, she skewered him with a look.

'Now, what are you up to, hanging around Ruthie's? You're not gonna find her there, you know.'

He stared at her. *She doesn't know.*

He began hesitantly, anxious for the old woman's heart, 'Mrs Connolly—'

'Peggy.'

'Peggy,' he repeated. 'I . . . I've got some bad news . . .'

'Jesus, they haven't *found* her, have they?'

'You know she's missing?'

'This isn't the dark ages – I've got the telly, haven't I?' she demanded, instantly belligerent. 'I've got me DAB radio.'

'She's still missing,' he said, feeling roundly cuffed about the ears.

She crossed herself. '*Jesus, Mary and Joseph*, I thought you was gonna say she was *dead*.' Quickly over the shock, her eyes narrowed and she tapped him on the arm.

'You've come to see what she's been getting up to, all hours of the night.' She must have seen the surprise in his face, because she added: 'I'm old, I don't sleep like I used to. She's in her kitchen till after midnight, up again before the milkman. I see the light across my back yard.'

Working through his unofficial case files, no doubt. Sooner or later, Parsons or Jansen or the PolSA would get it into their heads that it would be a good idea to search her place. He needed to get inside that house, if only to get rid of the evidence Ruth had stolen.

Peggy Connelly seemed to read his mind. She heaved the bunch of keys onto the kitchen table and picked through Yales and mortises, finally holding one brass key up by its tip.

'That'll get you in,' she said.

He stared at her, marvelling.

'I've lived here since Germany invaded Poland,' she said. 'Time was, you'd leave a key with a neighbour when you went away, for emergencies, like. Got keys to half the street on here.' She lifted the bundle by the one key, jangling it, smiling to herself. 'There's some good memories in this lot.'

She handed Carver the bunch so that he could wrestle the key off the ring.

"Course, there's hardly any of us oldies left,' she said, her smile tinged with sadness now. 'Some of the new kids coming in have swapped to them plastic doors, but I keep the keys anyway – for sentimental value.'

Carver stood carefully, and found his balance improved.

'It would be best if nobody knew I was here,' he said.

'I seen you getting out the taxi from the top of the street,' she said. 'No police cars. No sirens.' She gave him a knowing nod. 'Goes without saying, lad.'

He squeezed her hand gently and shambled to the kitchen door.

She called him, her tone business-like, no nonsense. 'Mr Carver?'

He turned to her, his hand on the door knob.

'I'll be wanting that back,' she said, eyeing the key in his hand. 'After you bring Ruthie home, safe.'

## 49

Inside the house, Carver noticed the faint nutty, chocolatey smell of coffee – Ruth always did like a good ground roast. It was cold, yet the house had a warmth that had nothing to do with the air temperature.

But he didn't have time for sentimentality.

He started at the back of the house, in the kitchen, since that was where Peggy seemed to think Ruth did most of her work. The cupboards contained nothing but kitchenware and cooking ingredients. The sitting room, up the hall on the right, had been knocked through to the dining room, and one end was occupied by a giant wall-mounted TV. A Blu ray player and an X-box 360 lay on a black glass stand below the TV screen. He hadn't known that Ruth was into gaming.

Two bookcases built into the alcoves of the front room were jammed with everything from popular science to forensic texts, the fiction almost exclusively science fiction and fantasy. More things he didn't know – hadn't bothered to get to know – about Ruth. But there would be time enough for guilt and self-recrimination. He squinted along the shelves, taking advantage of the lowering rays of the sun: a fine dusting on the exposed surfaces suggested the books hadn't been disturbed in a while; she couldn't have hidden the files here.

He moved upstairs, noticed that the front bedroom curtains were closed. He flicked the light switch in the gathering gloom, scoped out the room from the doorway, and almost immediately saw his box of files on top of the wardrobe. He lifted it down and set it on the bed before removing the lid. The pistol was gone. He'd half-expected that; as soon as DC Ivey said they'd found a .22 in Chris Lomax's car, his mind had gone to the pistol Ruth had lifted from his flat the night he was shot. It was only a matter of time till ballistics established it was the weapon that killed Adela Faraday.

Carver's hand went involuntarily to the healing wound in his chest. Most likely they would have matched the gun to the bullet lodged near his spine, too – if the surgeons had been able to dig it out of him. There must have been a spent bullet casing in his flat; Ruth would have taken that, too – he couldn't see her missing something so fundamental. The Thorn Killer might not have considered a shell casing, though. He lifted every file out of the box, but there was no sign of it.

The Thorn Killer had found a way to introduce the gun into evidence and implicate Lomax as the shooter, exonerating both Carver and Ruth Lake. But Carver didn't think for one moment that he had acted in the interests of justice. TK didn't do anything that didn't serve his own purpose; he had saved Ruth to use her as bait, to bring Carver back into the investigation.

He was just as certain that Ruth was the killer's next intended victim. What better way to keep Carver's undivided attention than to torment him with thoughts of what she was going through? The other victims had survived weeks of torture, so it was bitter consolation that Ruth's life was not in immediate danger, only for the horrible reason that the Thorn Killer's 'artistry' could not be rushed.

'Okay . . .' He took a breath and exhaled. He needed to stick with what he had, and decide where to go from there. The stolen evidence was gone; there was nothing he could do about that. But the rest was intact, as far as he could tell.

A destructive little voice whispered in his head: 'The files are useless – TK wouldn't leave them if he thought there was anything that might help you.' But arrogance was the greatest weakness of the psychopath: believing investigators far beneath their own intellect had snared many a killer.

So Carver forced himself to take his time to sift through the crime scene and post mortem reports, the photographs, his notes supplemented by Ruth's – hers more neatly filed. He found the notes he'd scratched on the transcripts of interviews with Kara Grogan's friends and fellow students. Re-reading them now, he saw them for what they were: desperate, alcohol-fuelled, rage-filled rants. He'd been out of control.

Ruth's additions, written in her concise, objective style, made it easy to catch up on details of her discoveries: that Kara had been preparing for a film role; that she had a terror about freezing on stage. He took time over Ruth's interviews with 'psychics' and her impressions of the people she had spoken to, and marvelled at her ability to old read the cold readers.

He found Ruth's handwriting among his charts and diagrams, too, and saw an echo of his own obsession. *Does she realise it's taken over her life, the way it did mine?* She had researched stage fright, psychics and cold readers, even tattoo symbolism. He found printouts of sigils and Celtic symbols he recognised from the victims' bodies. One image was a nine-teenth-century sampler. The text, laboriously stitched in the fabric by a teenaged girl, suggested that she had been a rape victim and had attempted suicide.

'Are the tattoos confessional samplers?' Ruth had written in the margin in her neat hand. She had made notes about the secrets the victims had held back from their families – they had known about Tali Tredwin's eating disorder and suicide attempts as a young adult, as well as Jo Raincliffe's double identity as stripper 'Joline', but hadn't connected them with their abduction and murder. Kara's stage fright, the job offer, the cruel trick her housemates had played on her were all new to him.

'The eye images tattooed on the victims are symbolic,' Ruth wrote in her research notes. 'The Eye of Providence represents knowledge, wisdom, the revealing of hidden truths.'

Beneath that, typed in bold and underlined: 'It's all about secrets for the Thorn Killer. But how is he finding his victims?'

A few lines further down, in her own hand, she'd added a note: 'Did we miss one of KG's lecturers?' She'd added an evidence number. 'CCTV, School Lane – after KG kicked out of theatre.' She'd noted the time log on the recording at 20:34:05. Eight thirty-four p.m., and five seconds. 'Woman spoke to Kara. Did K tell her where she was headed? Rendezvous with TK??? Talk to staff/students.'

Riffling through the rest, he discovered a set of email exchanges between Ruth and Dr Gaines – the man Ruth was supposed to interview earlier in the day. Her notes revealed that he was an anthropologist, a consultant brought in to advise the inquiry team.

In a separate document, headed, '*Interview notes, Dr Lyall Gaines*', Carver read with increasing concern that Gaines had posed as a psychic named 'Shadowman', concealing his identity until Ruth discovered it for herself.

*A Home Office-approved consultant acting like a carnival side-show performer – what the hell?*

Reading on, Carver discovered that the anthropologist had attended a psychic reading hosted by Jasmine Hart at the Epstein Theatre the night Kara was last seen. Even more alarmingly, that he'd made a repeat appearance when Ruth had attended another reading with the same psychic, and had followed Ruth after the event.

'Everything he says seems calculated to make me uneasy,' she'd written. 'He's glib, self-aggrandising and shallow.'

Dr Gaines seemed a good a place to start.

# 50

Ruth Lake comes to under lights so strong she can feel the heat of them.

*Am I in hospital?*

Something odd is happening: someone is circling beyond the intense, glaring white light. She squeezes her eyelids shut.

'At last.' The voice is distorted, deep and resonant, like a man talking down a drainpipe. 'It's a pity about the bruising,' he says, 'But it'll be gone by the time you're ready.'

*Ready?* Ruth's heart rate triples in the space of three seconds. She tries to move. Can't. Her head is propped up by some kind of moulded foam support; she can feel it supporting her neck. She is naked, except for her underwear. Her wrists, upper arms, thighs and ankles are strapped to the table, but she can't feel the restraints. Can't feel her limbs at all.

The inner aspect of her forearm already bears a symbol: a face, no eyes, nose or mouth. A mask on an elongated stem.

*Oh, God . . .*

'Background work,' the voice says. 'Different skin types take colour in different ways. Next time, you'll be awake.'

She tries to move, to struggle – to do *some* damn thing – but her body won't obey her, and it feels like a weight is pressing on her chest.

'The paralysing effect of the poison,' the killer says, interpreting her actions. 'Actually, I cheat a bit – I prep all my girls with a neuromuscular blocker. It's more reliable, less . . . risky.'

'Tali,' Ruth slurs. 'Thasss-why you dint f-finishhh.'

'Yes, Tali was . . . unfortunate. It's difficult to predict the potency of the aconitine decoction – and she was highly sensitive – succumbed before I'd really hit my stride.'

Ruth tries to remember how she'd got here. Recalls the office building, talking to Adela's former boss, the nervous PA. She'd looked down at his ID card. Pain exploding in her head.

'Lomax,' she murmurs. 'Bastard . . . They'll get you . . . I left word . . .'

'Poor Sergeant Lake. You're confused. 'I *rescued* you from Lomax – don't you remember?'

She does. She was in the boot of a car, thinking, *So this is how it ends*. Lomax drew his fist back. Then he turned, arm raised in defence. She remembered the wet thud of his skull as it hit the concrete floor.

'Lomax?' she says again.

'. . . is dead. You know he murdered Adela?'

Ruth tries to nod. Can't. 'Yes,' she says.

'That's my girl.' The man in the shadows pats her shoulder. His hand is rough, calloused. 'The police found the gun in the glove compartment of Lomax's car. His fingerprints are on it – I made sure of that.'

*How did he get the gun?* The fog lifts and she knows. *He was in my house.*

'You don't seem very pleased,' the killer says. 'Carver is exonerated, Adela's murderer is dead – you will be hailed as a hero. You should be happy.'

She forces disdain into her voice: 'So, you've been in my house. Well, good for you. D'you think you left anything of yourself there? Criminals are never as careful or as clever as they think they are.'

'I seem to've covered my tracks fairly effectively at Chief Inspector Carver's apartment.'

'So, Carver was right,' Ruth says. 'You *were* there the night he was shot.'

'No – I meant on previous occasions.'

He's been inside Carver's flat multiple times? How long has he been watching them?

'I did slip in a couple of nights later to pick something up on Greg's behalf,' he went on. 'But the night of the shooting there was only Chris Lomax – and you, of course. Yes, Sergeant, I was watching. Saw you arrive. Saw you empty the place of anything that might help the investigation. That piqued my curiosity, I'll admit.'

Ruth closes her eyes. *You screwed up, Ruth – you made such a terrible mess of everything.*

'No smart comeback, Sergeant?' The faceless voice says. 'Well, don't feel *too* badly. Carver is about to return the favour. He's inside your house as we speak, rooting through your files. The police should be there any moment now.'

*He's reading you. You need to do better, Ruth.*

'Carver's more resourceful than you give him credit for,' she says.

'Really?' The mocking tone is gone; she hears a hunger in his voice.

*He wants more.* Instinctively, she knows she needs to give less. She focuses on her facial muscles. She can feel her lips, her cheeks, in the way that you feel them as a dentist's injection wears off: they feel bigger, bulkier, only marginally under her control.

'You're a detective. You read crime scenes – and you say criminals don't cover their tracks very well,' he said. 'Well, I read people. And they are never as adept at covering their

372

feelings as they think they are. I eased up on the paralytics, too – that'll help.'

*Keep still, think of a blank sheet of white paper.* It isn't hard under the blinding white of the spotlights.

'All the others resisted at first,' her captor says. 'But eventually they revealed their secrets.'

'You're like a child, collecting Pokémon cards.' Ruth's tongue feels thick in her mouth; she has to work hard not to slur.

'This, from a former technician with a second-rate degree from a third-rate provincial university.'

*He's engaged with you – stopped seeing you as an object – he's trying to hurt you. You, personally, not some mannequin he's daubing with ink. And he's angry. Use that.*

She controls her breathing as she squints into the light. 'You think I'm provincial. Which makes you . . . what – a sophisticate? You're telling me torturing and murdering women is an intellectual pursuit?'

He leans in, and Ruth sees eyes, a nose like the snout of a muzzled dog. She flinches, waiting for the bite. But in the next instant, he's gone, and all she hears is the angry raggedness of his breathing.

She calms herself, says, 'I suppose it's true what they say: scratch a narcissist, find the damaged kid beneath.'

'You know what else they say?' The voice changer is acting against her abductor, picking up every growl and stutter of breath. "Criticise a narcissist, brace for an attack."'

She sees another flash of the snout.

*Be still; think straight. It's only the voice changer.*

She works hard on keeping her face and eyes empty of fear, but she can't slow the thud of blood in the arteries of her throat, and knows he has seen it.

'Anxious, Sergeant?'

'Yeah, well, you have me at a disadvantage,' she says.

'Best you don't forget that.'

Despite the warning, she feels the heightened tension in the room turn down a degree or two. *He knows he's in control. But he is curious.* She needs to tap into that curiosity.

'I'm puzzled,' she says.

He starts pacing again, his shadow flitting from one spotlight to the next. 'By what?'

Ruth hears a warning and a threat in those two words.

'Why did you rescue me from Lomax?' Using his own word to flatter his ego. 'Was it to draw DCI Carver back into the investigation?'

No answer.

'You know you have a better chance of getting away with what you're doing with DCI Parsons in charge.'

'Parsons has no fire.'

'So, you were bored?'

'That, and I wanted to see what Carver would do if I took you.'

'Manipulation,' Ruth says.

'A field experiment.'

*Field experiment.*

The shock of recognition must show in her face, because he chuckles softly. 'You don't think I rescued you because you're *worth* rescuing, do you?'

'Oh, I know I am,' she says, relieved that he has misinterpreted shock for disappointment. 'But there's a bit of the narcissist in all of us, isn't there?'

She hears a slight hiss, the voice changer mic picking up every subtle intake of breath. She doesn't need to see his face to know his reaction. In the silence that follows she can't tell where he is, and she experiences a panicky impulse to struggle against her bonds.

'See?'

His voice hisses in her ear and she tries not to cringe.

'Right now, you're suppressing the imperative to flee with every fibre of your being.' His breath on her skin is tormenting. 'I know you, Ruth Lake. I've been inside your suh-*weet* little house. I've seen the care you took tastefully renovating and modernising. I've seen your *bijou* courtyard garden. I found your scrapbook really rather moving.'

Her scalp tingles and she feels a sudden squeezing sensation around her heart. *He found the scrapbook.* Rollinson?

'Odd that you should hide it like that.'

Every nerve in Ruth's body rebels. It feels as if a thousand snakes are squirming over her exposed flesh; she wants to scream. But she forces it down.

'Too many painful memories?'

She wants to kill him.

He moves closer, whispers in her ear: 'I. See . . . you.'

'There's really not much to see,' she says, imposing control. 'I work, I run, I read a little.'

'No, no, no. There's more.'

'I do have a secret passion for eGaming . . .'

'Not so secret – your gaming gadgets are openly on display. In that context, I am curious as to why you would hide your family scrapbook.' He pauses and she sees his shadow flit from one lamp to the next, traversing the length of the table.

'Although some of those press cuttings are outside the scope of the average family album. So perhaps it's guilt.'

Her guts turn to iced water but she pushes back: 'Is it guilt that makes you hide your face? Or do you think it gives you more power over the women you brutalise?'

'That's trite and shallow.' He sounds affronted. 'Did you find a single bruise on any of my kills?'

'There's more than one way to brutalise a victim,' Ruth says. 'You stripped those women of their identity, carved them into a creation of your own twisted mind.'

'I *revealed* their true identity.'

'Five women. Humiliated, terrorised, tortured, and poisoned—'

'People,' he corrects. 'I am interested in *people* – in the secrets they withhold.'

'"People" implies men *and* women. You target only women.'

'Women are of necessity naturally inclined to secrecy. They withhold in order to survive, subjugating their needs, hiding their resentment from those closest to them, disguising their rage against the lot they have been stuck with by virtue of their gender, sublimating it into something rather beautiful: love of family and home. That makes them inherently more interesting.'

'"Women subjugate their needs"?' Ruth paraphrases. 'That's *not* trite?'

She hears a growl of disapproval, and briefly sees again the thrust of a chin the eyes – but only faintly, like a face pressed into a bedsheet, then he is gone again.

'So, why Kara, or Tali, or Jo, and not someone like Adela? She had more secrets than all of them combined.'

He scoffs. 'Adela's only *real* secret was she thought like a man.'

'Because she enjoyed sex without commitment?' she says, feeling more in control.

'Because she used sex as a weapon.'

'A weapon?' Ruth can't help herself; she is intrigued.

'Adela's financial inspirations were less spreadsheet, more bedsheet.'

'Pillow-talk?' Ruth says. '*That's* how she became a financial whizz?'

'I thought you would have worked *that* one out before now. Gives a new twist to insider trading, doesn't it?' He laughs, and the sound is guttural, ugly. 'She turned her charm on Chris Lomax after she discovered that Barrington wasn't big on post-coital chat.'

'She screwed the PA to get to the boss.'

'To be fair, it wasn't all about sex,' her abductor says. 'And Adela didn't *demand* information, she showed an interest – asked Lomax about his working day – which was, of course, centred around *Barrington's* working day. Adela used that information – used *him* – for three years. Just long enough to make sufficient cash to quit her job and set up on her own. And when she left the firm, she cut all ties.' He clicks his fingers. 'Just like that.'

Ruth recalls the nervy, insecure PA. 'Brutal,' she says.

'Women are dealt a shit hand right from the off,' he says. 'And if sex is about power – well, there's nothing in the rule book that says the power should always be in the hands of men.'

Ruth hears bitterness in her captor's tone, feeling she is missing something.

'How do you know all of this?' she asks.

He pauses, standing at the foot of the table, his outline grotesquely enlarged by the glare of the lights. 'I make it my business to know everything there *is* to know about Detective Chief Inspector Carver. He's investigating me.'

'You stalked him.'

'Surveilled,' he corrected. 'Him, and Adela, and Lomax, and Councillor Hill – who had quite the *pash* for Adela. And you, for a brief spell. Mr Hill's wife was a promising prospect for a while,' he adds, reflectively. 'But then I saw you, shivering in the snow outside Carver's apartment—'

'And you were smitten.'

'Let's say my curiosity was piqued. Until that point, you were always so closed, I thought you simply . . . dull. But on that night, I realised just how much you were hiding.'

## 51

Something flashed beyond the closed curtains of the bedroom, and Carver looked up. He didn't need to take a peek to recognise the blue lights of a police vehicle.

Leave the box of files, or take it?

*Leave it*, he thinks. *It could lead them to Gaines*.

He took a few quick snapshots on his phone camera, jammed the files in the box, and hobbled downstairs.

The doorbell rang, followed by an insistent hammering.

'Ruth Lake,' the officer shouted. 'Police. Please come to the door.'

Carver hesitated on the last step. It was a short distance from the stairs to the glazed interior door, and he could see three bulky silhouettes beyond the outer door.

*Can they see me?* Ruth's front door was one of the originals: wood, with narrow slats of glass. He just had to hope that he could blend with the shadows in the hallway.

He moved slowly around the newel post, ducking down and keeping close to the banister as he crept to the kitchen. The door was ajar and off-centre of the hall, so they might not see the extra light if he opened it wider, but he took no chances, squeezing through into the well-lit room without touching the door, praying they hadn't sent anyone around to the back, yet.

The hammering started up again.

The back door was a composite, triple-locked. No key.

*Shit*. Heart thudding, he rummaged in the drawer closest to it, came up with a key, jammed it in the lock at the instant he heard the crunch of a key in the lock of the front door. This was an injured police officer's home, not some scally's doss – of *course* they would send a locksmith.

Hoping they would take things slowly, not wanting to panic her, he stepped out into the freezing air and closed the door after him, crossing the yard as fast as his wobbly legs would carry him. There was no lock on the gate, only a bolt, top and bottom. He eased both back, and was through in seconds, into a narrow alley that stank of dog piss and overripe bins.

A few yards down, he saw a black grille at the near end. He'd forgotten the security gates.

He heard them calling Ruth's name inside the house, then, from the back door: 'Door's unlocked.' A pause. 'Ruth? Ruth Lake. Police – can you answer me?'

In the alley, Carver cast about for somewhere to hide. An unlocked gate, maybe. But he'd only find himself trapped in another back yard, and they *would* come looking, and they would find him.

At that moment, he heard the click of a latch as the next-door gate opened, and he braced himself. He had failed. He turned, and saw Peggy's grey head poke around the frame.

She beckoned him into her yard and silently pointed towards her back door, shooing him along impatiently. She stayed where she was in her carpet slippers, weatherproof jacket slung over her shoulders, unfastened.

'What's going on over there?' she demanded, calling indignantly over the wall. 'Yiz had better clear off coz I've rung for the police.'

'We *are* the police,' someone called back.

'Pull the other one, love, it's got bells on.'

Carver was safely inside her kitchen by then.

A second later, he heard Peggy exclaim, 'Jesus, you bloody great *ijit* – d'you wanna give an old lady a heart attack?'

He guessed that one of the uniforms had bobbed up over the wall to check the place out. He heard a muttered, 'Sorry love.'

'G'waan, get out of it,' Peggy snarled, then slammed the door and locked it.

When she turned to Carver, she was grinning. 'Don't think they'll be knocking at *my* door in a hurry,' she said. 'Did you get what you need?'

Carver nodded. 'Something, anyway.'

She led him through to the hallway and made him sit on the stairs while she went to the front door, opened it a crack.

'I'll keep dixie, let you know when the coast's clear.'

A couple of minutes later, she turned to him. 'They're all inside. Think you can manage a few minutes' walk?'

Carver stood, testing him limbs. 'Yeah. Yes, I think I can.'

'You sure? 'Cause I can borrow you my trolley if you want.'

'I'll manage,' he said with a smile.

She did one more sweep of the street before waving him forward. 'Turn left out the house – it's only about fifty yards to Smithdown Road. You can flag a cab there.'

Carver stared at her in admiration.

'Wha'?' she said.

'You're quite something, Peggy Connolly.'

'Should of seen me in me heyday,' she said.

## 52

Ruth Lake is burning. Awake, but without the muscle tone to enable her to move, her eyes are taped closed and she is strapped firmly to the table. Her forearm feels like second-day sunburn rubbed vigorously with sandpaper.

He is working on her forearm again. He has punctured her skin a thousand times, replacing the thorn styluses when they become blunted. She hears him toss them aside every fifteen minutes or so, rattling into a plastic tub like discarded pencils.

'A needle would be easier,' he says. 'But less authentic.' His voice has the deep growl of the voice distorter.

She wonders why is he still using it when she is blindfolded. *Because you know him, and he doesn't want you to be able to connect with him as a human being. He wants you to remain a mere object.*

Periodically, he pauses, rubs carbon powder into her skin. It sears like hot coals. Then he starts over again, pricking over the same swollen and inflamed patch of skin.

'Your first Eye of Truth is about halfway done.'

*Is that what he calls them?*

'How does it feel?'

Her breathing is shallow and rapid and sweat springs from every pore. Her heart beats painfully hard against her ribcage.

'Fuck off,' she says, and he laughs.

'When we really get into it, you won't be able to make a squeak, so feel free to yell, now.'

She suggests a better use for his thorns – one that involves an orifice and every discarded stylus in his sharps tub. 'Suit yourself,' he says. 'I've used muscle relaxants and barbiturates this time, so you're actually mildly sedated. You'll be completely paralyzed for the larger patches – intubated and ventilated, of course, but you won't have any anaesthesia or pain relief. You will be fully conscious.'

Feverish with pain, Ruth tries to tune him out, but his voice drills into her skull. She can't help it; a tear squeezes from under her eyelid.

'Stings, doesn't it,' he says.

*Distance yourself*, she thinks. *Disown the pain. You know how*.

She slows her breathing and focuses on a cloud she imagines into being. It carries her on a cool draught of air, miles away, and her tortured arm is no longer a part of her.

With the pain under control, she is free to think. Mind racing, she works back through their last exchange of words: he had been following Carver and Adela and Lomax. *And you*, her inner voice says. That was how he intercepted Lomax in the car park of LC&K Assets; that was how he stayed way ahead of them in the investigation. He'd been inside Carver's flat, her house – had probably read Carver's files as he wrote them up, witnessed his rapid disintegration after Kara's body was found.

*But he murdered Lomax in a city centre car park in broad daylight*. That seemed like a desperate act.

'You screwed up,' she says.

She hears a gasp of surprise, feels a stab of bruising pain as he inadvertently jabs the thorn deeper than he had intended.

'Careful,' he says. 'Wouldn't want to make a mess of this.'

'I wasn't supposed to make the connection between Lomax and Adela – you didn't think I was capable.'

'As I recall, you went to interview his boss,' he says.

But she notices that he hasn't gone back to work on the tattoo.

Ruth feels a hot numbness in her arm. The aconitine working its way into her system? *Don't let the fear control you.* She forces her mind back to the problem.

'How did Lomax find Adela? She was careful. She sold her house, moved into an apartment without even telling the concierge—' She breaks off. 'Is that how you did it? Did you send Lomax to Adela's hotel that night?'

A sharp scratch and the torture begins again. *Okay, you missed the mark this time.*

She leaves the pain where it is, and floats above it. He *did* mess up, that much is certain. Adela was known at the Old Bank Hotel – was a regular – but the desk manager said she'd been coming to the hotel for only about six months. So she must have switched from another venue. If Lomax didn't go to the hotel the night of the shooting, then he couldn't have followed Adela home. *Unless* . . .

'You gave Lomax the address of Adela's riverside apartment.'

'You're delirious,' he says.

'It was fun watching Carver fall apart, but Adela provided a release for him, a distraction from the case. You wanted her out of the way, so you sent Lomax after her. What you didn't bargain for was him coming after Carver as well.'

The killer's breath stutters behind the mask and she knows she's hit home.

'Lomax overreacted,' he says. 'I took care of him.'

'You murdered him.'

'I saved your life.'

'That's funny,' Ruth says.

'I don't hear you laughing.'

'You sent him an email in Adela's name. No,' she corrects herself. 'A text – probably on a burner phone to make it more like old times. Maybe even spun him a line about how she regretted breaking up with him. He went to Adela's apartment; my guess is she pulled the gun, they got into a wrestling match, he shot her by accident, decided to set Carver up for the murder.'

A moment's silence. 'There's a huge black hole in the centre of your theory,' he says, rubbing more powder, hard, into the fresh puncture-wounds with his thumb. 'How would Lomax know where Carver lived?'

Ruth groans in pain, despite herself. *He's distracting you because you've almost got it. Stay with it. Lomax was obsessive. What do obsessives do in relationships?* Suddenly, she knows.

'He stalked Adela before she dropped out of sight.'

He continues drilling into her skin, but she hardly feels it; her excitement anaesthetising the pain.

'Relevance?' he says.

'He did what stalkers do,' Ruth says. 'He followed her, watched her, got to know her routine: her business meetings, her hotel "dating", the room she booked into. Maybe he even sneaked up to her hotel room and listened. Watched her boyfriends come and go. Did he see you a few times, watching them? Were you afraid he would identify you?'

A click and the room is plunged into darkness, the intensity made even greater by the micropore strips over her eyes. Her body cooling, her left arm aflame with heat, Ruth listens for his footsteps, hardly daring to breathe.

A blast of cold air, then the door clangs shut, and she is alone again.

'Bull's-eye,' she murmurs.

## 53

Inside the taxi, Carver called Gaines's mobile number, which Ruth had carefully logged in her notes. No answer. He tried the landline; it went straight through to voicemail. It was a 727 number, the same area code as Carver's home phone, but 727 covered a large area of the city, from Sefton Park to Aigburth, and right along Ullet Road.

At the next set of traffic lights, the cab driver slid back the window and called through to him: 'D'you know where you're going, mate? 'Cause I'm due a tea break.'

Carver shoved a twenty-pound note through the dividing screen. 'Just keep circling,' he said.

He tried the university switchboard; they put him through to Gaines's office, but there was no answer there, either. Maybe he could blag an address out of the Human Resources section. He dialled the switchboard again, and was put through to a recorded message saying that the Human Resources section was closed after 4 p.m. 'for training'.

His only other option was a reverse look-up of the number. He tapped on the window and asked for Canning Place, arriving at the police headquarters in the last of the twilight. He used the rear entrance, relieved that his pass card still worked. He took the lift up to the Thorn Killer Major Incident Room, with nothing worse than a few funny looks to contend with. The room was deserted: every officer available must be out looking for Ruth. It had been rearranged to accommodate more staff, and he couldn't find Ruth's desk at first, but a kindly intelligence researcher helped him out, leading him to it and waiting until he was seated.

'How're you doing?' she asked.

'Not so good,' Carver admitted. 'Any news?'

'They sent a team round to her house. No sign of Ruth, but someone's been rooting around. CSIs are there, now.'

He nodded, feeling guilty that his actions had pulled resources from where they were needed.

'Can I get you anything?' she asked, still hovering.

'No,' he said. 'Thanks. I'll just . . .' He gestured to the stacks of papers on Ruth's desk without elaborating.

She left, but only after extracting a promise that he would give her a shout if he needed anything.

Using his password to log in at Ruth's computer he accessed the reverse look-up to get an address for Gaines, then called up the university website and found an image of the academic: a trim, grey-haired man, with hint of New Age hippy about him. He looked innocuous enough, but Carver knew from years of policing that looks could deceive. As he braced himself to stand, his eye snagged on an evidence bag in an in-tray at one corner of the desk. It was clearly marked 'CCTV, School Lane'. He flashed to the notes Ruth had made on the CCTV evidence. She'd logged an incident on the recording - a woman who had spoken to Kara Grogan the night she was last seen. Ruth wondered if Kara had told the woman where she was headed. He picked up the bag, and found four more under it.

*Hell*. He couldn't walk out with the lot. What was the evidence number Ruth had noted? He dug in his pocket and scrolled through the pictures he'd taken at her house, identified it by the number as the second in the pile. He swivelled the chair, ready to leave, and found DC Ivey blocking his way.

'You can't walk out of here with that in your possession, sir,' he said, polite, but implacable.

Carver said, 'The Thorn Killer has Ruth.'

The younger man's brow furrowed. 'No . . . *Lomax* tried to abduct her, and she—'

'I know what they're saying, and it's bollocks.'

Ivey shook his head.

'Think about it,' Carver said. 'Lomax's car was dumped in sight of Canning Place – why didn't she just cross the road and walk into police headquarters?'

'She was hit on the head – she was probably concussed.'

Carver took a breath. 'Okay . . . if she was concussed, she might wander the streets for bit – but with all the CCTV cameras around the city centre they'd have found her in ten minutes. They didn't. If she was concussed and *scared*, she might've jumped in a cab and headed for home. I know Parsons sent a team to her place; she isn't there, is she?'

Ivey shook his head.

'Did they find *anything*?'

Ivey glanced quickly around the room. 'Your um, unofficial file.' He lowered his voice, 'She's been working on the case at home – Parsons isn't happy.'

'I'd say that's the least of her worries, just now, wouldn't you?'

Ivey flushed.

'You're not gonna find anything on that recording, anyway,' Ivey said. 'Ruth would've said if there was anything important.'

'Sometimes you don't know how important a thing is,' Carver said. 'It's the *accumulation* of facts that gives it significance.'

Ivey's frown deepened, and Carver forced himself to remain calm and take the time to explain Ruth's theory about the woman who had spoken to Kara after she left the theatre.

Ivey shifted his weight from one foot to the other. 'I dunno . . . I've already stuck my neck out on this one, sir.'

Carver's head was beginning to swim. He took a breath and tried again: 'Look, if Kara *did* tell this woman where she was going, at the very least we would be able to seize CCTV footage on the route – which might help us locate where she was picked up. Which might give us a vehicle registration, even an image of the abductor . . .'

Ivey sighed. 'Okay . . . okay . . . I'll talk to DCI Parsons, see if we can get someone onto it.'

'Take a look around you, man,' Carver said, indicating the empty room. 'Everyone is out searching for Ruth – it could take *hours* to put together a team. There's you, and there's me. Here, now, with the evidence. Could it hurt to take a quick look?'

Ivey bowed his head, and Carver knew he'd won the argument. He offered the disk to the younger detective, and Ivey took it reluctantly.

'Focus on the minutes after Kara was kicked out of Jasmine Hart's psychic performance.' Carver closed his eyes, partly to concentrate, but partly because the room was turning in slow circles. 'Eight thirty-four p.m.,' he said.

When he heard Ivey break the evidence seal, he steadied himself and opened his eyes experimentally. The room was still. He planted his feet carefully, fixed his gaze on the doorway some fifteen feet away, and made ready to push off from the chair.

'Wait a minute, where are you going?' Ivey said.

'If I have to watch moving images, I might just throw up,' Carver said. 'What do you know about Dr Lyall Gaines?'

The younger man shrugged. 'Nothing.'

Clearly, he didn't even know the name.

'Okay,' Carver said. 'Find the woman on that CCTV footage; she might be able to help.'

## 54

Ruth's abductor is circling constantly, hiding in the shadows, stalking her like a cat, but always beyond the drenching curtain of light, so he is no more than a shadow, a shifting form as distorted as his electronically altered voice. The burning pain in her arm has receded a little, and she wonders if she is in shock. He has been working on her again, or the poison is working its way into her system, because the hot, dull throb extends from her forearm to just above her elbow.

'Why *do* you hide yourself?' she asks.

'A more interesting question is why do *you*?' he says.

Ruth ignores the bounce-back: 'We both know I'm not getting out of here. I won't be able to identify you – so, tell me – why?'

Her captor seems to think about this. 'Do you read your Bible, Sergeant?'

She doesn't answer, and he says, 'You really should. Your mother's name was Jacobs, I believe, and since matrilineal descent is the rule in Judaism, that makes you a Jew. The Old Testament is a vital part of your heritage.'

'I have no religion.'

'You may denounce your *religion*,' he says, 'but you cannot denounce your *race*. You should read the Book of Ruth: your namesake was a Moabite who married an Israelite. A loyal, self-reliant, resourceful woman. When her husband died, she could have returned to her own people, found a new husband, but she remained by her mother-in-law's side.' He paused. 'You see where this is leading?'

'No.' It was an honest answer, but Ruth was becoming more certain of the man with every word he spoke: the lecturing, pompous tone, the condescending attitude, the references to lineage and culture and heritage.

'Ah, well, we'll come back to that,' he says. 'Jo Raincliffe understood the benefits of anonymity in confession: she told me secrets and transgressions going back to her *childhood* – but she was Roman Catholic – they're fiends for confession.'

'So you're hiding your identity so that I can what – confess without *embarrassing* myself?'

'It's an opportunity. Will you embrace it?' he says, either not hearing, or refusing to acknowledge, her sarcasm.

'I'm no expert, but haven't you got it backwards? Doesn't the penitent usually *know* who she's confessing to?'

'This is not a conventional situation.' She hears amusement in his voice. 'But Jo ended her life with a clear conscience and a lighter heart.'

'*Jo* didn't end her life – *you* did.' Her voice lacks power, but her words seem to have hit their mark. He halts, and for a few seconds the fretful flicker of shadow and light stops.

'Fair point,' he says, at last. 'But they do say confession is good for the soul.'

Ruth says nothing, processing what she has just heard. Despite his careful modulation, there is tension – perhaps even irritation – in the distorted voice.

'Since you're anti-religious, perhaps you've read Kafka?' he says, beginning his awful pacing again. 'One of his stories, *In the Penal Settlement*, features an instrument of execution which pierces the body of the condemned person with hundreds of needles. It writes over and over the law they have broken, driving it deeper and deeper into the skin. It kills them over a period of twelve hours. The beauty of the process is the condemned person doesn't need to be told what they are charged with, or their punishment. The instrument does that, and eventually the condemned person understands, too. They gain enlightenment.'

'You see yourself as a judge and executioner?'

'That's a simplistic interpretation,' he said. 'You're not listening to what I'm trying to tell you.'

'Oh . . . I've disappointed you.'

'Does that concern you?' he asks. 'Did you disappoint your parents, Ruth? Becoming police when you could have entered one of the professions like a good Jewish girl?'

He has misread her. Ruth has been reading people since childhood. She learned it young and honed it every day of her life. This man doesn't have her skill – he uses pain and fear, digging confidences from his victims with cruelty. The notion gives her power.

'Jewish girl desperate to please her mother – is that the best you can do?' she says.

He laughs, softly. 'Deflections, misdirections, answering questions with questions; that's quite an armoury you have.'

Ignoring the pain in her arm, Ruth forces the corners of her mouth into the beginnings of a smile. 'I'm an open book. Read me.'

'Oh, I *am*.'

*Liar*.

'Okay. Tell me what I'm thinking, now.'

A hesitation. 'You're afraid.'

'Well, *duh* . . .'

She hears a sharp intake of breath. Distorted as it is, it sounds like water gurgling down a drain.

She used the offensive expression deliberately, knowing it would affront him.

'Anyway, it isn't fear you want for me, is it? It's *secrets* you get off on.'

'That is gross and uncalled-for.'

'Hey, you're the one who strapped me, practically naked, to a table,' Ruth says. Right now, she is terrified. But she makes herself go on, uses every ounce of her will to keep pushing, because if she stops, she might just break down and tell him everything he wants to know. 'How would you characterise it?'

'I'm not here to answer your questions.'

'No,' Ruth says. 'It's answers you want. Well, don't expect me to make it easy for you.'

'You sound so calm, but the pulse jumping in your throat betrays you.'

*Bastard. You bastard* . . . She works on her breathing, and when she is ready, she says, 'It's true – I don't seem to be able to control my heart rate. My breathing is a bit more controllable. But where I excel is with micro-expressions, micro-gestures, postural change, voice modulation – the whole gamut – I've been working on those for *years*.'

'You feel able to brag, strapped, "practically naked, to a table". *Good* for you.'

He pats her arm and Ruth feels the rough texture of his fingers again. She breathes through the urge to scream at the touch of his hand and tries to think ahead: it isn't enough just to stay alive – she has to find a way out of here.

'What I mean to discover is why you develop those strategies. Were you hiding *from* someone? Did Daddy play secret games with you when you were a girl?'

*He's clueless.* Gaining confidence, Ruth begins to think analytically. She has the details of every post mortem report by heart. Not one of the women showed any signs of pressure sores, so he must have allowed them to move about, or at least changed their position on the table from time to time. That meant removing the straps. Such times would be her chance to break free, but not while she's immobilised with drugs.

'Sergeant?'

'You know nothing about my father.'

'I know he's dead. I know *how* he died – have you forgotten I've seen your scrapbook?'

Ruth denies him an answer. Instead she lets her eyes drift closed.

'Answer me.'

Ruth feels the spiteful jab of a thorn, deep in her flesh. She gasps, but experiences a moment of triumph. That was a show of frustration and temper. *Just don't push him too far.*

She licks her lips, opens her eyes. 'What was the question again?'

'This little game won't work,' he says.

'Hey,' Ruth says, slurring her words. 'Pump all those muscle relaxants and narcotics into me, what do you expect?' Her message is clear: if he wants to read her, he'll have to ease up on the chemical cosh.

There is a long silence. She strains to hear him, but he must have turned off the voice-changer, because she can't even hear the exaggerated growl of his breathing.

After a while, she hears a distinct *click*, as he flips a switch.

'Is this a *negotiation*, Sergeant?'

'A challenge,' Ruth says. 'I give, you give.'

Another pause. 'This might be fun,' he says. 'You first.'

She laughs; it's no more than an out-push of breath, but she sees his shadow snap upright, as if she has physically struck him.

'Fair's fair,' she says. 'You've read my files, thumbed through my album – there's plenty of secrets in that lot. You owe me a few.'

She hears three, long breaths: in . . . out, in . . . out, in . . . out, like the artificial respirator of a space villain. Then, unexpectedly, he says, 'Ask away.'

'I haven't worked out how you found the victims, yet—'

'"Yet". Do you think you'll get the chance, Sergeant Lake?'

She closes her eyes so that the hope she cherishes will not betray her. 'No,' she says, putting a quiver into her voice. 'So, is it too much to ask for clarity?'

He pulls back, deeper into the shadows, a sure sign of vulnerability. Finally, he says, 'Go on.'

'I think they went to psychic readings.'

'You think I'm a psychic?'

'I think you're an opportunist.'

'Not bad. But Kara didn't believe in psychics, or mediums. Why would she ask for help from one?'

'She was about to audition for a film; she wanted to give a good performance.'

'Hm, the film . . . yes, that was resourceful of you, discovering her "big break".'

His tone is disparaging, and she matches it. 'Yeah, and I didn't have to torture her to find out.'

'Your question?'

397

'You sat in the audience, listening to people tell their tragic stories, and you singled out the most vulnerable.'

'I'm *really* not interested in attention-seekers who feel free to unburden themselves to a few hundred total strangers.'

Ruth thinks it through, framing what she says next as a statement, fearing he will only allow her the one question: 'You chose women who asked for a private reading.'

He snorts. 'Wrong again. That type is no better than the disgusting self-aggrandisers who pour out their tawdry lives for vulgar entertainment.'

'Then I don't get it,' Ruth says.

'Giving up so easily?' he says. 'You get it all right. You interview witnesses all the time.'

He has engaged with you. With *you* – now, think! Ruth recalls her interview with Kara's housemates. Angela, loud, abrasive, more than happy to talk about Kara's faults; Lia, mouthing platitudes about Kara's 'reserve'. But she'd homed in on silent, troubled Jake – and hadn't he provided the best intel?

'You chose the ones who held back, or *couldn't* go on.'

She hears a harsh exhalation. 'Those are secrets *worth* hearing.'

'How do you persuade them to talk to you?'

'And now, *finally*, we come to the question.' He seems to relish the moment. 'All right, I'll answer. All it takes is a discreet, sympathetic, *professional* approach – and a business card with a prestigious logo impressed upon it,' he adds with a roguish flourish.

'What logo?' she demands, thinking, *Gaines. I know it's you, Lyall Gaines*.

Silence.

Abruptly, the lights go out and the door clangs shut.

'Wrong question, Ruth,' she murmurs. *Or else he knows that I know who he is.*

She waits, listening for him to return, her body cooling rapidly. Weirdly, without the heat of the spotlamps, she feels more exposed, vulnerable.

Experimentally, she calls out, but her voice is weakened, and anyway the sound seems deadened, as though the place is soundproofed – or underground.

## 55

Out on the car park again, the cold air hit Carver like he'd downed a quarter of whisky. He focused on the brick security hut at the barrier, feeling the eyes of the duty officer on him behind the mirrored glass.

On Liver Street, he flagged down a taxi and gave the driver Dr Gaines's address.

He must have dozed off, because the next he knew, the cabbie had slid back the glass and was calling through to him. 'Wakey-wakey, Rip Van Winkle. This is where you get out.'

They were parked outside a well-kept house with a sand-stone wall and hedging at the front. 'Go up the drive, would you?' he said.

The driver gave him a look. 'What's up – legs not working or wha'?'

Carver handed him a ten-pound note for the fare, and held up a second. 'Another tenner in ten minutes – if you wait for me.'

The driver pocketed the cash and parked up in the driveway.

The side gate was open; it flapped in a slight breeze, juddering onto the latch, pausing, opening a few inches, then swinging shut again. The scent of wood smoke spiced the cold air.

Carver rang the front door bell. There were lights on in the hallway, and he peered in through the glass panelling on the front door, but couldn't make out any detail. He tried again, then turned the door handle. The front door was unlocked, and the inner one stood wide. He stepped inside, called Gaines's name. No answer.

The room immediately to the left was empty and cold. The one opposite was lit by table lamps, and the parquet floor glowed like sunlit honey in their mellow light. This room had been knocked through into the kitchen, but the glow of the lamplight did not penetrate far into the gloom.

Clusters of photographs on the walls were a horror show of heavily tattooed and scarred people. Alongside those, water-colours of plants: *Digitalis*; *Aconitum*; laurel; and *Pulsatilla*, the innocuous looking pasque flower. After a year of working this case, he knew that every one of them was poisonous.

The coffee table, chairs and floor were littered with sheets of paper. Celtic symbols, tattoos, sigils – pages and pages on symbolism. A laptop charger lead trailed off the coffee table. He scanned the room; no laptop. A reproduction black Bakelite phone squatted on the hearth next to an armchair, as if Gaines had been using it just minutes ago. Caught under one corner of the phone casing, a dozen sheets printed out from the Web showed a mummified body with what looked like tattoos at the wrists, on the arms, even on the ribcage. Notes, diagrams and printouts of the symbols inked on the Thorn Killer's victims spilled from the coffee table onto the floor. Among these were photographs of pyra-cantha, with close-ups of its thorns. And perched aslant an ashtray on a side table he found a twenty-centimetre pyra-cantha twig as thick as his thumb. Every side shoot and thorn had been sliced off, leaving only the terminal thorn, five centimetres long and wickedly sharp. No wonder Ruth had misgivings.

On a bookshelf he saw a framed photograph of a younger Gaines, stripped to the waist, his arm draped over the shoulder of a smaller man, possibly Malay. Gaines's free hand was curled around the hilt of a dagger, sheathed on his belt. He was laughing; he looked exhausted but happy, and he was sporting a fresh tattoo on his shoulder, the skin around the inking still red and inflamed.

Carver was hit by a sudden image of Gaines slicing a line with the dagger point through dark skin. Blue and orange colour formed a vortex around the photograph, sucking light into its centre. Carver reeled, nausea twisting his stomach, and he snatched hold of a chair-back to steady himself. He shut his eyes against the violence of the image, and mercifully, it vanished.

*Hallucination, or insight?* he wondered. He had pushed himself so hard today that it could be either. But one impression remained which he was certain he could trust: Gaines was a blood-sucking sadist.

Carver's face and body were drenched in sweat, he tasted bile at the back of his throat and his limbs were shaking. He wiped sweat from his face and looked around. The house was huge – did he have the strength to search every inch of it?

A breath of cold air shivered across the room, stirring the papers, raising gooseflesh on his arms and neck, and he realised that the French doors on the other side of the kitchen were open a crack. Swallowing hard against the nausea, he moved towards them, manoeuvring past the kitchen island. A step further and he stubbed his toe against something soft. He placed a hand flat on the granite surface to prevent a fall and, looking down, he saw a dark mass on the floor. A body.

*Ruth?*

His heart jumped; he felt the room tilt, and had to wait a moment before slowly lowering himself to a crouch, sliding down the cupboard for support.

*Not Ruth*. Thank God . . . He flicked on his phone flashlight app to get a better look, saw a man with grey hair; he wore braided bracelets on his wrists. It was Lyall Gaines.

His skin had a bluish tinge, and he didn't appear to be breathing.

Carver touched Gaines's face with the back of his hand. It was cold. But it was a cold evening, the French windows were open and he knew better than to assume a person was dead just because they were cold. An oft-used phrase of Ruth's came to him unbidden: 'You're not dead till you're warm and dead.'

Carver saw a tiny bead of blood on the dead man's throat, and moving around him crabwise, he saw an empty syringe on the floor on the other side of Gaines's body.

The over-exertion had caught up with him, and he wasn't sure he could stand without crashing back to the floor, so he stayed put to make the call to emergency services.

Call ended, he gave himself a few moments, breathing slowly, waiting for the nausea and dizziness to subside.

Suddenly, the patio was flooded with light. Carver tensed, a fresh surge of adrenaline giving him new energy. A cat crouched in the light, its ears flattened, lips drawn back in a snarl. Seeing that no threat was imminent, it stalked on with one haughty glance in his direction, crossing the patio and disappearing into the deep shadows beyond.

Watching it go, Carver saw a black smut drift across his line of vision, then another. He eased to his feet and went to the French doors to look out onto the floodlit garden. Curls of burnt paper chased in circles around the patio.

Abruptly, the lights went out.

Blinking away the after-image, he thought he saw a red point of light. He closed his eyes for a few seconds. It was still there when he opened them again; and another, and another. Three flickering red dots at the far end of the garden, near to the back wall. He stepped out, triggering the security lights and, phone flashlight at the ready for when they plunged him into darkness again, he made his way across the lawn. The scent of burning wood grew stronger; the source of the red glow seemed to be a large oil barrel standing on bricks amid piles of logs and sawn branches. As he drew closer, he realised he was looking at the glowing embers of a wood fire, seen through ventilation holes at the base of the barrel.

A second, smaller metal drum was inverted inside the barrel, the gap between them stuffed with twigs and sticks, most of which had burned down, leaving only a ten-centimetre layer at the base of the barrel. A few flakes of sooty paper rose from it, and shining the flashlight inside, he saw four or five sheets twisted and stuffed inside the drum. On this edge, the fire was almost out, but the metal was still hot, and he burned his knuckles trying to extract the papers.

The wind was getting up; it buffeted him, sending leaves and burned paper scurrying across the garden. He could feel the heat building; those last few remnants might flare and vanish any second. He grabbed a thickish section of sawn branch and used it to tilt the drum. Surprisingly light, it toppled easily, freeing the ash, which spiralled up in the breeze, rattling charcoal sticks from the inner drum onto the damp earth. Carver's prize remained stubbornly inside the outer barrel, but shining the phone flashlight on the remnants of ash and sticks, he saw the fragments of paper were now within his grasp. As he reached inside, a gust of wind whipped ash and soot into his eyes and the fire flared. Singeing his hair and eyebrows, he grabbed what he could and fell backwards, coughing. He wiped his eyes with his coat sleeve and carefully opened his fist. Ash, charred remains, a few bits of burnt twig.

And one tiny scrap of paper, no bigger than the corner of a postage stamp. He trapped it between finger and thumb and lifted it gingerly, tilting it to the light.

It was a logo of some kind. Green. Two letters at the bottom readable as 'NS', a third could be 'C' or 'G', the rest was too charred to tell. A line down the centre, between two thicker bands of green, pointed at the lower end. The one on the right was more complete; it was shaped like the head of a bird, its beak pointing downwards. Or maybe a flame. But a *green* flame? That didn't make sense. Okay, so a bird. Maybe. Three, tear-drop-shaped outlines radiated from the top of the centre line.

Carver heard the emergency sirens approaching; at least two cars and an ambulance by the sound of it.

He returned to the kitchen, placed the scrap of paper on the kitchen work surface and took a half-dozen pictures of it on his phone. Casting about for something suitable, he found a glass on the draining board and pinned the fragment under it. Then he returned to the taxi, still waiting outside, and told the driver to head towards Sefton Park.

The cabbie made the turn into Aigburth Drive just as the first police car flashed past in the opposite direction.

Carver called Parsons.

'Did you speak to Gaines when he postponed the interview this morning?'

'No – he emailed.' Parsons sounded distracted. 'What has that to do with anything?'

'I don't think he cancelled at all,' Carver said. 'I just found him on the floor of his kitchen. I think he's dead.'

'Jesus – have you called for an ambulance?'

'They're already at the scene. Look, there were some burned papers in the garden. I retrieved one piece that had some kind of logo on it; whoever got to Gaines tried to destroy it. You need to find out what it means.'

'I'm on my way,' Parsons said. 'If there are fingerprints on the paper—'

'The only prints you're likely to find are mine,' Carver interrupted. 'I had to salvage it from the fire.'

'Shit. All right. Stay where you are.'

'I'm already gone,' Carver said.

'What? You can't *leave* the scene of a crime!'

Parsons was right, but he couldn't allow himself to get tied up for hours.

'You'll find the paper under a tumbler on the kitchen island.' Carver heard a squawk of protest as he ended the call. He turned the phone off in case Parsons got it into his head to ping it and send someone out to arrest him.

He tapped on the window and the cabbie slid the screen back.

'Got a smartphone?' he said.

'Yeah . . .'

'How much to borrow it for an hour?'

## 56

Ruth Lake slips in and out of consciousness with the smell of earth and rotting wood in her nostrils, and dreams of her grandfather.

Mostly, when she visited their little house in Everton, he was too absorbed in reading the racing form or watching the races on TV for storytelling. Granddad was a betting man, had wagered on the horses every Saturday of his adult life. Grandma insisted that he watch the day's races from their own home, where she could keep an eye on him. 'Put a stop to his gallop,' in her words.

It was in this room that Ruth had begun discussing the chances of this horse or that as they warmed up in the paddock, and learned to merit more than the glossy sheen on a horse's flanks.

But Grandma wasn't always able to put a stop to his betting gallop, and on these occasions Granddad would end up sleeping in the Anderson shelter in the back yard. A relic of World War II, the shelter was dug into the ground and lined with sheet corrugated iron, covered over with topsoil. Granddad discovered it, rust-pitted and falling to bits, when they moved into that house. He had shored it up with wood planking and installed a couple of chairs and a primus stove under a make-shift chimney made from empty catering-size bean cans. Called it his 'Inner Sanctum' when he was in mellow mood, 'The Doghouse' when he was evading Grandma's wrath.

Granddad was seventy-six the year Ruth witnessed the stabbing in the alley. His quiet counsel, conducted in the stillness of his inner sanctum, had done more to heal her than the succession of counsellors the courts had appointed for her well-being in the run-up to the trial.

*Why am I thinking about this now?* Ruth wonders. Even as the thought forms in her head she knows: it's the smell. Earth and tree roots, the mulchy, autumnal odour of fungus and gently decomposing wood reminds her of Granddad's man cave. She *is* underground.

She listens in the pitch dark to the sound of her own breathing. It is cool in here, but not freezing. She can feel a tingling in her fingers, and experimentally she tries to move them. Her pinkie finger twitches. The numbness is receding.

Half an hour later, she can feel the leather straps, and can move her shoulders and legs, too. Perhaps there is a chance she will be able to fight back.

A sudden blast of cold air, the *click* of a switch, and powerful lights drench her skin again.

She deliberately relaxes her limbs, responding sluggishly, opening her eyes as if it's an effort.

'The Medicis had a Poison Garden in Padua,' her captor begins. He's still using the voice distorter, and he keeps out of her line of sight. 'The current Duchess of Northumberland laid one out at Alnwick Castle. It's gated and locked, and filled with toxic species; the gates have a skull and crossbones sculpted in metal, and bear the legend, "These plants can kill". She knew that people would be attracted by two things: secrecy, and risk. She was right – they come in their thousands to see it.'

'All things are poison and nothing is without poison,' Ruth quotes, consciously slurring her words.

'Paracelsus,' the killer says. 'Brava. But it's the *dose* makes the poison, Ruth.'

*Patronising bastard*. Ruth allows her eyes to close, opens then again, as if it is a tremendous strain, then lets them droop again, feigning sleep.

A sharp, hot needle of pain in her thigh.

She gasps, feeling a rush of clarity and energy.

Energy becomes anxiety, the tingling in her fingers suddenly terrifying. The fear spikes and she bucks against the restraints, hears them creak.

'Your heart is racing,' he says. 'Your blood pressure is raised.' He tosses an empty syringe onto her stomach and she flinches. 'Epinephrine – adrenaline, if you will. Now, if you're fully awake, it's your turn to talk.'

Panting, Ruth struggles to regain control. 'What – what do you want to know?'

'How did you feel when you saw Greg Carver slumped in his armchair, a bullet in his chest?'

'Shocked.'

'Liar.'

'I'm telling the *truth*.' She hears the panic in her voice, and experiences a scrabbling panic in her chest. *It's not your fear, it's the adrenaline. Ride with it.* 'It was horrible.'

'That's nearer the truth. But it can't have been a complete shock – you must have known something bad would happen, the way he'd been drinking, his reaction to Kara. I mean, he pretty much fell apart after that, didn't he?'

Ruth hesitates. 'Yes.'

'So . . . I'll ask the question again: how . . . did you . . . *feel*?'

'Angry,' Ruth says, hating herself for betraying her friend.

'Only angry?'

Ruth can't steady her nerves; the usual strategies that help her to disguise her feelings are not under her control. Her blood seems to hum through her arteries, and a high-pitched whine pierces her ears. 'That's what I said,' she says, and hears the doubt in her own voice.

'Just now, the epinephrine is doing you no harm,' he says. 'But repeated injections can cause a heart attack – even a stroke.' He removes the empty syringe and replaces it with an unused EpiPen. "The dose makes the poison", Ruth.'

She mutters the word that describes how she'd really felt, seeing Carver, slumped in his chair, reeking of booze.

'I can't hear you,' he says. 'Speak up.'

'I felt disgusted,' she admits. 'Contemptuous.'

He sighs, the outrush of breath drawn out, tremulous with emotion. 'Now we're getting somewhere.'


Ruth wakes, knowing that time has passed.

She had barely felt the sting of the hypodermic, wasn't even aware of drifting into unconsciousness, but she knows he has been working on her, because her arm is shrieking with pain, and her eyes are taped shut. She can't move.

He addresses her conversationally: 'A milestone, your first truth – your first open eye.' He rubs charcoal into the wound and she whimpers. 'But miles to go before you sleep,' he adds.

He pats her thigh. 'Now, let's get you properly compos mentis.'

'Nnnn . . .' Ruth tries to struggle, but although she can feel the pain in her arm, she can't make her limbs obey her.

She feels the needle go into her thigh. Then: mercury-cold liquid, racing through her body. She feels it rush from her thigh into her groin; from her stomach into her chest. Her heart hammers, pushing the drug to her brain.

He removes the micropore tape from her eyes.

Light, so intense she's sure it will blind her. And *pain*. Her flesh melting, her arm on fire. She screams, arches her back, hears the leather restraints creak as she strains against them, her entire mind and body focused on the agony in her arm.

He pushes her down. '*Shhhh* . . . Relax . . .'

Ruth wants to beg him to make it stop, but she will not give him that, so she screams again. '*Fuck* you!'

'Tell you what,' he says. 'If you're forthcoming this time, we'll see if you can do without the epinephrine for the next Q&A.'

He sounds flustered. Is he afraid of me? Is he *bargaining* with me?

'Fuck . . . you . . .' she says again, hearing her breath stutter in her throat. 'You want the truth?' she says. 'You're weak. That's why you hide. Because you're weak, and afraid.'

'Yet it's you that's trembling,' he says. 'The pulse in your throat is astonishingly fast. The pain of the tattoo feels like third-degree burns. You're in a cold sweat.'

She grits her teeth. 'Tell me . . . something I . . .' *God, the pain!* ' . . . don't . . . know.'

'All right. Your heart rate will come down in a minute or two, but the biggest risk is vasoconstriction of the small blood vessels in your brain. You could have a stroke at any moment.'

The pressure builds in her skull. She can't stop shaking. She should be going into shock, her body shutting down, numbing the pain centres, but it just keeps intensifying.

'Focus on my voice,' he says. 'Answer me truthfully, I'll give you something to ease the pain.'

He waits until she is ready to beg him to ask the question.

'You say you were disgusted, finding Carver that night. You thought he'd tried to kill himself.'

'Mm-nn,' Ruth manages.

'Then why did you destroy evidence of that? Why did you steal the gun from his apartment?'

'P-protect.' Ruth forces the word out through clenched teeth.

'Protect who? Carver? His reputation?'

'*Mmn.*'

'You must have known there would be repercussions. You're a trained CSI *and* a detective.'

'Not . . . then,' Ruth says, having to keep her answers short because her teeth are chattering, her entire body jangling against the restraints.

'You panicked.'

Ruth closes her eyes.

'Is it *really* so different, going into a crime scene when you know the victim?' He sounds genuinely curious.

'Yes.' She opens her eyes and stares into the bright disc of light surrounding the Thorn Killer's face. She hears a grunt of satisfaction.

*Now make this stop.*

She feels a slight pressure in her right arm and a sudden flush of warmth. The burning is still there, but it doesn't seem to matter as much. The shaking stops and she can breathe normally again.

'Morphine,' he says. 'Not too much – we'll crack on, now we've started to make progress.'

## 57

Carver risked switching his phone back on briefly so that he could Bluetooth the images to the taxi driver's phone. He switched off again and opened up the downloads on the borrowed phone, magnifying each one, but didn't find any more detail from the scrap of burned paper: only the three letters, 'NSC', and the stylised bird – a heron, maybe, or an exotic bird?

Of all the papers littered around Gaines's house, the killer had burned this – and he'd taken Gaines's laptop. Gaines must have found something on the Web that could implicate the Thorn Killer.

He searched the Web and found a security consultancy under NSC, also a computing specialist and a hi-tech composites manufacturer, but the logos were wrong: wrong colour, wrong shape.

He tapped on the driver's window. 'Pull over for a second, will you?

He handed the cabbie the phone with the image of the logo on-screen. 'What does that look like to you?'

'Not much, to be honest.' The driver screwed up his eyes. 'Pair of hands around a wheel cog?'

Carver took the phone back. He saw what the cabbie meant, but why would you symbolically cup hands either side of a wheel cog?

He Googled 'cupped hands logos'. There were hundreds. Okay, so what did cupped hands signify, symbolically? Protection?

Conservation? Again, the wheel cog didn't make sense. He tried 'bird conservation', but that was a dead end. Okay . . . Three teardrop shapes, point-in, forming an arc at the top of a line. Or a *stem*? Could it be a flower stem?

He Googled 'NSC' and 'plant conservation'. Six lines down was a national plant conservation society. He clicked the link, and there it was: the logo for the National Society for the Conservation of British Plant Species. The cabbie was right about the cupped hands. The line through the centre was, indeed, a plant stem, and the teardrops were petals. The 'plant' rested on the letters NSCBPS. But why was that significant? What was the killer trying to hide?

He clicked 'In your area' on the drop-down menu, then selected 'Merseyside'.

Listed under 'Collections Co-ordinator, Wirral' was a name he recognised.

For a few moments, he stared at the screen, his fingers numb. Then he roused himself, gave the driver instructions to the address, switched his phone back on and called up his contacts list. For a second, his thumb hovered over Parsons's entry, but at the last instant he changed his mind and scrolled back to Ivey: he didn't think Parsons would be in a listening mood.

'Where *are* you?' Ivey demanded, but he kept his voice low, and Carver imagined him ducking out of the incident room. 'Parsons is going *apeshit*. Jansen wants to hang you from the Liver Buildings by your balls.'

'What did you get from the security videos?'

'Nothing,' Ivey said.

'Ruth was very specific,' Carver said. 'A woman spoke to Kara.'

'I found the woman all right, but she only talked to Kara for a few seconds. I took a screen grab, showed it to Kara's flatmates and her tutors. No one knows her.'

'I think I do,' Carver said. 'Can you text me the image?'

Seconds later, he was staring at the photograph.

'Boss?' Ivey's voice came to him faintly.

'Listen carefully,' Carver said. 'The woman in the picture is Dr Laura Pendinning. She's a coordinator for a plant conservation society. She has rare subspecies of *Aconitum*, *Pulsatilla* and *Buxus* among her collections. They're all highly toxic plants, and we know that the Thorn Killer used aconite on his victims.' He took a breath. 'She has also been working on my rehab at the head injuries unit – she's a clinical psychologist.'

'Oh, my god . . .'

He gave Ivey the background and dictated Pendinning's address. He left the phone on and made sure that the GPS was activated: as of now, he *wanted* to be traceable. He just had to hope that Ivey could convince Parsons. After all, Pendinning's interest in plants could be entirely innocent, and anyway, Pendinning was with him when the Thorn Killer called him at the hospital.

*No*, he remembered, she came into the room just *after*. And it was Pendinning who had got him the mobile phone in the first place.

But she had tried to *stop* him leaving the hospital . . .

'Come off it, Carver,' he muttered. Arguing against the very thing you want a person to do was a simple psychological ploy – and he fell for it.

Pendinning did seem to know more than he'd told her: his brand of whisky, for one thing, and the significance of the photo he'd cherished of Emma on their honeymoon. Emma was contemptuous of him when he accused her of bringing the picture into the hospital. He'd convinced himself that Ruth was playing marriage counsellor again. But what if it was neither of them? The day he'd smashed the frame, hurling the picture after Emma, what had Pendinning said? 'Sometimes it's good to be reminded of what matters to us. Even if it causes us pain.'

He remembered the look on Pendinning's face when he'd tried to barge out of the hospital in search of Ruth. After days of looking exhausted, Pendinning was flushed, excited.

'There's nothing you can do, Greg,' she'd said.

He'd thought then that she was being rational, reasonable, but now he realised that she was taunting him.

His phone buzzed a second before it rang, and he gave a violent start. *Ivey*. He slid the icon to 'answer'.

'An armed Matrix team is on its way to Dr Pendinning's house,' Ivey told him.

# 58

A faint, percussive sound penetrates the walls of Ruth's prison, and the Thorn Killer turns. Her senses hyper-alert after the first warm flush of morphine, Ruth hears his shoes slither on the clay floor. He runs to the far end of the space and for a few seconds it is filled with the wail of a police siren, and further away, Ruth hears the drumming pulse of a phaser siren.

He whispers, 'No . . .'

*He's afraid.* Ruth experiences a rush of exhilaration.

'They're here,' Ruth says. 'They've found you.'

'Shut up.' He slams the door, shutting out the clamour, and the only sound is his ragged breathing, distorted by the voice changer.

'Give it up,' Ruth says. 'It's finished.'

'I said shut up!' He snatches up the EpiPen. 'It's finished when I say it is.'

Pendinning's house was swarming with police when Carver arrived. A Matrix Mercedes Sprinter van and two marked pursuit cars had torn past them at the Mersey Tunnel entrance ten minutes earlier.

The cabbie pulled up at the kerbside and the driver turned around. 'Bloody hell, mate. You sure you wanna go in there?'

'I don't have a choice.' Carver handed the driver his phone and a wodge of cash.

Pendinning's house was on a quiet lane, backing onto fields in Upton. They were still setting up the outer cordon and he slipped by without any trouble, but the scene log officer stopped him at the front door.

Carver flashed his ID.

'I know who you are, sir,' the officer said. 'But I can't let you in.'

'Have you found DS Lake?' Carver asked. 'Is she okay?'

The officer looked past him, his mouth set in a grim line.

'For God's sake, man . . . ' Carver's head was throbbing so hard that the ground seemed to advance and retreat, pulsing in time with the pain in his head.

One of the Matrix team came out of the house and trotted down the front steps. 'It's like a chuffing horror show in there,' he said to the guy on the door. He noticed Carver, and with an apologetic nod, hurried on.

Carver leant against the wall and willed the dizziness to pass.

A CSU van arrived a few minutes later and a team began kitting up. It started snowing as Crime Scene Manager John Hughes led the team towards the house.

Carver straightened up, tensing his muscles to control the shaking in his limbs.

'Greg.' Hughes looked shocked. 'You look terrible. Have they—?'

'I don't know, John. They won't tell me anything,' Carver said.

'Okay. Go and sit in the van,' Hughes said. 'I'll see what I can find out.'

He returned ten minutes later, peeling off his gloves and scene coveralls and bagging them before climbing into the driving seat.

'The house is empty,' he said. 'But it looks like you were right – she took trophies – hair and jewellery. And there are photographs – stage-by-stage as she tattooed the five victims.'

'Jesus . . .' Carver wiped a hand over his face. 'Ruth?'

'No.'

Carver looked at his trembling hands.

'Greg, are you listening? There's nothing of Ruth's in the place.' Hughes waited for Carver to look at him.

'Okay,' Carver said. 'I heard you.'

'She kept newspaper clippings about the murders. And . . .' Hughes hesitated.

Carver looked up. 'What?'

'There's a cabinet display with sections of tattooed skin – it's too early to say if they're human.'

'*Fuck*. Have they checked the loft space and cellar?'

'The Matrix team have searched every room, cupboard, cubby hole and crack in the place. They're about to clear out so we can process it. And I *promise* you, we will find anything that's here to be found. But as of this moment, there's no sign that Ruth was here.'

Carver nodded, acknowledging Hughes's reassurance, but thinking ahead: 'Computers, phones, tablets. If Pendinning stored information about the location where she—'

'Parsons has already given orders to have all e-devices seized,' Hughes said. 'Look, I know he's a shiny-arse who never leaves the office, but he's here today, and does know what he's doing.'

Carver opened the passenger door.

'Hey – where are you going?' Hughes demanded. 'You're in no fit state—'

'Need some air,' Carver mumbled.

He staggered to the garden wall dividing Pendinning's property from the next and perched there, half-sitting, fighting nausea and dread.

He had brought Ruth into this. His selfish, cowardly retreat into drink, his meaningless affair with Adela Faraday. If he'd done his job Ruth would never have become a target.

Two Matrix officers walked out of the house, then another; within a minute they were all in the van, ready to leave. Parsons was the next out. Carver couldn't face talking to him, so as John Hughes walked over to the house, he edged off into the shadow at the side of the building.


A spike of fear shoots pain through Ruth's heart, sends crackling shocks through her stomach and lower abdomen. *Stupid*, she thinks. 'Finished' was a stupid, stupid word to use. Ruth has seen the victims; she knows what he does to them when he's finished with them.

*DO something. Say something. He wants your secrets. Taunt him. Deny him.*

'I know who you are,' she says.

'You *think* you know.'

'Lyall Gaines,' Ruth says.

A curt laugh. 'That's what I wanted you to think. But DCI Carver has discovered that is not the case, and I do hate anyone taking credit for my work, so here it is: Gaines was a foolish man whose ability did not match his inflated ego.'

Reeling inside, Ruth tries to present an unshakable calm. 'Are you going to just sit here – wait for them to come for you?' she says. 'You know they'll tear this place apart to find me.'

'Why are you so concerned – wouldn't you *want* me to be caught?'

*You will never know how much.* But if he moves her, he'll have to free her hands and she will be in with a chance. If they stay, he might decide to take the easy way out, bring her along for company. And if he isn't already thinking along those lines, she doesn't want to put the idea in his head.

'If not Gaines, then who?'

'Oh, you know it's not going to be that easy. "You have to give to get".'

*Give him something – but make him want more.*

'The smell in this place,' Ruth says. 'Reminds me of the Anderson Shelter in my granddad's back yard.'

His breathing is hushed. He's listening.

'It was his bolthole when he was in trouble with Gran. Didn't even know it was there till he decided to dig it over and plant a vegetable patch.'

'Is that why you planted up your little garden, Ruth?'

It's the first time he's called her by her given name. The psych texts say it's a good sign if they give you your name. But Ruth isn't so sure. The Thorn Killer is unlike any serial killer she's ever read about: most killers do not want to think of their victims as people, couldn't be less interested in them as human beings.

The Thorn Killer needs to discover everything there is to know about his victims. And when he's harvested all that he can, he murders them.

*So, make sure he knows this is just a teaser – make him hungry for more.*

'Granddad always wanted a garden,' she says. 'All he got was a hole in the ground. When I was sixteen, I planted the back yard at my parents' house for him – to thank him, after . . .' She falters, hoping he won't see that she is exaggerating her emotion.

'*After*?' he demands. For a microsecond she sees a flash of that amorphous face as he breaks through the veil of blinding light, then he retreats.

'After something bad happened to me,' she says. 'He loved to sit in our back yard, smell the flowers, listen to the buzz of the insects.'

'The stabbing you witnessed as a child.'

'Yes.'

'But I already know about that. There are other, far more interesting possibilities in your secret scrapbook.'

'You've read it,' she says, trying to sound casual. 'You know everything there is to know.'

'Oh, I doubt that. I've read the press cuttings, but you didn't annotate them – and you *do* love to make notes, don't you, Ruth? So, either the marginal notes are burned into your memory. Or you're hiding something much bigger – and, knowing what's actually in the album, I'd say it would have to be something momentous.'

Ruth doesn't answer.

'Well, I didn't expect you to give up your secrets so easily. Let's start with an easier question: do you take it from its hidey hole and pore over it from time to time?'

What would he want to hear? 'Yes,' she lies.

'Hm, now *that* was a lie. You see, if it were true, it would be harder for you to admit to.' He presses the tips of his index and median fingers into the groove to the side of her windpipe and for a second she thinks he's going to choke her.

'Easy,' he says. 'Another question: When you covered up

what you believed to be evidence of Carver's attempted suicide, were you thinking of your father?'

Ruth's pulse thickens.

'You don't need to answer,' he says. '*That* was the truth.'

'Does Carver know that you delayed calling for the ambulance while you – removed evidence from his flat?'

Ruth bites her tongue to prevent a sob escaping her.

He takes his fingers away, and she gasps.

'Do you want to live, Ruth?'

'Yes,' she says. A humiliating tear slides from the corner of her eye.

'Then I want to know everything that happened. Every shameful thing you did.'

'All right.'

'No holding back?'

'Yes.'

'You're lying, of course,' he says. 'I do believe it's your default position.'

For the longest time, he is silent. It takes all of Ruth's experience and practise from years of masking her feelings to stay calm, to hide her fear.

Suddenly, his hand moves to her face. She holds her breath, bracing for an assault. It doesn't come. Instead, he removes the strap that holds her head still and loosens the bindings across her shoulders.

'I *will* extract the truth from you, even so,' he says. 'It will be a long, hard process, but I'm beginning to think you might be worth it.'

Ruth starts to breathe again.

'Now, here's what will happen next. In a moment, I will release your hands. On my order, you will sit up slowly and unfasten the straps binding your legs and ankles. You will place your hands behind your back so that I can bind them again, and then we will leave.'

Ruth stares straight ahead, all the while contracting and releasing the muscles of her arms, her torso, her legs, working muscle tone into them, readying herself for what is coming. If he gives her a chance, she has to act fast. Her head feels clear but if it comes to a fight, she's not sure she can take down a man. She hears the clink of a glass stopper in a bottle, the swish of liquid, a faint tinkle of metal on glass.

He shows her a syringe. 'This contains an extract of aconite, suspended in alcohol and water; I used it on all of the women – in lower doses, of course. Your pathologist will have told you the symptoms of aconite poisoning?'

Ruth swallows, hears a dry click at the back of her throat. 'Numbness, muscle weakness, low blood pressure, irregular heartbeat.'

'And death,' he says. 'Don't forget that.' He releases the strap on her left wrist. 'You do the other,' he says.

He's afraid to give her the advantage. Which means he's more nervous of her than it seems. Ruth tenses, ready to act.

He jabs the point of the needle into her neck and Ruth gasps, feeling its cold sting. She waits for the numbing effects of the poison, thinking, *I don't want to die. Not here. Not like this.*

'One false move, I *will* inject the entire syringe into your throat – you'll be dead in thirty seconds. Do you believe me?'

'Yes. Yes, I believe you. Completely.'

The snow was falling fast, now. Fat, soft flakes building fast on the icy ground. Carver moved to the back of the house; someone

424

had turned the patio lights on, and he saw that the frost on the lawn was criss-crossed with the Matrix team's boot-marks.

In the centre of the lawn was a parterre, divided into sections by low-growing box hedging. Carver had never been a gardener, but in the past year he had become quite the expert in poisonous plants, and they were here aplenty. The snow picked out hellebores, producers of highly toxic cardiac glycosides, already in bud, bowed under the weight of snow; snowdrops, in pristine bunches, contained scillitoxin, its effect on heart muscle as deadly as digitalis. Even the hyacinths, just poking their waxy spears above ground, contained dangerous alkaloids.

The far end of the garden looked untidy and wild. A tangle of brambles and berry-laden bushes clustered along the boundary wall.

*Pyracantha?* He wondered. *Is this where she got her stock of thorns?* He couldn't tell from this distance.

He shambled towards the stand of bushes. It was pyracantha, and sections had been cut. Next to the untidy hedge, a metal drum, like Gaines's home-made charcoal burner. Pendinning, crafting her own tools.

He walked on, skirting the edge of the thicket, and his ankle was snared by a trailing bramble shoot. He stumbled, fell, putting his hands out to save himself and plunged through a tangle of stems, the thorns scratching his hands and face, snagging and tearing his coat sleeves. Beneath the growth, he hit something cold and hard. He turned his head away and felt past the tangle of stems, feeling gritty stone. A low wall, perhaps, obscured by the scrubby growth.

He eased back, resting on his heels. Some of the stems had caught fast in the wool of his coat and he unhooked them. All were cut to the same length, and in the light of his phone, he saw that they had been cut clean across. There were more, cut, and then woven together to form a dense mat. He forced the fingers of his free hand between the weave, ignoring the pain, and pulled. It lifted, exposing a steep flight of steps down to a metal door.

He zipped off a quick text to DC Ivey and tiptoed down.

Ruth feels the pressure ease.

'Tell me what I want to hear.'

'I won't struggle,' she says. 'I know that you have the power to decide what happens to me.'

'Did they teach you that in hostage training?' he says. 'Acknowledge the power of the hostage taker?'

'I don't think they can train you for situations like this,' Ruth says.

A short bark of laughter. 'Now *that* is the truth. You know the problem with most psychologists?' he says. 'They oversimplify the complex nature of relationships by encoding behaviour. I never doubted that the women I chose were complex, rounded human beings. That is why they fascinated me. They chose anonymity, disguised their true selves; I revealed them – to themselves and to the world at large.'

'And what gave you the right?' Ruth says quietly.

'Nobody *gives* you the right,' he says. 'You have to *take* it. Surely you, of all people, must understand that?'

Ruth looks away. *Does he know what I did?*

'I can see that you do,' the killer says. 'It's the reason you conceal your feelings. You use that unreadable mask of yours to put men ill at ease. It's your defence and your weapon. It's how you establish your right to control and authority.'

Ruth said nothing. It terrified her that he knew so much.

'All right, go ahead,' he says. 'Undo the strap, sit up slowly.'

At the bottom of the steps, layers of mulch and leaf litter had accumulated. The door must open inwards. A quick turn of the lever and a shove should do it – use the element of surprise. *And if it's locked?* But Carver wouldn't allow himself to dwell on that.

He gripped the handle with both hands, depressed the lever and pushed.

It gave easily and Carver tumbled into a searingly bright space. In an instant, he saw concrete walls, lined with shelving, a surgical trolley, Ruth almost naked, sitting on it. Pendinning had her left arm across Ruth's chest; in her right hand, a syringe, the needle thrust deep into Ruth's neck. She had some kind of mask over her face and for a horrible moment he thought that it was a gas mask; that she had released a toxic gas into the room. But seeing him, Pendinning stripped off the mask.

'You've seen what this can do, injected into a vein,' she said.

'I know.' He stared into Ruth's eyes and saw terror and confusion. He spoke to Pendinning. 'Laura, there's no need to hide any more.'

'Not a step closer,' Pendinning said.

'Ruth, this is Laura Pendinning. I don't think you met at the hospital – she's a psychologist.'

'*She?*' Ruth said.

'Close the door,' Pendinning said.

Carver was about to comply when he saw orange light leap from Ruth like flame. Her left hand shot across and grabbed

427

Pendinning's right thumb, bending it back in one swift, decisive movement. Carver heard it snap like a twig.

Pendinning howled.

Ruth pulled the syringe from her neck and threw it aside, then struggled to release the strap on her legs.

Pendinning lunged for her and Carver leapt forward, lost his balance and clutched at the psychologist as he fell. They crashed into the shelving and he felt a sharp burst of pain in his back. He fell to his knees and saw the syringe, where it had rolled under the trolley. Pendinning scrabbled for it. He tried to get up, but his legs felt numb.

He yelled.

Ruth rolled off the table, stamped on Pendinning's injured hand as she reached for the syringe.

Pendinning screamed. 'Bitch! You fucking *bitch*!'

Ruth jammed her shoulder under Carver's arm. 'Move,' she yelled. But he couldn't make his legs obey. 'Greg, you *have* to move!'

She dragged him a little further and they stumbled towards the door.

Shouts rang out across the garden. Carver heard the thud of heavy boots. Ivey appeared at the top of the steps as Ruth half supported, half dragged him out of the bunker.

Ruth yelled, 'Help us!' and he threw himself down the steps, taking Carver's other arm.

Carver glanced back and saw Pendinning lunge forward. She slammed the door.

At the top of the steps, Ruth and Ivey lowered Carver to the ground and he gasped, 'I'm okay. Help Ruth.'

Ivey wrapped his coat around Ruth's Lake's shoulders as John Hughes and the scene log officer arrived.

'Poison,' Carver panted. He couldn't seem to catch his breath – the pain in his back. 'She's got poison in there. Tell Parsons you'll need gas-tight Hazmat suits. Body armour.'

The last thing he heard was Ruth, her teeth chattering, telling him to shut up and lie down, issuing an order to get the paramedics in.

# Epilogue

Carver stirred and moaned, and Ruth jolted awake. She had slept in the family room at the hospital for three nights, waiting for this moment.

'Hey,' he croaked.

She held a beaker of water to his lips and he took a sip.

'Are you awake, now?' she said. 'I mean properly?'

'I'm awake,' he said. 'But I feel like I got punched in the kidneys.'

'Close,' she said. 'Do you remember what happened?' The doctors had told her he might suffer retrograde amnesia again.

'Who's asking?' he murmured. The dismay on her face must have shown because he said, 'Joking. Sorry – I'm sorry, Ruth.'

'You should be.'

'Did they get her? Was anyone hurt?'

'Pendinning is dead. Used that syringe of poison on herself.'

'What about you? Are you—'

'I'm fine,' she said, though she couldn't help tugging at the sleeve that covered the tattoos on her arm. 'Better than you, anyway.'

'I'm just tired, that's all.'

'Greg, you've had surgery. You tried to fight her, d'you remember?'

He nodded uncertainly.

'The bullet near your spine got dislodged – the surgeon had no choice but to remove it. They were able to go through the back instead of cracking your chest, so they hope you'll recover quickly.'

He nodded. 'The bullet?'

'It's a match to the one they dug out of Adela Faraday.'

Another brief nod, and something in the reflective look on his face made her say, 'You remember what happened that night?'

'Fragments,' he said. 'I don't think I was drunk when I got back from the hotel, but I was woozy – I'd passed out in the car for a bit.'

'The concussion,' Ruth said.

'Could be. I went in and tried to work on the files. Poured a drink, maybe two, then called you. After that, there's a blank. Then . . . a man, forcing me to drink.'

'Lomax?' she said.

'Yeah. I was thinking, "Why are you doing this? I don't even know you."'

'Pendinning planned to use Lomax to get Adela out of the picture. Lomax had been stalking both you and Adela for weeks. He knew where you lived, where she was holed up. We tracked some of the text messages he sent to her. He was outside the hotel three times when you met her – including the night you were shot. In fact, he made a call to her minutes before security was called to your room.'

'Jesus . . .' Carver breathed.

'Did you fight with him there?'

'I . . . I don't remember.'

'The CSU is checking for trace,' she said. 'We'll know soon enough. We already know that Lomax showed up at her apartment – got him on CCTV at her building – security was lax over the holiday. I don't know what set him off that night:

maybe he'd heard the row between you and Adela at the hotel, thought he stood a chance with her. But whatever his plans were, they went to shit when she pulled the gun. Owning a gun, shooting a target with one – it's not the same as shooting another human being. Either she couldn't pull the trigger or he got the weapon from her before she had the chance. Then he came after you.'

Carver's eyes widened. 'I opened the door to him.'

Ruth held her breath: he was remembering – really remembering.

'I thought it was you,' Carver said. 'He shouldered past me, pulled the gun, held it on me to make me finish the Scotch. After I'd drunk about two thirds, I dropped the bottle; it rolled. He was distracted, and I took my chance, made a grab for the gun. We struggled, but I was no match for him.' His eyes clouded and he reached up with one hand, as if to fend off his attacker.

He blinked.

'I remember a flash. An impact. Like being punched, here.' He touched his chest.

'And after that?' Ruth dreaded to think that he was aware of her coming and going, removing evidence, apparently ignoring him while he lay dying. She was relieved to see a faint smile played at the corners of his mouth.

'The shadows terrified me. Then I saw you, and I thought, *Ruth's here. It'll be okay.*'

'How wrong could you be?' she said. 'I was just about ready to nod off to sleep when you rang. I thought you were maudlin drunk – only agreed to come round so I could kick your arse. And when I got there, someone'd beaten me to it.'

'I deserved a good kicking.' He looked penitent.

'Hey, I was joking.' She laughed, but it had a wet sound, and she turned away, not wanting to cry in front of him.

He was silent for a bit. 'You know, I really didn't go to Adela's apartment.'

'We know,' she said, turning back. 'Lomax planted the evidence there – stole stuff from your place – one of your dad's best whisky glasses with your fingerprints all over it; hairs, fibres, a few other things to implicate you. You messed up Lomax's plans when you didn't die.'

'Yeah, I can be a real killjoy. But you played your part, stealing the suicide weapon.'

She winced.

'Jesus, Ruth, I'm sorry.'

'You've got nothing to apologise for.' He didn't look convinced. Empathy wasn't going to lift him out of his gloom, so she went on the offensive: 'Except maybe the files – Parsons gave me a *lot* of grief about finding those in my spare bedroom – added to which, you were wrong about them.'

'Meaning?'

'You were obsessed with them: "Get me the files. The answer's in the files".'

'It was.'

She scoffed. 'We didn't find the Thorn Killer because of what was in the *files*, Greg. It was Gaines making the link between Pendinning and her deadly botanical collection.'

'But I wouldn't have found Gaines if it weren't for the files,' he countered.

'You mean if it weren't for *my notes* in the files.'

He wagged a finger at her. 'I know what this is. You're trying to distract from the fact that you were wrong about

Gaines. "Glib, self-aggrandising and shallow", you said. Admit it – you thought he was the Thorn Killer.'

'He was all of those things,' she said, 'But I don't remember saying anything about Gaines being the Thorn Killer. I *do* know my notes led you to Pendinning's door, however.'

They sat looking at each other for a while, Ruth reading affection for her in his eyes and in his smile. After a minute or two, the silence became uncomfortable and Ruth said, 'Are you looking at my aura? 'Cause if you are, *pal*, you'd better stop.'

He apologised and, feeling guilty, she said, 'Come on, Greg, I wasn't serious.'

He looked hurt. 'Would you make fun if I'd ended up with – I dunno, a squint or something?'

Now she knew he was winding her up.

'Maybe not,' she said with a sly smile. 'But this is a *lot* more freaky.'

'Well, you'd better get used to it,' he said with a twinkle. 'Because I don't think it's going away.'

'You *are* looking at my aura,' she said, with mock outrage.

'Soppy pinks and lilac, just now,' he said.

She shuddered theatrically, and he smiled, but it faded and Ruth knew his thoughts had turned inward.

'What?' she said.

He shook his head. 'I can't believe I didn't see Pendinning for what she was.'

'Of *course* you couldn't read her,' Ruth said. 'Pendinning was a psychopath – they don't have human feelings.' He didn't look much consoled and she added, 'I spoke with the consultant neurologist – he'd never had Pendinning in mind to help you with your hallucinations – she was a research psychologist, didn't even have clinical training. She only had a hospital ID because she was conducting research interviews with patients. Apparently, he was about to get her banned off the unit after a couple of families complained about dubious practices.'

'Like plying them with alcohol?' Carver said.

Ruth stared at him. 'This was the cognitive interview you mentioned?

'She said it might help to kick-start my memory.'

Ruth recalled how sick and frail he'd looked the day after.

'Don't feel bad,' he said. 'The one good thing to've come out of this is I can't be around alcohol any more – that's got to be good, hasn't it?'

She heard a forced jollity in his tone.

'There are easier ways to go teetotal,' she said.

Carver smiled. His eyes drifted closed.

'Why did Pendinning pick on you?' he asked.

He kept his eyes shut, and she was grateful for that.

'To get at you.'

'I don't need to see your aura to tell that's a barefaced lie,' he murmured, that smile playing over his face again. 'She wanted me back on the case, but she chose you, *specifically*, for a reason.'

Ruth couldn't think of a reply and he opened his eyes again.

'You said yourself, it was all about secrets with her. So, what's *your* secret?'

'The woman was crazy – who knows what she imagined she saw in me?' She shrugged. 'Anyway, don't you think some secrets are worth keeping?'

Ruth watched him search her face for hidden meaning and, emptying her mind of anything but the maddening itch from the tattoos on her forearm, she built a wall of white noise around herself and trusted that she was well concealed.

# Acknowledgments

Many are owed a huge debt of gratitude in the genesis of this book. I am in awe of the truly spectacular work done by Felicity Blunt and foreign rights marvel, Melissa Pimentel, at Curtis Brown; your combined brilliance in putting the book in front of all the right people has been dazzling. Sincere thanks to Jennifer Joel at ICM, for finding the book such a splendid home at William Morrow in the US. To James Gurbutt, my publisher and refreshingly straight-talking editor in the UK, thanks for being wonderful behind the scenes from the very early stages; an eminence grise with attitude. Thanks, too, to the rest of the amazing team at Corsair, Little, Brown whose enthusiasm and energy make so much difference.

To Ann Cleeves, Sue Mortimer, Mo Hayder and Sara MacDonald, I will always be grateful for your kinship, support, advice – and laughter.

This novel would never have seen the light of day if it weren't for the generous support of the Royal Literary Fund; thank you with all my heart.

Research is one of the joys of writing for a living, and *Hallucinations*, by Oliver Sacks, has been both an inspiration and a constant source of wonder in revealing the inventiveness, adaptability and resilience of the human mind. John Robertson's excellent poisons website, www.thepoisongarden.co.uk, proved a rich and reliable source of information; I guarantee that you'll be astounded by how many apparently innocuous garden plants harbour deadly secrets . . . Tattoos have always been an enigma to me, so I was delighted to discover anthropologist Lars Krutak's website, articles and YouTube talks, which were incredibly informative on the cultural heritage of tattoos and scarification.

Finally, I was recently asked to contribute to research on the importance of grit in achieving success (trust me, it's a 'thing' – just Google 'Grit, psychological factor'!). It's certainly true that my own perseverance and passion have been crucial, but the grit and determination of others must also be factored in to this complex equation. So, a special thank you is due to you, Felicity, for your steadfast support throughout all my incarnations; I hope to fully justify your faith in me.